SIMPLY
THE BEST
MYSTERIES

D0776513

SIMPLY THE BEST MYSTERIES

Edgar Award Winners and Front-Runners

**EDITED BY
JANET HUTCHINGS**

CARROLL & GRAF PUBLISHERS, INC.
NEW YORK

Introduction copyright © 1998 by Janet Hutchings

First Carroll & Graf edition 1998

Carroll & Graf Publishers, Inc.
19 West 21st Street
New York, NY 10010-6805

Library of Congress Cataloging-in-Publication Data

Simply the best mysteries : Edgar award winners and front runners /
  edited by Janet Hutchings.
     p.   cm.
    ISBN 0-7867-0483-7 (trade paper)
    1. Detective and mystery stories, American. I. Hutchings, Janet.
PS648.D4S555   1997
813'.0877208—dc21   97-21841
                                         CIP

We are grateful to the following for permission to reprint their copyrighted material:

"**Candles in the Rain**" by Doug Allyn, copyright © 1993 by Bantam Doubleday Dell Magazines, reprinted by permission of the author; "**And Already Lost . . .** " by Charlotte Armstrong, copyright © 1957 by Charlotte Armstrong, reprinted by permission of Brandt & Brandt Literary Agents, Inc.; "**Elvis Lives**" by Lynne Barrett, copyright © 1990 by Davis Publications, Inc., reprinted by permission of the author; "**The Judge's Boy**" by Jean B. Cooper, copyright © 1995 by Jean B. Cooper, reprinted by permission of the author; "**The Affair at Lahore Cantonment**" by Avram Davidson, copyright © 1961 by Davis Publications, Inc., reprinted by permission of the author; "**When Your Breath Freezes**" by Kathleen Dougherty, copyright © 1995 by Kathleen Dougherty, reprinted by permission of the author; "**The House Party**" by Stanley Ellin, copyright © 1954 by Stanley Ellin, reprinted by permission of Curtis Brown, Ltd.; "**The Blessington Method**" by Stanley Ellin, copyright © 1956 by Stanley Ellin, reprinted by permission of Curtis Brown, Ltd.; "**Goodbye, Pops**" by Joe Gores, copyright © 1969 by Joe Gores, reprinted by permission of the author; "**The Anderson Boy**" by Joseph Hansen, copyright © 1983 by Davis Publications, Inc., reprinted by permission of the author; "**The Purple Shroud**" by Joyce Harrington, copyright © 1972 by Davis Publications, Inc., reprinted by permission of the author; "**The Terrapin**" by Patricia Highsmith, copyright © 1962 by Patricia Highsmith, reprinted by permission of Grove/Atlantic, Inc.; "**Horn Man**" by Clark Howard, copyright © 1980 by Davis Publications, Inc., reprinted by permission of the author; "**Dream No More**", copyright © 1955 by Mercury Publications, Inc., from *Man Out of the Raw and Other Stories* by Philip MacDonald, used by permission of Doubleday, a division of Bantam, Doubleday, Dell Publishing Group, Inc.; "**The Cloud Beneath the Eaves**" by Barbara Owens, copyright © 1978 by Davis Publications, Inc., reprinted by permission of the author and the author's agents, Scott Meredith Literary Agency, Inc., 845 Third Avenue, New York, NY 10022; "**The Fallen Curtain**" by Ruth Rendell, copyright © 1974 by Davis Publications, Inc., reprinted by permissioin of the author; "**The New Girl Friend**" by Ruth Rendell, copyright © 1983 by Kingsmarkham Enterprises, Ltd., reprinted by permission of Kingsmarkham Enterprises, Ltd.; "**Like a Terrible Scream**" by Etta Revesz, copyright © 1976 by Davis Publications, Inc., reprinted by permission of the author; "**The Absence of Emily**" by Jack Ritchie, copyright © 1981 by Davis Publications, Inc., reprinted by permission of the author; "**H As in Homicide**" by Lawrence Treat, copyright © 1964 by Davis Publications, Inc., reprinted by permission of the author; "**Chance After Chance**" by Thomas Walsh Jr., copyright © 1977 by Davis Publications, Inc., reprinted by permission of the author; "**This Is Death**" by Donald E. Westlake, copyright © 1978 by Donald E. Westlake, reprinted by permission of the author; all stories previously appeared in *Ellery Queen's Mystery Magazine*, published by Dell Magazines, a division of Crosstown Publications.

Contents

CONTENTS

Introduction

The Edgar Allan Poe Awards, the most celebrated mystery awards in the world, have a rich history, with more than five decades of winners drawn from a great variety of publications. In the short story category, however, one name, *Ellery Queen's Mystery Magazine*, appears at nearly every turn. In this volume, we present a selection of *Ellery Queen's Mystery Magazine*'s Edgar winners and nominees, starting with the very first short story ever to win an Edgar and finishing with the Edgar winner for 1995.

The first Edgar to honor overall contributions to the short story field was given to Ellery Queen himself (really the two-cousin writing team of Frederic Dannay and Manfred Lee), in 1948, for founding and editing *Ellery Queen's Mystery Magazine* and for putting together the many mystery short story anthologies that grew out of the magazine. At the time, there was no award for best individual mystery short story, but the Mystery Writers of America, the organization responsible for the Edgars, felt that honor ought to be paid in some way to those persons, be they writers or editors, who made a significant contribution to the art of the mystery short story. Their choice of Ellery Queen as the first winner was amply vindicated in ensuing years when the magazine he founded produced winner after winner for best short story.

Ellery Queen had won the Edgar for outstanding contribution to

the mystery short story twice (in 1948 and 1950) before the nature
of that award was changed, in 1954, so as to recognize an individual
work of short fiction. There is no way of knowing whether Ellery
Queen concurred in the changing of a category that had twice recognized his genius as an editor, but he must have been delighted to
see the results of the very first polling for best individual short story,
for the winner was Stanley Ellin's "The House Party," a work that
not only first saw print in *Ellery Queen's Mystery Magazine* but was
written for a contest that was Ellery Queen's brainchild, the eighth
EQMM Worldwide Short Story Contest.

Although *EQMM*'s worldwide short story contests had no direct
connection to the Edgars, the history of the short story Edgar might
have been quite different had these contests never been run. From
1945 to 1956, and again in 1961, the editors of *Ellery Queen's Mystery Magazine* undertook the mammoth task of sponsoring and judg-
ing a series of mystery contests under the direction of Ellery Queen.
Submissions poured in from nearly every corner of the globe, many
from noted writers, including mystery legends such as Ngaio Marsh.
It is no surprise that the first three individual short story Edgar winners (Stanley Ellin's "The House Party," Philip MacDonald's "Dream
No More," and Stanley Ellin's "The Blessington Method") were also,
previously, winners or front-runners in the *EQMM* Worldwide Short
Story Contests, for the contests inspired superior work and helped to
set a standard for all short mystery fiction, and for the Edgar winners
that were to come.

One of the most wonderful things about the *EQMM* contests was
that despite the flock of already famous authors who entered, it was
sometimes relative newcomers who took the top spots. In fact, Ellery
Queen was so impressed by the high standard of submissions to the
contests by new authors that he launched a new *EQMM* feature, the
Department of First Stories, which remains in the magazine to this
day. In this book you will find three Edgar award winning stories that
were first published in *EQMM*'s Department of First Stories (Joyce
Harrington's "The Purple Shroud," Etta Revesz's "Like a Terrible
Scream," and Barbara Owens's "The Cloud Beneath the Eaves"). We
hope the knowledge that these tales were the first to be penned by
their promising new authors will cause you to enjoy them all the more.

Over the years *EQMM*'s Department of First Stories has been responsible for starting off the careers of many Edgar-winning or Edgar-nominated authors, not only those who went on to distinguish themselves in the short story category, but several who went on to write award-winning novels. While the success of everyone who got their start in *EQMM* gives us pleasure, we are proudest of the Edgar-winning stories that were actually published in our magazine. We present that select group of stories to you in this volume. We have chosen chronological order (with the year of nomination and/or win noted on the contents page) so that you will be able to get a sense of how tastes and styles have changed over the years.

One thing that has *not* changed over the years is the insistence of the Edgar committees on quality in writing as well as cleverness in the construction of a mystery/suspense plot. Out of the hundreds of stories published each year, only five are selected as nominees for the coveted award—five stories that entertain, surprise, and, often, enlighten. Selecting a winner from such formidable front-runners can be a near-impossible task, one which may leave amicable differences of opinion among the judges long after the decision is made. In this book, we have added six front-runners, or nominees, to our lineup of winners: Charlotte Armstrong's "And Already Lost," Patricia Highsmith's "The Terrapin," Donald E. Westlake's "This is Death," Joseph Hansen's "The Anderson Boy," Doug Allyn's "Candles in the Rain," and Kathleen Dougherty's "When Your Breath Freezes." Together with the other sixteen entries, all Edgar winners, they make up a collection that we hope you'll agree is simply the best.

—Janet Hutchings

SIMPLY THE BEST MYSTERIES

THE HOUSE PARTY

by Stanley Ellin

"He's coming around," said the voice.

He was falling. His hands were out-flung against the stone-cold blackness of space, and his body tilted head over heels, heels over head as he fell. If there were only a way of knowing what was below, of bracing himself against the moment of impact, the terror might not have been so great. This way he was no more than a lump of terror flung into a pit, his mind cowering away from the inevitable while his helpless body descended toward it.

"Good," the voice said from faraway, and it sounded to him as if someone were speaking to him quite calmly and cheerfully from the bottom of the pit. "Very good."

He opened his eyes. A glare of light washed in on him suddenly and painfully, and he squinted against it at the figures standing around him, at the faces, partly obscured by a sort of milky haze, looking down at him. He was lying on his back, and from the thrust of the cushions under him he knew he was on the familiar sofa. The milky haze was fading away now, and with it the panic. This was the old house at Nyack, the same living room, the same Utrillo on the wall, the same chandelier glittering over his head. *The same everything,* he thought bitterly, even to the faces around him.

That was Hannah, her eyes bright with tears—she could turn on tears like a faucet—and her hand was gripping his so hard that his

1

fingers were numb under the pressure. Hannah with the over-developed maternal instinct, and only a husband to exercise it on . . . That was Abel Roth chewing on a cigar—even at a time like this, that reeking cigar!—and watching him worriedly. Abel with his first successful production in five years, worrying about his investment . . . And that was Ben Thayer and Harriet, the eternal bumpkins . . . And Jake Hall . . . And Tommy McGowan . . . All the old familiar faces, the sickening familiar faces.

But there was a stranger, too. A short stout man with a look of amiable interest on his face, and splendidly bald, with only a tonsure of graying hair to frame his gleaming scalp. He ran his fingers reflectively over his scalp, and nodded at Miles.

"How do you feel now?" he asked.

"I don't know," Miles said. He pulled his hand free of Hannah's, and gingerly tried to raise himself to a sitting position. Halfway there he was transfixed by a shocking pain that was driven like a white-hot needle between his ribs. He heard Hannah gasp, and then the stranger's blunt fingers were probing deep into the pain, turning it to liquid, melting it away.

"See?" the man said. "It's nothing. Nothing at all."

Miles swung his legs around so that he sat erect on the sofa. He took a deep breath, then another. "For a second I thought it was my heart," he said. "The way it hit me—"

"No, no," the man said. "I know what you thought. You can believe me when I say it is of no concern." And then, as if it explained everything, he said, "I am Dr. Maas. Dr. Victor Maas."

"It was a miracle, darling," Hannah said breathlessly. "Dr. Maas was the one who found you outside and brought you in. And he's been an absolute angel. If it weren't for him—"

Miles looked at her, and then looked at all the others standing there and watching him with concern. "Well," he demanded, "what *did* happen? What was it? Heart? Stroke? Amnesia? I'm not a child, for God's sake. You don't have to play games with me."

Abel Roth rolled his cigar from the left-hand corner of his mouth to the right-hand corner. "You can't blame him for feeling that way, can you, Doc? After all, the man is out cold for fifteen minutes, he wants to know where he stands. Maybe there's some kind of checkup you could give him, like blood pressure and stuff like that. Maybe we'd all feel better for it."

Miles relished that, and relished even more the thought of what he had in store for Abel Roth. "Maybe we would, Abel," he said. "Maybe we've got a theater sold out sixteen weeks in advance, and the SRO sign up every night. Maybe we've got a real little gold mine to dig so long as I can keep swinging the shovel eight performances a week."

Abel's face turned red. "Ah, now, Miles," he said. "The way you talk—"

"Yes?" Miles said. "What about the way I talk?"

Ben Thayer shook his head slowly and solemnly. "If you'd only take the chip off your shoulder for one minute, Miles," he drawled. "If you'd try to understand—"

"Please!" Dr. Maas said sharply. "Gentlemen, please!" He frowned at them. "There is one thing I must make clear. Actually, I am not a medical physician. My interests, so to speak, lie more in the field of psychiatrics, and while I am, perhaps, qualified to make the examination of Mr. Owen that you suggest, I have no intention of doing so. For Mr. Owen's benefit I will also say that there is no need for me or anyone else to do so. He has my word on that."

"And Dr. Maas, I am sure," said Miles, "is an honorable man." He stood up flexing his knees gingerly, and noting the relief on the faces around him. "If you want to make yourself at home, Doctor, go right ahead. There seems to be some kind of buffet over there, and while I can't vouch for the food, I can promise that the liquor is very, very good."

The doctor's grin gave him a surprising resemblance to a plump and mischievous boy. "A delightful suggestion," he said, and immediately made his way toward the buffet. Abel followed, and, Miles observed, before the doctor had even reached the buffet, the cigar was perilously close to his ear. Abel spent three hours a week on a psychoanalyst's couch, and at least as much time pouring out lists of frightening and inconsequential symptoms to a sleek and well-fed Park Avenue practitioner. Dr. Maas, Miles thought with a wry sympathy, was in for some heavy going, whether he knew it or not.

The rest of the circle around the sofa broke up and eddied off, until only Hannah was left. She caught his arm in a panicky grip.

"Are you *sure* you're all right?" she demanded. "You know you can tell me if there's anything wrong."

There was something wrong. Every time she caught hold of him like that, tried to draw him close, he had the feeling of a web ensnaring him, closing over him so that he had to fight it savagely.

It had not been like that at the start. She had been so beautiful that he thought in her case it might be different. The rising together, the eating together, the talking together, the endless routine of marriage looked as if it might somehow be bearable as long as it was shared with that loveliness. But then after a year the loveliness had become too familiar, the affection too cloying, the routine too much of a crushing burden.

He had been unconscious for fifteen minutes. He wondered if he had babbled during that time, said something about Lily that could be seized on as a clue. It wasn't of much concern if he had; in fact, it might have been a good way of preparing Hannah for the blow. It was going to be quite a blow, too. He could picture it falling, and it wasn't a pleasant picture.

He shrugged off Hannah's hand. "There's nothing wrong," he said, and then could not resist adding, "unless it's this business of your throwing a house party the one time of the week when I might expect a little peace and quiet."

"I?" Hannah said uncertainly. "What did *I* have to do with it?"

"Everything, as long as you've got that damn yen to be the perfect hostess and everybody's friend."

"They're *your* friends," she said.

"You ought to know by now that they're not my friends either. I thought I made it clear a hundred different ways that I hate them all, individually and collectively. They're nobody's friends. Why is it my obligation to feed them and entertain them the one time of the week I can get rid of them?"

"I don't understand you," Hannah said. She looked as if she were about to break into tears. "I know you bought the house up here so you could get away from everybody, but you were the one—"

The web was closing in again. "All *right*," he said. "All *right!*"

The whole thing didn't matter, anyhow. After he cleared out she could throw a house party every night of the week if she wanted to.

She could burn the damn house down if that suited her. It wasn't of any concern to him. He'd had enough of this country-squire life between every Saturday and Monday performance to last him the rest of his life, and, as Lily had once remarked, Central Park had all the trees she wanted to see. Just the realization that he would soon be packed and out of here made any arguments pointless.

He shouldered his way to the buffet past Bob and Liz Gregory, who were mooning at each other as if doing it on the radio six mornings a week wasn't enough; past Ben Thayer, who was explaining to Jake Hall the trouble he was having with the final act of his new play; past Abel, who was saying something to Dr. Maas about psychosomatic factors. The doctor had a tall glass in one hand, and a sandwich in the other. "Interesting," he was saying. "Very interesting."

Miles tried to close his ears to all of them as he poured down two fingers of bourbon. Then he looked at his glass with distaste. The stuff was as flat as warm water, and as unpleasant to the palate. Obviously, one of the local help who took turns cleaning up the house had found the key to the liquor cabinet, and, after nearly emptying the bottle, had done a job on it at the kitchen tap. Damn fool. If you're going to sneak a drink, do it and forget it. But to ruin the rest of the bottle this way . . .

Abel poked him in the ribs. "I was just telling the doctor here," Abel said, "if he gets an evening off I'll fix him up with a house seat for *Ambuscade*. I was telling him, if he hasn't seen Miles Owen in *Ambuscade* he hasn't seen the performance of all time. How does that sound to you, Miles?"

Miles was lifting another bottle after making sure its seal was unbroken. He looked at Abel, and then set the bottle down with great care.

"As a matter of fact," he said, "I don't know how it sounds to me, Abel. It's something I've wanted to talk to you about, and maybe this is as good a time as any."

"Talk about what?" said Abel cheerfully, but there was a sudden worry in his eyes, a flickering of premonition on his face.

"It's private business, Abel," Miles said, and nodded to Dr. Maas, who stood by interestedly. "That is, if the doctor will excuse us."

"Of course, of course," the doctor said quickly. He waved his glass enthusiastically toward Miles. "And you were altogether right about the liquor, Mr. Owen. It is superb."

"Fine," Miles said. "This way, Abel."

He pushed his way through the crowd and crossed the room to the library, Abel trailing after him. When he closed the door of the library and switched on a lamp, the chill dampness of the room seemed to soak right into him, and he shivered. Logs and kindling had been laid on the fireplace, and he held a match to it until the wood crackled and caught. Then he lit a cigarette and drew deeply on it. He looked at the cigarette in surprise. There was a flatness about it, a lack of sensation which made him run his tongue over his lips questioningly. He drew again on the cigarette, and then flung it into the fire. First the liquor, he thought, and now this. Dr. Maas might be a handy man with Freudian complexes, but the first thing Monday an honest-to-God M.D. would be checking up on this little problem. It is discomforting to find out suddenly that you've lost your capacity to taste anything. Ridiculous maybe, but still discomforting.

Abel was standing at the window. "Look at that fog, will you. When I brought *Coxcomb* over to London I thought I saw the real thing there, but this makes it look like nothing. You could cut your way through this with a shovel."

The fog was banked solidly outside the window, stirring in slow waves, sending threads of damp smoke against the glass. Where the threads clung, little beads of water trickled down the pane.

"You get that around here a couple of times a year," Miles said impatiently. "And I didn't come in here to talk about the weather."

Abel turned away from the window and sat down reluctantly in an armchair. "No, I guess you didn't. All right, Miles, what's bothering you?"

"*Ambuscade,*" Miles said. "*Ambuscade* is what's bothering me."

Abel nodded wearily. "It figured. It figured. Well, what particular thing? Your billing? We're using the biggest letters they make. Your publicity? All you have to do is name the time and you have your pick of any TV or radio guest spot in town. Remember what I told you after opening night, Miles? You name it, and if I can get it for you, I will."

Miles found himself suddenly enjoying the scene. Ordinarily, he had a genuine horror of such scenes. "Funny," he said. "I didn't hear you say anything about money just now, did I? I mean, in all that pretty speech it couldn't have slipped past me, could it?"

Abel sank down in his chair and sighed like a man deeply stricken. "I thought it would come down to this. Even if I'm paying you twice as much as the biggest star I ever had, I could see it coming, Miles. All right, what's the beef?"

"As a matter of fact," Miles said, "there's no beef."

"No?"

"None at all."

"What are you getting at?" Abel demanded. "What's all this about?"

Miles smiled. "I'm not getting *at* anything, Abel. I'm getting *out*. I'm leaving the show."

Miles had seen Abel meet more than one crisis before; he could have predicted every action before it took place. The face becoming an impassive mask, the hand searching for a match, the thumbnail flicking the match into a light, the elaborate drawing on the cigar stump, the neat flick of the match across the room. Abel fooled him. The match was snapped with sudden violence between the fingers, and then slowly rolled back and forth, back and forth.

"You're a cute boy, Miles," Abel said. "This wouldn't be your idea of a joke, would it?"

"I'm getting out, Abel. Tonight was positively the last appearance. That gives you all day tomorrow to line up another boy for the Monday-night curtain."

"What other boy?"

"Well, you've got Jay Welker on tap, haven't you? He's been understudying me for five months, and hoping I'd break a leg every night of it."

"Jay Welker couldn't carry *Ambuscade* one week, and you know it, Miles. Nobody can carry that show but you, and you know that, too."

Abel leaned forward in his chair and shook his head from side to side unbelievingly. "And knowing that, you don't give a damn. You'd close the biggest thing on Broadway just like that, and to hell with the whole world, is that it?"

Miles felt his heart starting to pound heavily, his throat tightening. "Wait a second, Abel, before you start on the dirty words. One thing has already come through pretty well. In all this, you haven't yet asked me why I'm leaving. For all you know I might have some condition that's going to kill me an hour from now, but that would bother you less than keeping your show running! Have you thought about that side of it?"

"What side of it? I was standing right there when the doctor said you were in good shape. What am I supposed to do now? Get affidavits from the American Medical Association?"

"Then it's your idea that I'm pulling out because of a whim?"

"Let's not kid each other, Miles. You did this to Barrow five years ago, you did it to Goldschmidt after that, you did it to Howie Freeman last year, and I know, because that's how I got my chance to grab you for *Ambuscade*. But all the time I figured these others didn't know how to handle you, they didn't see just how much you meant to a show. Now I tell you they were right all along, and I was a prize sucker. They told me you would be going along fine, and then all of a sudden you would get a bug in your ear, and that was it. Bug in your ear, Miles. That's my low, ignorant way of saying whim, which is what it adds up to."

Abel paused. "The difference between me and them, Miles, is that I didn't take chances, and that's why you signed the first run-of-the-play contract you ever got since you were a nobody. You think you're walking out on that contract? Think again, my friend."

Miles nodded. "All right," he said thickly, "I'm thinking. Do you want to know about what?"

"They're your dice, my friend."

"I'm thinking about eight performances a week, Abel. Eight times a week I say the same lines, walk the same steps, make the same faces. I've done it for five months, which is the biggest break you ever got in your life, but if you had your way I'd be doing it for five years! Right now it's turned into one of those nightmares where you do the same thing over and over without being able to stop, but you wouldn't know about that because *you're* a guy in love with routine! But *I'm* not! After a while it's like being in jail with the key thrown away. What do you tell a man when he can walk out of jail? To stay there and like it?"

"Jail!" Abel cried. "Tell me somebody in this country who wouldn't give his right eye to be in the kind of jail you're in!"

"Listen," Miles said. He leaned forward urgently. "Do you remember before the show opened when we were rehearsing that kitchen scene? Do you remember when we ran through it that night ten times, fifteen times, twenty times? Do you know how I felt then? I felt as if I was plunked right down in hell, and all I would do for eternity was just play that scene over and over again. That's my idea of hell, Abel: a sweet little place where you do the same thing over and over, and they won't even let you go nuts at it, because that would spoil the fun for them. Do you get that? Because if you do, you can see just how I feel about *Ambuscade!*"

"I get it," Abel said. "I also get a certain little run-of-the-play contract tucked away in my safe deposit box. If you think rehearsing a scene a few times is hell, you'll find out different when Equity lands on you. They look at this a little different from you."

"Don't try to scare me, Abel."

"Scare you, hell. I'm going to sue you black and blue, and I'm going to make it stick. I'm dead serious about that, Miles."

"Maybe. But isn't it hard to sue a man who's too sick to work?"

Abel nodded with grim understanding. "I figured you'd get around to that angle. I'm the patsy, because to the rest of the world you're sick." His eyes narrowed. "And that explains something else, too. That little business of your little blackout on the front doorstep, with a doctor handy, and twenty witnesses to swear to it. I have to hand it to you, Miles, you don't miss a trick. Only it'll take more than a smart trick and a quack doctor to work things your way."

Miles choked down the rage rising in him. "If you think that was a trick—!"

"What was a trick?" Harriet Thayer's voice said gaily behind him. Harriet and Ben were standing in the doorway, regarding him with a sort of cheerful curiosity. They made an incongruous couple, Ben's gauntness towering high over Harriet's little-girl fragility, and they had an eager, small-town friendliness that grated on Miles's nerves like a fingernail drawn down a slate. "It sounds terribly exciting and interesting," Harriet said. "Don't let us stop you."

Abel pointed at Miles with a shaking forefinger. "This'll stop you all right," he said, "and I'll give it to you in one line. Our friend here is walking out on *Ambuscade*. Maybe *you* can do something to change his mind!"

Ben stared with slow incredulity, and Miles had to marvel, as he had done so many times before, that any man who could write even the few good lines to be found in *Ambuscade* could be so slow on his feet.

"But you can't," Ben said. "Your contract runs as long as the play does."

"Sure," Abel jeered, "but he's a sick man. He falls down and has fits. You saw him, didn't you?"

Harriet nodded dumbly. "Yes, but I never thought—"

"And you were right," Abel said. "He's faking it. He's just fed up with making all that money and having all those nice things printed about him, so he's going to close the show. That's all. Just fold it up tight."

Miles slammed his hand down hard on the arm of Abel's chair. "All right," he said, "now that you've made everything so clear, I'll ask you something. Do you think if *Ambuscade* was really a good play that any one person could close it up? Did it ever strike you that no one comes to see your crummy play; they come to see me walk through it? If you gave me *Jabberwocky* to read up there they'd come to see me! Who's to tell a one-man show that he has to keep playing when he doesn't want to!"

"It *is* a good play!" Harriet shouted at him. "It's the best play you ever acted in, and if you don't know that—"

Miles was shouting himself now. "Then get someone else to play it! It might be even better that way!"

Ben held his hands out, palms up, in a pleading gesture. "Now, Miles, you know you've been identified with that part so no one else could take it over," he said. "And try to see it my way, Miles. I've been writing fifteen years, and this is the first real break—"

Miles walked up to him slowly. "You clown," he said softly. "Don't you have any self-respect at all?"

When he walked out of the library he quickly slammed the door behind him to forestall any belated answer to that.

The party had broken into several small knots of people scattered around the room, a deafening rise and fall of voices, a haze of blue smoke which lay like a transparent blanket midway between floor and ceiling. Someone, Miles observed, had overturned a drink on the piano; the puddle ran down in a glittering string along the side of the mahogany and was leaving a damp stain on the Wilton rug beneath. Tommy McGowan and his latest, an overripe blonde—Norma or Alma or something—sat on the floor shuffling through piles of phonograph records, arranging some into a dangerously high stack, and carelessly tossing the others aside. The buffet looked as if a cyclone had hit it; only some empty platters and broken pieces of bread remained amidst the wreckage. From the evidence, Miles thought sardonically, the party would have to be rated a roaring success.

But even the sense of heat and excitement in the room could not erase the chill that he seemed to have brought with him from the library. He rubbed his hands together hard, but this didn't help any, and he felt a small pang of fright at the realization. What if there really were something wrong with him? Lily was not the kind of woman to take gracefully to the role of nursemaid to an invalid. Not that she was wrong about that, as far as he was concerned; if the shoe were on the other foot he couldn't see himself playing any Robert Browning to her Elizabeth Barrett either. Not for Lily or anyone else in the world. In that case it was better not to even bother about a checkup. If there was something, he didn't even want to know about it!

"You are disturbed about something, I think."

It was Dr. Maas. He was leaning casually against the wall, not an arm's length away, his hands thrust into his pockets, his eyes fixed reflectively on Miles. Taking in everything, Miles thought angrily, like some damn scientist looking at a bug under a microscope.

"No," Miles snapped. Then he thought better of it. "Yes," he said. "As a matter of fact, I am."

"Ah?"

"I don't feel right. I know you told me I was fine, but I don't feel fine."

"Physically?"

"Of course, physically! What are you trying to tell me? That it's all in my mind, or some claptrap like that?"

"I am not trying to tell you anything, Mr. Owen. You are telling me."

"All right. Then I want to know what makes you so sure of yourself. No examination, no X ray, no anything, and you come up with your answer just like that. What's the angle here? Do we somehow get around to the idea that there's nothing wrong physically, but if I put myself in your hands for a nice long expensive psychoanalysis—"

"Stop right there, Mr. Owen," Dr. Maas said coldly. "I will take for granted that your manners are abominable because you are clearly under some pressure. But you should rein in your imagination. I do not practice psychoanalysis, and I never said I did. I am not a healer of any sort. The people I deal with are, unfortunately, always past the point of any cure, and my interest in them, as you can see, must be wholly academic. To be taken for some kind of sharper seeking a victim—"

"Look," Miles said abruptly, "I'm sorry. I'm terribly sorry. I don't know what made me go off like that. Maybe it's this party. I hate these damn parties; they always do things to me. Whatever it is, I'm honestly sorry for taking it out on you."

The doctor nodded gravely. "Of course," he said. "Of course." Then he nervously ran his fingers over his shining scalp. "There is something else I should like to say. I am afraid, however, I would risk offending you."

Miles laughed. "I think you owe it to me."

The doctor hesitated, and then gestured toward the library. "As it happens, Mr. Owen, I heard much of what went on in there. I am not an eavesdropper, but the discussion got a little—well, heated, shall we say?—and it was impossible not to overhear it from outside the door here."

"Yes?" Miles said warily.

"The clue to your condition, Mr. Owen, lies in that discussion. To put it bluntly, you are running away. You find what you call routine unbearable, and so you are fleeing from it."

Miles forced himself to smile. "What do you mean, what *I* call routine? Is there another word for it in your language?"

"I think there is. I think I would call it responsibility. And since your life, Mr. Owen—both your profession and your private life— are very much an open book to the world, I will draw on it and say that most of this life has also been spent fleeing from responsibility of one sort or another. Does it strike you as strange, Mr. Owen, that no matter how far and fast you run, you always find yourself facing the same problem over and over again?"

Miles clenched and unclenched his fist. "After all," he said, "it's my problem."

"That is where you're wrong, Mr. Owen. When you suddenly leave your role in a play, it affects everyone concerned with that play, and, in turn, everyone concerned with those people. In your relations with women you may move on, but they do not stay motionless either. They move on, too, dangerous to themselves and perhaps to others. Forgive me if I seem sententious, Mr. Owen, but you cannot cast pebbles in the water without sending ripples to the far shore.

"That is why when you say *routine,* it is because you are thinking only of yourself caught in a situation. And when I say *responsibility,* I am thinking of everyone else concerned with it."

"And what's the prescription, Doctor?" Miles demanded. "To stay sunk in a private little hell because if you try to get away you might step on somebody's toes in the process?"

"Get away?" the doctor said in surprise. "Do you really think you can get away?"

"You've got a lot to learn, Doctor. Watch me and see."

"I am watching you, Mr. Owen, and I do see. In a wholly academic way, as I said. It is both fascinating and bewildering to see a man trying to flee, as he calls it, his private little hell, while all the time he is carrying it with him."

Miles's hand was half raised, and then it dropped limp at his side. "In other words, Doctor," he said mockingly, "you're replacing the good old-fashioned sulphur and brimstone hell with something even bigger and better."

The doctor shrugged. "Of course, you don't believe that."

"No," Miles said. "I don't."

"I have a confession to make, Mr. Owen." The doctor smiled, and suddenly he was the plump and mischievous boy again. "I knew you wouldn't. In fact, that is why I felt free to discuss the matter with you."

"In an academic way, of course."

"Of course."

Miles laughed. "You're quite a man, Doctor. I think I'd like to see more of you."

"I am sure you will, Mr. Owen. But right now I believe that someone is trying to attract your notice. There, by the door."

Miles followed the doctor's gesturing finger, and his heart stopped. All he could do was pray that no one else had noticed, as he swiftly crossed the room and blocked off the woman who was entering it from the hallway that led to the front door. He thrust her back against the door, and catching hold of her shoulders, he shook her once, sharply and angrily.

"Are you crazy?" he demanded. "Don't you have any more sense than to show up here like this?"

She twisted her shoulders away from his grasp, and carefully brushed at the collar of her coat with her fingertips. The coat had cost Miles a month's pay.

"Aren't you sweet, Miles. Do you invite all your guests in this way?"

Even in the dimness of the hallway she was startling to look at. The sulky lips against the gardenia pallor of the face, the high cheekbones, the slanted eyes darting fire at him. He quailed.

"All right, I'm sorry. I'm sorry. But, my God, Lily, there are two dozen of the biggest mouths on Broadway in that room. If you want the whole world to know about this, why don't you just tip off Winchell!"

She knew when she had him beaten. "I don't like that, darling. I don't like that at all. I mean, to make it sound as obscene and disgusting as all that. It really isn't supposed to be like that, is it?"

"You know damn well it isn't like that, Lily. But use your head, will you? There is such a thing as discretion."

"There's also such a thing as working a word to death, darling.

And I don't mind telling you that in the last two months you've filled me up to here with that one."

Miles said angrily, "I've been trying to make it clear that we'd work this thing out in the right way at the right time. I've already told Abel I was leaving the show. I was going to talk to Hannah, too, but this party has fouled everything up. Tomorrow, when I can be alone with her—"

"Ah, but tomorrow may be a long time away, darling. Much longer than you realize."

"What exactly does that mean?"

She fumbled through her purse and drew an envelope from it. She waved the envelope back and forth under his nose with a fine air of triumph.

"It means this, Miles. Two pretty little reservations, outward bound, for tomorrow's sailing. You see, you don't have nearly as much time as you thought, do you, darling?"

"Tomorrow! The agent said he couldn't possibly have anything for us within a month!"

"He didn't count on cancellations. This one came through just two hours ago, which is exactly how long it took me to get here. And if it wasn't for that awful fog on the road I would have been here that much sooner. I have the car outside, Miles. You can pack whatever is handy, and get the rest of what you need on the boat. When I go back I expect you to be with me, Miles, because whether you are or not I'll be sailing tomorrow. You can't really blame me for that, can you, darling? After all, none of us are getting any younger."

He tried to straighten out the aching confusion of his thoughts. He wanted to escape Hannah's web, and now it seemed, somehow or other, there was another waiting to be dropped around him. Running, the doctor had said. Always running and never getting anywhere. There was a great weight of weariness in his arms, his legs, his whole body. Running did that to you.

"Well," Lily said, "make up your mind, darling."

He rubbed his hand over his forehead. "Where's the car?"

"Right across the road."

"All right," Miles said, "you wait in it. Just stay there, and don't blow the horn for me, or anything like that. I'll be down in ten minutes. Fifteen minutes at the most. Most of my stuff is in town, anyhow. We'll pick it up on the way to the boat."

He opened the door and gently pushed her toward it.

"You'll have to feel your way to the car, Miles. I've never seen anything like what's outside."

"I'll find it," he said. "You just wait there."

He closed the door, then leaned against it, fighting the sickness that kept rising to his throat. The loud voices in the next room, the shrieks of idiot laughter that now and then cut through it, the roar of music from the phonograph tuned at its greatest volume—everything seemed conspiring against him, not allowing him to be alone, not allowing him to think things out.

He went up the stairs almost drunkenly, and into the bedroom. He pulled out his valise, and then at random started cramming it full. Shirts, socks, the contents of the jewel case on his dresser. He thrust down hard with all his weight, making room for more.

"What are you doing, Miles?"

He didn't look up. He knew exactly what the expression on her face would be, and he didn't want to meet it then. It would have been too much.

"I'm leaving, Hannah."

"With that woman?" Her voice was a vague, uncomprehending whisper.

He had to look at her then. Her eyes stared at him, enormous against the whiteness of her skin. Her hand fumbled with the ornament at her breast. It was the silver mask of comedy he had picked up for her on Fifth Avenue a week before their marriage.

She said wonderingly, "I saw you with her in the hallway. I wasn't prying or anything like that, Miles, but when I asked the doctor where you were—"

"Stop it!" Miles shouted. "What do you have to apologize for!"

"But she's the one, isn't she?"

"Yes, she's the one."

"And you want to go away with her?"

His hands were on the lid of the valise. He rested his weight on them, head down, eyes closed.

"Yes," he said at last. "That's what it comes to."

"No!" she cried with a sudden fervor. "You don't really want to. You know she's not good for you. You know there's nobody in the whole world as good for you as I am!"

He pressed the lid of the valise down. The lock caught with a tiny click.

"Hannah, it would have been better for you not to have come up just now. I would have written to you, explained it somehow—"

"Explained it? When it would be too late? When you'd know what a mistake you made? Miles, listen to me. Listen to me, Miles. I'm talking to you out of all my love. It would be a terrible mistake."

"I'll have to be the judge of that, Hannah."

He stood up, and she came toward him, her fingers digging into his arms frantically. "Look at me, Miles," she whispered. "Can't you see how I feel? Can't you understand that I'd rather have the both of us dead than to have you go away like this and leave the whole world empty for me!"

It was horrible. It was the web constricting around him so hard that it was taking all his strength to pull himself free. But he did, with a brutal effort, and saw her fall back against the dresser. Then she suddenly wheeled toward it, and when she faced him again he saw the pistol leveled at him. It shone a cold, deadly blue in her hand, and then he realized that her hand was trembling so violently that the gun must be frightening her as much as it did him. The whole grotesquerie of the scene struck him full force, melting away the fear, filling him with a sense of outrage.

"Put that thing down," he said.

"No." He could hardly hear her. "Not unless you tell me that you're not going."

He took a step toward her, and she shrank farther back against the dresser, but the gun remained leveled at him. She was like a child afraid someone was going to trick her out of a toy. He stopped short, and then shrugged with exaggerated indifference.

"You're making a fool of yourself, Hannah. People are paid for acting like this on the stage. They're not supposed to make private shows of themselves."

Her head moved from side to side in a slow, aimless motion. "You still don't believe me, do you, Miles?"

"No," he said. "I don't."

He turned his back on her, half expecting to hear the sudden explosion, feel the impact between his shoulder blades, but there was nothing. He picked up the valise and walked to the door.

"Goodbye, Hannah," he said. He didn't turn his head to look at her.

The weakness in his knees made each step a trial. He stopped at the foot of the staircase to shift the valise from one hand to the other, and saw Dr. Maas standing there, hat in hand, a topcoat thrown over his arm.

"Ah?" said the doctor inquiringly. "So you, too, are leaving the party, Mr. Owen?"

"Party?" Miles said, and then laughed short and sharp. "Leaving the nightmare, if you don't mind, Doctor. I hate to tell this to a guest, but I think you'll understand me when I say that this past hour has been a nightmare that gets thicker and thicker. That's what I'm leaving, Doctor, and you can't blame me for being happy about it."

"No, no," said the doctor. "I quite understand."

"The car is waiting for me outside. If I can give you a lift anywhere—?"

"Not at all," the doctor said. "I really do not have far to go."

They went to the doorway together and stepped outside. The fog moved in on them, cold and wet, and Miles turned up his jacket collar against it.

"Rotten weather," he said.

"Terrible," the doctor agreed. He glanced at his watch, and then lumbered down the steps to the walk like a walrus disappearing into a snowbank. "I'll be seeing you, Mr. Owen," he called.

Miles watched him go, then lifted the valise and went down the steps himself, burying his nose in his collar against the smothering dampness all around him. He was at the bottom step when he heard the sibilance of the door opening behind him, the faraway whisper of danger in his bones.

He turned, and, as he knew it would be, there was Hannah standing at the open door, still holding the gun. But the gun was gripped tightly in both hands now, and the menace of it was real and overwhelming.

"I tried to make you understand, Miles," she said, like a child saying the words. "I tried to make you understand."

He flung his arms out despairingly.

"No!" he cried wildly. "No!"

And then there was the roar of the explosion in his ears, the gout of flame leaping out toward him, the crushing impact against his chest, and the whole world dissolving. In it, only one thing stood sharp and definable: the figure of the doctor bending over him, the face strangely satanic in its cruel indifference.

For that single moment Miles understood everything. He had been here before. He had lived this hour a thousand times before, and would live it again and again for all eternity. The curtain was falling now, but when it rose again the stage would be set once more for the house party. Because he was in hell, and the most terrible thing of all, the terror which submerged all others, was this moment of understanding given him so that he could know this, and could see himself crawling the infinite treadmill of his doom. Then the darkness closed in with a rush, blotting out all understanding—until next time . . .

"He's coming around," said the voice.

He was falling. His hands were out-flung . . .

DREAM NO MORE

by Philip MacDonald

John Garroway and his passenger drove into El Morro Beach a little before noon. The convertible was open, and they could see everything as they rolled down the last hill toward the center of the clustered little town on the bay, with the cliffs and the sea to one side of it, the hillsides with their scattered houses to the other.

To John, whose home had been here since he was a small boy—since his father had died, in fact—the charm of the place was familiar, something you felt rather than noticed. But to his passenger, it was new and surprising and obviously delightful.

The passenger's name was Gavin Rhodes. He was a Ph.D., and, besides being John Garroway's friend, was also his English professor. He was one of those not-so-old, not-so-young men frequently found in the teaching profession. Actually, his age was forty-six, but he might have been five years younger or a couple older. He was tall and wide-shouldered and slender, with a gift for looking at once careless and well-groomed in anything he wore. He had sensitive, clearly cut features, with a mouth which seemed narrow only at moments of concentration, and his dark hair carried a nicely balanced flecking of gray at the temples. As he darted eager glances all around, his eyes sparkled. He said, "Enchanting, really enchanting . . ."

"Thought you'd like it," John said. "Wait till we get to the other side. It's even better."

Gavin said, "That, me lad, is hard to believe." It was one of his mannerisms, calling people he liked "me lad" or "me gal" according to gender. He went on looking about him with frank pleasure, but then, as they reached the bottom of the hill and slowed at the corner by the El Morro Hotel, he grew suddenly grave and said sharply, "John! Did you call your mother?"

"Oh-oh!" John's twenty-two-year-old face was sheepish. "Clean forgot." He glanced sideways at his companion. "Doesn't matter, though. Mom—Mother won't mind. She likes surprises."

"Won't do, John." The tone was decisive. "Park somewhere and find a telephone. Your mother may not mind being a surprised hostess. I, definitely, refuse to be a surprise guest!"

Frowning, John shrugged his big shoulders. But he pulled to the curb, just past the hotel entrance. He switched off the engine and ran a troubled hand over his blond, crew-cut hair.

"Don't pout, John." Gavin was laughing at him now. "It doesn't become your style of beauty, me lad!"

"Okay," John said. "Okay." He smiled suddenly, giving in completely, as he always did.

At the southern end of El Morro Beach, Espada Point juts out into the ocean, towering above the sand and surf. It is reached by a narrow private road which turns at right angles off the coast highway, and it is occupied, entirely, by the Garroway property—the rambling green-roofed gray house and its surrounding garden.

Mrs. Garroway was in the garden, standing by the top of the steps which ran down the almost sheer face of the cliff to the beach a hundred feet below. She was looking at the cobalt of the ocean and the gold of the sand and the little, sparsely dotted figures of the few people in Timber Cove. She had been cutting flowers, and a shallow basket filled with multicolored blooms was over her arm. She was a slim but still pleasantly rounded fifty, and frequently looked eight or nine years younger. She had an innocuous, regularly featured face which had been called pretty when she was a young woman, and now was saved from middle-aged insignificance by a pair of magnificent dark eyes.

She turned toward the house and was halfway across the lawn when she heard the telephone ringing. She began to run and burst in through the front door just as the telephone was on its fourth peal. She heard movement at the end of the passage and called breathlessly, "It's all right, Mollie, I'll get it."

She dumped the flower basket onto a chair, snatched up the phone, and said, "Hello—?" and then, after a moment, "*Johnnie!* Where are you, darling? I thought you'd be here by now."

She listened to a long speech, and the smile, which had made her look almost like a girl, slowly faded. She said, "Oh, John, I don't think—" and then checked herself.

She said, "But of course, darling! I'll be very glad to see any friend of yours. It was only—well, I'm a foolish old woman. I was just disappointed I wasn't going to have you to myself."

She listened some more, then said, "Don't be silly, dear. Of *course* it's all right! Bring him along right away."

She hung up gently and walked slowly to the kitchen.

She pushed open the swing door, but only a little, as if she didn't want to be seen by the small shrewd eyes in Mollie's copper-colored face.

She said gaily, "Set another place for lunch, Mollie. Mr. John's bringing a friend for the weekend."

It was six o'clock, and the slanting sun splashed a swath of gold across the sea and into Timber Cove.

John and Gavin lay on their towels just beneath the cliff. They lay without talking, soaking in peace and warmth and the silence which seemed only deepened by the murmur of the ocean and the occasional crying of a gull.

Gavin propped himself up on an elbow, looked around him, and said softly, " 'I sat beside the evening sea, and dreamed a dream that could not be'—"

"What's that from?" John sat up. "How's it go on?"

Gavin laughed. "I've forgotten," he said. "And it's a misquotation anyway. It's 'I *walked*.' "

"Sure you've forgotten? Or don't you like the rest?"

"Bit of both, me lad." Gavin lay down again, stretching out on his back with hands locked behind his head. His slim taut body, its tan smooth and dark, looked like a Greek bronze.

John said, "What was the dream about? You can remember if you try."

"The poet's I wouldn't know. My own was definitely a compliment—to the Garroway family."

"How?" John said. He looked eager and enjoyably puzzled, like a child watching a conjuror.

"Are you utterly insensible to what you have here, me lad!" Gavin made a little, all-embracing gesture. "That house—that garden—this cove! . . . All this, I might say, and Sanctuary too!"

"I *knew* you'd like it," John said, and then, "Sanctuary? What from?"

"My cherished infant!" Gavin laughed. "From everything that you and I don't want. Everything that grates. All the—the *bru-ha-ha* of our ill-fated century, including the H-bomb!"

"Yes. I see what you mean. . . ." John's young face was grave.

"Now for the compliment," Gavin said. "My dream that couldn't be was—well, put in simple words for the young, it was just that I was going to stay here for the rest of my life."

He laughed, and looked up at the sun. "Hey! It must be after six!"

"Guess we'd better get back," John said. He heaved his big body to its feet and picked up his towel. He said suddenly:

"Look, Gavin, you don't *have* to go Monday, do you?"

Gavin rose in one smooth movement. His lithe body made John's look clumsy and overmuscled. "I'm afraid I do," he said. "The Stones are expecting me. It's not that I wouldn't like to stay, but—" He broke off, smiling. "I've remembered the next two lines of that stanza—'The waves that plunged along the shore said only, Dreamer, dream no more.'"

"Now look," John said, "you could send a wire and say you were sick—"

"Don't be mulish, me lad!" Gavin's tone was sharp. He turned and started for the steps in the cliff, but John caught up to him in two strides.

"Now don't get mad," John said. "Please . . ."

Gavin stopped at the foot of the steps, his hand on the white post which carried a PRIVATE PROPERTY sign. He laughed and said, "You tend to forget I'm a testy old man. Sorry."

"What've *you* got to apologize about!" Relief was painted on John's face with a broad-stroked brush. "I was just nervous, I guess. All I wanted to say was that if Mother seemed—well, sort of stiff and social and—and artificial, it's only because she's really awfully shy. You'd never think so, but—"

"Johannes, Johannes!" Gavin cut him short. "It's nothing to do with your mother—who is charming, perfectly charming. It is simply that it would be impolitic for me to offend a senior member of the faculty like Bob Stone. You young plutocrats don't realize the economic situation of the paupers who endeavor to instruct you."

"Okay," John said. "Okay." And then he said, "It's a damn shame!"

Gavin was eyeing the steps, running his glance up their steepness. They were concrete built into the rock; their risers were high but the treads were wide enough for two to use abreast. He said, "A challenge, me lad! Race you to the top!"

John grinned. "You'll be sorry!"

"So?" said Gavin, and maneuvered into position for the inside track. "You ready? All right, then—*off!*"

It was close for half the ascent, and then Gavin forged ahead, to arrive at the top a winner by some half a dozen steps. He was about to turn and jeer at John, puffing and panting behind him, when he looked across the lawn and saw a car roll down the private road and stop outside the garage. It was a coupé—very clean, very shining, but at least twenty years old. Enid Garroway was erect at the wheel, and behind her, its head thrust out of the window, was a big dog with a dark and saturnine face.

Gavin heard John at his shoulder and turned to smile at him. John said, still puffing, "Isn't that—a god-awful jalopy—of Mother's. She won't—get rid of it—"

The dog bayed at them, and Gavin said, "Who's her friend?"

"That's Gill. He was at the vet's—for a bath—" John sounded worried. "Watch him till he knows you."

Her back to them, Mrs. Garroway was getting out of the car. The dog bayed again, and John's mother tilted the car seat forward to let him out.

"Hold it, Mother!" John shouted, but the dog was already streaking across the lawn toward them. It was heavy and powerfully built, standing as high as a collie, but with a flat wiry coat, almost black.

John ran ahead of Gavin and roared, "Gill! Gill! Down, sir!" But the dog swerved out of John's reach and came on.

Mrs. Garroway ran onto the lawn. She looked frightened. Her son's big back was blocking her view; then she moved past him, and stopped dead.

Gill was sitting erect on his short stub of a tail, with both his forepaws in Gavin's hands; the dog reached up the full stretch of his neck so that he could lick Gavin's face.

John said, "For God's sake, Mom, will you look at that!" His eyes were fixed on Gavin and the dog, and there was a sort of awed quality to his smile. Mrs. Garroway turned away and walked quickly toward the house.

John called, "Wait a minute, Mother—" and she said, without turning around, "I have several things to do before dinner." She was frowning, and there was a cold stiffness in her voice which she seemed unable to control.

She got rid of the frown before cocktail time, but the stiffness persisted. Whatever she said or did, or omitted to do or say, the stiffness persisted. She didn't seem able to help it—in spite of the effect it was having on John.

If Gavin Rhodes noticed anything, however, he gave no sign. He was the perfect guest, never speaking unless it was plain he should, and then talking well and easily. And the dog Gill, having started by following him wherever he moved, at last sat motionless beside his chair at the dining-table.

Mrs. Garroway commented on this early in the meal. She said sharply, "*Look* at that dog, John! Make him go away and lie down!"

Her son glared at her and said, "He's perfectly all right, Mother. Unless Gavin doesn't like him sitting there."

Gavin, blandly ignoring the crackling static of conflict, said he was flattered, and slid smoothly into talk of dogs in general and of Gill in particular. It was a useful topic, and lasted quite a while, with John relating how he and his mother had bought Gill as a mongrel pup from a drunken Swedish sailor in San Diego, and Gavin cutting in, astonished, saying, "Mongrel! He's an aristocrat!"

John stared, and even Mrs. Garroway showed signs of interest.

Gavin said, "He's a Rottweiler, me lad—and a damn good one." He launched upon a brief history of the breed, from its beginnings as cattle guard for Roman invading armies, through its adoption and development by the livestock breeders of Würtemberg, down to its recrudescence as a police and war dog.

"That's *fascinating!*" John said. "Isn't it, Mother?" He was beaming.

And that was the end of that—because Mrs. Garroway said, "Most interesting," and the stiffness overwhelmed everything once more. She shot a miserable glance at John, and then made matters worse by trying again and saying, "You seem to have a remarkable fund of information, Doctor Rhodes."

John groaned, "Oh, *Mother!*" Then he closed his mouth as Gavin looked at Mrs. Garroway and said easily, "My dear lady, I'm a mine of smatterings—none of them economically utile. It's a sort of parlor trick . . ."

He went on talking and managed to keep discomfort at bay until the meal was practically over and Mollie brought in the coffee. On the tray she also brought a squat dark bottle which she placed firmly in front of Mrs. Garroway with the words, "Now don't you go forgettin' these tonight!"

John winced as Mrs. Garroway opened the bottle and shook two big yellow capsules into her palm. The procedure seemed to have for him a last-straw quality, and he said, almost savagely, "For God's sake, Mother! Do you *have* to dose yourself?"

Enid Garroway stared at him. Her face flushed, then paled. Deliberately, she put the capsules into her mouth, took a sip of water, and swallowed them. She didn't speak.

Gavin slid into the breach. He took a small flat box from a pocket, opened it, tipped out two white tablets, and casually swallowed them. He smiled at Mrs. Garroway and said, "The trouble with the young is really a matter of psychostomachies. They can't conceive the importance of the digestive tract."

It was his first conversational failure. John, still glaring at his mother, didn't seem to hear, and Mrs. Garroway herself merely said, "It's a vitamin and mineral mixture I'm supposed to take. . . ."

Gavin seemed to shrug without moving his shoulders. He didn't talk anymore, and it was in miserable silence, with the stiffness surrounding them like invisible plastic, that they moved into the living room. John, muttering something no one could hear, lost himself in the corner by the radio-phonograph and began to search through albums of records. Mrs. Garroway sat, very straight, in her usual chair by the piano. Gavin lounged on the big sofa, scratching Gill's head until the dog suddenly put out a forefoot and rested it on his knee in a gesture of dignified supplication.

Gavin looked at Mrs. Garroway. "I have a notion our friend here would like to take me for a walk. You won't mind, will you?" He said it easily, and then, just as easily, stood up and walked out of the room, the dog at his side. The door closed behind them.

John slammed the record album shut, scrambled to his feet, and strode across the room to stand over his mother. His face was white and pinched-looking around the mouth. He was breathing fast. He said unsteadily:

"Look, Mother, what exactly are you trying to do? Why not be honest? If you don't like my friends, come clean with it. Tell them— or me. Or if you can't do that, at least remember there *are* rules of hospitality!"

Enid Garroway looked up at him. Her eyes fell from his. She said, "I—I don't know what you're talking about, Johnnie—" and then couldn't go on.

John said, "Oh yes, you do!" He drew a deep breath. "Either be honest, and tell me—or him!—that you don't want Gavin Rhodes in the house. *Or* behave with ordinary courtesy!"

She said, weakly, "I—I still don't follow, Johnnie—"

"For God's sake, Mother, *will* you remember I'm not a child!" John's hands clenched at his sides. "If it's of any interest to you at all, the man you've been so—so vilely rude to is the best friend I'll ever have! A better friend than I've any right to!"

He turned away. Hands thrust into pockets, head down, he began to pace the room. Mrs. Garroway's eyes were glistening, and now a tear trickled from the corner of one of them. She said, "I didn't mean—I didn't know I was being—being uncivil to Doctor Rhodes . . . I—I'm awfully sorry, darling."

John stopped in the middle of the room. His hands were out of his pockets now, and he was beating a fist into a palm. He said, "I can't understand why you're behaving like this! It's not *you!* It isn't you at all!"

Enid Garroway went to her son and put her hands on his shoulders. She said, "I'm a silly old woman, Johnnie—I was jealous. Don't you see? I—I'd made a lot of plans—of things we were going to do together, when you weren't out with Betty Lou—" Her voice wavered and broke, and she was suddenly in his arms, her face buried against his shoulder.

Slowly, John's frown dissolved. He said huskily, "It's all right, Mom, it's all right."

She pulled away from him, desperately found a handkerchief, and dabbed at her eyes and kissed him. "I'm sorry, Johnnie, I'm so sorry."

John made her sit down again, and brought her a pony of brandy and sat on the arm of her chair. Very soon he had steered the talk back to Gavin, telling her the whole story of the friendship from the time when they had met in Gavin's first class of the semester and had immediately liked each other. . . .

John's eyes were alight, and he gestured as he talked. He said, "I can't begin to explain what it means to me, having Gavin for a friend. If you knew even a part of what he has done for me, Mother—"

He broke off. Mrs. Garroway looked at him and said, "Tell me, Johnnie—do tell me."

He said, in a sudden rush of words, "For one thing, he's shown me what I'm going to do with my life! . . . I'm going to write, Mother! Write—and write—and write! Until I've written something worthwhile." He glared at her, then suddenly smiled. "Listen to me, for God's sake! The boy genius, huh? . . . Look, Mother, just forget all the trimmings and remember your son's going to be a writer."

Enid Garroway reached up, took his hand, and squeezed it. "That's wonderful, darling," she said. "Could I possibly read something . . . sometime?"

"Sure," said her son. "Sure. I'll dig out something tomorrow."

"You know what I think?" Mrs. Garroway said. "I think we ought to have a drink on this—" And, as if on cue, they heard Gill bark outside and the crunching of Gavin's feet on the gravel. She added quickly, "Oh, isn't that lucky! Now Doctor Rhodes can have one with us!"

John bent down and kissed her. "Attagirl!" he said. He was at the other end of the room, mixing drinks, when Gavin came in with the dog at his heels.

There was no stiffness in the atmosphere now, and Gavin was full of quiet gaiety. He took a highball from John, and described how Gill had taken him along the beach. He said, "He's quite a fellow," reaching down a hand and patting the dog's shoulder. "Quite a fellow! . . . What impressed me most was the steps. You see, I ran down them—I hate *walking* any kind of stairs, either way—and instead of getting in my way, or trying to pass, he kept a safe four steps behind me. As I say, I was impressed."

The dog raised its head and stared up at him, resting its chin on the arm of the chair.

"*Look* at that, Mother!" John said.

Mrs. Garroway said, "It's—it's unbelievable!" She smiled at Gavin. "There's one thing, Doctor Rhodes—you'll never need a character reference with Gill around!"

Gavin looked across at her. "My *dear* lady! Surely you don't subscribe to that misleading cliché about dogs and children!"

John laughed, and Mrs. Garroway said, "I've always thought the most frightening thing about clichés was that they were true."

"Only in the main," Gavin said. "One might almost say—when they are true they are very very true; but when they are bad they are horrid."

"Like the little girl with the curl," said Mrs. Garroway.

Gavin went on looking at her with mock gravity. "Exactly," he said. "And let me warn you that the horridest of all is the dangerous, the fatal idea that persons to whom dogs and children take a fancy must *ipso facto* be sterling and trustworthy characters."

He said, "For all you know, I might be planning some skulduggery right now. Such as stealing the silver." He smiled suddenly, impishly. "Or something on a larger scale, maybe . . ."

The next day passed pleasantly, except for one minor cloud which arose at lunchtime and was concerned with John's reluctance to keep a dinner engagement with a childhood girlfriend. But when Gavin added a biting comment to Mrs. Garroway's pleas the boy gave in.

Which explains how it was that John's mother and John's friend dined *à deux* that night, seeming to enjoy each other's company as much as the excellent food.

It was almost at the end of the meal that Mrs. Garroway said suddenly: "I ought to thank you, Doctor Rhodes, for persuading John to go out with Betty Lou." She hesitated. "She's a nice child, really. And she's terribly in love with him."

Gavin smiled. "That shows good taste, at least."

There was a silence, and during it Mollie brought in coffee. After she had poured it, Mrs. Garroway took her two capsules from the bottle on the tray, and Gavin, smiling at her, took his tablets from the box in his pocket.

He said, "Don't worry about John, Mrs. Garroway. He's merely going through that tiresome process known as growing up."

"I know," Mrs. Garroway said, "I know." She sighed, and her face seemed older. She sat straighter and said abruptly, "John seems determined to make a career out of writing. What do you think about it? About his chances?"

Gavin looked at her shrewdly. "You've been reading some of his stuff, haven't you?"

"Yes. This morning. I—I didn't like it." She drew a deep breath. "I thought it was—well, not very well written."

Gavin said, "Don't be discouraged. The boy has talent. Latent— but lots of it . . ." He hesitated. "As to a career, let me put it this way: *If* John has to earn his living when he leaves college, then I couldn't practically recommend writing for his profession. But, if he hasn't—if there's enough money, to put it vulgarly—then I most definitely do! As I said, there's talent in him."

He had been looking down, but now he raised his eyes to Mrs. Garroway's. "You'll have to forgive my bluntness," he said.

"There's nothing to forgive," Mrs. Garroway said, and smiled at him. "Now I'll answer *your* question. John does *not* have to worry about earning his way. We live quietly, as you see, but then I'm naturally unostentatious. There's plenty of money. More than enough." She stopped abruptly, as if she had intended to say more, then decided not to.

Gavin said slowly, "Then let him write—*make* him write."

Mrs. Garroway looked at him steadily. She said, "Thank you. You've made me feel better. Ever so much better!"

That was at eight o'clock. Two and a half hours later, John Garroway turned his convertible into the private road and swooped down toward the house.

His headlights showed him the open maw of the garage, with his mother's ancient but gleaming coupé parked neatly at the left. They also showed the unexpected sight of a man's figure, its back to him, bent over at one side of the open door. John braked, and the figure straightened, turned, and revealed itself as Gavin. Beside him was the dark shape of Gill, a short heavy stick between his jaws.

John pulled up on the apron of the garage. He leaned out and said, "Hi! . . . What you doing?" and Gavin came nearer to the car. He was drying his hands on a handkerchief, and he grinned and said, "Washing. Any rule against it?"

John looked past him and saw the tin of powdered soap under the faucet in the wall. He grinned and said, "What's the matter with a bathroom?" and Gavin looked down at the dog and said, "Gill, you explain."

The dog made a sound in his throat, refusing to release the stick. Gavin grinned at John. "It's all his fault. We found that stick on the beach and he brought it up. I was throwing it for him and it went under your mother's car." He looked at his hands, then ruefully down at the knees of his trousers. "I, of course, did the retrieving."

John laughed. "You and that dog!" he said, and drove slowly into the garage.

As he came out, Gavin was putting the can of soap back on the shelf. They stepped out onto the apron together and John jerked a contemptuous thumb at the coupé. "I *wish* Mother would get rid of that heap," he said, and reached up, pulled down the garage door, and bolted it.

Gavin tucked away his handkerchief. "Got off early, didn't you?" he said. "How was the young woman?"

John's big shoulders lifted in a shrug. "Oh, all right, I guess."

They walked slowly to the house, and on the porch Gavin stopped, looking around him. He said, "God, it's beautiful here!"—and sighed.

John said, "How did you and Mother get on?" He said it awkwardly, as if he'd had to force himself to say it.

But Gavin didn't seem to notice. He said, "Like a house afire, me lad. . . . She was kind enough to ask me to stay on."

"That's wonderful!" John beamed. "Now I can go ahead with that 'Turtle Dove' story. You could sort of steer me on every day's work—"

Gavin smiled. "After I've spent a couple of days with the Stones," he said. "But I could be back on Wednesday, around lunchtime."

John's smile vanished. He said, "Oh, hell—" and Gavin threw a casual arm around John's shoulders.

The morning came, promising another gemlike day, and Gavin Rhodes, adamant in turning down all John's offers to drive him the sixty-odd miles to Coronado, packed a suitcase, had breakfast, and allowed John to take him down to the Greyhound station in El Morro. Gavin promised he'd be back by the noon bus on Wednesday. . . .

The rest of Monday passed, and all Tuesday. On Wednesday, just after noon, the Greyhound from San Diego rolled down the highway into El Morro, turned left on Pine Avenue, and hissed to a stop.

Gavin, suitcase in hand, was the first passenger to alight. He looked quickly around, and then started across the street to where John's convertible was parked at the curb, conspicuous by the shining cream of its paint and the scarlet spokes of its wire wheels. Gavin stared at its driver—and broke into a run which took him across the road in long strides.

He reached the side of the car and said, "John—for God's sake—what've you done to yourself?"

John grinned. "You ought to see the other guy!" he said. There was a broad band of adhesive tape across a dressing on his forehead, and two similar patches on cheek and jaw. And his right forearm, as it lay on the wheel, was bandaged from wrist to elbow.

Gavin threw his suitcase into the backseat and climbed into the car. His face was gray-pale under its heavy tan. He said, sharply, "Don't play the fool. What happened?"

John said, "Okay, okay, keep your shirt on. Little car trouble, that's all. That jalopy of Mother's turned on me. . . ." He laughed, and started the engine.

Over the whir of the starter Gavin's voice was loud. "What the hell are you talking about? You never drive the thing!"

John let the motor idle. He said, "Well, I did. Day before yesterday. Only a couple hours after you'd left, as a matter of fact." He grinned at Gavin again, plainly delighted to be the focal point of an adventure. "Mother wanted me to pick her up a new tire. So I climbed in the heap and started to bring it downtown here. I thought the brakes seemed on the spongy side, but I didn't really worry about them." His laugh was almost a giggle. "Then I started down the steep stretch past the golf club. I was doing about forty, I guess—maybe a little better—when I saw the signal against me at the bottom, *and* a couple of damn big oil trucks turning out of the canyon road. So I started to brake. Only there weren't any brakes! I mean, not any!"

He giggled again and looked at Gavin, who muttered under his breath.

"So I had to think pretty fast," John said. "I steered as close as I could to the shoulder—it's real soft along there—and I jumped. . . ."

Gavin muttered again. Some of the color was back under his tan, but his face was still set, unsmiling.

"Well, I rolled quite a way," John said. "I ended up in the ditch, a little woozy but all in one piece." He grinned. "Good day's work, really—you know how I hated that heap."

"What happened to it?" Gavin said.

"What didn't!" John laughed. "Scratch one jalopy! . . . I'd tried to head it into the side, but somehow it went on and hit one of the trucks square amidships. Fortunately nothing exploded—but, brother, the thing sure wrecked itself!"

Gavin said, "What had happened to the brakes?" He was pulling a pack of cigarettes from his pocket, looking down at it as he spoke.

"There wasn't any fluid," John said. "The master cylinder must have sprung a leak. The crate was pretty ancient, and that sort of thing is always happening."

"Yes," Gavin said, "I suppose it is." He shook his head. "Thank God it wasn't your mother! She might—she might have been killed!"

A little shudder shook John's shoulders. "She would have been," he said.

The days ran into each other in gold-and-blue sequence, and now, after ten days which seemed to have passed like two, there were only forty-eight hours left before Gavin must leave, to return to the University and take up the summer-school teaching which, as he explained with a wry smile, was necessitated by the inevitable penury, in this day and age, of a tutor of the young.

He broke the news at breakfast. John dropped his knife and fork and said, "Gavin, you can't go! Isn't there any way you can duck it?" And Mrs. Garroway, who had long since dropped the "Doctor," said, "Oh *no*, Gavin! You mustn't leave us like this." And Gill chose this exact moment to emit one of what John called his "lost lone wolf" whines, and even Mollie, who happened to be in the breakfast room at the time, said, "Why, Mister-Doctor-Rhodes, sir, you ain't never goin' to up an' run out on us!"

But Gavin Rhodes made it clear that leave he must. He had, it seemed, already booked plane passage for the day after tomorrow.

"Which brings me," he said, "to the real point. Which is an invitation—an invitation to which I'll brook no refusal!" He smiled at the Garroways, and explained. The Tollers were at the Grand Theater in Los Angeles, winding up a triumphal tour in *Paradise for Fools,* and he wanted Mrs. Garroway and John to be his guests at the performance tonight, after they'd been his guests at dinner.

"There's a catch in it, of course," he said. "There always is with me. John, I hope, will drive us up, but I want to see my lawyer, so I'd have to be in town a couple of hours before dinnertime."

And it was arranged that way. They left El Morro at three-fifteen and reached Los Angeles just before five. They separated outside the Biltmore Garage with an agreement to meet at Escoffier's at seven on the dot. John and his mother took a taxi for parts west, where Mrs. Garroway would do some feminine shopping and John would browse in his favorite bookstore. Gavin set off on foot in the direction of Spring Street.

But he never reached it. As soon as he had turned the corner into Pershing Square, he changed his course, cutting over to Seventh. Instead of seeming pressed for time and a trifle on edge about his appointment, he now strolled easily along the crowded sidewalks until he came to a big chain drugstore sandwiched between a newsreel theater and a restaurant.

He went into the drugstore and came out, five minutes later, stowing a small package into his hip pocket. He started strolling again, this time striking south, but all the time keeping to the bigger, more crowded thoroughfares.

He visited in turn a jewelry store, another druggist, a giant establishment labeled *Helstrom's Hardware—Everything for the Home and Garden,* then back again to Pershing Square—to a quiet tobacco-and-pipe shop.

When he left the last, it was barely six o'clock and he still had an hour to kill. Disposed in the pockets of his loosely cut suit were his purchases from the drugstores and the Helstrom emporium. In one neat parcel which he carried openly were the separate packages from the other stores.

He struck over to Fifth again and to the Biltmore Garage. He found John's car and put one parcel in the glove compartment. He crossed back to the hotel, went to the bar, and had two quiet, quick drinks. When he lifted the first, there was a faint tremor in his fingers, but when he set the glass down the hand was as steady as a watchmaker's.

He then took a taxi to Escoffier's. Ten minutes after his arrival he was joined by Mrs. Garroway and John, and then began a highly successful evening, with Gavin as perfect a host as he had proved himself a guest. The dinner was good, their seats at the theater better, and the play itself best of all.

They were home by twenty to one and, to John's and Gavin's astonishment, found supper waiting for them. It was laid out in the living room, in front of a log fire which had been lighted long enough to be cheerful and recently enough not to be giving off too much heat. It was a good and imaginative meal, with everything ready to be heated and eaten, or opened and drunk. They served themselves, Mrs. Garroway controlling the chafing dishes, Gavin in charge of the liquor, and John feeding the Victrola with suitable music.

It was just after they had finished that Gavin, detaching Gill's adoring head from his knee, left the room suddenly, to return with the parcel he had stored in the glove compartment of the car. He opened it to reveal two small gift packages which he carried to the hearth, where he stood between Mrs. Garroway and John. He said, *"Timeo Danaes—"* and made the presentations on just the right note of mock ceremony—for John the latest in wickless lighters, for Mrs. Garroway a miniature flashlight for her purse, surprisingly efficient and charming to look at in its case of hammered silver.

They thanked him, Mrs. Garroway with a flush in her cheeks which made her look younger than ever, John with a wide embarrassed grin and eyes which—perhaps because of the drinks he had had—were suspiciously moist. . . .

It was an hour later that Mrs. Garroway, pulling a robe around her over her nightgown, went into her son's room. John was in bed, reading. She sat on the edge of it as John said, "Hi, Mother, come to tuck me in?" He was a trifle high, but in spite of the smile he didn't look happy.

Mrs. Garroway put out a hand as if to touch him, but then drew it back into her lap. She said, "Wasn't that a lovely evening? I don't know when I've enjoyed myself more!"

John said, "It was swell—" and then frowned at himself for juvenility. "I mean it was—perfect. It was *whole*—a sort of *entity* of a party."

"That sounds awfully clever, darling." Mrs. Garroway laughed softly. "But I think I know what you mean."

"It was Gavin, of course," John said. "When he does something, he does it *right!*"

He sat up and locked his arms around his knees under the covers. He gave up all pretense of sophistication, looked at his mother, and said, "Isn't he terrific, Mom? Isn't he?"

Mrs. Garroway's hand came out again, and this time it did touch him, for one brief instant passing across his forehead and sliding down his cheek. She said, "Darling, I think he's perfectly charming. In fact," she added, "I'm not sure he isn't *the* most charming person I ever met."

She stood up then, bent over the bed, and kissed her son. "You'd better go to sleep, hadn't you, Johnnie?" she said. "Didn't I hear you promising Gavin you'd finish that story before he left?"

"That's right," John said, and as she reached the door he put down his book and turned out the light.

Mrs. Garroway went back to her own room, passing the head of the stairs. She didn't see Gill—whom she'd put to bed on the back porch half an hour ago—crouching at the foot.

Her door closed, and the dog began noiselessly to mount the stairs. He reached the landing and padded along the corridor of the ell, toward the guest rooms. He stopped at the last door and raised a tentative foot to scratch at the lower panel.

Inside the room, Gavin Rhodes started involuntarily at the sound. In pajamas, he was seated at the writing table in the window. Spread out over the blotter in front of him was a newspaper upon which, open and spilling their contents, were the packages he had carried back in his pockets from Los Angeles.

The scratch at the door came again. Gavin smiled and got to his feet. He opened the door silently, and Gill flowed into the room.

Gavin said quietly, "Hello, chum—late tonight, aren't you?"

Gill wagged the whole rear half of his big body. Gavin stroked his head, then pointed to the corner by the head of the bed. Without hesitation, the dog padded over, settled himself on the rug, and lay down. One contented sigh escaped him, and then he slept.

Gavin sat down at the writing table again. He lifted a hand and saw that it was trembling. Then he leaned back, deliberately relaxing, closing his eyes and letting his arms hang down almost to the floor.

After a few moments he opened his eyes and sat up. He held both hands out, looking at them. The fingers were steady now. He hitched his chair closer to the table, picked up a small cardboard box which had come out of one of the packages, opened it, and shook out the upper and lower halves of several gelatin capsules, ready to be filled and put together. The capsules were yellow.

Gavin picked out two halves and placed them in the middle of the newspaper. From another package he took a small envelope which he opened carefully. It was filled with a fine-grained, dark-gray powder, which he spooned into the lower half of the capsule with the blade of a penknife until the gelatin container was half full. . . . Now the last of the packages—and another envelope—and a little pile of brownish crystals which he added to the powder . . .

And then he was staring down at a complete capsule, dark yellow against the white paper, which was identical in size and color with the capsules which Enid Garroway took every night with her coffee.

It was over. It was done. At the first try. He examined it carefully, holding it this way and that against the light. Satisfied, he crossed to the closet and very carefully put the capsule into a pocket of his dark jacket.

He crossed the room and picked up a traveling clock from the bed-side table. Its hands stood at twenty minutes past three. He pondered a moment, set the alarm for seven-thirty, then went back to the writing table and carefully wrapped the remains of all the packages in the newspaper, making a neat parcel which he slid under his pillow.

Five minutes later he was in bed.

The alarm went off, faithfully, at half-past seven.

Gavin dragged himself out of bed, shaved, and took a shower, making a minimum of noise in the process.

He was out of the house, Gill beside him, at five minutes to eight—having heard vague sounds of Mollie beginning to move about in her room behind the garage. Beneath his coat was the parcel wrapped in newspaper.

He circled the garden and came to the latticed enclosure which hid the big incinerator. Quietly, he lifted the iron lid and slipped the parcel into the dark maw.

He struck a match, touched it to the edge of the paper, and stood by, picking up the iron bar which served for a poker and continually stirring at the flaming mass until, with hardly a wisp of smoke, it was completely consumed.

He raked over the pile of ash, then put the poker back as he had found it. With Gill at his heels, he left the latticed enclosure and went along the path beside the privet hedge and came to the steps to the beach.

He trotted down their steepness, not quite so fast as usual. Gill, who had dropped behind, followed four steps behind.

They reached the sand and started along it, southward. The dog shed his staidness and raced around Gavin in furious, ever-widening circles. The beach was deserted, and the little breeze off the ocean was light and heady, like a good champagne, and the climbing sun sparkled on the crests of the little rippling waves.

Gavin breathed deeply as he walked. At first his hands were thrust into his pockets, but presently he took them out and, still walking, held them in front of him, eyeing them critically. They were steady, absolutely steady, and he smiled to himself. He spotted a piece of driftwood, picked it up, and threw it into the gentle foam of the surf as Gill plunged delightedly after it. . . .

They reached the house again at nine-thirty, Gavin looking as fresh as if he had had eight hours of undisturbed sleep; Gill was drenched and ecstatic. Gavin left him outside to dry off, went in, found Mollie, and within minutes was eating an enormous breakfast.

It was eleven before Mrs. Garroway came downstairs, and nearly noon before there was any sight of John. He appeared in robe and pajamas, announcing that he had a hangover and regarding Gavin's obvious well-being with admiring awe.

Gavin laughed at him. "All you need, me lad, is a good honest sweat." He outlined a program: John would eat; John would change; John and Gavin would visit the tennis club and play two hard sets of singles, after which they would drive straight back, go down to the beach, and swim.

John blinked. "But I've got to work," he said. "You wanted me to finish that thing—"

Gavin cut him short. "You'll never write a line worth anything, me lad, with a head full of cotton!"

As it turned out, Gavin's program was carried out to the full, so that it was past midafternoon before John could get back to his own room and start to write. He felt better. He felt, as he said, wonderful; but time is time and it was with a worried look that he appeared for cocktails several minutes late.

He said, "Gavin, I just can't finish it in time!"

Gavin said, "In the remote days of my infancy, I had an English nurse. She used to say, 'There's no such word as *cahn't* in the diction'ry, Mister Gavin.' I think she had something there. . . ."

Mrs. Garroway said, "*You* can make it, John."

John grinned ruefully. "I guess I can," he said, and the topic wasn't touched upon again until the end of dinner, when Gavin suddenly said, looking at his watch:

"Why don't you take your coffee upstairs and start in, me lad. I'll

be on the beach in an hour and a half, and you can meet me there."
He smiled at Mrs. Garroway. "If you don't mind my taking Gill for a
farewell walk?" he said.

"Of course I don't!" Mrs. Garroway said.

"But look, Gavin—" John checked abruptly as Gavin looked at
him with one eyebrow raised. "Okay, okay!" He picked up his coffee
cup, grinned, and said, "What a slave driver!" to his mother and went
quickly out of the room.

They heard his footsteps going up the stairs, and Gavin glanced at
Mrs. Garroway apologetically. He said, "I'm sorry. Perhaps I
shouldn't ride him so hard."

Mrs. Garroway said, "It's good for him, Gavin." She smiled. "And
you know it."

Gavin said, "You're very understanding," and smiled back at her,
gratefully.

Mrs. Garroway said, "Oh, my pills—" and reached for the bottle
on the tray. She wasn't looking at Gavin as she unscrewed the top
and shook out two capsules—and for one flickering instant his face
paled and contorted, like the face of a man before making some
tremendous and dangerous effort. But then he was himself again. As
the woman put the capsules into her mouth and reached for her water
glass, he said lightly, "Ah yes, medicine time!" and pulled out his
box of tablets—

And fumbled it, most realistically. The little box flew up into the
air. He reached out, grabbing for it, and as he caught it, his hand
came quickly down, his wrist striking against Mrs. Garroway's bottle
of capsules and knocking it off the tray.

The capsules spilled over the table, some of them rolling. As if
flustered, Gavin grabbed at the bottle itself, apparently righting it but
in the process shaking out the remaining capsules. They were now
strewn all around, yellow against the white of the cloth.

He said, "I'm so sorry—how clumsy of me!" and dropped his box
of tablets back into his pocket with his right hand, holding the bottle
in his left.

Mrs. Garroway laughed. She said, "No harm done," and began to
collect the few capsules which had fallen onto the tray.

As she spoke, Gavin's right hand came out of his pocket, and hidden in its cupped palm was the capsule he had made himself during the night.

He stood up, saying, "Now don't you bother. The least I can do is to collect them for you."

He was very busy—and very careful. The first capsule that went into the bottle was the one from his pocket, and he kept the bottle motionless until there were enough other capsules on top of the first to hold it in place at the bottom.

He was very busy—and very careful. He even counted the capsules as he picked them up. At the end he said, "That's seventy-six. . . . Would that be right?"

Mrs. Garroway smiled. "Just about, I should think. Please don't worry about it."

Gavin put the bottle back on the tray. He sat down, one hand casually in a jacket pocket. He let the extra capsule, which he had replaced with his, slip from his fingers inside the pocket. He saw Mrs. Garroway reaching for the cigarettes and was quick to hand them to her, then hold a light.

In a little while they moved into the living room, and, as he had known she would, she said, "Is it too warm for a fire, do you think?"

"Not a bit," he replied easily. He crossed to the hearth and lit the gas jets under the logs. When he came back to his chair, the extra capsule was no longer in his pocket; in fact, it was no longer in existence—except as ashes.

They chatted—about the theater last night, about John, about Gill, about the new car Mrs. Garroway was buying. He forced himself to go slowly, but at last the moment arrived when he could properly glance at his watch in such a way that the woman was bound to say, as she did, "Isn't it about time for Gill's walk?"

Hearing his name, the dog jumped up, his head turned to look expectantly at his idol.

Gavin smiled at his hostess and spoke to the dog. "All right," he said. "All right, you bully!" He got to his feet. "I'll just go and change my shoes," he said, and Mrs. Garroway asked, "Do you think John's finished?"

Gavin tilted his head toward the ceiling, holding up a finger for silence. Faintly from above came the sound of a typewriter, working in hesitant bursts.

Gavin said, "He's trying, anyway."

"He'll get it done," Mrs. Garroway said. Gavin nodded and got himself out of the room, Gill ahead of him, as she picked up a book.

He went upstairs quietly. He could hear the boy's typewriter still going. He reached his room, shut himself into it, and dropped into a chair as if his legs suddenly had lost the strength to hold him upright. He found he was shaking, shaking all over, and determinedly he relaxed his whole body, dropping his arms down to his sides, thrusting out his feet, letting his head loll back as he drew deep breaths into his lungs.

Gill crouched beside the chair. After a minute or two he whined low in his throat.

Gavin sat up. He looked at his hands, then down at the dog. He said, "You blackguardly old villain!" and pulled himself out of the chair, quite steadily, went to the closet, found his beach shoes, and put them on.

As he tied the laces, his lips were moving, reflecting the simple arithmetic running through his head—

Seventy-six at two per day . . . that equals thirty-eight days . . . which is a week over a month . . . and I'll have been away from here so long I'll be just a friend of the bereaved . . .

He heard the whispers coming from his mouth and cut them off abruptly. He finished tying the lace of the second shoe, straightened and called loudly, "Come on, Gill!" and marched out of the room and along the passage of the ell to the head of the stairs. He could still hear the typewriter stammering from John's room.

He ran down the stairs with Gill behind him. They left the house and struck out over the lawn, toward the steps to the beach. He was halfway across, the dog at his heels, when he saw Mrs. Garroway coming toward him. In the bright pale moonlight he could see her clearly. There was a bunch of roses in her hand, and she held them up as she neared him.

She said, "Growing flowers is a vice, almost. One can't ever leave the poor things alone."

Gavin said, "Maybe they prefer you to pick them," and she laughed softly, "You ought to have been a diplomat, Gavin!" Then she started for the house as he gave her a mock salute and went on toward the steps to the beach.

He reached them, and Gill fell behind. Gavin was now in full command of himself again; he was even whistling as he started down the steps at his usual trot.

He reached the bend in the cliff, where the steps took their only curve.

His whistling was cut off, in the middle of a bar. He seemed to stumble—and pitched outward and downward in a curving, head-foremost, terrifying arc. A strange sound, half scream, half shout, came from him—followed by an instant of eerie silence which mingled with the hush-hushing noise of the gentle surf and was then broken by a series of soft and crushing semi-liquid thuds from seventy feet below.

And then no sound—no sound at all except the surf.

But the cry that had come from him—that half-shouted scream—seemed to hang in the air as if it were fighting not to die away into nothingness. On the porch, Mrs. Garroway stood with her head half-turned. The sound seemed to have frozen her—but after a moment she dropped the flowers and ran toward the steps.

As she reached the head of them, another sound broke through the murmur of the surf. It was the lost and lonely and brokenhearted baying of a dog.

She started down, reached the curve, and stopped on the angled step. She bent quickly—and from the tough, two-inch-thick trunk of a laurel in the cliffside unwound the double strand of garden wire that was wrapped around the laurel trunk and stretched across, four inches above the tread of the step, to a post on the other side.

One end free, she moved quickly to the far side of the step, starting to untie the other end of the wire from the post. From below, the howling of the dog mounted in crescendo—and through it she heard a window being flung open in the house above—and then John's voice shouting, "Gill—Gill! . . . Is there anyone down there? . . . What's going on?"

Mrs. Garroway stood up. The cliff-face hid her from the house. She called, frantically, "John—John—*hurry!* . . . Gavin's hurt!"

Her hands, steady and certain, coiled the wire neatly and slipped it into a side-pocket of her dress.

It was midnight—and it was all over.

Mrs. Garroway closed the front door behind Doctor Gundarsen and leaned against it, closing her eyes. Around her, the quietness of the house closed in.

She was tired—but it was all over. The body of Gavin Rhodes had been taken away. It was all over—the sirens, the ambulance, the questions, the sympathy. It was finished.

Upstairs, John was sleeping like a weary child under the shot of sedation Doctor Gundarsen had given him. Off in her room, the exhausted Mollie also slept soundly.

Mrs. Garroway was alone. She opened her eyes and stood away from the door and walked slowly across the hall to the shelves beside the telephone. On the bottom shelf, where it always stood, was her gardening basket. She took the coil of wire from the pocket of her dress and dropped it into the basket, on top of her pruning shears.

Then she walked along the passage to the dark kitchen. As she entered, she could hear the surf below. She switched on a light and crossed to the screen door of the back porch. She peered through the screen and could see Gill lying on his bed. She said, "Poor Gill!" But the dog gave no sign of hearing her. It lay there, seeming somehow to look smaller, its heavy head slumped hopelessly between outspread forepaws.

Mrs. Garroway crossed back to the sink. She turned on the cold water, then reached up to a cupboard and took down the dark bottle which held her capsules.

For a long moment she looked at it meditatively—and then unscrewed the top, and reached under the sink and switched on the garbage disposal. The blades whirred grindingly as she upended the bottle over the sink and watched the capsules disappear.

She switched off the motor, and let the water run for a long moment while she put the top back on the bottle and put it into her pocket.

Then she turned off the water, turned off the light, and went slowly out . . .

THE
BLESSINGTON
METHOD

by Stanley Ellin

Mr. Treadwell was a small, likeable man who worked for a prosperous company in New York City, and whose position with the company entitled him to an office of his own. Late one afternoon of a fine day in June a visitor entered this office. The visitor was stout, well-dressed, and imposing. His complexion was smooth and pink, his small, nearsighted eyes shone cheerfully behind heavy, horn-rimmed eyeglasses.

"My name," he said, after laying aside a bulky portfolio and shaking Mr. Treadwell's hand with a crushing grip, "is Bunce, and I am a representative of the Society for Gerontology. I am here to help you with your problem, Mr. Treadwell."

Mr. Treadwell sighed. "Since you are a total stranger to me, my friend," he said, "and since I have never heard of the outfit you claim to represent, and, above all, since I have no problem which could possibly concern you, I am sorry to say that I am not in the market for whatever you are peddling. Now, if you don't mind—"

"Mind?" said Bunce. "Of course, I mind. The Society for Gerontology does not try to sell anything to anybody, Mr. Treadwell. Its interests are purely philanthropic. It examines case histories, draws up reports, works toward the solution of one of the most tragic situations we face in modern society."

"Which is?"

"That should have been made obvious by the title of the organization, Mr. Treadwell. Gerontology is the study of old age and the problems concerning it. Do not confuse it with geriatrics, please. Geriatrics is concerned with the diseases of old age. Gerontology deals with old age as the problem itself."

"I'll try to keep that in mind," Mr. Treadwell said impatiently. "Meanwhile, I suppose, a small donation is in order? Five dollars, say?"

"No, no, Mr. Treadwell, not a penny, not a red cent. I quite understand that this is the traditional way of dealing with various philanthropic organizations, but the Society for Gerontology works in a different way entirely. Our objective is to help you with your problem first. Only then would we feel we have the right to make any claim on you."

"Fine," said Mr. Treadwell more amiably. "That leaves us all even. I have no problem, so you get no donation. Unless you'd rather reconsider?"

"Reconsider?" said Bunce in a pained voice. "It is you, Mr. Treadwell, and not I who must reconsider. Some of the most pitiful cases the Society deals with are those of people who have long refused to recognize or admit their problem. I have worked months on your case, Mr. Treadwell. I never dreamed you would fall into that category."

Mr. Treadwell took a deep breath. "Would you mind telling me just what you mean by that nonsense about working on my case? I was never a case for any damned society or organization in the book!"

It was the work of a moment for Bunce to whip open his portfolio and extract several sheets of paper from it.

"If you will bear with me," he said, "I should like to sum up the gist of these reports. You are forty-seven years old and in excellent health. You own a home in East Sconsett, Long Island, on which there are nine years of mortgage payments still due, and you also own a late-model car on which eighteen monthly payments are yet to be made. However, due to an excellent salary you are in prosperous circumstances. Am I correct?"

"As correct as the credit agency which gave you that report," said Mr. Treadwell.

Bunce chose to overlook this. "We will now come to the point. You have been happily married for twenty-three years, and have one daughter who was married last year and now lives with her husband in Chicago. Upon her departure from your home your father-in-law, a widower and somewhat crotchety gentleman, moved into the house and now resides with you and your wife."

Bunce's voice dropped to a low, impressive note. "He is seventy-two years old, and, outside of a touch of bursitis in his right shoulder, admits to exceptional health for his age. He has stated on several occasions that he hopes to live another twenty years, and according to actuarial statistics which my Society has on file, *he has every chance of achieving this.* Now do you understand, Mr. Treadwell?"

It took a long time for the answer to come. "Yes," said Mr. Treadwell at last, almost in a whisper. "Now I understand."

"Good," said Bunce sympathetically. "Very good. The first step is always a hard one—the admission that there *is* a problem hovering over you, clouding every day that passes. Nor is there any need to ask why you make efforts to conceal it even from yourself. You wish to spare Mrs. Treadwell your unhappiness, don't you?"

Mr. Treadwell nodded.

"Would it make you feel better," asked Bunce, "if I told you that Mrs. Treadwell shared your own feelings? That she, too, feels her father's presence in her home as a burden which grows heavier each day?"

"But she can't!" said Mr. Treadwell in dismay. "She was the one who wanted him to live with us in the first place, after Sylvia got married, and we had a spare room. She pointed out how much he had done for us when we first got started, and how easy he was to get along with, and how little expense it would be—it was she who sold me on the idea. I can't believe she didn't mean it!"

"Of course, she meant it. She knew all the traditional emotions at the thought of her old father living alone somewhere, and offered all the traditional arguments on his behalf, and was sincere every moment. The trap she led you both into was the pitfall that awaits anyone who indulges in murky, sentimental thinking. Yes, indeed, I'm sometimes inclined to believe that Eve ate the apple just to make the serpent happy," said Bunce, and shook his head grimly at the thought.

"Poor Carol," groaned Mr. Treadwell. "If I had only known that she felt as miserable about this as I did—"

"Yes?" said Bunce. "What would you have done?"

Mr. Treadwell frowned. "I don't know. But there must have been something we could have figured out if we put our heads together."

"What?" Bunce asked. "Drive the man out of the house?"

"Oh, I don't mean exactly like that."

"What then?" persisted Bunce. "Send him to an institution? There are some extremely luxurious institutions for the purpose. You'd have to consider one of them, since he could not possibly be regarded as a charity case; nor, for that matter, could I imagine him taking kindly to the idea of going to a public institution."

"Who would?" said Mr. Treadwell. "And as for the expensive kind, well, I did look into the idea once, but when I found out what they'd cost I knew it was out. It would take a fortune."

"Perhaps," suggested Bunce, "he could be given an apartment of his own—a small, inexpensive place with someone to take care of him."

"As it happens, that's what he moved out of to come live with us. And on that business of someone taking care of him—you'd never believe what it costs. That is, even allowing we could find someone to suit him."

"Right!" Bunce said, and struck the desk sharply with his fist. "Right in every respect, Mr. Treadwell."

Mr. Treadwell looked at him angrily. "What do you mean—right? I had the idea you wanted to help me with this business, but you haven't come up with a thing yet. On top of that you make it sound as if we're making great progress."

"We are, Mr. Treadwell, we are. Although you weren't aware of it, we have just completed the second step to your solution. The first step was the admission that there was a problem; the second step was the realization that no matter which way you turn, there seems to be no logical or practical solution to the problem. In this way you are not only witnessing, you are actually participating in the marvelous operation of The Blessington Method, which, in the end, places the one possible solution squarely in your hands."

"The Blessington Method?"

"Forgive me," said Bunce. "In my enthusiasm I used a term not yet in scientific vogue. I must explain, therefore, that The Blessington Method is the term my co-workers at the Society for Gerontology have given to its course of procedure. It is so titled in honor of J. G. Blessington, the Society's founder, and one of the great men of our era. He has not achieved his proper acclaim yet, but he will. Mark my words, Mr. Treadwell, some day his name will resound louder than that of Malthus."

"Funny I never heard of him," reflected Mr. Treadwell. "Usually I keep up with the newspapers. And another thing," he added, eyeing Bunce narrowly, "we never did get around to clearing up just how you happened to list me as one of your cases, and how you managed to turn up so much about me."

Bunce laughed delightedly. "It does sound mysterious when you put it like that, doesn't it? Well, there's really no mystery to it at all. You see, Mr. Treadwell, the Society has hundreds of investigators scouting this great land of ours from coast to coast, although the public at large is not aware of this. It is against the rules of the Society for any employee to reveal that he is a professional investigator—he would immediately lose effectiveness.

"Nor do these investigators start off with some specific person as their subject. Their interest lies in *any* aged person who is willing to talk about himself, and you would be astonished at how garrulous most aged people are about their most intimate affairs. That is, of course, as long as they are among strangers.

"These subjects are met at random on park benches, in saloons, in libraries—in any place conducive to comfort and conversation. The investigator befriends the subjects, draws them out—seeks, especially, to learn all he can about the younger people on whom they are dependent."

"You mean," said Mr. Treadwell with growing interest, "the people who support them."

"No, no," said Bunce. "You are making the common error of equating *dependence* and *finances*. In many cases, of course, there is a financial dependence, but that is a minor part of the picture. The important factor is that there is always an *emotional* dependence.

Even where a physical distance may separate the older person from the younger, that emotional dependence is always present. It is like a current passing between them. The younger person by the mere realization that the aged exist is burdened by guilt and anger. It was his personal experience with this tragic dilemma of our times that led J. G. Blessington to his great work."

"In other words," said Mr. Treadwell, "you mean that even if the old man were not living with us, things would be just as bad for Carol and me?"

"You seem to doubt that, Mr. Treadwell. But tell me, what makes things bad for you now, to use your own phrase?"

Mr. Treadwell thought this over. "Well," he said, "I suppose it's just a case of having a third person around all the time. It gets on your nerves after a while."

"But your daughter lived as a third person in your home for over twenty years," pointed out Bunce. "Yet, I am sure you didn't have the same reaction to her."

"But that's different," Mr. Treadwell protested. "You can have fun with a kid, play with her, watch her growing up—"

"Stop right there!" said Bunce. "Now you are hitting the mark. All the years your daughter lived with you, you could take pleasure in watching her grow, flower like an exciting plant, take form as an adult being. But the old man in your house can only wither and decline now, and watching that process casts a shadow on your life. Isn't that the case?"

"I suppose it is."

"In that case, do you suppose it would make any difference if he lived elsewhere? Would you be any the less aware that he was withering and declining and looking wistfully in your direction from a distance?"

"Of course not. Carol probably wouldn't sleep half the night worrying about him, and I'd have him on my mind all the time because of her. That's perfectly natural, isn't it?"

"It is, indeed, and, I am pleased to say, your recognition of that completes the third step of The Blessington Method. You now realize that it is not the *presence* of the aged subject which creates the problem, but his *existence*."

Mr. Treadwell pursed his lips thoughtfully. "I don't like the sound of that."

"Why not? It merely states the fact, doesn't it?"

"Maybe it does. But there's something about it that leaves a bad taste in the mouth. It's like saying that the only way Carol and I can have our troubles settled is by the old man's dying."

"Yes," Bunce said gravely, "it is like saying that."

"Well, I don't like it—not one bit. Thinking you'd like to see somebody dead can make you feel pretty mean, and as far as I know it's never killed anybody yet."

Bunce smiled. "Hasn't it?" he said gently.

He and Mr. Treadwell studied each other in silence. Then Mr. Treadwell pulled a handkerchief from his pocket with nerveless fingers and patted his forehead with it.

"You," he said with deliberation, "are either a lunatic or a practical joker. Either way, I'd like you to clear out of here. That's fair warning."

Bunce's face was all sympathetic concern. "Mr. Treadwell," he cried, "don't you realize you were on the verge of the fourth step? Don't you see how close you were to your solution?"

Mr. Treadwell pointed to the door. "Out—before I call the police."

The expression on Bunce's face changed from concern to disgust. "Oh, come, Mr. Treadwell, you don't believe anybody would pay attention to whatever garbled and incredible story you'd concoct out of this. Please think it over carefully before you do anything rash, now or later. If the exact nature of our talk were even mentioned, you would be the only one to suffer, believe me. Meanwhile, I'll leave you my card. Anytime you wish to call on me I will be ready to serve you."

"And why should I ever want to call on you?" demanded the white-faced Mr. Treadwell.

"There are various reasons," said Bunce, "but one above all." He gathered his belongings and moved to the door. "Consider, Mr. Treadwell: Anyone who has mounted the first three steps of The Blessington Method inevitably mounts the fourth. You have made remarkable progress in a short time, Mr. Treadwell—you should be calling soon."

"I'll see you in hell first," said Mr. Treadwell.

Despite this parting shot, the time that followed was a bad one for Mr. Treadwell. The trouble was that having been introduced to The Blessington Method, he couldn't seem to get it out of his mind. It incited thoughts that he had to keep thrusting away with an effort, and it certainly colored his relationship with his father-in-law in an unpleasant way.

Never before had the old man seemed so obtrusive, so much in the way, and so capable of always doing or saying the thing most calculated to stir annoyance. It especially outraged Mr. Treadwell to think of this intruder in his home babbling his private affairs to perfect strangers, eagerly spilling out details of his family life to paid investigators who were only out to make trouble. And, to Mr. Treadwell in his heated state of mind, the fact that the investigators could not be identified as such did not serve as any excuse.

Within very few days Mr. Treadwell, who prided himself on being a sane and level-headed businessman, had to admit he was in a bad way. He began to see evidences of a fantastic conspiracy on every hand. He could visualize hundreds—no, thousands—of Bunces swarming into offices just like his all over the country. He could feel cold sweat starting on his forehead at the thought.

But, he told himself, the whole thing was *too* fantastic. He could prove this to himself by merely reviewing his discussion with Bunce, and so he did, dozens of times. After all, it was no more than an objective look at a social problem. Had anything been said that a *really* intelligent man should shy away from? Not at all. If he had drawn some shocking inferences, it was because the ideas were already in his mind looking for an outlet.

On the other hand—

It was with a vast relief that Mr. Treadwell finally decided to pay a visit to the Society for Gerontology. He knew what he would find there: a dingy room or two, a couple of underpaid clerical workers, the musty odor of a piddling charity operation—all of which would restore matters to their proper perspective again. He went so strongly imbued with this picture that he almost walked past the gigantic glass-and-aluminum tower which was the address of the Society, rode its softly humming elevator in confusion, and emerged in the anteroom of the main office in a daze.

And it was still in a daze that he was ushered through a vast and seemingly endless labyrinth of rooms by a sleek, long-legged young woman, and saw, as he passed, hosts of other young women, no less sleek and long-legged, multitudes of brisk, square-shouldered young men, rows of streamlined machinery clicking and chuckling in electronic glee, mountains of stainless-steel card indexes, and, over all, the bland reflection of modern indirect lighting on plastic and metal —until finally he was led into the presence of Bunce himself, and the door closed behind him.

"Impressive, isn't it?" said Bunce, obviously relishing the sight of Mr. Treadwell's stupefaction.

"Impressive?" croaked Mr. Treadwell hoarsely. "Why, I've never seen anything like it. It's a ten-million-dollar outfit!"

"And why not? Science is working day and night like some Frankenstein, Mr. Treadwell, to increase longevity past all sane limits. There are fourteen million people over sixty-five in this country right now. In twenty years their number will be increased to twenty-one million. Beyond that no one can even estimate what the figures will rise to!

"But the one bright note is that each of these aged people is surrounded by many young donors or potential donors to our Society. As the tide rises higher, we, too, flourish and grow stronger to withstand it."

Mr. Treadwell felt a chill of horror penetrate him. "Then it's true, isn't it?"

"I beg your pardon?"

"This Blessington Method you're always talking about," said Mr. Treadwell wildly. "The whole idea is just to settle things by getting rid of old people!"

"Right!" said Bunce. "That is the exact idea. And not even J. G. Blessington himself ever phrased it better. You have a way with words, Mr. Treadwell. I always admire a man who can come to the point without sentimental twaddle."

"But you can't get away with it!" said Mr. Treadwell incredulously. "You don't really believe you can get away with it, do you?"

Bunce gestured toward the expanses beyond the closed door. "Isn't that sufficient evidence of the Society's success?"

"But all those people out there! Do they realize what's going on?"

"Like all well-trained personnel, Mr. Treadwell," said Bunce reproachfully, "they know only their own duties. What you and I are discussing here happens to be upper echelon."

Mr. Treadwell's shoulders drooped. "It's impossible," he said weakly. "It can't work."

"Come, come," Bunce said not unkindly, "you mustn't let yourself be overwhelmed. I imagine that what disturbs you most is what J. G. Blessington sometimes referred to as the Safety Factor. But look at it this way, Mr. Treadwell: Isn't it perfectly natural for old people to die? Well, our Society guarantees that the deaths will appear natural. Investigations are rare—not one has ever caused us any trouble.

"More than that, you would be impressed by many of the names on our list of donors. People powerful in the political world as well as the financial world have been flocking to us. One and all, they could give glowing testimonials as to our efficiency. And remember that such important people make the Society for Gerontology invulnerable, no matter at what point it may be attacked, Mr. Treadwell. And such invulnerability extends to every single one of our sponsors, including you, should you choose to place your problem in our hands."

"But I don't have the right," Mr. Treadwell protested despairingly. "Even if I wanted to, who am I to settle things this way for anybody?"

"Aha." Bunce leaned forward intently. "But you do want to settle things?"

"Not this way."

"Can you suggest any other way?"

Mr. Treadwell was silent.

"You see," Bunce said with satisfaction, "the Society for Gerontology offers the one practical answer to the problem. Do you still reject it, Mr. Treadwell?"

"I can't see it," Mr. Treadwell said stubbornly. "It's just not right."

"Are you sure of that?"

"Of course I am!" snapped Mr. Treadwell. "Are you going to tell me that it's right and proper to go around killing people just because they're old?"

"I am telling you that very thing, Mr. Treadwell, and I ask you to look at it this way. We are living today in a world of progress, a world of producers and consumers, all doing their best to improve our common lot. The old are neither producers nor consumers, so they are only barriers to our continued progress.

"If we want to take a brief, sentimental look into the pastoral haze of yesterday we may find that once they did serve a function. While the young were out tilling the fields, the old could tend to the household. But even that function is gone today. We have a hundred better devices for tending the household, and they come far cheaper. Can you dispute that?"

"I don't know," Mr. Treadwell said doggedly. "You're arguing that people are machines, and I don't go along with that at all."

"Good heavens," said Bunce, "don't tell me that you see them as anything else! Of course, we are machines, Mr. Treadwell, all of us. Unique and wonderful machines, I grant, but machines nevertheless. Why, look at the world around you. It is a vast organism made up of replaceable parts, all striving to produce and consume, produce and consume until worn out. Should one permit the worn-out part to remain where it is? Of course not! It must be cast aside so that the organism will not be made inefficient. It is the whole organism that counts, Mr. Treadwell, not any of its individual parts. Can't you understand that?"

"I don't know," said Mr. Treadwell uncertainly. "I've never thought of it that way. It's hard to take in all at once."

"I realize that, Mr. Treadwell, but it is part of The Blessington Method that the sponsor fully appreciate the great value of his contribution in all ways—not only as it benefits him, but also in the way it benefits the entire social organism. In signing a pledge to our Society a man is truly performing the most noble act of his life."

"Pledge?" said Mr. Treadwell. "What kind of pledge?"

Bunce removed a printed form from a drawer of his desk and laid it out carefully for Mr. Treadwell's inspection. Mr. Treadwell read it and sat up sharply.

"Why, this says that I'm promising to pay you two thousand dollars in a month from now. You never said anything about that kind of money!"

"There has never been any occasion to raise the subject before this," Bunce replied. "But for some time now a committee of the Society has been examining your financial standing, and it reports that you can pay this sum without stress or strain."

"What do you mean, stress or strain?" Mr. Treadwell retorted. "Two thousand dollars is a lot of money, no matter how you look at it."

Bunce shrugged. "Every pledge is arranged in terms of the sponsor's ability to pay, Mr. Treadwell. Remember, what may seem expensive to you would certainly seem cheap to many other sponsors I have dealt with."

"And what do I get for this?"

"Within one month after you sign the pledge, the affair of your father-in-law will be disposed of. Immediately after that you will be expected to pay the pledge in full. Your name is then enrolled on our list of sponsors, and that is all there is to it."

"I don't like the idea of my name being enrolled on anything."

"I can appreciate that," said Bunce. "But may I remind you that a donation to a charitable organization such as the Society for Gerontology is tax-deductible?"

Mr. Treadwell's fingers rested lightly on the pledge. "Now just for the sake of argument," he said, "suppose someone signs one of these things and then doesn't pay up. I guess you know that a pledge like this isn't collectible under the law, don't you?"

"Yes," Bunce smiled, "and I know that a great many organizations cannot redeem pledges made to them in apparently good faith. But the Society for Gerontology has never met that difficulty. We avoid it by reminding all sponsors that the young, if they are careless, may die as unexpectedly as the old. . . . No, no," he said, steadying the paper, "just your signature at the bottom will do."

When Mr. Treadwell's father-in-law was found drowned off the foot of East Sconsett pier three weeks later (the old man fished from the pier regularly although he had often been told by various local authorities that the fishing was poor there), the event was duly entered into the East Sconsett records as Death By Accidental Submersion, and Mr. Treadwell himself made the arrangements for an exceptionally elaborate funeral. And it was at the funeral that Mr. Treadwell first had the Thought. It was a fleeting and unpleasant thought, just disturbing enough to make him miss a step as he entered the church. In all the confusion of the moment, however, it was not too difficult to put aside.

A few days later, when he was back at his familiar desk, the Thought suddenly returned. This time it was not to be put aside so easily. It grew steadily larger and larger in his mind, until his waking hours were terrifyingly full of it, and his sleep a series of shuddering nightmares.

There was only one man who could clear up the matter for him, he knew; so he appeared at the offices of the Society for Gerontology burning with anxiety to have Bunce do so. He was hardly aware of handing over his check to Bunce and pocketing the receipt.

"There's something that's been worrying me," said Mr. Treadwell, coming straight to the point.

"Yes?"

"Well, do you remember telling me how many old people there would be around in twenty years?"

"Of course."

Mr. Treadwell loosened his collar to ease the constriction around his throat. "But don't you see? I'm going to be one of them!"

Bunce nodded. "If you take reasonably good care of yourself there's no reason why you shouldn't be," he pointed out.

"You don't get the idea," Mr. Treadwell said urgently. "I'll be in a spot then where I'll have to worry all the time about someone from this Society coming in and giving my daughter or my son-in-law ideas! That's a terrible thing to have to worry about all the rest of your life."

Bunce shook his head slowly. "You can't mean that, Mr. Treadwell."

"And why can't I?"

"Why? Well, think of your daughter, Mr. Treadwell. Are you thinking of her?"

"Yes."

"Do you see her as the lovely child who poured out her love to you in exchange for yours? The fine young woman who has just stepped over the threshold of marriage, but is always eager to visit you, eager to let you know the affection she feels for you?"

"I know that."

"And can you see in your mind's eye that manly young fellow who is her husband? Can you feel the warmth of his handclasp as he greets you? Do you know his gratitude for the financial help you give him regularly?"

"I suppose so."

"Now, honestly, Mr. Treadwell, can you imagine either of these affectionate and devoted youngsters doing a single thing—the slightest thing—to harm you?"

The constriction around Mr. Treadwell's throat miraculously eased; the chill around his heart departed.

"No," he said with conviction, "I can't."

"Splendid," said Bunce. He leaned far back in his chair and smiled with a kindly wisdom. "Hold on to that thought, Mr. Treadwell. Cherish it and keep it close at all times. It will be a solace and comfort to the very end."

AND ALREADY LOST . . .

by Charlotte Armstrong

Miss Murphy often made reasons to be in the corridor when the four of them were due to come by. She knew their schedules. She could anticipate. She was to be found, looking vague, with papers in her hand, just turning into Mr. Madden's office, or perhaps just leaving her own, and she would hesitate and frown and pretend to be preoccupied; but her pale green eyes under dust-colored lashes would secretly watch them. After they had passed, she would go about her business, concealing the depth of her pleasure.

As assistant principal of the high school, she ought to have been, without exception, on the side of society. But when the four of them went by in their inevitable formation, something lively and stubborn and sly, something that contradicted everything Miss Murphy lived by, lifted up a voice to say inside her, "Nevertheless, this is magnificent!"

Miss Murphy was a little woman who had looked about the same age for the last fifteen years—ever since she had first lost the bloom of youth. She was a pale redhead, with pale freckled skin, and the flesh of her face did not cling cleanly to the bones; it was rather doughy and lumpy, as if a sculptor had thrown clay on the framework in careless preliminary and then never had got around to refining his work. Miss Murphy was everything law-biding, anxious, and reliable. She was destined to be "good old Miss Murphy," and she knew this

61

and was even rather pleased about it. What was it in her that responded? What clapped impious applause in her heart—to see the four of them go by?

Miss Murphy was not, of course, the only one who watched them in their peculiar habit of march—that strange phenomenon—and pretended not to see it. New students were sometimes impelled to jeer in astonishment, but they soon learned that it was better not to notice.

The faculty, the principal's office staff, the adults—all deplored but could not forbid the walking ritual. It was simply four seniors walking by. That was all. In their passage they did nothing against the rules. But they did do something. And they did it in the long corridors of the school between classes, whenever all four were able to travel together in the same direction. And on the campus too— sometimes when they arrived in the morning, and every day as they departed. The four of them—the girl and the three boys . . .

One spring Tuesday, just before the end of fourth period, Miss Murphy found herself compulsively gathering up a packet of record cards. In a moment the bell would ring, the individual cells of the orderly hive would erupt, and there would be the periodical roar of voices, thump of feet, and rush of bodies. Miss Murphy knew she was deliberately waiting out the necessary minutes before The Four would pass her door. She rested her wrists on the edge of her desk, the record cards loosely held but ready in her hands, and her quiet waiting like meditation before a dubious god.

When the clock had moved enough, she rose and opened her door. She did not step out into the humming traffic. She stood still and began to sort the cards.

They were coming. She knew because the hum lessened. The Four traveled in a shell of lesser noise.

It was always exactly the same. First, by a single step, came the girl, Ivy Vole. She was tall. She had a small head held high on a neck that was disproportionately thick. Her forehead was rounded and high, and her dark hair went straight back from this bold brow to hang in a limp mass between her shoulder blades. She walked proudly on small feet that almost crossed over each other to follow a straight line and create a swagger in her narrow hips. Ivy Vole looked dead ahead, her eyes like a sleepwalker's. This was the strange, the subtly evil thing. Although she led the pack, she walked as if she was also its prisoner.

A step behind her and a step to the left loomed Stan Fuller, constituting himself a wall at her back. He was taller than she, a fierce burly boy. His dark frown went over her left shoulder to warn anyone from interfering, from crossing their immediate path.

Ranging on the flanks were Ross and Tentor. Greyhounds both, they slouched loosely along, their heads held forward, restless, turning, fending, guarding. Ross, with his long, straight, slick blond hair, his predatory nose, his narrow eyes, walked on the left, his feet even with Stan's but the forward bend of his torso and neck guarding the girl. Tentor, a less blond version with a nose less sharp and eyes that were always puffed and sleepy—as if he never slept at night but engaged instead in some nameless dissipation—Tentor ranged on the right flank; in the pattern, he walked on the halfway line, a bit ahead of the other two boys, and half a step behind the girl.

In this curious phalanx they swept along. If anyone chanced or dared to stand in their path, the whole formation could veer without altering their relative positions. The girl simply kept stepping in that strange, proud, blind way of hers, and the three escorts kept bulking, just behind—as if The Four defied all who might break them apart even when, as a unit and quite flexibly, they yielded and then threaded through. The sweep and rhythm, the rigidity of their march—and something in their cold eyes—made it unnecessary for them to swerve very often.

When they had gone by, Miss Murphy feigned a decision, closed her hand around the cards, and turned toward the principal's office. The little shivering ride along her nerves was like the effects of a drug she took in secret.

Wasn't there an integrity in them? In their very scorn? In the imperial air itself—the nerve it took, the calm arrogance of their strange and self-sufficient alliance, the very coldness of their eyes? Was this not somehow magnificent? What would it be to live like that? To have no truck with a thousand nervous little conformities, to resign from the anxiety to please those in authority, to walk so proudly, to be like Ivy Vole, Queen and Head Slave, of however small a kingdom, however evil? What could goodness, civilization, propriety, offer that could compare . . . ?

Mr. Madden came up behind her. "Coming to see me? After you, Miss Murphy."

She had an uneasy feeling that she had been caught this time.

The principal sat down behind his desk. He was a thin man, with a stiff body and stiff white hair. He took off his glasses and massaged his eyes. "How I wish we could reach those four," he sighed, "before we lose them. Do you have any ideas, Miss Murphy?"

"I? Why, no, I'm afraid not," she said, knowing that she had indeed been caught since he spoke directly of what he knew was in her mind. "I have these for your file, sir."

He did not even look at the cards. "Have you ever tried to get at them individually?"

"I think everyone has tried," she said in her bright everyday voice.

Privately she didn't think it was any use. For taken one by one, neither the girl nor any of the three boys was formidable. Ivy Vole was of no importance in the school's society. She was an indifferent student, and did not compete in any of the usual ways. None of the boys were competing athletes, none of them politicians or joiners. It was their alliance alone that gave them identity. And the alliance was old. She seemed to remember its taking shape during the last quarter of their freshman year. Now they were seniors. So the alliance was old and it was strong and Miss Murphy did not think that Mr. Madden or any of his staff could break it up before spring came.

"If we do not help them . . ." He shook his head.

Help them? thought Miss Murphy. Help them to what? To obscurity and a humbler place? After this strange, almost mystic thing that gives them status?

"I am asking your advice because it seems to me—I don't quite know how to put this, Miss Murphy—but it seems to me that *your* approach might be a little different."

Miss Murphy flushed. "It's true that I have tried very hard to understand them—from their point of view," she said tolerantly.

"Yes?" he said.

Sometimes Miss Murphy shuddered to think of any possible point of view for the girl, Ivy . . . or of her possible relationship with those three males, which could scarcely be that of three *parfait* gentle knights to a fair lady. But this was only one facet of the problem. Not much had been proved against the four this year, although much was believed and even more suspected. They were almost certainly still vandals. The year before they had been caught twice, lectured, and let off. This year they had learned how not to leave any clues behind them. They were bullies, of course, and had been openly so last year. This year they were more skillful, using pressure and threats instead of blows.

Nevertheless, Miss Murphy said earnestly, "Mr. Madden . . . separately they aren't significant. They have welded themselves into this unit because *it* gives them *meaning.*"

"I don't like the meaning," he interrupted sharply.

"No, no, of course not," she said hastily, "but just the same they have some qualities we *can* admire."

"And what are those?" the principal asked flatly.

"They are loyal to each other."

"Are they? Have they ever been really tested?"

"They show," said Miss Murphy, "a certain courage."

"Many criminals have courage," said Mr. Madden, "and often they have power—and power is glamorous."

It was a fair hit and Miss Murphy knew she was blushing.

"And these four," the principal went on, "have achieved a certain amount of power *and* glamor. Tell me how to jolt them out of that. Tell me how to make them substitute the kind of power and glamor that one has to work for—for fifty years."

Miss Murphy found herself thinking: Yes, you can work for it and *hard* for fifty years, or a hundred years, and never get it. And then she thought: Just the same, there is something strong and bold and magnificent—about *taking* it. Taking it *now*.

"I've talked to their families myself," the principal was saying wearily, "and it got nowhere. The parents simply do not *know*. Ivy's mother and father think of her as a perfectly ordinary young girl, not too bright, not too enthusiastic, not doing too well in her studies . . . but 'popular.' Lord help us! Stan's father thinks he is grown up and is quite complacent about it. 'Let the kid alone,' *he* says. Ross's folks are financially harassed this year and they are so frantically absorbed in their troubles that the boy goes almost unnoticed. He merely appends to them. As for Tentor, he lives with grandparents who write him off in one sentence. He is seventeen. They were once seventeen, and they survived. They expect him to do the same."

He sighed and raised his eyes to her. "So they've grown up like weeds. And we have failed them. I wish you could tell me how to change the wrong and rotten things inside them."

"They defy the group," she stammered, "they don't conform."

He stared at her and said, "My soul, my soul . . . if only that were all." Then he got out of his chair and shook off that moment of despair. "I will tell you this," he said. "The moment, if it ever comes, that they are caught red-handed, I will do all I can to blacken their records. I will feed them into the hands of juvenile experts and police psychiatrists. I can afford no more weak and hopeful *wishes* about these four. There isn't time."

He smiled at her to let down the tension. "Thanks, anyway," he said gently.

Miss Murphy went away in some confusion.

Just the same, just the same, her mind kept saying. The four of them are so strong. The world, she thought, will use them, just as they are—out there where the wicked sometimes flourish like the green bay tree.

She did not think the school could change them anymore. She herself would miss the sight of them. The school would miss something when next year The Four would not be back.

Miss Murphy wished she could, in the few weeks remaining, make contact with them. What she had long tried to do was to project to them the friendly, give-and-take attitude she proffered to other students . . . even as they looked through her with those icy eyes. Their eyes could pass over you so blankly that you wanted to pinch yourself. Maybe she had been wrong not to betray how she felt, how she *truly* understood them.

But maybe someday, somehow, and yet . . . she *could* reach them— without any motive to change them. There was a wicked excitement in the very thought.

*   *   *

Miss Murphy lived with her widowed sister, Diane, who was not well and in Miss Murphy's memory never had been. Diane was weak and low that evening. She had been sitting in the sun and had received an irritation of the skin. It was one of the misfortunes of Diane that nature never did her any good. Sun, air, wind—all these usually turned out to have harmed her delicate sensibilities.

About a quarter of nine Diane discovered that her peach-colored pills had run out—the ones she took before bed. So Miss Murphy set out for the neighborhood drugstore, with her normal willingness to serve.

It was a pleasant evening and she enjoyed walking the few blocks, looking into other people's houses now that the lights were on, glimpsing a bridge game or a lonely TV watcher or a family dinner party lingering late at table because everyone was reluctant to leave the quips and the teasings to wash the dishes. Miss Murphy enjoyed her pleasant suburban world.

The little cluster of shops was darkened. Only the drugstore was still open at this hour. Miss Murphy had a cheerful exchange of commonplaces with the clerk, received her package, and left with a polite "Good night."

But as she drew near the dark and silent gas station, she began to wonder about Diane's lotion. Was that low, too? From old experience, Miss Murphy felt she had better call up home and ask. For the drugstore was about to close, at nine o'clock, and she would not be able to return tonight . . .

So Miss Murphy, both kind and shrewd in the matter, left the sidewalk, stepped into the green phone booth, and stood against the stucco outside wall of the service station.

As she pulled the thin flaps of the door shut, the light failed to go on but, after firming the door as best she could, Miss Murphy thought nothing of the semi-darkness and hopefully put her dime in.

Nothing happened. The phone was dead. It must be out of order. Turning her mind to the prospect of going back and calling from the drugstore itself, Miss Murphy took a full minute to discover and realize that she could not open the door of the booth. It was out of order, too, in a very stubborn way. She could not get out; she was imprisoned in this upright coffin with no way to telephone for help.

It was a ridiculous entrapment.

Nine o'clock of a spring evening and Miss Delphine Murphy had got herself locked into a telephone booth!

Peering out through the glass, she fought a sudden feeling of suffocation which was purely subjective. She could tell by reflections on the sidewalk that some of the lights in the drugstore were going out. Then she was able to make out the figure of the clerk as he emerged and locked the door. Miss Murphy rapped on the glass with the metal clasp of her purse, making all the noise she decorously could, but he strode away in the opposite direction.

Never in her life had Miss Murphy been in a position to cry out for help, to lift up her voice. She couldn't decide what to shout. To shout "Help" seemed quaint and ridiculous, like something out of a comic strip. Nevertheless, she had to shout something, so she called, "Hi . . . hi . . . hi there!" The clerk vanished in the reaches of the parking lot at the other side of the drugstore, and in a little while his car rattled out into the street and turned to go off the other way, so that it did not pass her. Now the whole small business section was abed for the night.

Traffic on the street was rather thin. Miss Murphy was not in absolute darkness because the streetlight was shedding down on the gas station corner. But neither was she very visible in her little prison, and the passing cars paid no attention to the fact that the door to the phone booth was shut. Perhaps they could not even see that this was so.

Miss Murphy resolved that she must take the desperate measure of breaking the glass. It was a shock to discover that she could not break it, that the glass was very tough, and besides, had a wire mesh embedded in it. When the heel of her shoe had no more effect than had her elbow, she began to be afraid.

The fear whistled around her head like a bird and lit upon the name of her sister, Diane. Miss Murphy had the medicine. Diane was alone and not feeling well and was easily visited by swarms of wild dreads and melodramatic forebodings. Diane would miss her soon. Diane would think that something terrible had happened to her. Diane would know that her sister never deliberately delayed her return with the medicine. So Diane would be frantic, and to be frantic was very bad for her.

Miss Murphy felt frantic for Diane's sake. But after a minute or two, she knew she was frantic for herself. She was feeling claustrophobic. How was she going to get out . . . *get out* . . . the words began to shout in her consciousness . . . *GET OUT!*

She caught herself turning and twisting and pounding unreasonably on the glass when there was no one who could possibly hear her. Miss Murphy took hold of herself and tried to think. The thing to do was stop someone. There did not seem to be any pedestrians. But there were cars. How could she stop a car? Peering with her cheek tight on the cold glass, Miss Murphy saw a convertible come gliding down the street. It was cruising, going softly. It seemed, almost, as if this car, in the gentle evening, in the quiet streets of the town, was looking for trouble.

Miss Murphy rapped on the glass and cried, "Hi! Hi! Hi!"

As the car went by, she saw who was in it.

Stan Fuller was driving. The car—no cheap rattletrap of a jalopy, but a modern, shining, expensive car—was his. It was hard to say how the kids got these cars—they just did. It seemed that the intense desire, the absolute necessity of the young American to own a car, generated its own fulfillment. Stan Fuller sat behind the wheel but it was as if the common agreement of the four of them directed the car's prowling. Ivy Vole sat in the middle and on the edge of the front seat, a little forward of the others, as was her assigned position. Tentor sat on her right, cooly watching and guarding. Ross, who belonged on the left, was draped across the back of the seat behind Stan where he could project his watchfulness to the left, as was his usual station.

Miss Murphy saw them go by, saw Stan and Ivy hold their heads to look straight forward, saw only Tentor peering to the right where she was so helplessly hidden.

The sight of the four of them, on the prowl in a car, intrigued her briefly. But she was not out of her prison and she could not think how to get out.

In about four minutes she was astonished to see the convertible approach once more and from the same direction, as if it had circled the block.

Then she was thrilled when it rocked gently over the break in the gutter and slipped onto the pavement of the service station. It rolled into the shadow of the laundry building that was next to the gas station. It stopped. The four of them sat there.

Miss Murphy, filled with relief and also with the shame of being caught, especially by them, in so undignified a situation, tapped primly upon the glass. She called out, "The door is jammed. Stan? Would you please try to open it? This is Miss Murphy. Jim Tentor? Ivy?"

They did not seem to hear her.

Miss Murphy kept on tapping and calling to them, repeating and repeating in a curious suspension of her own attention. She chose not to notice how much time was going by. But at last her wrist weakened and felt tired and her hand fell and her voice failed. She could see their heads. She began to think she could see their cold eyes, as cold and baleful as wolves'. She saw Stan put one huge foot up and hang it by the ankle over the side of the car. She knew Ross had relaxed, for he had nothing to watch on the left but the brick wall of the laundry. She saw Tentor, his neck arched, watching the street behind them. Ivy sat with her head high. Ivy lit a cigarette. The Four seemed to have settled themselves, as if this were a drive-in movie. Were they going to sit there and watch Miss Murphy turning in her trap?

She did turn. She revolved in her cage. She tried the phone again. But nothing had happened to put it suddenly and obligingly back in working order. She braced herself to make no more appeals, to wait with some kind of dignity.

But the thought of Diane came again and she felt her nerve crack, her dignity wash out in rage.

"Listen!" she cried. "*Listen* to me. My sister is ill. I have her medicine with me. I must get out. My sister is ill. Don't you hear me—my sister needs her medicine! *Medicine!*" It should have moved them, the appeal to medical necessity. It always did among the civilized. Didn't planes fly with the serums, ambulances race, cops clear the way to the hospital?

But The Four were not moved.

In a kind of last grasp at reason, Miss Murphy supposed she could not be heard. So she stopped her useless noises.

She heard Ross say restlessly, "What say? Shall we stripe out?"

Ivy said, "What's the hurry?"

They spoke in ordinary conversational voices. Miss Murphy heard *them*. Therefore, *they* had heard everything she had been shouting— every frantic word of hers that still rang in her own ears.

Miss Murphy's head became filled with a red rage.

She sank down, missed the seat, went all the way to the floor, and felt, at first, an enormous relief. To be so degraded as to be kneeling on a dirty floor and leaning her clean forehead against a worn wooden seat . . . to feel the first comforting rush of self-pity . . . Soon Miss Murphy was weeping.

She would not look at them again. But *they* were looking at her. *They* could see her, crumpled where she was. *They* could even hear her sobbing. A little of her pride came back. She hushed herself and looked at her watch as best she could. It was 9:22. Twenty-two minutes had reduced her to this?

She put her chin on her forearm, stared at the back wall of the booth, and forced her mind to turn over. The gas station opened, she guessed, not much earlier than eight in the morning. This then was her earliest firm hope of release.

Now she trembled and felt ill. She could endure. She must endure. But it was horrifying and primitive: it called on reserves she had not used in years, if ever. Long shudders of rage were going up and down her spine. She must not think, for even one moment, of the four of them or she might begin to pound her head on the glass and hurt herself.

Then she heard a motor. Were they leaving? She would not look. Then she heard a scream of brakes. A car had come. Then she heard a voice crying in concern for *her*, "Hey, lady! Gee—I'm sorry! Look, I'm getting you out right away!"

She looked then and saw a man beyond the glass with a heavy tool in his hands. She struggled upright, feeling weary and soiled, and she heard the wonderful crunching of breaking wood. Then suddenly she was free.

It was the owner of the gas station. "Say, listen, that's a nasty thing to happen," he said, supporting her with his strong arm. "How long were you in there? I got here as soon as I could. I had to put some clothes on, and I had to come all the way across town. Guess it took me about twenty minutes. . . . Well, I'm sorry, really sorry."

Miss Murphy looked toward the laundry building. No convertible was there. The Four had vanished.

She heard the owner say, "The minute the girl called me I came as fast as I could. . . ."

"The minute who called you?"

"Some girl—said her name was Ivy Vole."

"Called you! Twenty minutes ago!"

"That's right. Say, are you okay?" He thought she might faint. He led her to his car. "I want to wedge this door so nobody else gets into trouble. Then I'll take you home," he promised.

"Yes, my sister . . . I have her medicine. . . ."

Miss Murphy got weakly into the man's car and sat there and the cold air sharpened the chill of the sweat at her hairline. Then they had learned to do that much. They *had* conformed. They *had* acted to save her. And people would believe that they had saved her. But if they had sat and watched her for twenty minutes *and had not told her so* . . . simply watched her suffering . . . It was too subtle and refined a cruelty. And it was not because they were so cold and so callous that they did not recognize her suffering. Nor that they were too young or too self-centered . . . or too ignorant. On the contrary. They had not only recognized her suffering, they had prolonged it deliberately. They had enjoyed it.

When she reached home, her sister Diane looked up from the novel in which she had become lost. "What kept you, Delphine?" asked Diane, lazily. And then jealously, "I suppose it's nice out."

"Very nice," said Miss Murphy, whose legs were like water.

In the morning, soon after the first bell rang, a message summoned Miss Murphy to Mr. Madden's office. When she got there, she found the room full. There was a man who could be nothing on earth but a police officer. And standing, in formation, but like culprits before judgment, were The Four.

Miss Murphy's lumpy little face was very pale this morning. She felt no new shock to see the four of them—the older shock that had rocked her whole system was still operating. Now she seemed to look through them—all the way through them—with cold green eyes.

"Last night," said Mr. Madden, in a voice of restrained anger and excitement, "this office was wrecked—vandalized, as you can see."

Miss Murphy saw the torn papers, the broken drawers, the ink on the walls.

"These four students, as you know, have done this sort of thing before. Last year they were forgiven. This time Police Officer Davis here and I feel that something a bit different is going to have to be done about them. Now, I called you in, Miss Murphy, because *they* say . . ." there was a small but distinct sneer in Mr. Madden's thin cultivated voice, "that *you* can give them an alibi."

"I?" she said.

The eyes of The Four were on her. For once she stood in the range of their eye-beams and was solid and seen by them.

"You know . . ." began Stan.

"Quiet," snapped Mr. Madden. A wave of something like alarm went through the phalanx. Mr. Madden was on the warpath. No one could doubt it.

"These four," he said ostensibly to Miss Murphy but really to the policeman, "have got away with just about enough. We can no longer help them here at school with the measures at our command. And they need help. They need it from experts and someday they will realize how fortunate they were to get it at the right time." Mr. Madden glanced about him. "This handkerchief," he went on, "was found here in my office. And it gives them away. Now, let's forget all this nonsense about an alibi and get on with it."

Miss Murphy looked at the handkerchief, a grimy scrap of cotton with IV in one corner. IV. For Ivy Vole. For Ivy. And the Roman way to write a four. She brooded on the symbolism. . . . The Four . . .

"Better let me put this to her," said the policeman Davis, courteously, for Mr. Madden was obviously not wholly objective this morning. "Now, Miss Murphy, it seems that last night, up until nine P.M., there was somebody in this building."

"Adult education class, out nine-oh-two," snapped Mr. Madden. "Mr. Collins locked up after it. No trouble then. But when *I* came here, for some papers I needed at home, *I* walked right into them. They were at work, all right. In the dark. One of them hit me. . . ."

Miss Murphy now saw the slight bruise on the principal's face.

"That," said Madden with satisfaction, "will make it enough of a crime so that we can really . . ."

"Let's—er—get at this alibi business," said Davis, clearing his throat. "Now, Miss Murphy. Mr. Madden came here and caught them in the act, although of course they got away in the dark . . . at about nine-twenty. Where were you at that time? Do you remember?"

Miss Murphy did not speak. But she remembered.

"*They* say you were locked in a phone booth," said Davis. "*They* say that they called the man to come and let you out. *They* say they stayed by you. . . ."

"Is that what they say?" There was a sick chill in her voice. The four rippled slightly—like a sensitive plant recoiling from a touch.

"We have checked with the owner of the gas station," said Davis in his calm voice, "and he corroborates that much of their story. The girl called him close after nine. Now he let you out at nine twenty-five, or a few moments later, but he says these four *were not there.* Not at nine twenty-five."

Miss Murphy remained silent. The times marched stately in her mind—9:00 . . . 9:25. She recalled reading her watch in the poor light, with her knees on the dirty floor of the telephone booth . . . at exactly 9:22.

"You see how it stands, Miss Murphy?" Davis said. "They could have come here to the school after phoning the gas station owner. . . ."

"They did," said Madden positively.

"Somebody . . ." began Ivy.

"Be still," the principal said. "Miss Murphy, I can only warn you very carefully. Don't make a mistake about this."

Miss Murphy stood there with power.

"You saw us," Stan said accusingly.

"Sure she did," said Ross.

The eyes of the girl, Ivy, bored into Miss Murphy's. Well? they said. There was even a little scorn in them. You are trapped, they said. You have to speak the truth and you know it.

Miss Murphy smiled and spoke the truth. "Yes, they were there.

All four of them. They stayed by me." She said it without bitterness, as if she spoke in a not unpleasant dream. "So," she continued, "they couldn't have done this damage. Not between nine and nine twenty-five. Is that what you wanted of me?"

"Gee, thanks!" she heard one say. Was it Tentor?

"If she gives them an alibi . . ." Davis said and opened his hands.

"Miss Murphy," said the principal in a tired voice, "if this is mercy on your part, if you mistakenly think that they ought to be let off again . . ."

"No, sir," she said quietly.

"Get back to your classes," Madden snapped at them.

The Four, with a sudden scurry of feet, went away.

"If you are trying to be friendly and lying for them . . . Oh, I know you have had a certain sneaking fondness . . ." Mr. Madden's mouth looked as if it might froth and Davis had his ears pricked. "Then you are so wrong," said Madden fiercely. "This was our last chance to save them. Don't you realize that? They'll lie low, now, till the end of the year."

"I know it was the last chance," Miss Murphy said softly. "But the truth is the truth. And besides, it doesn't matter. They are trash."

Both men looked at her, a little shocked and startled, and then they let her go.

A little later she sat at her own desk and heard them knock. She called, "Come in." The Four came in and arranged themselves before her. She knew at once what they had come to do. They were conforming. They would throw a sop to good manners, to civilization. They had grown shrewd. So they would, in cold blood and on the surface, pretend to conform.

"Gee, Miss Murphy," Stan said, "we wanted to tell you that we think it was swell of you."

"To tell the truth?" said Miss Murphy lightly.

"Somebody just put my handkerchief there," said Ivy in her small whine. "On purpose. Because we get blamed anyway."

"Trying to frame us," Ross said.

Tentor smiled, but his puffy eyes were sleepless in evil.

"Oh yes, you have been framed," Miss Murphy said. Her green eyes looked them over indifferently from under her dusty lashes.

"You may go now," she said and her mouth curved slightly. She might just as well have said, *Go now—go on to hell.*

The icy mystery of her own cruelty—for she saw where they were going and did not care—intrigued them. They blinked at her; then their eyes shifted, puzzled. But they left. Outside they fell into formation again. The girl, Ivy, put her small feet proudly down and assumed that sleepwalker's look, and Stan seemed as fierce as ever, and the greyhounds ranged on the flanks, defying anyone to touch them . . . or to teach them.

Miss Murphy could see them in her mind's eye. She watched for the last time. She thought: What waste! Born, raised, grown so high, and already lost . . .

THE AFFAIR AT LAHORE CANTONMENT

by Avram Davidson

It is some time before dawn, in the late spring, as I write this. The seagulls have more than an hour before it will be their moment to fly in from the river, screeing and crying, and then fly back. After them, the pigeons will murmur, and it will be day, perhaps a hot, sticky day. Right now the air is deliciously cool, but I find myself shivering. I find myself imagining the cold, the bitter cold, of that morning when Death came in full panoply, like one dressed for dinner. That morning so very long ago . . .

In the winter of 1946-7 it was cold enough to suit me, and more, although the thermometer was well above what I used to consider a cold winter at home. But I was then in England, and the wet and the chill never seemed to leave me. The cottage where I was staying had the most marvelous picturesque fireplaces—it had them in every single room, in fact. But coal was rationed and firewood seemed not only unavailable, it seemed unheard of. There was an antique electric heater, but it emitted only a dull coppery glow which died out a few inches away. The only gas fire was, naturally enough, in the kitchen, a cramped and tiny room, where it was impossible to write.

And it was in order to write that I was in England. In the mornings I visited the private library, fortunately unbombed, where lay a mass of material unavailable in America. Afternoons I did the actual writing. In the early evenings I listened to the Third Program while I looked over what I had written, and revised it.

Late evenings? It was, as I say, cold. Raw and damp. I could retire to bed with a brace of hot water bottles and read. I could go to the movies. I could go to the local, see if they had any spirits left, or, failing that—and it usually failed—have a mug of cider. Beer, I don't care for. The local was named . . . well, I won't say exactly what it was named. It may have been called The Green Man. Or The Grapes. Or The Something Arms. A certain measure of reticence is, I think, called for, although by now the last of the principals in the story must surely be dead. But for those who are insatiably curious there are always the newspaper files to check.

But be all that as it may. It was eight o'clock at night. The Marx Brothers were playing at the cinema, but I had seen this one twice before the War and twice during the War. My two hot water bottles gaped pinkly, ready to preserve my feet from frostbite if I cared to retire early to bed. I would have, but it happened that the only reading matter was a large and illustrated work on Etruscan tombs.

So the local won. It was really no contest.

It was warm there, and noisy and smoky and sociable. True, almost none of the sociability was directed my way, but as long as I wasn't openly being hated, I didn't care. Besides, we were all in luck: There *was* whiskey on hand. Gin, too. I drank slowly of the stuff that keeps the bare knees of Scotland warm and watched the people at their quaint native rituals—darts, football pools, even skittles.

A large, rather loutish-looking man at my right, who had made somewhat of a point of ignoring me, said suddenly, "Ah, Gaffer's heard there's gin!" A sort of ripple ran through the crowded room, and I turned around to look.

A man and a woman had come in. A little husk of a shriveled old man, wrapped almost to the tip of his rufous nose. An old woman, evidently his wife, was with him, and she helped undo the cocoon of overcoat, pullover, and muffler that, once removed, seemed to reduce him by half. They were obviously known and liked.

"Hello, Gaffer," the people greeted him. "Hello, Ma."

"I don't know if I'll be able to come fetch him when it's his going-home time," she said.

"I can manage meself, missus," the old man said querulously.

"If I don't turn up, some of you give him a hand and see he has all his buttons buttoned. One gin and two ales, Alfred—no more, mind!" And with a brisk, keen look all around she was off.

She seemed the younger of the two, but it may not have been a matter of years. Thin, she was, white-haired and wrinkled; but there was no pink or gray softness about her. Her black eyes snapped as she looked around. Her back was straight. There was something not quite local in the accents of her speech—a certain lilting quality.

The old man was given a seat at a table near me and the fellow who had first announced the old man's entrance now said, "Got your pension today, eh, Gaffer? Stand us a drink, there's a good fellow."

The old man stared at a palmful of change, then stirred it with a twisted finger. "My missus hasn't given me but enough for the gin and the two ales," he said.

"Ah, Tom's only having his games with you, Gaffer," someone said. "He does with everyone. Pay no mind." And they resumed their conversation where they'd left off, the chief topic of the night being that the English wife of an American serviceman stationed in the county had given birth to triplets. "Ah, those Yanks," they said indulgently.

" 'Ah, those Yanks,' " Tom mimicked. His spectacles were mended on the bridge with tape. "They get roaring drunk on the best whiskey that you and me can't find and couldn't afford to buy it if we could; they smash up cars like they cost nothing—you and me couldn't buy them if we saved forever. Curse and brawl like proper savages, they do."

There was an embarrassed silence. Someone said, "Now, Tom—" Someone looked at me, and away, quickly. And someone muttered, rather weakly, about there being "good and bad in all nations." I said nothing, telling myself that there was no point in getting into a quarrel with a middle-aged man whose grievances doubtless would be as great if all Americans, civil and military, vanished overnight from the United Kingdom.

To my surprise, and to everyone else's, it was the Gaffer who spoke up against the charge.

"You don't know what you're talking about, laddie-boy," he said to Tom, who must have been fifty, at least. " 'Tisn't that they're Yanks at all. 'Tis that they're soldiers, and in a strange land. That's a wicked life for a man. I've seen it meself. I could tell you a story—"

"Sweet Fanny Adams, no, don't!" Tom said loudly—an outburst which did nothing to increase his popularity. "I heard 'em all, millions of times. The old garrison at Lahore and the Pay-thans and the Af-gains and the Tarradiddles, mountain guns and mules, and, oh, the whole bloody parade. Give us a rest, Gaffer!"

He could have killed the old man with a slap of his hand, I suppose, the Gaffer looked that feeble. But he couldn't shut the old man up, now he'd had his sip of gin.

"No, you don't want to hear naught about it, but I'll tell it anyway. Me, that was fighting for the flag before you was born." For a moment his faded blue eyes seemed puzzled. "Oh, but I have seen terrible things," he said in a voice altogether different from his vigorously annoyed tone of a second before. "And the most terrible thing of all—to see my friend die before my eyes, and he died hard, and not to be able to do aught to help him." His words died off with a slow quiver.

Tom wasn't giving up that easily. "What's the football news?" he asked at large. No one answered.

"And not just the fighting in the Hills," the Gaffer went on. "What was that all for? India? They're giving India away now. No—other things . . . My *best* friend."

"How about a game of darts?" Tom urged, gesturing toward the back room, through the open door of which we could see the darts board and a frieze of old pictures which dated back six reigns or more. I'd often meant to examine them with attention, but never had.

". . . and it's all true, for I've got cuttin's to prove it. Young chap from newspaper was there and saw it and wrote it all up. Oh, it was terrible!" Tears welled to the reddened edges of his eyes. "But it had to be."

"Anyone for *darts?*"

Someone said, "Shut up, Tom. Go on, Gaffer."

And this was many years ago.

As you went along the Mall in Lahore (which was the local section of the Grand Trunk Road from Calcutta to Peshawur), you passed the museum and the cathedral and the Gardens and Government House and the Punjab Club. And you kept on passing, because you were an enlisted man and the Club was for officers and civilians of high rank. And then for three dusty miles there was nothing to speak of (natives hardly counted), and then there was the Cantonment, and in the Cantonment was the garrison.

"Head-bloody-quarters of the Third bloody Division of the Northern bloody Army," said the Docker. He spat into the dust. "And you can 'ave it all for one bloody yard of the Commercial Road of a Saturday night," he said. "Or *any* bloody night, for that matter!"

But his friend, the Mouse, knew nothing of the glories of the Commercial Road. He had taken the Queen's shilling in the market town that all his life he had regarded as if it were London, Baghdad, and Babylon. Lahore? He would have 'listed to go serve in Kamtchatka, if it had only got him away from his brute of a father, a drunken farm laborer in a dirty smock. How, he often wondered, had he got the courage to take the step at all?

"It frightens me sometimes, Docker," he confessed. "It's all so strange and different."

The Docker gave him a look on which his habitual sneer was half overcome by affection. "Don't you 'ave no bloody fear while *I'm* wiv you!" And he touched him, very lightly, on the shoulder. The Docker was tall and strong, with straight black hair and sallow skin and a mouth that was quick to anger and quick to foul words even without anger, and a mind that was quick to take offense and slow—very slow—to forgive.

Sergeant-Major had shouted, "I'll teach you to look at me!" and had kicked him hard. That night in the lanes on the other side of the little bazaar, past the tank and the place where the hafiz taught, someone hit Sergeant-Major with a piece of iron, thrown with main force. Split his scalp open. Who? No one ever knew. When Sergeant-Major came off sick list and went round telling about it, spreading his hair with his thick fingers to show the long and ugly wound with its black scab, the Docker passed by, walking proper slow. And Sergeant-Major looked up, suddenly, as if he recognized the footfalls, and there was a look passed between them that had murder in it. But nothing was said, nothing at all.

And no one kicked the Docker after that, and when it became

known that he was the pal of the little private everyone called the Mouse, because of his coloring and his timid ways, why, no one kicked the Mouse either, after that.

"See that blackie there, Docker?" the Mouse demanded. "See that white bit of string round his waist and over? He's what they call a braymin. Like our parson back 'ome—only, fancy a parson with not more clothes on than that!"

A mild interest stirred the big soldier's face. "Knew a parson give me sixpence once, when I was a nipper," he said. "Only I 'ad to come to church and let 'im christen me, like, afore 'e'd leave me 'ave it. Nice old chap. Bit dotty."

The crowd was thick on the road, but somehow there was always space where the soldiers walked. They passed a blind Jew from Peshawur, with a gray lambskin cap on his head, playing music on the harmonium. It wasn't like any music the Mouse had ever heard, but it stirred him all the same. The Docker grandly threw a few pice in the cup and his little friend admired the gesture.

"That lane there—" The Mouse drew close, dropped his voice. "—They say there's women there. They say some of'm won't look at sojers. But they say that some of'm will."

The Docker set his cap acock on his head. "Let's 'ave a look, then, kiddy," he said. "And see which ones will." But they never did—at least, not that day. Because they met Lance-Corporal Owen going to the bazaar and with him were three young ladies, with ruffles and fancy hats and parasols. They were going to the bazaar to help Lance-Corporal Owen buy gifts to send home to his mother and sisters. And this was quite a coincidence, because when the Docker heard it he at once explained that he and the Mouse were bound on the same errand.

"Only they say the best prices are at the places where they don't speak English. And Alf, 'ere, and me, we don't know none of this Punjabee-talk, y'see."

And because the young ladies—two of whom were named Cruceiro and one De Silva, and they were cousins—said that they knew a few words and would be pleased to help Lance-Corporal Owen's friends, and because Owen was very decent about it all—and why not, seeing that he had three of them?—they all walked off, three pairs of them.

The Mouse had the youngest Miss Cruceiro on his arm, and the Docker had Miss De Silva. Perhaps Owen wasn't quite so pleased with this arrangement, but he smiled.

That was how it began, many years ago.

Harry Owen was a proper figure of a man: broad shoulders, narrow waist, chestnut-colored hair, eyes as bright blue as could be. Always smiling and showing his good white teeth. Not many men had teeth that good. Even the wives of the officers didn't feel themselves too proud to say, "Good morning, Owen." It was as if there was a sun inside of him, shining all the time.

The three of them became friends. The *six* of them. The Docker and Leah De Silva, Harry and Margaret Cruceiro, and the Mouse and Lucy Cruceiro. To be sure, Lucy was rather dim and didn't say much, but that suited her escort well enough: He had little to say to her. But he would have felt all sorts of things bubbling up inside of him— if he had been walking with Miss De Silva.

But that, he knew, was impossible. Miss De Silva was so clever, so handsome, so self-assured; he would have been tongued-tied beside her. Besides, she walked with the Docker. And so, for all that she was pleasant to the Mouse, he was too shy to do much more than nod.

Later on he was to think that if the Docker had known that Leah De Silva was not really English, and that she and her cousins and all the others of their class were not regarded by the soldiery as . . . well . . .

But he did not know. Chasteness was not a highly prized attribute in Cat's-meat Court, where the Docker's wild, slumb-arab childhood had been largely spent—indeed, it was a quality almost completely unknown. He had no experience of respectable girls, neither half-caste nor quarter-caste nor simon-pure English. The daughters of the officers lived in a world sealed off from him, and the few daughters of NCOs almost as much so.

To men like Lance-Corporal Owen, Eurasian girls may have seemed to lack that certain quality which spelled Rude Hands Off, which the English girls at home had had. But the Docker knew nothing of afternoon teas and tiny sandwiches, of strict papas and watchful mamas, of prim and chaperoned walks in country towns. For him the

Victorian Age had never existed, raised as he had been in a world little changed from the fierce and savage eighteenth century.

But this did not bring him to take liberties now. On the contrary. To the Docker a railroad telegrapher (for such was Mr. De Silva, burly and black-moustached) was a member of a learned profession. He little noticed that the ever-blooming Mrs. De Silva wore no corsets and let her younger children run about the house naked. And little cared. He knew that there were girls to be had for a thrupney-bit and there were girls who were not. All the latter were respectable. No cottage in Kensington could have been more respectable, in the Docker's eyes, than the old house where the De Silvas lived, three or four generations of them, in dark and not always orderly rooms smelling of incense and odd sorts of cooking. That the girls were not exactly bleached-white in complexion was nothing to him; the Docker was dark himself. When Mr. and Mrs. De Silva boasted of their ancestry—of Portuguese generals and high-ranking officials of the old East India Company—the Docker felt no desire to doubt. He felt humble.

Miss Leah De Silva was quiet and ladylike enough when talking to the Docker. But she could be fierce and sudden when someone in her family did anything she thought not right. Perhaps her parents had been something less than keen as mustard about the Docker. He was only a corporal. Did they feel that their daughter should look higher? A sentence like a shower of swords from Leah, in a language which had once been Portuguese, silenced them.

One afternoon, when the barracks were almost deserted, the Docker summoned Owen and the Mouse to consult with. He produced a bottle and offered it.

"And risk my stripe? Thanks, my boy, but no thanks," said Owen. The Mouse took a small sip. The Docker's manner was very odd, he thought. He was proud and he was abashed; he was happy and he was uneasy.

" 'Ere's the thing," he said. "I mean to marry Miss De Silva." And he gave them a challenging look.

"Good!" said the Mouse.

"I know she'll 'ave me," the Docker went on. "But . . . well . . . there's Susanna."

"Oh, ah," agreed Owen. "There's Susanna."

Susanna was a girl who had a little house of her own, often visited by soldiers, one of whom had been the Docker. Her mother was a woman of some tribe so very deep in the Hills that they were neither Hindu nor Moslem. Heaven only knew how she had come to Lahore, or where she had gone after leaving it—for leave it she did, after her baby was born; and heaven, presumably, knew who the father had been.

Susanna had been raised and educated by the Scottish Mission and had once been employed in the tracts department of its printing establishment. The officials of the Mission had been willing to forgive Susanna once, then twice—they had even been willing to forgive Susanna a third time—but not to retain her in the printing establishment. Whereupon Susanna had renounced the Church of Scotland and all its works, and had gone altogether to the bad.

"I'm going to break off wiv 'er," said the Docker determinedly. "I shan't give 'er no present neither—no money, I mean. I know it's the custom, but if I'm going to be married I shall need all the money I've got."

"That's rather hard on Susanna," said Owen.

"Can't be 'elped," said the Docker briefly. "Now I'm going to write 'er a letter." He wanted assistance, but he also was strong for his own style. The letter, in its third and least-smudged version, was brief.

Dear Friend,

It's been a great lark but now it's all over, for I am getting married to someone else. Best not to see each other again. Keep merry and bright.

Respectfully,

"That'll do it," the Docker said, with satisfaction. "Here's two annas—give 'em to a bearer, one of you, and send the letter off directly. I'm going to start tidying up meself and me kit, as I mean to speak to Mr. De Silva tonight."

But he never spoke to Mr. De Silva that night. Sergeant-Major came striding in, big as Kachenjunga, and swollen with violent satisfaction, and found the bottle in with the Docker's gear. The Docker drew three weeks, and was lucky not to lose his stripes.

There was a note waiting for him when he came out.

Dear Docker,

I hope you will take it in good part but Miss De Silva and I are going to be married Sunday next. Perhaps it was not quite the thing for me to do—to speak during your absence—but Love knows no laws as the poet says and we do both hope you will be our friend,

Sincerely,
Harry Owen

For a long time the Docker just sat and stared. Then he said to the Mouse, "Well, if it must be. I should 'ave known a girl of 'er quality wouldn't ever marry a brute like me."

"Ah, but Docker," the Mouse said. Then in a rush of words: "It isn't that at all! Don't you see what it was? The note you meant for Susanna—Owen sent it off to Miss De Silva instead! And then went and proposed 'imself! And it must've been 'im who peached that you 'ad the bottle."

The Docker's face went dark, but his voice kept soft. "Oh," he said, "that was how it was." And said nothing more. That night he got drunk, wildly, savagely drunk, wrecked twenty stalls in the little bazaar, half killed two Sikhs who tried to stop him, and coming into the sleeping barracks as silently as the dust, took and loaded his rifle and shot Harry Owen through the head. . . .

"Yarn, yarn, yarn!" said Tom. "I don't believe you was ever in India in your life!"

The Gaffer, who had been sipping his beer silently, fired up.

"Ho, don't you! One of you fetch that pict're—the one directly under the old king's—"

He gestured toward the rear room. In very short time someone was back and handed over an old cardboard-backed photograph. It was badly faded, but it showed plainly enough three soldiers posed in front of a painted backdrop. They wore ornate and tight-fitting uniforms and had funny, jaunty little caps perched to one side of their heads.

"That 'un's me," said the Gaffer, pointing his twisted old finger.

The faces all looked alike, but the one in the middle was that of the shortest.

When it was passed to me I turned it over. The back was ornately printed with the studio's name and sure enough, it was in Lahore— a fact I pointed out, not directly to Tom, but in his general direction; and in one corner, somehow bare of curlicues, was written in faded ink a date in the late eighties, and three names: *Lance-Corporal Harry Owen, Corporal Daniel Devore, Private Alfred Graham.*

". . . young chap from newspaper was talking about it to the Padre Sahib," the Gaffer was saying. "Earnest young fellow, 'ad spectacles, young's 'e was. 'But a thing like that, sir,' says 'e, 'so unlike a British soldier—what could've made him do a thing like that?' And the Chaplain looks at 'im and sighs and says, 'Single men in barracks don't turn into plaster saints.' The writing-wallah thought this over a bit, then, 'No,' 'e says, 'I suppose not,' and wrote it down in 'is notebook."

"Well," Tom said grudgingly, "so you've been to India. But that doesn't prove the rest of the story."

"It's true, I tell you. I've got cuttin's to prove it. *Civil and Military Gazette* of Lahore."

Tom began singing:
"All this happened in Darby
(I never was known to lie.)
And if you'd 'a' been there in Darby
You'd 'a' seen it, the same as I."

Someone laughed. Tears started in the old man's weak blue eyes, and threatened to overflow the reddened rims. "I've got cuttin's."

Tom said, "Yes, you've always got cuttin's. But nobody does see 'em but you."

"You come 'ome with me," the Gaffer said, pushing his nobby old hands against the table top and making to rise. "You come 'ome with me. The cuttin's are in my old trunk and you ask my missus—for she keeps the keys—you just ask my missus."

"What!" cried Tom. "Me ask your missus for anything? Why, I'd as soon ask a lion or a tiger at Whipsnade Zoo for a bit o' their meat, as ask your missus for anything. She's a Tartar, *she* is!"

The Gaffer's mind had evidently dropped the burden of the conversation. He began to nod and smile as if Tom had paid him a very acceptable compliment. But he seemed to recall the object of Tom's remarks, rather than their tone.

"Oh, she was a lovely creature," he said softly. "Most beautiful girl you ever saw. And it was me that she married, after all, y'see. Not either of them two others, but *me,* that they called the Mouse!" And he chuckled. It was not a nice chuckle, and as I looked up, sharply, I caught his eye, and there was something sly and very ugly in it.

I went cold. In one second I was all but certain of two things. "Gaffer," I said, trying to sound casual. "What was your wife's maiden name?"

The Gaffer seemed deep in thought, but he answered, as casually as I'd asked, "Her name? Her name was Leah De Silva. Part British, part Portugee, and part—but who cares about that? Not I. I married her in church, I did."

"And how," I asked, "do you pronounce D-e-v-o-r-e?"

The dim eyes wavered. "Worked in the West India Docks, was why we called him the Docker," said the old man. "But his Christian name, it was Dan'l Deever."

"Yes," I said. "Of course it was. And it wasn't Harry Owen who peached about the whiskey bottle in Dan'l's gear, so as to get him in the guardhouse—and it wasn't Harry Owen who sent the note to the wrong young lady—was it? It was someone who knew what Harry would do if he had the chance. Someone who knew that the Docker would certainly kill Harry, if told the right set of lies. And he did, didn't he? And then the way was all clear and open for you, wasn't it?"

For just a second there was fear in Gaffer Graham's face. And there was defiance, too. And triumph. Then, swiftly, all were gone, and only the muddled memories of old age were left.

"It was cold," he whimpered. "It was bitter cold when they hanged Danny Deever in the morning. There was that young chap from the newspaper, that wrote about it. Funny name 'e 'ad—somethin' like Kipling—Ruddy Kipling, 'twas."

"Yes," I said, "something like that."

*   *   *

EDITORS' NOTE: *Here, to refresh your memory, is the full text of Rudyard Kipling's famous poem—which is so vitally connected with Avram Davidson's fascinating story . . .*

DANNY DEEVER   *by Rudyard Kipling*

"What are the bugles blowin' for?" said Files-on-Parade.
"To turn you out, to turn you out," the Color-Sergeant said.
"What makes you look so white, so white?" said Files-on-Parade.
"I'm dreadin' what I've got to watch," the Color-Sergeant said.
For they're hangin' Danny Deever, you can 'ear the Dead March play,
The regiment's in 'ollow square—they're hangin' him to-day;
They've taken of his buttons off an' cut his stripes away,
An' they're hangin' Danny Deever in the mornin'.

"What makes the rear-rank breathe so 'ard!" said Files-on-Parade.
"It's bitter cold, it's bitter cold." the Color-Sergeant said.
"What makes the front-rank man fall down?" says Files-on-Parade.
"A touch of sun, a touch of sun," the Color-Sergeant said.
They are hangin' Danny Deever, they are marchin' of 'im round,
they 'ave 'alted Danny Deever by 'is coffin on the ground;
An' 'e'll swing in 'arf a minute for a sneakin', shootin' hound—
O they're hangin' Danny Deever in the mornin'!

"'Is cot was right-'and cot to mine," said Files-on-Parade.
"'E's sleepin' out an' far to-night," the Color-Sergeant said.
"I've drunk 'is beer a score o' times," said Files-on-Parade.
"'E's drinkin' bitter beer alone," the Color-Sergeant said.
They are hangin' Danny Deever, you must mark 'im to 'is place,
For 'e shot a comrade sleepin'—you must look 'im in the face;
Nine 'undred of 'is countr an' the regiment's disgrace,
While they're hangin' Danny Deever in the mornin'.

"What's that so black agin the sun? said Files-on-Parade.
"It's Danny fightin' 'ard for life," the Color-Sergeant said.
"What's that that whimpers over'ead?" said Files-on-Parade.
"It's Danny's soul that's passin' now," the Color-Sergeant said.
For they're done with Danny Deever, you can 'ear the quickstep play.
The regiment's in column an' they're marchin' us away;
Ho! the young recruits are shakin', an' they'll want their beer to-day,
After hangin' Danny Deever in the mornin'.

THE TERRAPIN

by Patricia Highsmith

Victor heard the elevator door open, his mother's quick footsteps in the hall, and he flipped his book shut. He shoved it under the sofa pillow, and winced as he heard it slip between sofa and wall and fall to the floor with a thud. Her key was in the lock.

"Hello, Veector-r!" she cried, raising one arm in the air. Her other arm circled a big brown-paper bag, her hand held a cluster of little bags. "I have been to my publisher and to the market and also to the fish market," she told him. "Why aren't you out playing? It's a lovely, lovely day!"

"I was out," he said. "For a little while. I got cold."

"Ugh!" She was unloading the grocery bag in the tiny kitchen off the foyer. "You are seeck, you know that? In the month of October, you are cold? I see all kinds of children playing on the sidewalk. Even I think that boy you like. What's his name?"

"I don't know," Victor said.

His mother wasn't really listening, anyway. He pushed his hands into the pockets of his too-small shorts, making them tighter than ever, and walked aimlessly around the living room, looking down at his heavy, scuffed shoes. At least his mother had to buy him shoes that fit him, and he rather liked these shoes, because they had the thickest soles of any he had ever owned, and they had heavy toes that rose up a little, like mountain climbers' shoes.

Victor paused at the window and looked straight out at a toast-colored apartment building across Third Avenue. He and his mother lived on the eighteenth floor, just below the top floor where the penthouses were. The building across the street was even taller than this one. Victor had liked their Riverside Drive apartment better. He had liked the school he had gone to there better. Here they laughed at his clothes. In the other school they had got tired of laughing at them.

"You don't want to go out?" asked his mother, coming into the living room, wiping her hands briskly on a wadded paper bag. She sniffed her palms. "Ugh! That stee-enk!"

"No, Mama," Victor said patiently.

"Today is Saturday."

"I know."

"Can you say the days of the week?"

"Of course."

"Say them."

"I don't want to say them. I know them." His eyes began to sting around the edges with tears. "I've known them for years. Years and years. Kids five years old can say the days of the week."

But his mother was not listening. She was bending over the drawing table in the corner of the room. She had worked late on something last night. On his sofa bed in the opposite corner of the room, Victor had not been able to sleep until two in the morning, when his mother had finally gone to bed on the studio couch.

"Come here, Victor. Did you see this?"

Victor came on dragging feet, hands still in his pockets. No, he hadn't even glanced at her drawing board this morning, hadn't wanted to.

"This is Pedro, the Little Donkey. I invented him last night. What do you think? And this is Miguel, the little Mexican boy who rides him. They ride and ride over all of Mexico, and Miguel thinks they are lost, but Pedro knows the way home all the time, and . . ."

Victor did not listen. He deliberately shut his ears in a way he had learned to do from many years of practice; but boredom, frustration—he knew the word frustration, had read all about it—clamped his shoulders, weighed like a stone in his body, pressed hatred and tears up to his eyes as if a volcano were seething in him.

He had hoped his mother might take a hint from his saying he was too cold in his silly shorts. He had hoped his mother might remember what he had told her—that the fellow he had wanted to get acquainted with downstairs, a fellow who looked about his own age, eleven, had laughed at his short pants on Monday afternoon. *They make you wear your kid brother's pants or something?* Victor had drifted away, mortified. What if the fellow knew he didn't even own any longer pants, not even a pair of knickers, much less *long* pants or even blue jeans!

His mother, for some cockeyed reason, wanted him to look "French," and made him wear shorts and stockings that came up to just below his knees, and dopey shirts with round collars. His mother wanted him to stay about six years old, forever, all his life.

She liked to test out her drawings on him. *Victor is my sounding board,* she sometimes said to her friends. *I show my drawings to Victor and I* know *if children will like them.* Often Victor said he liked stories that he did not like, or drawings that he was indifferent to, because he felt sorry for his mother and because it put her in a better mood if he said he liked them. He was quite tired now of children's book illustrations, if he had ever in his life liked them—he really couldn't remember; and now he had only two favorites—Howard Pyle's illustrations in some of Robert Louis Stevenson's books and Cruikshank's in Dickens.

It was too bad, Victor thought, that he was absolutely the last person his mother should have asked an opinion of, because he simply *hated* children's illustrations. And it was a wonder his mother didn't see this, because she hadn't sold any illustrations for books for years and years—not since *Wimple-Dimple,* a book whose jacket was all torn and turning yellow now from age, which sat in the center of the bookshelf in a little cleared spot, propped up against the back of the bookcase so that everyone could see it.

Victor had been seven years old when that book was printed. His mother liked to tell people—and remind him, too—that he had watched her make every drawing, had shown his opinion by laughing or not, and that she had been absolutely guided by him. Victor doubted this very much, because first of all the story was somebody else's and had been written before his mother did the drawings, and her drawings had had to follow the story closely.

Since *Wimple-Dimple,* his mother had done only a few illustrations now and then for children's magazines—how to make paper pumpkins and black paper cats for Halloween and things like that—though she took her portfolio around to publishers all the time.

Their income came from his father, who was a wealthy businessman in France, an exporter of perfumes. His mother said he was very wealthy and very handsome. But he had married again, and he never wrote, and Victor had no interest in him, didn't even care if he never saw a picture of him, and he never had. His father was French with some Polish, his mother said, and she was Hungarian with some French. The word Hungarian made Victor think of Gypsies, but when he had asked his mother once, she had said emphatically that she hadn't any Gypsy blood, and she had been annoyed that Victor had brought the question up.

And now she was sounding him out again, poking him in the ribs to make him wake up, as she repeated, "Listen to me! Which do you like better, Victor? 'In all Mexico there was no bur-r-ro as wise as Miguel's Pedro,' or 'Miguel's Pedro was the wisest bur-r-ro in all Mexico'?"

"I think—I like it the first way better."

"Which way is that?" demanded his mother, thumping her palm down on the illustration.

Victor tried to remember the wording, but realized he was only staring at the pencil smudges, the thumbprints on the edges of his mother's illustration board. The colored drawing in its center did not interest him at all. He was not thinking. This was a frequent, familiar sensation to him now; there was something exciting and important about not-thinking, Victor felt, and he thought that one day he would find out something about it—perhaps under another name—in the public library or in the psychology books around the house that he browsed in when his mother was out.

"Veec-tor! What are you doing?"

"Nothing, Mama."

"That is exactly it! Nothing! Can you not even *think?*"

A warm shame spread through him. It was as if his mother read his thoughts about not-thinking. "I am thinking," he protested. "I'm thinking about *not*-thinking." His tone was defiant. What could she do about it, after all?

"About what?" Her black, curly head tilted, her mascaraed eyes narrowed at him.

"Not-thinking."

His mother put her jeweled hands on her hips. "Do you know, Victor, you are a leetle bit strange in the head?" She nodded. "You are seeck. Psychologically seeck. And retarded, do you know that? You have the behavior of a leetle boy five years old," she said slowly and weightily. "It is just as well you spend your Saturdays indoors. Who knows if you would not walk in front of a car, eh? But that is why I love you, little Victor."

She put her arm around his shoulders, pulled him against her, and for an instant Victor's nose pressed into her large, soft bosom. She was wearing her flesh-colored knitted dress, the one you could see through a little where her breast stretched it out.

Victor jerked his head away in a confusion of emotions. He did not know if he wanted to laugh or cry.

His mother was laughing gaily, her head back. "Seeck you are! Look at you! My lee-tle boy still, lee-tle short pants—ha! ha!"

Now the tears showed in his eyes, and his mother acted as if she were enjoying it! Victor turned his head away so that she would not see his eyes. Then suddenly he faced her. "Do you think I *like* these pants? *You* like them, not me, so why do you have to make fun of them?"

"A lee-tle boy who's crying!" she went on, laughing.

Victor made a dash for the bathroom, then swerved away and dove onto the sofa, his face toward the pillows. He shut his eyes tight and opened his mouth, crying but not-crying in a way he had also learned through long practice. With his mouth open, his throat tight, not breathing for nearly a minute, he could somehow get the satisfaction of crying, screaming even, without anybody knowing it.

He pushed his nose, his open mouth, his teeth, against the tomato-red sofa pillow, and though his mother's voice went on in a lazily mocking tone, and her laughter went on, he imagined that it was getting fainter and more distant from him.

He imagined, rigid in every muscle, that he was suffering the absolute worst that any human being could suffer. He imagined that he was dying. But he did not think of death as an escape, only as a concentrated and painful instant. This was the climax of his not-crying.

Then he breathed again, and his mother's voice intruded: "Did you hear me? *Did you hear me?* Mrs. Badzerkian is coming over for tea. I want you to wash your face and put on a clean shirt. I want you to recite something for her. Now what are you going to recite?"

" 'In winter when I go to bed,' " said Victor. She was making him memorize every poem in *A Child's Garden of Verses*. He had said the first one that came in his head, and now there was an argument, because he had recited that the last time Mrs. Badzerkian came to tea. "I said it because I couldn't think of any other one right off the bat!" Victor shouted.

"Don't yell at me!" his mother cried, storming across the room at him.

She slapped his face before he knew what was happening.

He was up on one elbow on the sofa, on his back, his long, knobby-kneed legs splayed out in front of him. All right, he thought, if that's the way it is, that's the way it is. He looked at her with loathing.

He would not show her that the slap had hurt, that it still stung. No more tears for today, he swore, not even any more not-crying. He would finish the day, go through the tea, like a stone, like a soldier, not wincing.

His mother paced the room, turning one of her rings round and round, glancing at him from time to time, looking quickly away from him. But his eyes were steady on her. He was not afraid. She could even slap him again and he wouldn't move.

At last she announced that she was going to wash her hair, and she went into the bathroom.

Victor got up from the sofa and wandered across the room. He wished he had a room of his own to go to. In the apartment on Riverside Drive there had been two rooms, a living room and his mother's bedroom. When she was in the living room, he had been able to go into the bedroom, and vice versa, but here— They were going to tear down the old building they had lived in on Riverside Drive. It was not a pleasant thing for Victor to think about.

Suddenly remembering the book that had fallen, he pulled out the sofa and reached for it. It was Menninger's *The Human Mind*, full of fascinating case histories of people. Victor put it back in its place on the bookshelf between a book on astrology and *How to Draw*.

His mother did not like him to read psychology books, but Victor loved them, especially ones with case histories in them. The people in the case histories did what they wanted to do. They were natural. Nobody bossed them. At the local branch library he spent hours browsing through the psychology shelves. They were in the adults' section, but the librarian did not mind him sitting at the tables there, because he was always so quiet.

Victor went into the kitchen and got a glass of water. As he was standing there drinking it, he heard a scratching noise coming from the paper bags on the counter. A mouse, he thought, but when he moved a couple of the bags he didn't see any mouse. The scratching was coming from inside one of the bags.

Gingerly, he opened the bag's end with his fingers and waited for something to jump out. Looking in, he saw a white paper carton. He pulled it out slowly. Its bottom was damp. It opened like a pastry box. Victor jumped in surprise. In the box was a turtle—a live turtle!

It was wriggling its legs in the air, trying to turn over. Victor moistened his lips, and frowning with concentration, took the turtle by its sides with both hands, turned him over, and let him down gently into the box again. The turtle drew its feet in then and its head stretched up a little and it looked right at him.

Victor smiled. Why hadn't his mother told him she'd brought him a present? A live turtle! Victor's eyes glazed with anticipation as he thought of taking the turtle down, maybe with a leash around its neck, to show the fellow who'd laughed at his short pants. The boy might change his mind about being friends with him if he learned that Victor owned a live turtle.

"Hey, Mama! Mama!" Victor yelled at the bathroom door. "You brought me a turtle?"

"A what?" The water shut off.

"A turtle! In the kitchen!" Victor had been jumping up and down in the hall. He stopped.

His mother had hesitated, too. The water came on again, and she said in a shrill tone, *"C'est une terrapène! Pour un ragout!"*

Victor understood, and a small chill went over him because his mother had spoken in French. His mother addressed him in French only when she was giving an order that had to be obeyed, or when she anticipated resistance from him.

So the terrapin was for a stew. Victor nodded to himself with a stunned resignation, and went back to the kitchen. For a stew. Well, the terrapin was not long for this world, as they say. What did a terrapin like to eat? Lettuce? Raw bacon? Boiled potato? Victor peered into the refrigerator.

He held a piece of lettuce near the terrapin's horny mouth. The terrapin did not open its mouth, but it looked at him. Victor held it near the two little dots of its nostrils, but if the terrapin smelled the lettuce, it showed no interest. Victor looked under the sink and pulled out a round wash pan. He put two inches of water into it. Then he gently dumped the terrapin into the pan. The terrapin paddled for a few seconds, as if it had to swim; then finding that its stomach sat on the bottom of the pan, it stopped, and drew its feet in.

Victor got down on his knees and studied the terrapin's face. Its upper lip overhung the lower, giving it a rather stubborn and unfriendly expression; but its eyes—they were bright and shining. Victor smiled when he looked hard at them.

"Okay, *Monsieur terrapène,*" he said, "just tell me what you'd like to eat and we'll get it for you. Maybe some tuna?"

They had had tuna fish salad yesterday for dinner, and there was a small bowl of it left over. Victor got a little chunk of it in his fingers and offered it to the terrapin. The terrapin was not interested.

Victor looked around the kitchen, wondering; then seeing the sunlight on the floor of the living room, he picked up the pan and carried it to the living room and set it down so that the sunlight would fall on the terrapin's back. All turtles liked sunlight, Victor thought. He lay down on the floor on his side, propped up on an elbow.

The terrapin stared at him for a moment, then, very slowly and with an air of forethought and caution, put out its legs and advanced, found the circular boundary of the pan, and moved to the right, half its body out of the shallow water.

Obviously it wanted to get out, so Victor took it in one hand, by the sides, and said, "You can come out and have a little walk."

He smiled as the terrapin started to disappear under the sofa. He caught it easily, because it moved so slowly. When he put it down on the carpet, it was quite still, as if it had withdrawn a little to think what it should do next, where it should go.

The terrapin was brownish green. Looking at it, Victor thought of river bottoms, of river water flowing. Or maybe oceans. Where did terrapins come from? He jumped up and went to the dictionary on the bookshelf. The dictionary had a picture of a terrapin, but it was a dull black-and-white drawing, not so pretty as the live one. He learned nothing except that the name was of Algonquian origin, that the terrapin lived in fresh or brackish water, and that it was edible.

Edible. Well, that was bad luck, Victor thought. But he was not going to eat any *terrapène* tonight. It would be all for his mother, that ragout, and even if she slapped him, scolded him, and made him learn an extra two or three poems, he would *not* eat any terrapin tonight.

His mother came out of the bathroom. "What are you doing there?—Victor?"

Victor put the dictionary back on the shelf. His mother had seen the pan. "I'm looking at the terrapin," he said, then realized the terrapin had disappeared. He got down on hands and knees and looked under the sofa.

"Don't put it on the furniture. It makes spots," said his mother. She was standing in the foyer, rubbing her hair vigorously with a towel.

Victor found the terrapin between the wastebasket and the wall. He put it back in the pan.

"Have you changed your shirt?" asked his mother.

Victor changed his shirt, and then at his mother's order sat down on the sofa with *A Child's Garden of Verses* and tackled another poem, a brand-new one for Mrs. Badzerkian. He learned two lines at a time, reading it aloud in a soft voice to himself, then repeating it, then putting two, four, and six lines together, until he had memorized the whole poem. He recited it to the terrapin. Then Victor asked his mother if he could play with the terrapin in the bathtub.

"No! And get your shirt all splashed?"

"I can put on my other shirt."

"No! It's nearly four o'clock now. Get that pan out of the living room!"

Victor carried the pan back to the kitchen. His mother took the terrapin quite fearlessly out of the pan, put it back into the white paper box, closed its lid, and stuck the box in the refrigerator.

Victor jumped a little as the refrigerator door slammed. It would be awfully cold in there for the terrapin. But then, he supposed, fresh or brackish water was cold too.

"Victor, cut the lemon," said his mother. She was fixing the big round tray with cups and saucers. The water was boiling in the kettle.

Mrs. Badzerkian was prompt as usual, and his mother poured the tea as soon as her guest had deposited her coat and pocketbook on the foyer chair and sat down. Mrs. Badzerkian smelled of cloves. She had a small, straight mouth and a thin moustache on her upper lip which fascinated Victor, as he had never seen one on a woman before—not at such short range, anyway. He never had mentioned Mrs. Badzerkian's moustache to his mother, knowing it was considered ugly; but in a strange way, her moustache was the thing he liked best about Mrs. Badzerkian.

The rest of her was dull, uninteresting, and vaguely unfriendly. She always pretended to listen carefully to his poetry recitations, but he felt that she fidgeted, thought of other things while he recited, and was glad when it was over. Today, Victor recited very well and without any hesitation, standing in the middle of the living room floor and facing the two women, who were then having their second cup of tea.

"*Très bien,*" said his mother. "Now you may have a cookie."

Victor chose from the plate a small round cookie with a drop of orange goo in its center. He kept his knees close together when he sat down. He always felt that Mrs. Badzerkian looked at his knees and with distaste. He often wished she would make some remark to his mother about his being old enough for long pants, but she never had—at least, not within his hearing.

Victor learned from his mother's conversation with Mrs. Badzerkian that the Lorentzes were coming for dinner tomorrow evening. It was probably for them that the terrapin stew was going to be made.

Victor was glad that he would have one more day to play with the terrapin. Tomorrow morning, he thought, he would ask his mother if he could take the terrapin down on the sidewalk for a while, either on a leash or, if his mother insisted, in the paper box.

"—like a chi-ild!" his mother was saying, laughing, with a glance at him, and Mrs. Badzerkian smiled shrewdly at him with her small, tight mouth.

Victor had been excused, and was sitting across the room with a book on the studio couch. His mother was telling Mrs. Badzerkian how he had played with the terrapin. Victor frowned down at his book, pretending not to hear. His mother did not like him to speak to her or her guests once he had been excused. But now she was calling him her "lee-tle ba-aby Veec-tor. . . ."

He stood up with his finger in the place in his book. "I don't see why it's childish to look at a terrapin!" he said, flushing with sudden anger. "They are very interesting animals. They—"

His mother interrupted him with a laugh, but at once the laugh disappeared and she said sternly, "Victor, I thought I had excused you. Isn't that correct?"

He hesitated, seeing in a flash the scene that was going to take place when Mrs. Badzerkian had left. "Yes, Mama. I'm sorry," he said. Then he sat down and bent over his book again.

Twenty minutes later Mrs. Badzerkian left. His mother scolded him for being rude, but it was not a five or ten minute scolding of the kind he had expected. It lasted barely two minutes. She had forgotten to buy heavy cream, and she wanted Victor to go downstairs and get some.

Victor put on his gray woolen jacket and went out. He always felt embarrassed and conspicuous in the jacket, because it came just a little bit below his short pants, and it looked as if he had nothing on underneath the coat.

Victor looked around for Frank on the sidewalk, but he didn't see him. He crossed Third Avenue and went to a delicatessen in the big building that he could see from the living room window. On his way back, he saw Frank walking along the sidewalk, bouncing a ball. Victor went right up to him.

"Hey," Victor said. "I've got a terrapin upstairs."

"A what?" Frank caught the ball and stopped.

"A terrapin. You know, like a turtle. I'll bring it down tomorrow morning and show you, if you're around. It's pretty big."

"Yeah? Why don't you bring it down now?"

"Because we're gonna eat now," said Victor. "See you."

He went into his building. He felt he had achieved something. Frank had looked really interested. Victor wished he could bring the terrapin down now, but his mother never liked him to go out after dark, and it was practically dark now.

When Victor got upstairs, his mother was still in the kitchen. Eggs were boiling and she had put a big pot of water on a back burner. "You took it out again!" Victor said, seeing the terrapin's box on the counter.

"Yes. I prepare the stew tonight," said his mother. "That is why I need the cream."

Victor looked at her. "You're going to—you have to kill it tonight?"

"Yes, my little one. Tonight." She jiggled the pot of eggs.

"Mama, can I take it downstairs to show Frank?" Victor asked quickly. "Just for five minutes, Mama. Frank's down there now."

"Who is Frank?"

"He's that fellow you asked me about today. The blond fellow we always see. *Please,* Mama."

His mother's black eyebrows frowned. "Take the *terrapène* downstairs? Certainly not. Don't be absurd, my baby! The *terrapène* is not a toy!"

Victor tried to think of some other lever of persuasion. He had not removed his coat. "You wanted me to get acquainted with Frank—"

"Yes. What has that got to do with the *terrapène?*"

The water on the back burner began to boil.

"You see, I promised him I'd—" Victor watched his mother lift the terrapin from the box, and as she dropped it into the boiling water his mouth fell open. *"Mama!"*

"What is this? What is this noise?"

Victor, open-mouthed, stared at the terrapin, whose legs were now racing against the steep sides of the pot. The terrapin's mouth opened, its eyes looked right at Victor for an instant, its head arched back in torture, then the open mouth sank beneath the seething water—and that was the end.

Victor blinked. The terrapin was dead. He came closer, saw the four legs and the tail stretched out in the water. He looked at his mother.

She was drying her hands on a towel. She glanced at him, then said, "Ugh!" She smelled her hands, then hung the towel back.

"Did you have to kill it like that?"

"How else? The same way you kill a lobster. Don't you know that? It doesn't hurt them."

He stared at her. When she started to touch him, he stepped back. He thought of the terrapin's wide-open mouth, and his eyes suddenly flooded with tears. Maybe the terrapin had been screaming and it hadn't been heard over the bubbling of the water. The terrapin had looked at him, wanting him to pull it out, and he hadn't moved to help it. His mother had tricked him, acted so fast that he couldn't save it. He stepped back again. "No, don't touch me!"

His mother slapped his face, hard and quickly.

Victor set his jaw. Then he about-faced and went to the closet and threw his jacket onto a hanger and hung it up. He went into the living room and fell down on the sofa. He was not crying now, but his mouth opened against the sofa pillow. Then he remembered the terrapin's mouth and he closed his lips. The terrapin had suffered, otherwise it would not have moved its legs so terribly fast to get out.

Then Victor wept, soundlessly as the terrapin, his mouth open. He put both hands over his face, so as not to wet the sofa. After a long while he got up.

In the kitchen his mother was humming, and every few seconds he heard her quick, firm steps as she went about her work. Victor had set his teeth again. He walked slowly to the kitchen doorway.

The terrapin was out on the wooden chopping board, and his mother, after a glance at him, still humming, took a knife and bore down on the blade, cutting off the terrapin's little nails. Victor half closed his eyes, but he watched steadily. His mother scooped the nails, with bits of skin attached to them, off the board into her palm and dumped them into the garbage bag.

Then she turned the terrapin on its back and with the same sharp, pointed knife she began to cut away the pale bottom shell. The terrapin's neck was bent sideways. Victor wanted to look away, but still he stared. Now the terrapin's insides were all exposed, red and white and greenish.

Victor did not listen to what his mother was saying—something about cooking terrapins in Europe before he was born. Her voice was gentle and soothing, not at all like what she was doing.

"All right, don't look at me like that!" she cried out suddenly, stomping her foot. "What's the matter with you? Are you crazy? Yes, I think so! You are seeck, you know that?"

Victor could not touch any of his supper, and his mother could not force him to, even though she shook him by the shoulders and threatened to slap him. They had creamed chipped beef on toast. Victor did not say a word. He felt very remote from his mother, even when she screamed right into his face. He felt very odd, the way he did sometimes when he was sick to his stomach, but he was not sick to his stomach.

When they went to bed that night, he felt afraid of the dark. He saw the terrapin's face very large, its mouth open, its eyes wide and full of pain. Victor wished he could walk out the window and float, go anywhere he wanted to, disappear, yet be everywhere. He imagined his mother's hands on his shoulders, jerking him back, if he tried to step out the window. He hated his mother.

He got up and went quietly into the kitchen. The kitchen was absolutely dark, as there was no window, but he put his hand accurately on the knife rack and felt gently for the knife he wanted. He thought of the terrapin, in little pieces now, all mixed up in the sauce of cream and egg yolks and sherry in the pot in the refrigerator.

His mother's cry was not silent—it seemed to tear his ears off. His second blow was in her body, and then he stabbed her throat again.

Only tiredness made him stop, and by then people were trying to bump the door in. Victor at last walked to the door, pulled the chain bolt back, and opened it for them.

He was taken to a large old building full of nurses and doctors. Victor was very quiet and did everything he was asked to do, and answered the questions they put to him, but only those questions; and since they didn't ask him anything about a terrapin, he did not bring it up.

H As in Homicide

by Lawrence Treat

She came through the door of the Homicide Squad's outer office as if it were a disgrace to be there, as if she didn't like it, as if she hadn't done anything wrong—and never could or would.

Still, here she was. About twenty-two years old and underweight. Wearing a pink sleeveless dress. She had dark hair pulled back in a bun; her breasts were close together; and her eyes ate you up.

Mitch Taylor had just come back from lunch and was holding down the fort all alone. He nodded at her and said, "Anything I can do?"

"Yes. I—I—" Mitch put her down as a nervous stutterer and waited for her to settle down. "They told me to come here," she said. "I went to the neighborhood police station and they said they couldn't do anything, that I had to come here."

"Yeah," Mitch said. It was the old runaround and he was willing to bet this was Pulasky's doing, up in the Third Precinct. He never took a complaint unless the rule book said, "You, Pulasky—you got to handle this or you'll lose your pension."

So Mitch said, "Sure. What's the trouble?"

"I don't like to bother you and I hope you don't think I'm silly, but—well, my friend left me. And I don't know where, or why."

"Boyfriend?" Mitch said.

She blushed a deep crimson. "Oh no! A real *friend*. We were traveling together and she took the car and went, without even leaving me a note. I can't understand it."

"Let's go inside and get the details," Mitch said.

He brought her into the squad room and sat her down at a desk. She looked up shyly, sort of impressed with him. He didn't know why, because he was only an average-looking guy, of medium height, on the cocky side, with stiff, wiry hair and a face nobody remembered, particularly.

He sat down opposite her and took out a pad and pencil. "Your name?" he said.

"Prudence Gilford."

"Address?"

"New York City, but I gave up my apartment there."

"Where I come from too. Quite a ways from home, aren't you?"

"I'm on my way to California—my sister lives out there. I answered an ad in the paper—just a moment, I think I still have it." She fumbled in a big canvas bag, and the strap broke off and the whole business dropped. She picked it up awkwardly, blushing again, but she kept on talking. "Bella Tansey advertised for somebody to share the driving to California. She said she'd pay all expenses. It was a wonderful chance for me. . . . Here, I have it."

She took out the clipping and handed it to Mitch. It was the usual thing: woman companion to share the driving, and a phone number.

"So you got in touch?" Mitch prodded.

"Yes. We liked each other immediately, and arranged to go the following week."

She was fiddling with the strap, trying to fix it, and she finally fitted the tab over some kind of button. Mitch, watching, wondered how long *that* was going to last.

Meanwhile she was still telling him about Bella Tansey. "We got along so well," Prudence said, "and last night we stopped at a motel—The Happy Inn, it's called—and we went to bed. When I woke up, she was gone."

"Why did you stop there?" Mitch asked sharply.

"We were tired and it had a Vacancy sign." She drew in her breath and asked anxiously, "Is there something wrong with it?"

"Not too good a reputation," Mitch said. "Did she take all her things with her? Her overnight stuff, I mean."

"Yes, I think so. Or at least, she took her bag."

Mitch got a description of the car: a dark blue Buick; 1959 or 1960, she wasn't sure; New York plates but she didn't know the number.

"Okay," Mitch said. "We'll check. We'll send out a flier and have her picked up and find out why she left in such a hurry."

Prudence Gilford's eyes got big. "Yes," she said. "And please, can you help me? I have only five dollars and the motel is expensive. I can't stay there and I don't know where to go."

"Leave it to me," Mitch said. "I'll fix it up at the motel and get you a place in town for a while. You can get some money, can't you?"

"Oh yes. I'll write my sister for it."

"Better wire," Mitch said. "And will you wait here a couple of minutes? I'll be right back."

"Of course."

Lieutenant Decker had come in and was working on something in his tiny office, which was jammed up with papers and stuff. Mitch reported on the Gilford business and the lieutenant listened.

"Pulasky should have handled it," Mitch said, finishing up. "But what the hell— The kid's left high and dry, so maybe we could give her a little help."

"What do you think's behind this?" Decker asked.

"I don't know," Mitch said. "She's a clinger—scared of everything and leans on people. Maybe the Tansey woman got sick and tired of her, or maybe this is lesbian stuff. Hard to tell."

"Well, go ahead with an S-Four for the Buick. It ought to be on a main highway and within a five-hundred-mile radius. Somebody'll spot it. We'll see what cooks."

Mitch drove Prudence out to the motel and told her to get her things. While she was busy, he went into the office and spoke to Ed Hiller, who ran the joint. Hiller, a tall, stoop-shouldered guy who'd been in and out of jams most of his life, was interested in anything from a nickel up, but chiefly up. He rented cabins by the hour, day, or week, and you could get liquor if you paid the freight; but most of his trouble came from reports of cars that had been left unlocked and rifled. The police had never been able to pin anything on him.

He said, "Hello, Taylor. Anything wrong?"

"Just want to know about a couple of dames that stayed here last night—Bella Tansey and Prudence Gilford. Tansey pulled out during the night."

"Around midnight," Ed said. "She came into the office to make a phone call, and a little later I heard her car pull out."

Time for the missing girl to pack, Mitch decided. So far, everything checked. "Who'd she call?" he asked. "What did she say?"

Hiller shrugged. "I don't listen in," he said. "I saw her open the door and then I heard her go into the phone booth. I mind my own business. You know that."

"Yeah," Mitch said flatly. "You heard the coins drop, didn't you? Local call, or long distance?"

Hiller leaned over the counter. "Local," he said softly. "I think."

"Got their registration?" Mitch asked. Hiller nodded and handed Mitch the sheet, which had a record of the New York license plates.

That was about all there was to it. Nobody picked up Bella Tansey and her Buick, Prudence Gilford was socked away in a rooming house in town, and Mitch never expected to see her again.

When he got home that night, Amy kissed him and asked him about things, and then after he'd horsed around with the kids a little, she showed him a letter from her sister. Her sister's husband was on strike and what the union paid them took care of food and rent and that was about all; but they had to keep up their payments on the car and the new dishwasher, and the TV had broken down again, and could Mitch and Amy help out for a little while—they'd get it back soon.

So after the kids were in bed, Mitch and Amy sat down on the sofa to figure things out, which took about two seconds and came to fifty bucks out of his next paycheck. It was always like that with the two of them: They saw things the same way and never had any arguments. Not many guys were as lucky as Mitch.

The next morning Decker had his usual conference with the Homicide Squad and went over all the cases they had in the shop. The only thing he said about the Gilford business was, the next time Pulasky tried to sucker them, figure it out so he had to come down here, personally, and then make him sweat.

Mitch drew a couple of minor assault cases to investigate, and he'd finished up with one and was on his way to the other when the call came in on his radio. Go out to French Woods, on East Road. They had a homicide and it looked like the missing Tansey woman.

He found a couple of police cars and an oil truck and the usual bunch of snoopers who had stopped out of curiosity. There was a kind of rough trail going into the woods. A couple of hundred yards in, the lieutenant and a few of the boys and Jub Freeman, the lab technician, were grouped around a dark blue car. It didn't take any heavy brainwork to decide it was the Tansey Buick.

When Mitch got to the car, he saw Bella Tansey slumped in the front seat with her head resting against the window. The right-hand door was open and so was the glove compartment, and Decker was looking at the stuff he'd found there.

He gave Mitch the main facts. "Truck driver spotted the car, went in to look, and then got in touch with us. We've been here about fifteen minutes, and the medical examiner ought to show up pretty soon. She was strangled—you can see the marks on her neck—and I'll bet a green hat that it happened the night before last, not long after she left the motel."

Mitch surveyed the position of the body with a practiced eye. "She wasn't driving either. She was pushed in there, after she was dead."

"Check," Decker said. Very carefully, so that he wouldn't spoil any possible fingerprints, he slid the junk he'd been examining onto the front seat. He turned to Jub Freeman, who was delicately holding a handbag by the two ends and scrutinizing it for prints.

"Find anything?" the lieutenant asked.

"Nothing," Jub said. "But the initials on it are B. T. W."

"Bella Tansey What?" the lieutenant said. He didn't laugh and neither did anybody else. He stooped to put his hands on the door sill, leaned forward, and stared at the body. Mitch, standing behind him, peered over his head.

Bella had been around thirty and she'd been made for men. She was wearing a blue dress with a thing that Amy called a bolero top, and, except where the skirt had pulled up, maybe from moving the body, her clothes were not disturbed. The door of the glove compartment and parts of the dashboard were splotched with fingerprint powder.

Mitch pulled back and waited. After about a minute the lieutenant stood up.

"Doesn't look as if there was a sex angle," Decker said. "And this stuff—" He kicked at the dry leaves that covered the earth. "—doesn't take footprints. If we're lucky, we'll find somebody who saw the killer somewhere around here." He made a smacking sound with his thin, elastic lips and watched Jub.

Jub had taken off his coat and dumped the contents of the pocketbook onto it. Mitch spotted nothing unusual—just the junk women usually carried; but he didn't see any money. Jub was holding the purse and rummaging inside it.

"Empty?" the lieutenant asked sharply.

Jub nodded. "Except for one nickel. She must have had money, so whoever went through this missed up on five cents."

"Couldn't be Ed Hiller, then," Mitch said, and the gang laughed.

"Let's say the motive was robbery," Decker said. "We got something of a head start on this, but brother, it's a bad one. Why does a woman on her way to California make a phone call and then sneak off in the middle of the night? Leaving her girlfriend in the lurch too. Doesn't sound like robbery now, does it?"

"Sounds like a guy," Mitch said. "She had a late date, and the guy robbed her, instead of—"

"We'll talk to Ed Hiller about that later," the lieutenant said. "Taylor, you better get going on this. Call New York and get a line on her. Her friends, her background. If she was married. How much money she might have had with her. Her bank might help on that."

"Right," Mitch said.

"And then get hold of the Gilford dame and pump her," Decker said.

Mitch nodded. He glanced into the back of the car and saw the small overnight bag. "That," he said, pointing. "She packed, so she didn't expect to go back to the motel. But she didn't put her bag in the trunk compartment, so she must have expected to check in somewhere else, and pretty soon."

"She'd want to sleep somewhere, wouldn't she?" Decker said.

"That packing and unpacking doesn't make sense," Mitch said.

Decker grunted. "Homicides never do," he said grimly.

Mitch drove back to headquarters thinking about that overnight bag, and it kept bothering him. He didn't know exactly why, but it was the sort of thing you kept in the back of your mind until something happened or you found something else, and then everything clicked and you got a pattern.

But, what with organizing the questions to ask New York, he couldn't do much doping out right now. Besides, there was a lot more information to come in.

He got New York on the phone and they said they'd move on it right away; so he hung up and went to see Prudence. He was lucky to find her in.

She was shocked at the news, but she had nothing much to contribute. "We didn't know each other very long," she said, "and I was asleep when she left. I was so tired. We'd been driving all day, and I'd done most of it."

"Did she mention knowing anybody around—anybody in town?" Mitch asked. Prudence shook her head, but he put her through the wringer anyhow—it was easy for people to hear things and then forget them. You had to jog their memories a little. And besides, how could he be sure she was telling all she knew?

He felt sorry for her, though—she looked kind of thin and played out, as if she hadn't been eating much. So he said, "That five bucks of yours isn't going to last too long, and if you need some dough—"

"Oh, thanks!" she said, sort of glowing and making him feel that Mitch Taylor, he was okay. "Oh, thanks! It's perfectly wonderful of you, but I have enough for a while, and I'm sure my sister will send me the money I wired her for."

By that afternoon most of the basic information was in. Locally, the medical examiner said that Bella Tansey had been strangled with a towel or a handkerchief; he placed the time as not long after she'd left the motel. The lieutenant had questioned Ed Hiller without being able to get anything "hot." Hiller insisted he hadn't left the motel, but his statement depended only on his own word.

Jub had used a vacuum cleaner on the car and examined the findings with a microscope, and he'd shot enough pictures to fill a couple of albums.

"They stopped at a United Motel the first night," he recapitulated, "and they had dinner at a Howard Johnson place. They ate sandwiches in the car, probably for lunch, and they bought gas in Pennsylvania and Indiana, and the car ate up oil. There was a gray kitten on the rear seat some time or other. They both drove. Bella Tansey had ear trouble and she bought her clothes at Saks Fifth Avenue. I can tell you a lot more about her, but I'm damned if I've uncovered anything that will help on the homicide. No trace in that car of anybody except the two women."

The New York police, however, came up with a bombshell. Bella Tansey had drawn $1800 from her bank, in cash, and she'd been married to Clyde Warhouse and they'd been divorced two years ago. She'd used her maiden name—Tansey.

"Warhouse!" the lieutenant said.

Everybody knew that name. He ran a column in the local paper— he called it "Culture Corner"—and he covered art galleries, visiting orchestras, and egghead lectures. Whenever he had nothing else to write about, he complained how archaic the civic architecture was.

"That's why she had the W on her bag," Mitch said. "Bella Tansey Warhouse. And Ed Hiller didn't lie about the phone call. She made it all right—to her ex-husband."

Decker nodded. "Let's say she hotfooted it out to see him. Let's say she still had a yen for him and they scrapped, that he got mad and lost his head and strangled her. But why would he take her dough? She must've had around seventeen hundred with her. Why would he rob her?"

"Why not?" Mitch said. "It was there, wasn't it?"

"Let's think about this," Decker said. "Prudence says Bella unpacked. Did Bella start to go to bed, or what?"

"Prudence doesn't know," Mitch said. "I went into that for all it was worth, and Prudence *assumes* Bella unpacked—she can't actually remember. Says she was bushed and went right to sleep. Didn't even wash her face."

"Well," Decker said, "I guess Warhouse is wondering when we'll get around to him. I'll check on him while you go up there." The lieutenant's jaw set firmly. "Bring him in."

Mitch rolled his shoulders, tugged on the lapels of his jacket, and went out. The first time you hit your suspect, it could make or break the case.

Clyde Warhouse lived in a red brick house with tall white columns on the front. Mitch found him at home, in his study. He was a little guy with big teeth, and he didn't really smile; he just pulled his lips back, and you could take it any way you pleased.

Warhouse came right to the point. "You're here about my former wife," he said. "I just heard about it on the radio, and I wish I could give you some information, but I can't. It's certainly not the end I wished for her."

"What kind of end were you hoping for?" Mitch asked.

"None." The Warhouse lips curled back, telling you how smart he was. "And certainly not one in this town."

"Let's not kid around," Mitch said. "You're coming back with me. You know that, don't you?"

The guy almost went down with the first punch. "You mean—you mean I'm being arrested?"

"What do *you* think?" Mitch said. "We know she phoned you and you met her. We know you saw her."

"But I didn't see her," Warhouse said. "She never showed up."

Mitch didn't even blink.

"How long did you wait?" he asked.

"Almost an hour. Maybe more."

"Where?"

"On the corner of Whitman and Cooper." Warhouse gasped, then put his head in his hands and said, "Oh God!" And that was all Mitch could get out of him until they had him in the squad room, with Decker leading off on the interrogation.

The guy didn't back down from that first admission. He knew he'd been tricked, but he stuck to his guns and wouldn't give another inch. He said Bella had called him around midnight and said she must see him. He hadn't known she was in town, didn't want to see her, had no interest in her, but he couldn't turn her down. So he went, and he waited. And waited and waited. And then went home.

They kept hammering away at him. First, Mitch and Decker, then Bankhart and Balenky, then Mitch and Decker again.

In between, they consulted Jub. He'd been examining Warhouse's car for soil that might match samples from French Woods; for evidence of a struggle, of Bella's presence—of anything at all. The examination drew a blank. Warhouse grinned his toothy grin and kept saying no. And late that night they gave up on him, brought him across the courtyard to the city jail, and left him there for the night. He needed sleep—and so did the Homicide Squad.

At the conference the next morning, Decker was grim. "We have an ex-wife calling her ex-husband at midnight and making an appointment; we have his statement that he went and she never showed up; and we have a homicide and that's all."

"The dough," Bankhart said.

Decker nodded. "When we find that seventeen hundred, then we might have a case. We'll get warrants and we'll look for it, but let's assume we draw another blank. Then what?"

"Let's have another session with Ed Hiller," Mitch said.

They had it, and they had a longer one with Warhouse, and they were still nowhere. They'd gone into the Warhouse background thoroughly. He earned good money, paid his bills promptly, and got along well with his second wife. He liked women, they went for him, and he was a humdinger with them, although he was not involved in any scandal. But in Mitch's book, he'd humdinged once too often. Still, you had to prove it.

For a while they concentrated on The Happy Inn. But the motel guests either couldn't be found, because they'd registered under fake names with fake license numbers, or else they said they'd been asleep and had no idea what was going on outside.

The usual tips came in—crank stuff that had to be followed up. The killer had been seen, somebody had heard Bella scream for help, somebody else had had a vision. Warhouse had been spotted waiting on the corner, which proved nothing except he'd arrived there first.

Every tip checked out either as useless or a phony. The missing $1700 didn't show up. Decker ran out of jokes, and Mitch came home tired and irritable.

The case was at full stop.

Then Decker had this wild idea, and he told it to Jub and Mitch. "My wife says I woke up last night and asked for a drink of water, and I don't even remember it."

"So you were thirsty," Mitch remarked.

"Don't you get it?" Decker exclaimed. "People wake up, then go back to sleep, and in the morning they don't even know they were awake. Well, we know Bella packed her bag, and she was in that motel room with Prudence and must have made some noise and possibly even talked. I'll bet a pair of pink panties that Prudence woke up, and then forget all about it. She has a clue buried deep in her mind."

"Granted," Jub said, "but how are you going to dig it up?"

"I'll hypnotize her," Decker said, with fire in his eyes. "I'll ask a psychiatrist to get her to free-associate. Taylor, ask her to come in tomorrow morning, when my mind is fresh. And hers too."

Mitch dropped in on Prudence and gave her the message, but the way he saw things, the lieutenant was sure reaching for it—far out. Mitch told Amy about this screwy idea of Decker's, but all she said was that tomorrow was payday and not to forget to send the fifty dollars to her sister.

That was why Mitch wasn't around when Prudence showed up. He took his money over to the post office and there, on account he liked to jaw a little, make friends, set up contacts—you never knew when you might need them—he got to gabbing with the postal clerk.

His name was Cornell and he was tired. Mitch figured the guy was born that way. Besides, there was something about a post office that dragged at you. No fun in it, nothing ever happened. All the stamps were the same (or looked the same) and all the clerks were the same (or looked the same) and if anything unusual came up, you checked it in the regulations and did what the rules said, exactly. And if the rules didn't tell you, then the thing couldn't be done, so you sent the customer away and went back to selling stamps.

Which people either wanted, or they didn't. There were no sales,

no bargains. A damaged stamp was never marked down—it was worth
what it said on its face, or nothing. There was nothing in between.

Still, the post office was a hell of a lot better than what Decker was
doing over at the Homicide Squad, so Mitch handed in his fifty bucks
for the money order and said, "It's not much dough, I guess. What's
the most you ever handled?"

The clerk came alive. "Ten thousand dollars. Six years ago."

"The hell with six years ago. Say this week."

"Oh. That dame with seventeen hundred dollars. That was the
biggest."

Click.

Mitch said cautiously, "You mean Prudence Gilford?"

"No. Patsy Grant."

"P. G.—same thing," Mitch said with certainty. "Same girl. And
I'll bet she sent the dough to herself care of General Delivery, somewhere in California."

Cornell looked as if he thought Mitch were some kind of magician.
"That's right," he said. "How did you know?"

"Me?" Mitch said, seeing that it all fitted like a glove. Prudence—
or whatever her name was—had strangled Bella for the dough, then
packed Bella's bag, dragged her out to the car, driven it to the woods,
and left it there. And probably walked all the way back. That's why
Prudence had been so tired.

"Me?" Mitch said again, riding on a cloud. "I know those things.
That's what makes me a cop. Ideas—I got bushels of 'em." He
thought of how the lieutenant would go bug-eyed. Mitch Taylor, Homicide Expert.

He walked over to the phone booth, gave his shield number to the
operator so he could make the call free and save himself a dime, and
got through to the Homicide Squad.

Decker answered. "Taylor?" he said. "Come on back. The Gilford
dame just confessed."

"She—*what?*"

"Yeah, yeah, confessed. While she was in here, the strap on her
bag broke and she dropped it. Everything fell out—including a
money-order receipt for seventeen hundred dollars. We had her cold

and she confessed. She knew all about Warhouse and planned it so we'd nail him."

There was a buzz on the wire and Lieutenant Decker's voice went fuzzy.

"Taylor," he said after a couple of seconds. "Can you hear me? Are you listening?"

"Sure," Mitch said. "But what for?"

And he hung up.

Yeah, Mitch Taylor, Homicide Expert.

GOODBYE, POPS

by Joe Gores

I got off the Greyhound and stopped to draw icy Minnesota air into my lungs. A bus had brought me from Springfield, Illinois, to Chicago the day before; a second bus had brought me here. I caught my passing reflection in the window of the old-fashioned depot—a tall hard man with a white and savage face, wearing an ill-fitting overcoat. I caught another reflection, too, one that froze my guts: a cop in uniform. Could they already know it was someone else in that burned-out car?

Then the cop turned away, chafing his arms with gloved hands through his blue stormcoat, and I started breathing again. I went quickly over to the cab line. Only two hackies were waiting there; the front one rolled down his window as I came up.

"You know the Miller place north of town?" I asked.

He looked me over. "I know it. Five bucks—now."

I paid him from the money I'd rolled a drunk for in Chicago and eased back against the rear seat. As he nursed the cab out ice-rimed Second Street, my fingers gradually relaxed from their rigid chopping position. I deserved to go back inside if I let a clown like this get to me.

"Old man Miller's pretty sick, I hear." He half turned to catch me with a corner of an eye. "You got business with him?"

"Yeah. My own."

119

That ended that conversation. It bothered me that Pops was sick enough for this clown to know about it; but maybe my brother Rod being vice president at the bank would explain that. There was a lot of new construction and a freeway west of town with a tricky overpass to the old county road. A mile beyond a new subdivision were the 200 wooded hilly acres I knew so well.

After my break from the federal pen at Terre Haute, Indiana, two days before, I'd gotten outside their cordon through woods like these. I'd gone out in a prison truck, in a pail of swill meant for the prison farm pigs, had headed straight west, across the Illinois line. I'm good in open country, even when I'm in prison condition, so by dawn I was in a hayloft near Paris, Illinois, some twenty miles from the pen. You can do what you have to do.

The cabby stopped at the foot of the private road, looking dubious. "Listen, buddy, I know that's been plowed, but it looks damned icy. If I try it and go into the ditch—"

"I'll walk from here."

I waited beside the road until he'd driven away, then let the north wind chase me up the hill and into the leafless hardwoods. The cedars that Pops and I had put in as a windbreak were taller and fuller; rabbit paths were pounded hard into the snow under the barbed-wire tangles of wild raspberry bushes. Under the oaks at the top of the hill was the old-fashioned, two-story house, but I detoured to the kennels first. The snow was deep and undisturbed inside them. No more foxhounds. No cracked corn in the bird feeder outside the kitchen window either. I rang the front doorbell.

My sister-in-law Edwina, Rod's wife, answered it. She was three years younger than my thirty-five, and she'd started wearing a girdle.

"Good Lord! Chris!" Her mouth tightened. "We didn't—"

"Ma wrote that the old man was sick." She'd written, all right. *Your father is very ill. Not that you have ever cared if any of us lives or dies* . . . And then Edwina decided that my tone of voice had given her something to get righteous about.

"I'm amazed you'd have the nerve to come here, even if they did let you out on parole or something." So nobody had been around asking yet. "If you plan to drag the family name through the mud again—"

I pushed by her into the hallway. "What's wrong with the old man?" I called him Pops only inside myself, where no one could hear.

"He's dying, that's what's wrong with him."

She said it with a sort of baleful pleasure. It hit me, but I just grunted and went by into the living room. Then the old girl called down from the head of the stairs.

"Eddy? What—who is it?"

"Just—a salesman, Ma. He can wait until Doctor's gone."

Doctor. As if some damned croaker was generic physician all by himself. When he came downstairs Edwina tried to hustle him out before I could see him, but I caught his arm as he poked it into his overcoat sleeve.

"Like to see you a minute, Doc. About old man Miller."

He was nearly six feet, a couple of inches shorter than me, but outweighing me forty pounds. He pulled his arm free.

"Now see here, fellow—"

I grabbed his lapels and shook him, just enough to pop a button off his coat and put his glasses awry on his nose. His face got red.

"Old family friend, Doc." I jerked a thumb at the stairs. "What's the story?"

It was dumb, dumb as hell, of course, asking him; at any second the cops would figure out that the farmer in the burned-out car wasn't me after all. I'd dumped enough gasoline before I struck the match so they couldn't lift prints off anything except the shoe I'd planted, but they'd make him through dental charts as soon as they found out he was missing. When they did they'd come here asking questions, and then the croaker would realize who I was. But I wanted to know whether Pops was as bad off as Edwina said he was, and I've never been a patient man.

The croaker straightened his suitcoat, striving to regain lost dignity. "He—Judge Miller is very weak, too weak to move. He probably won't last out the week." His eyes searched my face for pain, but there's nothing like a federal pen to give you control. Disappointed, he said, "His lungs. I got to it much too late, of course. He's resting easily."

I jerked the thumb again. "You know your way out."

Edwina was at the head of the stairs, her face righteous again. It seems to run in the family, even with those who married in. Only Pops and I were short of it.

"Your father is very ill. I forbid you—"

"Save it for Rod; it might work on him."

In the room I could see the old man's arm hanging limply over the edge of the bed, with smoke from the cigarette between his fingers running up to the ceiling in a thin unwavering blue line. The upper arm, which once had measured an honest eighteen and had swung his small tight fist against the side of my head a score of times, could not even hold a cigarette up in the air. It gave me the same wrench as finding a good foxhound that's gotten mixed up with a bobcat.

The old girl came out of her chair by the foot of the bed, her face blanched. I put my arms around her. "Hi, Ma," I said. She was rigid inside my embrace, but I knew she wouldn't pull away. Not there in Pops's room.

He had turned his head at my voice. The light glinted from his silky white hair. His eyes, translucent with imminent death, were the pure, pale blue of birch shadows on fresh snow.

"Chris," he said in a weak voice. "Son of a biscuit, boy . . . I'm glad to see you."

"You ought to be, you lazy devil," I said heartily. I pulled off my suit jacket and hung it over the back of the chair, and tugged off my tie. "Getting so lazy that you let the foxhounds go!"

"That's enough, Chris." She tried to put steel into it.

"I'll just sit here a little, Ma," I said easily. Pops wouldn't have long, I knew, and any time I got with him would have to do me. She stood in the doorway, a dark indecisive shape; then she turned and went silently out, probably to phone Rod at the bank.

For the next couple of hours I did most of the talking; Pops just lay there with his eyes shut, like he was asleep. But then he started in, going way back, to the trapline he and I had run when I'd been a kid; to the big white-tail buck that followed him through the woods one rutting season until Pops whacked it on the nose with a tree branch. It was only after his law practice had ripened into a judgeship that we began to draw apart; I guess that in my twenties I was too wild, too much what he'd been himself thirty years before. Only I kept going in that direction.

About seven o'clock my brother Rod called from the doorway. I went out, shutting the door behind me. Rod was taller than me, broad and big-boned, with an athlete's frame—but with mush where his guts should have been. He had close-set pale eyes and not quite enough chin, and hadn't gone out for football in high school.

"My wife reported the vicious things you said to her." It was his best give-the-teller-hell voice. "We've talked this over with Mother and we want you out of here tonight. We want—"

"*You* want? Until he kicks off it's still the old man's house, isn't it?"

He swung at me then—being Rod, it was a right-hand lead—and I blocked it with an open palm. Then I backhanded him, hard, twice across the face each way, jerking his head from side to side with the slaps, and crowding him up against the wall. I could have fouled his groin to bend him over, then driven locked hands down on the back of his neck as I jerked a knee into his face; and I wanted to. The need to get away before they came after me was gnawing at my gut like a weasel in a trap gnawing off his own paw to get loose. But I merely stepped away from him.

"You—you murderous animal!" He had both hands up to his cheeks like a woman might have done. Then his eyes widened theatrically, as the realization struck him. I wondered why it had taken so long. "You've *broken out!*" he gasped. "*Escaped!* A fugitive from— from justice!"

"Yeah. And I'm staying that way. I know you, kid, all of you. The last thing any of you want is for the cops to take me here." I tried to put his tones into my voice. "*Oh! The scandal!*"

"But they'll be after you—"

"They think I'm dead," I said flatly. "I went off an icy road in a stolen car in downstate Illinois, and it rolled and burned with me inside."

His voice was hushed, almost horror-stricken. "You mean—that there *is* a body in the car?"

"Right."

I knew what he was thinking, but I didn't bother to tell him the truth—that the old farmer who was driving me to Springfield, because he thought my doubled-up fist in the overcoat pocket was a gun, hit a patch of ice and took the car right off the lonely country road. He was impaled on the steering post, so I took his shoes and put one of mine on his foot. The other I left, with my fingerprints on it, lying near enough so they'd find it but not so near that it'd burn along with the car. Rod wouldn't have believed the truth anyway. If they caught me, who would?

I said, "Bring me up a bottle of bourbon and a carton of cigarettes. And make sure Eddy and Ma keep their mouths shut if anyone asks about me." I opened the door so Pops could hear. "Well, thanks, Rod. It *is* nice to be home again."

Solitary in the pen makes you able to stay awake easily or snatch sleep easily, whichever is necessary. I stayed awake for the last thirty-seven hours that Pops had, leaving the chair by his bed only to go to the bathroom and to listen at the head of the stairs whenever I heard the phone or the doorbell ring. Each time I thought: *This is it.* But my luck held. If they'd just take long enough so I could stay until Pops went; the second that happened, I told myself, I'd be on my way.

Rod and Edwina and Ma were there at the end, with Doctor hovering in the background to make sure he got paid. Pops finally moved a pallid arm and Ma sat down quickly on the edge of the bed—a small, erect, rather indomitable woman with a face made for wearing a lorgnette. She wasn't crying yet; instead, she looked purely luminous in a way.

"Hold my hand, Eileen." Pops paused for the terrible strength to speak again. "Hold my hand. Then I won't be frightened."

She took his hand and he almost smiled, and shut his eyes. We waited, listening to his breathing get slower and slower and then just stop, like a grandfather clock running down. Nobody moved, nobody spoke. I looked around at them, so soft, so unused to death, and I felt like a marten in a brooding house. Then Ma began to sob.

It was a blustery day with snow flurries. I parked the Jeep in front of the funeral chapel and went up the slippery walk with wind plucking at my coat, telling myself for the hundredth time just how nuts I was to stay for the service. By now they *had* to know that the dead farmer wasn't me; by now some smart prison censor *had* to remember Ma's letter about Pops being sick. He was two days dead, and I should have been in Mexico by this time. But it didn't seem complete yet, somehow. Or maybe I was kidding myself, maybe it was just the old need to put down authority that always ruins guys like me.

From a distance it looked like Pops but up close you could see the cosmetics and that his collar was three sizes too big. I felt his hand: It was a statue's hand, unfamiliar except for the thick, slightly down-curved fingernails.

Rod came up behind me and said, in a voice meant only for me, "After today I want you to leave us alone. I want you out of my house."

"Shame on you, brother," I grinned. "Before the will is even read, too."

We followed the hearse through snowy streets at the proper funeral pace, lights burning. Pallbearers wheeled the heavy casket out smoothly on oiled tracks, then set it on belts over the open grave. Snow whipped and swirled from a gray sky, melting on the metal and forming rivulets down the sides.

I left when the preacher started his scam, impelled by the need to get moving, get away, yet impelled by another urgency, too. I wanted something out of the house before all the mourners arrived to eat and guzzle. The guns and ammo already had been banished to the garage, since Rod never had fired a round in his life; but it was easy to dig out the beautiful little .22 target pistol with the long barrel. Pops and I had spent hundreds of hours with that gun, so the grip was worn smooth and the blueing was gone from the metal that had been out in every sort of weather.

Putting the Jeep on four-wheel, I ran down through the trees to a cut between the hills, then went along on foot through the darkening hardwoods. I moved slowly, evoking memories of Korea to neutralize the icy bite of the snow through my worn shoes. There was a flash of brown as a cotton-tail streaked from under a deadfall toward a rotting woodpile I'd stacked years before. My slug took him in the spine, paralyzing the back legs. He jerked and thrashed until I broke his neck with the edge of my hand.

I left him there and moved out again, down into the small marshy triangle between the hills. It was darkening fast as I kicked at the frozen tussocks. Finally a ringneck in full plumage burst out, long tail fluttering and stubby pheasant wings beating to raise his heavy body. He was quartering up and just a bit to my right, and I had all the time in the world. I squeezed off in mid-swing, knowing it was perfect even before he took that heart-stopping pinwheel tumble.

I carried them back to the Jeep; there was a tiny ruby of blood on the pheasant's beak, and the rabbit was still hot under the front legs. I was using headlights when I parked on the curving cemetery drive. They hadn't put the casket down yet, so the snow had laid a soft blanket over it. I put the rabbit and pheasant on top and stood without moving for a minute or two. The wind must have been strong, because I found that tears were burning on my cheeks.

Goodbye, Pops. Goodbye to deer-shining out of season in the hardwood belt across the creek. Goodbye to jump-shooting mallards down in the river bottoms. Goodbye to woodsmoke and mellow bourbon by firelight and all the things that made a part of you mine. The part they could never get at.

I turned away, toward the Jeep—and stopped dead. I hadn't even heard them come up. Four of them, waiting patiently as if to pay their respects to the dead. In one sense they were: To them that dead farmer in the burned-out car was Murder One. I tensed, my mind going to the .22 pistol that they didn't know about in my overcoat pocket. Yeah. Except that it had all the stopping power of a fox's bark. If only Pops had run to handguns of a little heavier caliber. But he hadn't.

Very slowly, as if my arms suddenly had grown very heavy, I raised my hands above my head.

THE PURPLE SHROUD

by Joyce Harrington

Mrs. Moon threw the shuttle back and forth and pumped the treadles of the big four-harness loom as if her life depended on it. When they asked what she was weaving so furiously, she would laugh silently and say it was a shroud.

"No, really, what is it?"

"My house needs new draperies." Mrs. Moon would smile and the shuttle would fly and the beater would thump the newly woven threads tightly into place. The muffled, steady sounds of her craft could be heard from early morning until very late at night, until the sounds became an accepted and expected background noise and were only noticed in their absence.

Then they would say, "I wonder what Mrs. Moon is doing now."

That summer, as soon as they had arrived at the art colony and even before they had unpacked, Mrs. Moon requested that the largest loom in the weaving studio be installed in their cabin. Her request had been granted because she was a serious weaver, and because her husband, George, was one of the best painting instructors they'd ever had. He could coax the amateurs into stretching their imaginations and trying new ideas and techniques, and he would bully the scholarship students until, in a fury, they would sometimes produce works of surprising originality.

127

George Moon was, himself, only a competent painter. His work had never caught on, although he had a small loyal following in Detroit and occasionally sold a painting. His only concessions to the need for making a living and for buying paints and brushes were to teach some ten hours a week throughout the winter and to take this summer job at the art colony, which was also their vacation. Mrs. Moon taught craft therapy at a home for the aged.

After the loom had been set up in their cabin, Mrs. Moon waited. Sometimes she went swimming in the lake, sometimes she drove into town and poked about in the antique shops, and sometimes she just sat in the wicker chair and looked at the loom.

They said, "What are you waiting for, Mrs. Moon? When are you going to begin?"

One day Mrs. Moon drove into town and came back with two boxes full of brightly colored yarns. Classes had been going on for about two weeks, and George was deeply engaged with his students. One of the things the students loved about George was the extra time he gave them. He was always ready to sit for hours on the porch of the big house, just outside the communal dining room, or under a tree, and talk about painting or about life as a painter or tell stories about painters he had known.

George looked like a painter. He was tall and thin, and with approaching middle age he was beginning to stoop a little. He had black snaky hair which he had always worn on the long side, and which was beginning to turn gray. His eyes were very dark, so dark you couldn't see the pupils, and they regarded everything and everyone with a probing intensity that evoked uneasiness in some and caused young girls to fall in love with him.

Every year George Moon selected one young lady disciple to be his summer consort.

Mrs. Moon knew all about these summer alliances. Every year, when they returned to Detroit, George would confess to her with great humility and swear never to repeat his transgression.

"Never again, Arlene," he would say. "I promise you, never again."

Mrs. Moon would smile her forgiveness.

Mrs. Moon hummed as she sorted through the skeins of purple and deep scarlet, goldenrod yellow and rich royal blue. She hummed as she wound the glowing hanks into fat balls, and she thought about George and the look that had passed between him and the girl from Minneapolis at dinner the night before. George had not returned to their cabin until almost two in the morning. The girl from Minneapolis was short and plump, with a round face and a halo of fuzzy red-gold hair. She reminded Mrs. Moon of a teddy bear; she reminded Mrs. Moon of herself twenty years before.

When Mrs. Moon was ready to begin, she carried the purple yarn to the weaving studio.

"I have to make a very long warp," she said. "I'll need to use the warping reel."

She hummed as she measured out the seven feet and a little over, then sent the reel spinning.

"Is it wool?" asked the weaving instructor.

"No, it's orlon," said Mrs. Moon. "It won't shrink, you know."

Mrs. Moon loved the creak of the reel, and she loved feeling the warp threads grow fatter under her hands until at last each planned thread was in place and she could tie the bundle and braid up the end. When she held the plaited warp in her hands she imagined it to be the shorn tresses of some enormously powerful earth goddess whose potency was now transferred to her own person.

That evening after dinner, Mrs. Moon began to thread the loom. George had taken the rowboat and the girl from Minneapolis to the other end of the lake where there was a deserted cottage. Mrs. Moon knew he kept a sleeping bag there, and a cache of wine and peanuts. Mrs. Moon hummed as she carefully threaded the eye of each heddle with a single purple thread, and thought of black widow spiders and rattlesnakes coiled in the corners of the dark cottage.

She worked contentedly until midnight and then went to bed. She was asleep and smiling when George stumbled in two hours later and fell into bed with his clothes on.

Mrs. Moon wove steadily through the summer days. She did not attend the weekly critique sessions for she had nothing to show and was not interested in the problems others were having with their work. She ignored the Saturday night parties where George and the girl from Minneapolis and the others danced and drank beer and slipped off to the beach or the boathouse. Sometimes, when she tired of the long hours at the loom, she would go for solitary walks in the woods and always brought back curious trophies of her rambling. The small cabin, already crowded with the loom and the iron double bedstead, began to fill up with giant toadstools, interesting bits of wood, arrangements of reeds and wild wheat.

One day she brought back two large black stones on which she painted faces. The eyes of the faces were closed and the mouths were faintly curved in archaic smiles. She placed one stone on each side of the fireplace.

George hated the stones. "Those damn stonefaces are watching me," he said. "Get them out of here."

"How can they be watching you? Their eyes are closed."

Mrs. Moon left the stones beside the fireplace and George soon forgot to hate them. She called them Apollo I and Apollo II.

The weaving grew and Mrs. Moon thought it the best thing she had ever done. Scattered about the purple ground were signs and symbols which she saw against the deep blackness of her closed eyelids when she thought of passion and revenge, of love and wasted years and the child she had never had. She thought the barbaric colors spoke of these matters, and she was pleased.

"I hope you'll finish it before the final critique," the weaving teacher said when she came to the cabin to see it. "It's very good."

Word spread through the camp and many of the students came to the cabin to see the marvelous weaving. Mrs. Moon was proud to show it to them and received their compliments with quiet grace.

"It's too fine to hang at a window," said one practical Sunday-painting matron. "The sun will fade the colors."

"I'd love to wear it," said the life model.

"You!" said a bearded student of lithography. "It's a robe for a pagan king!"

"Perhaps you're right," said Mrs. Moon, and smiled her happiness on all of them.

The season was drawing to a close when in the third week of August, Mrs. Moon threw the shuttle for the last time. She slumped on the backless bench and rested her limp hands on the breast beam of the loom. Tomorrow she would cut the warp.

That night, while George was showing color slides of his paintings in the main gallery, the girl from Minneapolis came alone to the Moons' cabin. Mrs. Moon was lying on the bed watching a spider spin a web in the rafters. A fire was blazing in the fireplace, between Apollo I and Apollo II, for the late summer night was chill.

"You must let him go," said the golden-haired teddy bear. "He loves me."

"Yes, dear," said Mrs. Moon.

"You don't seem to understand. I'm talking about George." The girl sat on the bed. "I think I'm pregnant."

"That's nice," said Mrs. Moon. "Children are a blessing. Watch the spider."

"We have a real relationship going. I don't care about being married—that's too feudal. But you must free George to come and be a father image to the child."

"You'll get over it," said Mrs. Moon, smiling a trifle sadly at the girl.

"Oh, you don't even want to know what's happening!" cried the girl. "No wonder George is bored with you."

"Some spiders eat their mates after fertilization," Mrs. Moon remarked. "Female spiders."

The girl flounced angrily from the cabin, as far as one could be said to flounce in blue jeans and sweatshirt.

George performed his end-of-summer separation ritual simply and brutally the following afternoon. He disappeared after lunch. No one knew where he had gone. The girl from Minneapolis roamed the camp, trying not to let anyone know she was searching for him. Finally she rowed herself down to the other end of the lake, to find that George had dumped her transistor radio, her books of poetry, and her box of incense on the damp sand, and had put a padlock on the door of the cottage.

She threw her belongings into the boat and rowed back to the camp, tears of rage streaming down her cheeks. She beached the boat, and with head lowered and shoulders hunched she stormed the Moons' cabin. She found Mrs. Moon tying off the severed warp threads.

"Tell George," she shouted, "tell George I'm going back to Minneapolis. He knows where to find me!"

"Here, dear," said Mrs. Moon, "hold the end and walk backwards while I unwind it."

The girl did as she was told, caught by the vibrant colors and Mrs. Moon's concentration. In a few minutes the full length of cloth rested in the girl's arms.

"Put it on the bed and spread it out," said Mrs. Moon. "Let's take a good look at it."

"I'm really leaving," whispered the girl. "Tell him I don't care if I never see him again."

"I'll tell him." The wide strip of purple flowed garishly down the middle of the bed between them. "Do you think he'll like it?" asked Mrs. Moon. "He's going to have it around for a long time."

"The colors are very beautiful, very savage." The girl looked closely at Mrs. Moon. "I wouldn't have thought you would choose such colors."

"I never did before."

"I'm leaving now."

"Goodbye," said Mrs. Moon.

George did not reappear until long after the girl had loaded up her battered bug of a car and driven off. Mrs. Moon knew he had been watching and waiting from the hill behind the camp. He came into the cabin whistling softly and began to take his clothes off.

"God, I'm tired," he said.

"It's almost dinnertime."

"Too tired to eat," he yawned. "What's that on the bed?"

"My weaving is finished. Do you like it?"

"It's good. Take it off the bed. I'll look at it tomorrow."

Mrs. Moon carefully folded the cloth and laid it on the weaving bench. She looked at George's thin naked body before he got into bed, and smiled.

"I'm going to dinner now," she said.

"Okay. Don't wake me up when you get back. I could sleep for a week."

"I won't wake you up," said Mrs. Moon.

*   *   *

Mrs. Moon ate dinner at a table by herself. Most of the students had already left. A few people, the Moons among them, usually stayed on after the end of classes to rest and enjoy the isolation. Mrs. Moon spoke to no one.

After dinner she sat on the pier and watched the sunset. She watched the turtles in the shallow water and thought she saw a blue heron on the other side of the lake. When the sky was black and the stars were too many to count, Mrs. Moon went to the toolshed and got a wheelbarrow. She rolled this to the door of her cabin and went inside.

The cabin was dark and she could hear George's steady heavy breathing. She lit two candles and placed them on the mantelshelf. She spread her beautiful weaving on her side of the bed, gently so as not to disturb the sleeper. Then she quietly moved the weaving bench to George's side of the bed, near his head.

She sat on the bench for a time, memorizing the lines of his face by the wavering candlelight. She touched him softly on the forehead with the pads of her fingertips and gently caressed his eyes, his hard cheeks, his raspy chin. His breathing became uneven and she withdrew her hands, sitting motionless until his sleep rhythm was restored.

Then Mrs. Moon took off her shoes. She walked carefully to the fireplace, taking long quiet steps. She placed her shoes neatly side by side on the hearth and picked up the larger stone, Apollo I. The face of the kouros, the ancient god, smiled up at her and she returned that faint implacable smile. She carried the stone back to the bench beside the bed, and set it down.

Then she climbed onto the bench, and when she stood, she found she could almost touch the spider's web in the rafters. The spider crouched in the heart of its web, and Mrs. Moon wondered if spiders ever slept.

Mrs. Moon picked up Apollo I, and with both arms raised, took careful aim. Her shadow, cast by candlelight, had the appearance of a priestess offering sacrifice. The stone was heavy and her arms grew weak. Her hands let go. The stone dropped.

George's eyes flapped open and he saw Mrs. Moon smiling tenderly down on him. His lips drew back to scream, but his mouth could only form a soundless hole.

"Sleep, George," she whispered, and his eyelids clamped over his unbelieving eyes.

Mrs. Moon jumped off the bench. With gentle fingers she probed beneath his snaky locks until she found a satisfying softness. There was no blood and for this Mrs. Moon was grateful. It would have been a shame to spoil the beauty of her patterns with superfluous colors and untidy stains. Her mothlike fingers on his wrist warned her of a faint uneven fluttering.

She padded back to the fireplace and weighed in her hands the smaller, lighter Apollo II. This time she felt there was no need for added height. With three quick butter-churning motions she enlarged the softened area in George's skull and stilled the annoying flutter in his wrist.

Then she rolled him over, as a hospital nurse will roll an immobile patient during bed-making routine, until he rested on his back on one half of the purple fabric. She placed his arms across his naked chest and straightened his spindly legs. She kissed his closed eyelids, gently stroked his shaggy brows, and said, "Rest now, dear George."

She folded the free half of the royal cloth over him, covering him from head to foot with a little left over at each end. From her sewing box she took a wide-eyed needle and threaded it with some difficulty in the flickering light. Then kneeling beside the bed, Mrs. Moon began stitching across the top. She stitched small careful stitches that would hold for eternity.

Soon the top was closed and she began stitching down the long side. The job was wearisome, but Mrs. Moon was patient and she hummed a sweet, monotonous tune as stitch followed stitch past George's ear, his shoulder, his bent elbow. It was not until she reached his ankles that she allowed herself to stand and stretch her aching knees and flex her cramped fingers.

Retrieving the twin Apollos from where they lay abandoned on George's pillow, she tucked them reverently into the bottom of the cloth sarcophagus and knelt once more to her task. Her needle flew faster as the remaining gap between the two edges of cloth grew smaller, until the last stitch was securely knotted and George was sealed into his funerary garment. But the hardest part of her night's work was yet to come.

She knew she could not carry George even the short distance to the door of the cabin and the wheelbarrow outside. And the wheelbarrow was too wide to bring inside. She couldn't bear the thought of dragging him across the floor and soiling or tearing the fabric she had so lovingly woven. Finally she rolled him onto the weaving bench, and despite the fact that it only supported him from armpits to groin, she managed to maneuver it to the door. From there it was possible to shift the burden to the waiting wheelbarrow.

Mrs. Moon was now breathing heavily from her exertions, and paused for a moment to survey the night and the prospect before her. There were no lights anywhere in the camp except for the feeble glow of her own guttering candles. As she went to blow them out she glanced at her watch and was mildly surprised to see that it was ten minutes past three. The hours had flown while she had been absorbed in her needlework.

She perceived now the furtive night noises of the forest creatures which had hitherto been blocked from her senses by the total concentration she had bestowed on her work. She thought of weasels and foxes prowling, of owls going about their predatory night activities, and considered herself in congenial company. Then taking up the handles of the wheelbarrow, she trundled down the well-defined path to the boathouse.

The wheelbarrow made more noise than she had anticipated and she hoped she was far enough from any occupied cabin for its rumbling to go unnoticed. The moonless night sheltered her from any wakeful watcher, and a dozen summers of waiting had taught her the nature and substance of every square foot of the camp's area. She could walk it blindfolded.

When she reached the boathouse she found that some hurried careless soul had left a boat on the beach in defiance of the camp's rules. It was a simple matter of leverage to shift her burden from barrow to boat and in minutes Mrs. Moon was heaving inexpertly at the oars. At first the boat seemed inclined to travel only in wide arcs and head back to shore, but with patient determination Mrs. Moon established a rowing rhythm that would take her and her passenger to the deepest part of the lake.

She hummed a sea chanty which aided her rowing and pleased her sense of the appropriate. Then, pinpointing her position by the silhouette of the tall solitary pine that grew on the opposite shore, Mrs. Moon carefully raised the oars and rested them in the boat.

As Mrs. Moon crept forward in the boat, feeling her way in the darkness, the boat began to rock gently. It was a pleasant, soothing motion and Mrs. Moon thought of cradles and soft enveloping comforters. She continued creeping slowly forward, swaying with the motion of the boat, until she reached the side of her swaddled passenger. There she sat and stroked the cloth and wished that she could see the fine colors just one last time.

She felt the shape beneath the cloth, solid but thin and now rather pitiful. She took the head in her arms and held it against her breast, rocking and humming a long-forgotten lullaby.

The doubled weight at the forward end of the small boat caused the prow to dip. Water began to slosh into the boat—in small wavelets at first as the boat rocked from side to side, then in a steady trickle as the boat rode lower and lower in the water. Mrs. Moon rocked and hummed; the water rose over her bare feet and lapped against her ankles. The sky began to turn purple and she could just make out the distant shape of the boathouse and the hill behind the camp. She was very tired and very cold.

Gently she placed George's head in the water. The boat tilted crazily and she scrambled backward to equalize the weight. She picked up the other end of the long purple chrysalis, the end containing the stone Apollos, and heaved it overboard. George in his shroud, with head and feet trailing in the lake, now lay along the side of the boat, weighting it down.

Water was now pouring in. Mrs. Moon held to the other side of the boat with placid hands and thought of the dense comfort of the muddy lake bottom and George beside her forever. She saw that her feet were frantically pushing against the burden of her life, running away from that companionable grave.

With a regretful sigh she let herself slide down the short incline of the seat and came to rest beside George. The boat lurched deeper into the lake. Water surrounded George and climbed into Mrs. Moon's lap. Mrs. Moon closed her eyes and hummed "Nearer My God to Thee." She did not see George drift away from the side of the boat, carried off by the moving arms of water. She felt a wild bouncing, a shuddering and splashing, and was sure the boat had overturned. With relief she gave herself up to chaos and did not try to hold her breath.

Expecting a suffocating weight of water in her lungs, Mrs. Moon was disappointed to find she could open her eyes, that air still entered and left her gasping mouth. She lay in a pool of water in the bottom of the boat and saw a bird circle high above the lake, peering down at her. The boat was bobbing gently on the water, and when Mrs. Moon sat up she saw that a few yards away, through the fresh blue morning, George was bobbing gently too. The purple shroud had filled with air and floated on the water like a small submarine come up for air and a look at the new day.

As she watched, shivering and wet, the submarine shape drifted away and dwindled as the lake took slow possession. At last, with a grateful sigh, green water replacing the last bubble of air, it sank just as the bright arc of the sun rose over the hill in time to give Mrs. Moon a final glimpse of glorious purple and gold. She shook herself like a tired old gray dog and called out, "Goodbye, George." Her cry echoed back and forth across the morning and startled forth a chorus of bird shrieks. Pandemonium and farewell. She picked up the oars.

Back on the beach, the boat carefully restored to its place, Mrs. Moon dipped her blistered hands into the lake. She scented bacon on the early air and instantly felt the pangs of an enormous hunger. Mitch, the cook, would be having his early breakfast and perhaps would share it with her. She hurried to the cabin to change out of her wet clothes, and was amazed, as she stepped over the doorsill, at the stark emptiness which greeted her.

Shafts of daylight fell on the rumpled bed, but there was nothing for her there. She was not tired now, did not need to sleep. The fireplace contained cold ashes, and the hearth looked bare and unfriendly. The loom gaped at her like a toothless mouth, its usefulness at an end. In a heap on the floor lay George's clothes where he had dropped them the night before. Out of habit she picked them up, and as she hung them on a hook in the small closet she felt a rustle in the shirt pocket. It was a scrap of paper torn off a drawing pad; there was part of a pencil sketch on one side, on the other an address and telephone number.

Mrs. Moon hated to leave anything unfinished, despising untidiness in herself and others. She quickly changed into her town clothes and hung her discarded wet things in the tiny bathroom to dry. She found an apple and munched it as she made up her face and combed her still-damp hair. The apple took the edge off her hunger, and she decided not to take the time to beg breakfast from the cook.

She carefully made the bed and tidied the small room, sweeping a few scattered ashes back into the fireplace. She checked her summer straw pocketbook for driver's license, car keys, money, and finding everything satisfactory, she paused for a moment in the center of the room. All was quiet, neat, and orderly. The spider still hung inert in the center of its web and one small fly was buzzing helplessly on its perimeter. Mrs. Moon smiled.

There was no time to weave now—indeed, there was no need. She could not really expect to find a conveniently deserted lake in a big city. No. She would have to think of something else.

Mrs. Moon stood in the doorway of the cabin in the early sunlight, a small frown wrinkling the placid surface of her round pink face. She scuffled slowly around to the back of the cabin and into the shadow of the sycamores beyond, her feet kicking up the spongy layers of years of fallen leaves, her eyes watching carefully for the right idea to show itself. Two grayish-white stones appeared side by side, half covered with leaf mold. Anonymous, faceless, about the size of canteloupes, they would do unless something better presented itself.

Unceremoniously she dug them out of their bed, brushed away the loose dirt and leaf fragments, and carried them back to the car.

Mrs. Moon's watch had stopped sometime during the night, but as she got into the car she glanced at the now fully risen sun and guessed the time to be about six thirty or seven o'clock. She placed the two stones snugly on the passenger seat and covered them with her soft pale-blue cardigan. She started the engine, and then reached over and groped in the glove compartment. She never liked to drive anywhere without knowing beforehand the exact roads to take to get to her destination. The road map was there, neatly folded beneath the flashlight and the box of tissues.

Mrs. Moon unfolded the map and spread it out over the steering wheel. As the engine warmed up, Mrs. Moon hummed along with it. Her pudgy pink hand absently patted the tidy blue bundle beside her as she planned the most direct route to the girl in Minneapolis.

THE FALLEN CURTAIN

by Ruth Rendell

The incident happened in the spring after his sixth birthday. His mother always referred to it as "that dreadful evening," and always is no exaggeration. She talked about it a lot, especially when he did well at anything, which was often since he was good at school and at passing exams.

Showing her friends his swimming certificate or the prize he had won for being top at geography: "When I think we might have lost Richard that dreadful evening! You have to believe there's Someone watching over us, don't you?" Clasping him in her arms: "He might have been killed—or worse." (A remarkable statement, this one.) "It doesn't bear thinking about."

Apparently, it did bear talking about. "If I'd told him once, I'd told him fifty times never to talk to strangers or get into cars. But boys will be boys and he forgot all that when the time came. He was given sweets, of course, and *lured* into this car." Whispers at this point, meaningful glances in his direction. "Threats and suggestions—persuaded into goodness knows what—I'll never know how we got him back alive."

What Richard couldn't understand was how his mother knew so much about it. She hadn't been there. Only he and the Man had been there, and Richard himself couldn't remember a thing about it. A curtain had fallen over the bit of his memory that held the details of

141

that dreadful evening. He remembered only what had come immediately before it and immediately after.

They were living then in the South London suburb of Upfield, in a
little terraced house on Petunia Street, he and his mother and his
father. His mother had been over forty when Richard was born and he
had no brothers or sisters. ("That's why we love you so much, Richard.") He wasn't allowed to play in the street with the other kids. ("You
want to keep yourself to yourself, dear.") Round the corner in Lupin
Street lived his Gran, his father's mother. Gran never came to their
house, though he thought his father would have liked it if she had.

"I wish you'd have my mother to tea on Sunday," he once heard
his father say.

"If that woman sets foot in this house, Stan, I go out of it."

So Gran never came to tea.

"I hope I know what's right, Stan, and I know better than to keep
the boy away from his grandmother. You can have him round there
once a week with you, so long as I don't have to come in contact with
her."

That made three houses Richard was allowed into—his own, his
Gran's, and the house next door on Petunia Street where the Wilsons
lived with their Brenda and their John. Sometimes he played in their
garden with John, though it wasn't much fun as Brenda, who was
much older, nearly sixteen, was always bullying them and stopping
them from getting dirty.

He and John were in the same class in school, but his mother
wouldn't let him go to school alone with John, although it was only
three blocks away. She was very careful and nervous about him, was
his mother, waiting outside the gates before school ended to walk
him home with his hand tightly clasped in hers.

But once a week he didn't go straight home. He looked forward to
Wednesdays because Wednesday evening was the one he spent at
Gran's, and because the time between his mother's leaving him and
his arrival at Gran's house was the only time he was ever free and
by himself.

This was the way it was. His mother would meet him from school
and they'd walk down Plumtree Grove to where Petunia Street started.
Lupin Street turned off the Grove a bit farther down, so his mother

would see him across the road, waving and smiling encouragingly, till he turned the corner into Lupin Street. Gran's house was about 100 yards down. That 100 yards was his free time, his alone time.

"Mind you run all the way," his mother always called after him.

But round the corner he always stopped running and began to dawdle—stopping to play with the cat that roamed about the bit of waste ground or climbing on the pile of bricks the builders never came to build into anything. Sometimes, if she wasn't bad with arthritis, Gran would be waiting for him at her gate, and he didn't mind having to forgo the cat and the climbing because it was so nice in Gran's house.

Gran had a big TV set—unusually big for those days—and he'd watch it, eating chocolate, until his father came from the factory in time for tea. Tea was lovely, and fish and chips that Gran didn't buy at the shop but cooked herself, and cream meringues and chocolate eclairs, and tinned peaches with evaporated milk, all of it washed down with fizzy lemonade. ("It's a disgrace the way your mother spoils that boy, Stan.")

They were supposed to be home by seven, but every week when it got to seven, Gran would remember there was a cowboy film coming up on TV and there'd be cocoa and biscuits and potato crisps to go with it. They'd be lucky to be home in Petunia Street before nine.

"Don't blame me," said his mother, "if his schoolwork suffers next day."

That dreadful evening his mother left him as usual at the corner and saw him cross the road. He could remember that, and remember too how he'd looked to see if Gran was at her gate. When he'd made sure she wasn't, he'd wandered on to the building site to cajole the cat out of the nest she'd made for herself in the rubble.

It was late March, a fine afternoon and still broad daylight at four. He was stroking the cat, thinking how thin and bony she was and how some of Gran's fish and chips would do her good, when—what? What next? At this point the curtain came down. Three hours later it lifted, and he was in Plumtree Grove, walking along quite calmly ("Running in terror with that Man after him!") when whom should he meet but Mrs. Wilson's Brenda out for the evening with her boyfriend.

Brenda had pointed at him, stared and shouted. She ran up to him and clutched him and squeezed him till he could hardly breathe. Was that what had frightened him into losing his memory? They said no. They said he'd been frightened before that ("Terrified out of his life!") and that Brenda's grabbing him and the dreadful shriek his mother gave when she saw him had nothing to do with the curtain coming down.

Petunia Street was full of police cars and there was a crowd outside their house. Brenda hustled him in, shouting, "I've found him, I've found him!"—and there was his father all white in the face, talking to the policeman, his mother half dead on the sofa being given brandy, and—wonder of wonders—his Gran there, too. That had been one of the strangest things of that whole strange evening, that his Gran had set foot in their house and his mother hadn't left it.

They all started asking him questions at once. Had he answered them? All that remained in his memory was his mother's scream. That endured, that shattering sound, and the great open mouth from which it issued as she leaped upon him. Somehow, although he couldn't have explained why, he connected that scream and her seizing him as if to swallow him with the descent of the curtain.

He was never allowed to be alone after that, not even to play with John in the Wilsons' garden, and he was never allowed to forget those events he couldn't remember. There was no question of going to Gran's even under supervision, for Gran's arthritis had got so bad they had put her in the old people's ward at Upfield Hospital. The Man was never found. A couple of years later a little girl from Plumtree Grove got taken away and murdered. They never found that Man either, but his mother was sure it was the same one.

"And it might have been our Richard. It doesn't bear thinking of, that Man roaming the streets like a wild beast."

"What did he do to me, Mum?" asked Richard, trying.

"If you don't remember, so much the better. You want to forget all about it, put it right out of your life."

If only she'd let him. "What did he *do*, Dad?"

"I don't know, Rich. None of us knows, me nor the police nor your mum, for all she says. Women like to set themselves up as knowing all about things, but it's my belief you never told her no more than you told me."

She took him to school and fetched him home until he was twelve. The other kids teased him mercilessly. He wasn't allowed to go to their houses or have any of them to his. ("You never know who they know or what sort of connections they've got.") His mother only stopped going everywhere with him when he got taller than she was, and anyone could see he was too big for any Man to attack.

Growing up brought no elucidation of that dreadful evening but it did bring, with adolescence, the knowledge of what might have happened. And as he came to understand that it wasn't only threats and blows and stories of horror which the Man might have inflicted on him, he felt an alien in his own body or as if his body were covered with a slime which nothing could wash away. For there was no way of knowing how, there was nothing to do about it but wish his mother would leave the subject alone, and to avoid getting friendly with people, and to work hard at school.

He did very well there, for he was naturally intelligent and had no outside diversions. No one was surprised when he got to a good university, not Oxford or Cambridge but nearly as good, ("Imagine, all that brainpower might have been wasted if that Man had had his way.") where he began to read for a science degree. He was the first member of his family ever to go to college, and the only cloud in the sky was that his Gran, as his father pointed out, wasn't there to see and share his glory.

She had died in the hospital when he was fourteen and she'd left her house to his parents. They'd sold it and theirs and bought a much bigger one with a proper garden and a garage in a suburb some five miles farther out from Upfield. The little bit of money Gran had saved she left to Richard, to come to him when he was eighteen. It was just enough to buy a secondhand car, and when he came down from university for the Easter holidays, he bought a two-year-old Ford, took his driving test, and passed it.

"That boy," said his mother, "passes every exam that comes his way. It's as if he *couldn't* fail if he tried. He's got a guardian angel watching over him, has had ever since he was six." Her husband had admonished her for her too-excellent memory and now she referred only obliquely to that dreadful evening. "When you-know-what happened and he was spared."

She watched him drive expertly round the block, her only regret that he didn't have a nice girl beside him, a sensible hard-working fiancée—not one of your tarty ones—and saving up for the deposit on a house and furniture. Richard had never had a girl. There was one at college he liked and who, he thought, might like him. But he didn't ask her out. He was never quite sure if he was fit for any girl to know, let alone to love.

The day after he'd passed his test he thought he'd drive over to Upfield and look up John Wilson. There was more in this, he confessed to himself, than a wish to revive an old friendship. John was the only friend he'd really ever had, but he'd always felt inferior to him, for John had been (and had had the chance to be) easy and sociable and had had a girl to go out with when he was only fourteen. He rather liked the idea of arriving outside the Wilsons' house, fresh from his first two terms at the university and in his own car.

It was a Wednesday in early April, a fine, mild afternoon and still, of course, broad daylight at four. He chose a Wednesday because that was early closing day in Upfield and John wouldn't be in the hardware store where he'd worked ever since he left school three years before.

But as he approached Petunia Street up Plumtree Grove from the southerly direction, it struck him that he'd like to take a look at his Gran's old house and see if they'd ever built anything on that bit of waste ground. For years and years, half of his lifetime, those bricks had lain there, though the thin old cat had disappeared or died long before Richard's parents moved. And the bricks were still there, overgrown now by grass and nettles.

He drove into Lupin Street, moving slowly along the pavement edge until he was within sight of his Gran's house. There was enough of his mother in him to stop him from parking directly outside the house ("Keep yourself to yourself and don't pry into what doesn't concern you.") so he stopped the car some few yards this side of it.

It had been painted a bright pink, the window woodwork picked out in sky blue. Richard thought he liked it better the way it used to be, cream plaster and brown wood, but he didn't move away. A strange feeling had come over him, stranger than any he could remember having experienced, which kept him where he was, staring at the wilderness of rubble and brick and weeds. Just nostalgia, he thought, just going back to those Wednesdays which had been the highspots of his weeks.

It was funny the way he kept looking in the rubble for the old cat to appear. If she were alive, she'd be as old as he by now and not many cats live that long. But he kept on looking just the same, and presently, as he was trying to pull himself out of this dreamy, dazed feeling and go off to John's, a living creature did appear behind the shrub-high weeds. A boy, about eight. Richard didn't intend to get out of the car. But he found himself out of it, locking the door and then strolling over onto the building site.

You couldn't really see much from a car, not details. That must have been why he'd got out, he thought, to examine more closely this scene of his childhood pleasures. It seemed very small, not the wild expanse of brick hills and grassy gullies he remembered, but a scrubby bit of land twenty feet wide and perhaps twice as long. Of course it had seemed so much bigger because he had been so much smaller—smaller even than this little boy who now sat on a brick mountain, eyeing him.

He didn't mean to speak to the boy, for Richard wasn't a child anymore but a Man. And if there is an explicit rule that a child mustn't speak to strangers, there is an implicit, unstated one that a Man doesn't speak to children. If he had *meant* to speak, his words would have been very different, something about having played there himself once, or having lived nearby. The words he did use came to his lips as if they had been placed there by some external (or deeply internal) ruling authority.

"You're trespassing on private land. Did you know that?"

The boy began to ease himself down. "All the kids play here, mister."

"Maybe, but that's no excuse. Where do you live?"

On Petunia Street, but I'm going to my Gran's . . . No.

"Upfield High Road."

"I think you'd better get in my car," the Man said, "and I'll take you home."

Doubtfully the boy said, "There won't be no one there. My mum
works late Wednesdays and I haven't got no dad. I'm to go straight
home from school and have my tea and wait for when my mum comes
at seven."

Straight to my Gran's and have my tea and . . .

"But you haven't gone straight home, have you? You've hung about
trespassing on other people's property."

"You a cop, mister?"

"Yes," said the Man.

The boy got into the car quite willingly. "Are we going to the cop
shop?"

"We may go to the police station later. I want to have a talk to you
first. We'll go—" Where should they go? South London has many
open spaces, commons they're called—Wandsworth Common, Toot-
ing Common, Streatham Common . . . What made him choose Drywood Common, so far away, a place he'd heard of but hadn't visited,
so far as he knew, in his whole life? The Man had known, and he
was the Man now, wasn't he?

"We'll go to Drywood and have a talk. There's some chocolate on
the dashboard shelf. Have a piece if you like." He started the car
and they drove off past Gran's old house. "Have it all," he said.

The boy ate it all. He introduced himself as Barry. He was eight
and he had no father or brothers or sisters, just his mum who worked
to keep them both. His mum had told him never to get into a stranger's
car, but a cop was different, wasn't he?

"Quite different," said the Man. "Different altogether."

It wasn't easy finding Drywood Common because the signposting
was bad around there. But the strange thing was that, once there, the
whole layout of the common was remarkably familiar to him.

"We'll park," he said, "down by the pond."

He found the pond with ease, driving along the main road that
bisected the common, then turning left onto a smaller lane. There
were ducks on the pond. It was surrounded by trees, quite a wood of
trees, but in the distance you could see houses and a row of shops.
He parked the car by the water and switched off the engine.

Barry was very calm and trusting. He listened intelligently to the
"policeman's" lecture on behaving himself and not trespassing, and

he didn't fidget or seem bored when the Man stopped talking about that and began to talk about himself. The Man had had a lonely life, a bit like being in prison, and he'd never been allowed out alone. Even when he was in his own room doing his homework, he'd been watched ("Leave your door open, dear, we don't want any secrets in this house.") and he hadn't had a single real friend. Would Barry be his friend, just for a few hours, just for this evening? Barry would.

"But you're grown up now," Barry said.

The Man nodded, but as if that didn't make much difference, and then he began to cry. He cried as grownups do, almost tearlessly but with shame and self-disgust.

A small and rather dirty hand touched the Man's hand and held it. No one had ever held his hand like that before. Not possessively or commandingly ("Hold onto me tight, Richard, while we cross the road.") but gently, sympathetically—lovingly? Their hands remained clasped, the small one covering the large, then the large one enclosing and gripping the small. A tension, as of time stopped, held the two people in the car quiet, motionless. Then the boy broke it, and time moved again.

"I'm getting hungry," the boy said.

"Are you? It's past your teatime. I'll tell you what, we could have some fish and chips. One of those shops over there is a fish and chip shop."

Barry started to get out of the car.

"No, not you," the Man said. "It's better if I go alone. You wait here. Okay?"

"Okay," Barry said.

He was gone only ten minutes—for he knew exactly and from a distance which one of the shops it was—and when he got back Barry was waiting for him. The fish and chips were good, almost as good as those Gran used to cook. By the time they had finished eating and had wiped their greasy fingers on his handkerchief, dusk had come. Lights were going on in those far-off shops and houses but here, down by the pond, the trees made it quite dark.

"What's the time?" said Barry.

"A quarter past six."

"I ought to be getting back."

"How about a game of hide and seek first? Your mum won't be home yet. I can get you back to Upfield in ten minutes."

"I don't know. . . . Suppose she gets in early?"

"Please," the Man said. "Please, just for a little while. I used to play hide and seek down here when I was a kid."

"But you said you never played anywhere. You said—"

"Did I? Maybe I didn't. I'm a little confused."

Barry looked at him gravely: "I'll hide first," he said.

He watched Barry disappear among the trees. Grownups who play hide and seek don't keep to the rules; they don't bother with that counting-to-100 bit. But the Man did. He counted slowly and seriously, then he got out of the car and began walking round the pond.

It took him a long time to find Barry, who was more proficient at this game than he, a proficiency which showed when it was his turn to do the seeking. The darkness was deepening, and there was no one else on the common. He and the boy were quite alone.

Barry had gone to hide. In the car the Man sat counting—97, 98, 99, 100. When he stopped he was aware of the silence of the place, alleviated only by the faint, distant hum of traffic on the South Circular Road, just as the darkness was alleviated only by the red blush of the sky radiating the glow of London. Last time round it hadn't been this dark. The boy wasn't behind any of the trees or in the bushes by the waterside.

Where the hell had the stupid kid got to? Richard's anger was irrational, for he had suggested the game himself. Was he angry because the boy had proved better at it than he? Or was it something deeper and fiercer—rage at rejection by this puny and ignorant little savage?

"Where are you, Barry? Come on out. I've had about enough of this."

There was no answer. The wind rustled, and a tiny twig scuttered down out of a treetop to his feet. God, that little devil! What will I do if I can't find him?

When I do find him I'll—I'll kill him.

He shivered. The blood was throbbing in his head. He broke a stick off a bush and began thrashing about with it, infuriated, shouting into the dark silence. "Barry, Barry, come out! Come out at once, d'you hear me?" He doesn't want me, he doesn't care about me, no one will ever want me—

Then he heard a giggle from a treetop, and suddenly there was a crackling of twigs, a slithering sound. Not quite above him—over there. In the giggle, he thought, there was a note of jeering. But where, where? Down by the water's edge. The boy had been up in the tree that almost overhung the pond.

There was a thud as of small feet bouncing onto the ground, and again that maddening, gleeful giggle. For a moment the Man stood still. His hands clenched as around a frail neck, and he held them pressed together, as if crushing out life.

Run, Barry, run . . . *Run, Richard, to Plumtree Grove and Brenda, to home and Mother who knows what dreadful evenings are.*

The Man thrust his way through the bushes, making for the pond. The boy would be away by now, but not far away. And the Man's legs were long enough to outrun the boy, his hands strong enough to insure there would be no future of doubt and fear and curtained memory . . .

But the boy was nowhere, nowhere. And yet—what was that sound, as of stealthy, fearful feet creeping away? He wheeled round, and there was the boy coming toward him, walking a little timidly between the straight, gray tree trunks *toward* him. A thick constriction gripped his throat. There must have been something in his face, some threatening gravity made more intense by the half dark, that stopped the boy in his tracks.

Run, Barry, run, run . . .

They stared at each other for a moment, for a lifetime, for twelve long years. Then the boy gave a merry laugh, fearless and innocent. He ran forward and flung himself into the Man's arms, and the Man, in a great release of pain and anguish, lifted the boy up, lifted him laughing into his own laughing face. They laughed with a kind of rapture at finding each other at last, and in the dark, under the whispering trees, each held the other in a close embrace.

"Come on," Richard said, "I'll take you home. I don't know what I was doing, bringing you here in the first place."

"To play hide and seek," said Barry. "We had a swell time."

They got back into the car. It was after seven when they reached Upfield High Road, but not much after.

"I don't reckon my mum's got in yet."

"I'll drop you here. I won't go up to your place. Barry?"

"What is it, mister?"

"Don't ever take a lift from a Man again, will you? Promise me?"

Barry nodded. "Okay."

"I once took a lift from a stranger, and for years I couldn't remember what had happened. It sort of came back to me tonight, meeting you. I remember it all now. He was all right, just a bit lonely like me. We had fish and chips on Drywood Common and played hide and seek like you and me, and he brought me back nearly to my house—the way I've brought you. But it wouldn't always be like that."

"How do you know?"

Richard looked at his strong young man's hands. "I just know," he said.

He drove away, turning once to see that the boy was safely in his house. Barry told his mother all about it, but she insisted it must have been a nasty experience and called the police. Since Barry didn't know the license number of the car and had no idea of the stranger's name, there was little the police could do. They never found the Man.

LIKE A TERRIBLE SCREAM

by Etta Revesz

Me, I just sit here and wait until the man outside push the little button and the door open with a small click and the Father walk out. The Father, I know him since I be five, which is now eight years. I bet he never think he come to see me in lockup. Kid lockup they call it but look like real grown-up jail to me.

I look out the little window for two days now. All I see is sky and maybe a airplane go by. The bed is clean but the floor is cement stone and hard on my leg. It is the door that I hate with much feeling. It is gray and iron, like the brace I wear on my leg. The little square window is high and I am yet too little to see out it and down the hall. I know a man sits there by a high desk and pushes buttons for many doors like I have to my cell. Yesterday I push up tight against the door because I am afraid. I think maybe I am the only one left here. But all I see is the ceiling of the hall and it is gray and not so clean.

It is hard to sit here and see the Father leave. He try. He try hard to make me tell why I do it.

"Confess, my son," Father Diaz say. "Tell me why did you do that terrible thing? You could not have realized. You were not thinking right!"

The good Father he lean his head way down and I think he cry,

153

but I shake my head. How can I tell him? If I tell him the reason why I have done this it would be all for nothing. So I let him put his hand on my head and I say nothing.

"Kneel, my son," the Father say. "If you cannot tell me, tell God. It will help."

"No, Father," I say. "I cannot kneel."

He look very unhappy then, almost I think he will slap me when he take his hand away from my head. But he does not.

"A boy that cannot kneel and ask forgiveness from God is lost," he say and then go to my iron door and punch the little black button that tell the man at the desk to open up.

Now I sit here on my cot and wait for the Father to leave. My leg is out straight with my iron brace beginning to hurt me. Always at this time when night sounds start, Rita come home and take it off for me and rub my leg. Her hands, always so soft, rub away the stiffness. She talk to me about things outside. Always she ask to see my picture that I make that day. It was Rita that buy the paper and black crayon for me to draw. And last Christmas she bring me a box of paints! How much I do not guess it cost, but I know it cost much.

I feel in my eyes the water begin, but I want not to cry. I look again at Father Diaz's black suit. Like a crow he looks, standing with his arms folded close to his side like wings. I cannot stop my eyes from making tears. I pretend it is because my leg hurts and I try not to think of Rita.

I decide to tell Father Diaz that I cannot kneel because my iron brace does not bend. Then he would not think that all his teaching about God and the Blessed Virgin was for nothing. But it is too late. I hear the click and the door pop open and I am alone again.

Soon they will bring me food. I do not like noodles and cheese. Cheese should be on enchiladas. Noodles and cheese and maybe wheat bread with edges curled up like a dried leaf. Next to it a spoonful of peanut butter which I hate. It glues my tongue to my teeth. I think back to what Rita always bring to me.

Every night before she go to her job she come by the house with a surprise. First she take off my iron brace and rub my leg and then she put the brown bag in my lap and we stick both our heads close to see what big pleasure is there. Sometimes I look up and see her eyes big on me and smiling when I find a bag of candy or a pomegranate or even a new paint brush. At such time I feel a big pain over my heart and my jaw hurt from not crying. Rita she hate for me to cry. How can she know that it is for love of her that I cry?

Sometimes when only Mama and I are home I stop my painting and look out the window. We are high, two stairs up, but I can see the branches of the tree growing from the brown square of land in our sidewalk. It is not very healthy this poor tree, and has dry brown limbs with no leaves much. But still I watch the sun on what leaves are still there. It is when the sun is low and shines even with my tree that I like it best. Long fingers of white light run sharp from the center and when the wind blows everything shoots gold and shining. It is like a sign from God that the day is gone and Rita will run soon into the room and call out.

"Pepito," she calls, "I am here again. Your ugly old sister is here again!"

I pretend I do not hear her and then she come and put her hands around to cover my eyes from behind.

"Guess who it is?" she ask in make-believe man voice.

"My ugly old sister!" I say and then we both laugh. My sister Rita is not ugly. Sometimes she have a day off and she let me draw her picture. She sit by the window quiet while I look at her and put my markings on my paper. Sometimes I forget to move my hand when I look at her. Rita have long black hair and she tie it back so her neck looks very thin. Her mouth is still but when she think I am not watching, her lips move a little and I think she is telling secrets to herself. It is her eyes that I cannot draw so well.

When I look once they are laughing and show a joke ready to be said, but when I look again, I feel I must weep. Once I really start to cry at least a year ago when I was only twelve. Rita rush over and hug me.

"My little Pepito." She touch my cheek. "Does your leg hurt? I will work hard and save—oh, I will save so and will take you to a big hospital where the finest doctors will make a miracle on your leg."

"No," I tell her. I can never lie to Rita even when I want pity. "It is my love for you that make me cry. You are like Sunday music."

She just laugh then and the next day when she come she say, "Here is your Sunday music for your ears to hear on Wednesday!"

I love my Mama and Papa almost as much as I love Rita. But Mama sigh often as she count her beads and wears black instead of colors bright and gay like Rita. I remember long time before, when we first come to city, Mama sing always. Sometimes she dance with Papa when Papa say about the big job he going to get.

"No more driving the junk truck for me," say Papa. "Lucerno family will be on easy street soon."

When Papa finish driving truck for Mr. George Hemfield he go to night school. When I wake up at night from the couch where I sleep because my leg hurt, I see Papa sitting at the kitchen table with books. All is quiet. Only sleeping sounds and the tick-ting of the wake-up clock and the hush sound of the books when Papa close them. Then I hear him push the chair and walk to his bed.

Carlos and Mikos, my big brothers, sleep in the bedroom. They have the big bed and Rita sleep with little Rosa in the little bed. Rosa is very small, only three years, and Rita call her Little Plum. Mama and Papa have the back porch for them. Papa fix it up and when Mama say, "What about the heat, my husband, when the winter come?" Papa he laugh and grab Mama as she pass him to the stove and say, "I will keep you warm—like always!"

"You crazy fellow, not before the children!" And Mama push his hand away like she is mad but I see her lips smile. Mama think I know nothing about life because I stay at home, because I do not run the streets and only walk outside for special days like Easter and Christmas and Cinque de Mayo when the world is spinning to guitar music.

At first when we come to city I go to school but after a while the stairs and long walk is too much. Rita try to carry me but the iron prison on my leg make her tired and once she drop me and the iron bend and cut into my leg. I learn, but not very much. It is hard for me to read the words and the teacher do not call my name very often.

Rita try to help. She is in the high school and she show me to make my letters. But I cannot do well. At my desk I draw pictures of what I want to say. It is much easier and soon the school hall show them on the walls.

One day the Principal give Rita a note for Mama to come and talk with him. Papa he go instead and after a long time in the Principal's office he come out and we walk home. Papa walk very small steps and not even holds my hand from sidewalk to car street. When we get to house Papa pick me up and carry me up to Mama. He hold me very tight and push my face to look behind him but I know he angry, sad angry. He tell Mama that a special teacher is going to teach me at home because they have no place for me at my school.

The teacher come but not for long. After a while another lady come to talk to Mama about budget and say that if Mama bring me to Down-Town I go to special school. Papa get mad and go Down-Town but come back soon. He say nothing and now I stay home and draw much.

I hear the pop of my iron door and a kid like me come in. He is an old one in experience at this place and they let him bring the food. He push open my door with a foot and carry in the tray. I watch him look where to put it.

"Here's your supper, Crip," he say. "Where d'ya want it?"

I sit up and look at what there is to eat, but all I see is red jello and two pieces of brown bread poked into a sauce of broken meat. I take off the square paper box of milk and tell him to take the tray. He looks worried at me.

"Look, Mex," he speak low. "Not eating won't help."

I shake my head and lean back on my cot and he leaves. It is almost dark now in my little gray room. I can put on a light. It is held away from me in a wire basket like a muzzle for a dog, but I have nothing to look at anyway. So I stand and press against the stone wall so I see up and out the window into the soon night.

In the sky is fuzzy lines of color, like the cotton when you pull it out of the box and it spread fine in your hand. Somewhere I hear a noise and the red and green light of a airplane pass my eyes. So small it is, like a ladybug. So far away and such a small spot, much bigger looks the bird that flies closer to my window, not knowing that night is close and he should be in his nest. I am all alone now in my darkness.

It is like the darkness that came to our house the day Papa come home from new job hunting. For long days Papa try for new job, after he come home from school and hold high his beautiful piece of paper with gold words saying he is a educated man.

"This is just the beginning," say Papa. "I am just the number one to bring home the High School Certificate. Look, kids," say Papa, "this little piece of paper will be our passport to a new life."

We have a good dinner that night and Mama make a toast. "My man, with all this education, will be *presidenti* yet!" Papa kiss Mama then and she let us all watch. Rita dance that day. She was fifteen and the next one who would bring home such a paper. But it was not to be.

Papa's paper was only words and no one pull Papa in by the arm and give him a good job. Each day it was harder and harder to see his face at night and each night he have more and more red wine. At last Papa go back to his old job. It was a big truck and Papa was very tired at night after filling it with broken cars and iron and rusty pipes. Soon Mama cry all the time and then Rita stop her school. She come home one day and say she have a fine job that pay much money but she have to work at night. Papa ask who boss is, but Rita say he is Up-Town man and that Papa would not know him.

Rita sleep late now every morning and sometimes she look sad at me when she say goodbye to go for job. Always she look tired and one day she and Mama have big fight. Rita say she move out nearer her job and Mama say, "No," but Rita go anyway. She tell Mama she come every day to see me and bring money every week. The house seem so still now and Mama sit long times with little Rosa on her lap and I hear her say "Little Plum" over and over.

Now for me the day begins when Rita come, for Rita keep her promise. One day she come and after we eat the caramel corn she bring, Rita tell me of a secret she and I will have. It is a plan to make me walk straight without iron brace.

"Pepito," Rita say and put three dollars in my hand, "I want you to hide this and every week I will give you more until there is enough and then we will visit the doctor who fixes legs."

We find empty box that oatmeal come in and cut a hole in the round top big enough to fold money into. It is our secret hiding place and I push the box under the couch where I sleep. Each week Rita add more money, sometimes even more at one time.

Our home is not very happy now. With Rita the smiles have gone. Carlos and Mikos are big now. Carlos is in the high school but want to stop and he and Papa fight now. Carlos say to Papa, "Old man, you live on your daughter's hustling!"

I watch as he pull himself up and like a bear try to squeeze the words back into Carlos's mouth. Papa's big hand slaps out at Carlos but he is quick and runs out and down the steps to the street. For the first time I see Papa cry, and when Mama come in and ask, he will not tell her what hurts him.

I cannot sleep that night. I know what hustling is. It is the walking of the streets that a woman does to offer her body to any man who will pay. I have hear Carlos and Mikos talk when they think I sleep. I hear the names of some girls and then rough words and then small swallowed laughter. I am much older than the pain in my legs. I am as old as the new leaves on my poor tree on the sidewalk.

My pillow is hard that night and I close my eyes against my fear. It is then that Rita's face come before my mind. I see her smooth skin and the quick way her body moves and the softness of her breast. I have watched her grow more beautiful in form as in heart. I have made the curve of her with my crayon on white paper. Do not think I look upon her with more than a brother should. But is it wrong to see beauty when it grows before your eyes? Her name is really Margarita, like the white flower with the golden center.

I cannot bear the evil pictures that pass before my eyes, and I cross myself and insist to my mind that Carlos spoke in anger and said a lie. I prefer it so.

When Rita come that next evening I want to tell her what Carlos say so we could laugh about it together and she could slap his face. But I keep silent. When she ask me why I do not smile I tell her a lie. I say my foot hurt.

"Come," she say, "get our box and let us count the money."

We open the top and count it in her lap. "We need more," Rita say. "I will work overtime."

I nod for I am afraid to ask and afraid not to ask. For the first time I want Rita to leave.

It is weeks before I sleep well and I blame it on my leg but I know it is Rita that worry me. Now I look at her more closely as if I expect to see a sign that all was a lie. Once I start to say something.

"A woman that sells her body." I stutter over the words. "What would one call her?"

Rita look at me quick and pulls her lips tight, then smiles. "Don't tell me that my little Pepito is growing up!"

She put her hand on my head and push my hair off my face.

"You do not answer me," I say.

"A prostitute." She turn away from me and her hand drop.

"That is an evil thing for a woman to do, isn't it?" I say.

"It all depends."

She turns and picks up a big bag. "Look what I brought you to-night."

After we eat the big oranges she lean her head against mine and speaks into the room.

"You must not concern yourself with ugly things. You must see only beauty and put it on paper. I do not know any prostitutes and neither do you."

She leave soon after and before I sleep that night I curse my brother Carlos and his vile tongue.

It goes on as before now with Rita and me. Soon it is her birthday. She is to be eighteen in a week and I decide to buy her a present. Mama has said that eighteen is a special age for a girl and I want to make it fine for her birthday. The only money I have is under my couch in the oatmeal box. I decide within myself that it would not be wrong to use some of it for Rita's birthday present.

Mama is surprised when I tell her I will go down the stairs and on the street until I explain to her what I want to do. I tell her I have saved some money and I show her the $20 I have in my pocket. She helps me down the first steps and watches me as I walk down the street to where the stores are.

The stores are filled with fine things and I move slowly from one window to the other. Before one I stop a long time and almost decide to buy a small radio. But I think maybe a pretty dress would be better for Rita. A white dress to make her hair blacker than the midnight and the white like snow against her golden skin.

Now I look for a dress shop. Across the street is a large store with dresses like a flower garden. At the corner I stand waiting for the street light to change when I hear voices behind me. It is what they say that makes me turn and follow them instead of crossing the street.

I do not know all of them but one boy is Luis. He is older than Rita but was in school with her and sometimes Carlos bring him to the house. It is when I hear him say the name Rita that I decide to follow them.

"Yeah, that damn Rita," one boy say. "Since she move Uptown into the big time, you can't even touch her anymore."

"I hear she's hooked up with some pimp who is really rolling in clover." They all laugh.

My blood! I feel it leave my body and sink to the sidewalk. Surely the earth will open up and these boys will fall into hell! I cannot walk anymore. They turn the corner and disappear. My heart is dead inside of me. No longer can I doubt what I feared. No longer can I doubt.

I feel people shove at me as they pass me and still I cannot move. Long later I take steps, slowly down the sidewalk. All the time in the center of my throat is a sore spot I cannot swallow away. Like a terrible scream that has no sound.

It was when my leg hurt so much that I stop and lean my face against the smooth glass of a store window. Cool it feels on my hot cheeks. My eyes I close tight—so tight it hurt. Colors dance in my head and run to stab my heart. My leg beats out the music of pain.

No longer can I stand the ache so I open my eyes again. There, under my look, I see the guns. Like soldiers ready to march when the general shout out a command. They wait quietly, these black snails that carry death inside a shell.

For a long time I look at these guns. Has not Father Diaz said that death is only another life? And a better one?

I move to the store door. It is glass with a wire across it, like the knitting Mama does, all looped together. I put two hands on the door handle. It is stiff and cold like a gun, I think. Down I push and shove open the door. I stumble on a mat and my iron brace rips at the rubber as I pull my leg free. A small bell shakes and makes a ringing. I walk in.

When the police ask me I shake my head and when Mama and Papa cry in the courtroom for children and the judge ask me why I kill my sister on her birthday I still am quiet. They would not understand how hard a thing it was to do. To lose your star when you are thirteen is to walk blind on the earth. Better this way than to see your star fall from the heavens and end in mud. Always to me Margarita will be like her name, pure white on the outside and golden in the center.

And that is why I lie here on this cot with the black of my little room hiding me from the night of nothingness and I am called a murderer.

CHANCE AFTER CHANCE

by Thomas Walsh

Padre, everybody in Harrington's called him. Year after year he dropped in from his furnished room about seven at night, then drank steadily until three in the morning, closing time; and one Christmas Eve, very drunk, he curled both arms around his shot glass, put his head down, and began chanting some kind of crazy gibberish. Nobody in Harrington's knew what it was—but maybe, Harrington himself thought later on, maybe it was Latin. Because little by little, from remarks he let drop about his earlier life, it became rumored that he had once been a Roman Catholic priest in a small New England town somewhere near Boston.

He was perhaps in his fifties and in youth must have been a lusty and physically powerful man. Now, however, the whiskey had almost finished him. His hands trembled; his face was markedly lined, weary and sunken; his shabby alcoholic's jauntiness had a forced ring to it; and he was almost never without a stubble of dirty gray beard on his cheeks.

One night Jack Delgardo on the next stool inquired idly as to why they had kicked him out of the church. Was it the whiskey, Jack wanted to know, or was it women? Did he mean to say they never even gave him a second chance?

"Well, a chance," Padre admitted, always a bit genially boastful in man-of-the-world conversation. "They found out about a certain

French girl over in Holyoke, Massachusetts, and because of her and the booze they told me I'd have to go down to a penitential monastery in Georgia for two years. But bare feet and long hours of prayerful communion with the Lord God would be the only ticket for me in that place, not to mention the dirtiest sort of physical labor day after day. They had no conception at all, however, about the kind of man they were dealing with. So naturally, when I told the monsignor straight out where to go, since I discovered that I had lost the faith by that time, there was no more point in discussing the matter. A long time past, Jack—twenty-odd years."

But Jack Delgardo was not much interested in the Lord God. Besides which, he had just seen his new girl bob in, very dainty and elegant, through Harrington's front door.

"Yeah," he said, rising briskly. "Can't blame you a bit, Padre, for getting the hell out. See you around, huh?"

"Very probably," Padre said, blessing him with humorously overdone solemnity for the free drink. "Always here, Jack. Could you spare me a dollar or two until the first of the month?"

Because the first of the month was when his four checks arrived. In Harrington's he never mentioned that part of his life, but he came from a large and very prosperous family of Boston Irish—Robert the surgeon, Michael the chemist, Edward the engineer, and Kevin Patrick the businessman; and three married sisters and their families who had all settled down years ago in one or another of the more well-to-do Boston suburbs.

But Padre had eventually found himself unable to endure his family any more than he had been able to endure his monsignor. He never failed to detect a slight but telltale flush of shame and apology when they had to introduce him to some friend who dropped by, and he could all too easily imagine the sly knowledge of him that would be whispered from mouth to mouth later on—the weakling of the family, the black sheep, the spoiled youngest of them, and now the drunken, profligate, defrocked priest.

Although having been the spoiled youngest, Padre occasionally thought, might have been the beginning of all his troubles. Like Robert he might well have been the surgeon, or like Michael the chemist, but as little Joey, always too much loved, always dearest and closest of anyone to the mother, he seemed never once to have had his own life in his hands. As far back as he could remember anything, he could remember Mama and him in a church pew, with sunlight streaming in over them through a stained-glass window, her face lifted up to the high dim altar before them, her lips moving silently, and the rosary beads slipping one by one through her fingers.

Only three or four years old then, Padre had been young enough to believe anything he was told; young enough, in fact, to have believed everything. Only in seminary days had come his first questioning, his first resentment, his first rebellion. So he had written a long letter to his favorite uncle, Uncle Jack, and announced dramatically that he was unable to take the life anymore. So if Uncle Jack could not get Mama to see some sense, he had made up his mind to run away, or even to kill himself.

But in the end he had done neither. He had gone on, and he could also remember, if he ever wanted to, a winter night soon afterward in the kitchen at home, with Uncle Jack and his mother shouting angrily at each other from opposite sides of the table.

"Don't try to make the boy do what he has no inclination at all for," Uncle Jack had cried out at her. "Damn it to hell, Maggie, can't you understand there's nothing half so contemptible in this world as a bad priest? Where in God's name are your brains? It's his life, don't you see? It's not yours. Then let him do what he wants with it, or you'll have to answer for that yourself. It's just the pride you'd feel at having a son in the church—that's why you're bound and determined on it! Why, you're forcing him to—"

Leaning forward shakily, his mother had rested both hands on the table in front of her.

"He'll do what I say!" she had cried back. "He'll have the only true happiness there is in this world. He'll have the collar, I tell you! And you daring to come here tonight and lead him on like this when you never once had the faith that I do, and you never will! What were you all your days but a shame and disgrace to yourself and to the Holy Roman Catholic Church? I know what he wants and what he needs, and better than you. I've prayed to the Blessed Lady every night of my life for it—and she'll answer me! And you'll change that, will you, with your mad carrying on here tonight, and your cursing and swearing at us! Then I take my vow on the thing here and now. From this day on I swear to Almighty God that you and yours will never again enter this house, as I swear to Almighty God that I and mine will never again enter yours! Is that the answer you want? Then there it is. Never again!"

But after that had come the sudden horrible twist of her whole face to one side and her clumsy lurch forward halfway across the table. And after that, Padre could also remember, there had been the family doctor hurriedly summoned, and old Father O'Mara, and up in her bedroom a few minutes after, all the family down on their knees, with Bonnie and Eileen and Agnes all crying, and Father O'Mara leading them on solemnly and gravely in the Litany for the Dying. But Padre had been closest of all to her, as he knew from the day of his birth he had always been, and holding her hand. So . . .

So. He had gone on. He had done what he had promised her in that moment, if without words. He had got the collar at last. But now, on the first of every month, what he got were the $50 checks mailed in, one apiece, from the surgeon and the chemist and the engineer and the businessman. To earn them, tacitly understood, he had only to keep himself well away from the city of Boston for as long as he lived. So Harrington's, as the finale of all; so his regular stool at the end of the bar, nearest the rest rooms; so Padre, now hardly more than a shaky and alcoholic shadow of his former self, at the age of not quite fifty-three years old.

There, year after year, he troubled no one and bothered no one, making no friends and no enemies. So he was rather surprised when he was invited up to Jack Delgardo's apartment on Lexington Avenue one January night to meet two of Jack's friends, with a promise that the whiskey would be free and liberally provided for him. And it was. They all had a lot to drink, one after another—a lot even for Padre; and then in half an hour or so, surprisingly enough, it appeared that the conversation had turned to theology.

"But at least you have to believe in God," Jack argued, refilling the glass for him. "You can't kid me, Padre—because a guy has to believe in something, that's all, no matter what he says. And I can still remember what they taught me in parochial school. Once a priest always a priest, the way I got it."

"Quite true," Padre had to agree, smacking his lips over the fine bourbon. "Although I believe the Biblical terminology is a priest forever, according to the order of the high priest Melchizedek."

"Yeah, I guess," Eddie Roberts grinned—Steady Eddie, as Jack often referred to him. "Only how do you mean high, Padre? The way you get every night in the week down at Harrington's?"

At that they all laughed, including Padre, although the third man, Pete, did not permit the laugh to change his expression in any way. He had said little so far. He appeared to be studying Padre silently and intently, though not openly, dropping his eyes down to the cigarette in his hand every time Padre happened to glance at him.

"No, not quite like me," Padre said, very jovial about it. "In seminary we used to paraphrase a poem about him, or at least I did. 'Melchizedek, he praised the Lord and gave some wine to Abraham; but who can tell what else he did is smarter far than what I am.' "

"Oh, sometimes you seem smart enough," Steady Eddie put in. "Almost smart enough to know the right score, Padre. I wonder, are you?"

"Classical education," Padre assured him. "Only the best, Eddie, Latin, Greek, and Advanced Theology."

"Yeah, but I thought the theology never took," Jack said, exchanging a quick glance with Pete. "That's what you're always claiming around at Harrington's, isn't it?"

"Well, yes," Padre had to agree once more. "At least these days. Years ago it just happened to strike me all of a sudden that the Lord God Almighty, granting that He exists at all, isn't what most of us are inclined to believe about Him. Look at His record for yourself. Who else, one by one, has killed off every life that He ever created?"

"Yeah, but Sister Mary Cecilia," Jack objected, "used to tell us that no human being ever died, actually. They were transported."

"No, no," Padre corrected grandly. "Transformed, Jack. Into a higher and more superior being, into the spirit; or else, conversely, down into eternal and everlasting hell. And very useful teaching too, let me tell you. Nothing like it for keeping in line everyone who still believes."

"Only you don't believe it anymore?" Pete asked softly.

Padre finished his drink, again smacking his lips over it with great relish. He was very cunning in defending himself at these moments. He'd had much practise.

"I believe," he said, indicating the glass to them, "in what a man sees, hears, tastes, touches, and feels. That's what I believe, gentlemen, and all I believe. Is your bourbon running out, Jack?"

"Yeah, sure," Steady Eddie grinned. "But of course lots of guys talk real big with a few drinks in them. Sometimes you never know whether to believe them or not, Padre."

"So you don't believe in nothing," Pete said, while Jack hurriedly refilled Padre's glass. "Nothing at all. How about money, though? You believe in that?"

"Oh, most emphatically. And in God too. Or at least," Padre amended, trying his new drink, "at least God in the bottle. Which of course means God in the wallet too."

"Yeah, but old habits," Pete said, even more softly. "Hard to break, Padre. Let's suppose somebody ast you to hear a guy's confession, say—and for maybe five or ten thousand dollars? Your specialty too. Right up your alley. Only it wouldn't bother you even one bit?"

"Shrive the penitent," Padre beamed, knowing that he was somewhat overdoing it, as always in discussions of this kind, but unable to restrain himself. Why? He did not know. He did not, as a matter of fact, want to know. It simply had to be done, that was all. Someone had to know the kind of a man He was dealing with. "Solace the afflicted and comfort the dying. I've heard many a confession in my day, and for nothing at all. Very juicy listening too, some of them. You wouldn't believe the things that—"

Pete and Jack exchanged quick glances. Steady Eddie inched forward a bit.

"And then tell us," he whispered, "tell us what the guy said to you afterwards?"

Padre, hand up with the refilled glass, felt an altogether absurd catch of the heart. He had broken many vows in his time, but there was one he had not. He looked over at Eddie, as if a bit startled, then up at Jack, then around at Pete. But this was not fair, something whispered in him. This was active and deliberate malevolence. All his life he had been tried and tried, and beyond his strength; tested and tested; but now at last to betray the only thing he had never betrayed . . .

Yet he managed to nod calmly. There had to be considered, after all, the kind of man that he was, and what five or ten thousand dollars would mean to him. Could he admit now that he had lied and lied even to himself all these years, and lied to everyone else too? Never! It was not to be thought of for one instant.

"I see," he murmured. "And tell you afterwards. So that's the condition?"

"That's the condition," Pete said. "You still got a priest's shirt and a Roman collar, Padre?"

"Here or there," Padre said, still smiling brightly at them, which was very necessary now; nothing but the bold face for it. "Only it's been a very long time, of course. As the old song has it, there's been a few changes made. So I don't know that I could quite—"

Jack Delgardo rubbed a savage hand over his mouth. Steady Eddie replaced his grin with a cold ominous stare. But Pete proved much more acute than either of them. He understood at once why the protest had been made by Padre—not out of strength, but from sudden shrinking weakness; the hidden and unadmitted desire, probably, to be persuaded now even against himself.

"Easiest thing in the world," Pete remarked quietly. "Guy you know, too—so no question about you being a priest, Padre. All you'd have to say is that you've gone back to the church and he'd believe it. Remember Big Lefty Carmichael?"

And Padre did, four or five years ago from Harrington's, but not clearly. He was trying to get the name straight in his head when Jack Delgardo leaned forward to him.

"Well, they let him out," Jack whispered, resting his right hand on Padre's arm, then shaking it, as if to give the most perfect assurance of what he said. "He got sick up in Dannemora Prison, Padre, and now he's dying in a cheap little furnished room over on Ninth Avenue. They can't do a damned thing for him anymore now. They can't even operate. He's just sick as hell and ready to holler cop, see? A friend of his told us. He said that Lefty asked him to bring a priest tomorrow night. So where's any problem?"

That time Padre decided only to sip from his glass. He had begun to feel all drunkenly confused.

"Because what happened," Pete drawled, apparently observing that Padre could not quite place the name, "is that Lefty and two other guys got away with a potful of money three years ago—only they piled up into a trailer truck on Second Avenue, and no one but Lefty got out alive.

"Then the cops grabbed him that night, soon as they identified the two dead guys he always worked with. Grabbed him, Padre—but not the bank money. Well, he couldn't have spent it, of course. No time. And he wouldn't have given it to anyone to hold for him, because he wasn't that stupid. He must have stashed it away somewhere real cute, and wherever he put it, it's still there. They only let him out of Dannemora yesterday morning and he ain't left the house on Ninth Avenue since he got there. He couldn't have. We've been watching it. We'd have seen.

"Okay. So now he wants somebody like you, old Lefty does. No more of the old zip in him, Padre. So if we have the friend tell him about you rejoining the church and all, he's gonna believe it. You're the kind of a priest he wouldn't mind telling his confession to, you know what I mean? You're just like him, the way he'll look at it. You're both losers. Then when he confesses about the bank holdup, all you have to do is tell him he's got to make restitution for what he stole. That's what you'd do, anyway, isn't it? Only this time, of course, soon as he tells you where the money is hid—"

Padre picked up his drink from the coffee table and this time he emptied it. His mind still worked slowly, which irritated him. He could not understand why. So he took good care to conceal whatever he felt, and to smile back at Pete even more arrogantly than before. He reached over to the bourbon bottle with his right hand, lifted it, and solemnly blessed the assembly.

"Absolvo te," he announced then, and in a tone that successfully gave just the right touch of derisive priestly unction to what he said. " 'Blessed is he that comes in the name of the Lord.' If it's as simple as that, gentlemen, then I think we're just about agreed on the matter. Let's say somewhere about nine o'clock tomorrow night, then. What's the address?"

*   *   *

Pete was behind the steering wheel, Eddie beside him. Jack Delgardo was crouched forward in the middle of the backseat. It was nine-thirty the next night and they were all watching the entrance to a tenement house directly opposite.

About fifteen minutes later Padre came out of the house. He was now shaved cleanly; he wore the black shirt and the Roman collar; and Steady Eddie at once reached back to open the rear door.

"Hey, Padre," he called guardedly. "Over here. We decided to wait for you."

It was a cold January night, with misty rain in the air, but Padre removed his hat a bit wearily in the vestibule doorway. They could see his gray hair then, and the thinly drawn pale face under it—the alcoholic's face. He glanced about, right and left, but did not move until Pete impatiently tapped on the car horn.

Even then, when Jack Delgardo had made room on the backseat, there was a kind of funny look on his face, Steady Eddie thought— a look, for a couple of long seconds, just like he had never seen them before and did not know who they were.

"So how did it go?" Jack Delgardo whispered. "Come on and tell us, Padre. He make his confession to you?"

But for another moment or so Padre only fingered the black hat on his knees, lightly and carefully.

"Yes," he said then. "Yes, he did. He made his confession."

"Then open up," Steady Eddie urged. "What did he tell you? Where's the money, Padre?"

"What?" Padre said. He appeared to be thinking of other matters; like in some damn fog, Jack thought furiously. He did not answer the question. All he did was to keep smoothing the black hat time after time while looking down at it, as if he had never seen that before either. "But first," he added, "I decided that I'd better talk to him a little—to get him into the right mood for the thing. And I had to think up the words to do that, of course—only pretty soon they seemed to be coming out of me all by themselves. Father, he kept calling me—" and he had to laugh here, with a kind of shakily nervous unsteadiness. "It's almost thirty years since anybody called me that, in that way. With respect, I mean. With a certain kind of dependence on me . . . Father."

Eddie got hold of him by the throat angrily and yanked his head up.

"You listen to me, you old lush! Jack asked you something. Where's that money?"

"What?" Padre repeated. He did not seem to understand the question. He was frowning absently. "I had to tell him I'd be around first thing tomorrow morning with the Host," he said. "I think I may have helped him a little. When I gave him absolution afterwards, he kissed my hand. He actually—"

Pete, who had been staring fixedly ahead through the windshield, his lips compressed, started the car. Nothing more was said. It must have been all decided between them, just as they had decided to wait for Padre while he was still in the house.

They drove onto a dingy street farther west under the shadows of an overhead roadway that was being constructed, and there they drove up and around on a half-finished approach ramp. There was a kind of platform at the top of it, with lumber and big concrete mixers scattered about; before them a waist-high stone parapet; and beyond that the river.

No other cars could be seen, and no other people; no illumination except the intermittent gleam of a blinker light down on the next corner. Red, dark, red, dark. Padre found himself thinking with a curious and altogether aimless detachment of mind. Bitter cold cheer this night against the January rain and against the cluster of faint lights way over on the Jersey side—or not cheer at all, really . . . Father.

"Padre," Pete said, and unlike Eddie in a calm, perfectly controlled manner. "Where's the money?"

Padre might not have heard him at all.

"I had to—comfort him," he said. "But the only thing that came to me was what I had read once in the words of a French Jesuit priest—that a Christian must never be afraid of death, that he must welcome it, that it was the greatest act of faith he would ever make in this life, and that he must plunge joyfully into death as into the arms of his living and loving God. Then I led him on into the Act of Contrition—after I remembered it myself. And somehow I did remember it. Hoist by my own petard, then—" and once more he had to laugh softly. " 'Oh, my God, I am heartily sorry for having offended Thee—' That's how it starts, you know. And once I'd repeated that for him—would any of you have a drink for me?"

Pete got out of the car. So did Eddie. So did Jack Delgardo. One of them opened the door for Padre and took his arm. He got out obediently and then stood there.

"Padre," Pete said. "Where's the money?"

"What?" Padre said. The third time.

There were no more words wasted, just Eddie and Jack Delgardo closing in on him. They were quick about it and very efficient. They got Padre back against the stone parapet, which was some eighty or ninety feet above the river at this point, and there Eddie used his hands, and Jack Delgardo the tip of his right shoe.

There were almost no sounds, just the quick scrape of their feet on the paving, then a gasp, and then Padre falling. After that they allowed him to sit up groggily, muddy brown gutter water all over his black suit, his hat knocked off so that his gray hair could again be seen, and blood on his mouth.

"Now you just come on," Steady Eddie gritted. "We ain't even started on you. You ain't getting away with this, not now. We didn't make you come in with us. You promised you would. So do what we tell you, you phony old lush, or we'll—*Where's that money?*"

By then Padre had straightened against the parapet, supporting himself by his two hands, and breathing with shallow and labored effort.

"But it was never fair," he cried out. "Never fair! I was tempted not in one way during my life but in every possible way—and time after time! And now tonight, up in that room back there, I had to listen to myself saying something—whatever kept coming into my head. And not for him either—but for myself, don't you see? That it didn't matter how often we failed. That we only had to succeed at the end! That it wasn't trial after trial that was given to us. That it was chance after chance! And that if only once, if only once and at the very finish of everything, we could say to Almighty God that we accepted the chance—"

Pete gestured Eddie and Jack Delgardo off and then moved back himself into somewhat better light so that the knife in his hand became clearly visible.

"You know what this is?" he said. "This is a knife. And you know, if you want to go ahead and make me, what I can do with it?"

He proceeded to say. He spoke in a clinically detached manner of various parts of the human body, of their extreme vulnerability to pain, and of what he could do with the knife—if he was forced. Very soon Padre, still hanging onto the parapet, had to turn shuddering away from that voice, and in blind panic. But on one side there was Steady Eddie waiting for him. On the other was Jack Delgardo.

"We'll even give you a square count," Steady Eddie urged, obviously thinking that part important, and at the same time offering a pint bottle of whiskey out of his overcoat pocket. "Honest to God, Padre. Just take a good long drink for yourself—and then think for a minute. Nothing like it, remember? God in a bottle."

And Padre needed that drink. He was beginning to feel the pain now—in his face, in the pit of his stomach, in his right knee. Which would be nothing at all, he realized, to the pain of the knife. Yes, then, he would tell. In the end, knowing himself, he knew he would have to tell.

But was it test after test that had always been demanded of him, venomously and to no purpose? Or was it, as he had found himself saying earlier tonight, chance after chance after chance that was offered—and the chance even now, it might be, to admit finally and for the first time in his life a greater love which, being the kind of man he was, or had insisted he was, he had always denied?

He still could not say. But how queer, it came to him, that the last denial of all, the only promise he had never violated, was now being demanded of him. But as proof of what? Of a thing he believed in his heart even yet, or of a thing he did not believe?

His hands were shaking. He looked at them, at the pint bottle they held, and then at the jagged cluster of rocks almost a hundred feet straight down that he could see at the very edge of the river. He had not drunk from the bottle yet. Now he attempted to and it had rolled out of his hands, as if accidentally, onto the parapet.

He wailed aloud, scrambling up desperately for the bottle, and before Steady Eddie could lose his contemptuous grin, before Jack Delgardo, turning his back to the wind, could light the match for his cigarette, and before Pete, now more distant than either of them, could move, Padre was standing erect on top of the parapet.

Pete shouted a warning. Steady Eddie rushed forward. But plunge joyfully, Padre was thinking—the chance taken, the trust maintained, the greater love at last and beyond any question admitted by him. Plunge joyfully!

That was the final thought in his head. After it, avoiding a frantic outward grab for his legs by Steady Eddie, Father Joseph Leo Shanahan moved quickly but calmly to the edge of the parapet, crossed himself there, put up the other hand in a last moment of weakness to cover his eyes—and stepped straight out.

Then the blinker light shone down on a stone ledge empty save for the still corked whiskey bottle, and there were left only the three men, but not the fourth, to gape stupidly and unbelievingly from back in the shadows.

THE CLOUD
BENEATH
THE EAVES

by Barbara Owens

May 10: I begin. At last. Freshborn, dating only from the first of May. New. A satisfying little word, that "new." A proper word to start a journal. It bears repeating: I am new. What passed before never was. That unspeakable accident and the little problem with my nerves are faded leaves, forgotten. I will record them here only once and then discard them. Now—it's done.

I have never kept a journal before and am not sure why I feel compelled to do so now. Perhaps it's because I need the proof of new life in something I can touch and see. I have come far and I am filled with hope.

May 11: This morning I gazed long at myself in the bathroom mirror. My appearance is different, new. I can never credit myself with beauty, but my face is alive and has lost that indoor pallor. I was not afraid to look at myself. That's a good sign.

I've just tidied up my breakfast things and am sitting at my little kitchen table with a steaming cup of coffee. The morning sun streams through my kitchen curtains, creating lacy, flowing patterns on the cloth. Outside it's still quiet. I'm up too early, of course—difficult to break years of rigid farm habits. I miss the sound of birds, but there are several large trees in the yard, so perhaps there are some. Even a city must have some birds.

I must describe my apartment. Another "new"—my own apartment. I was lucky to find it. I didn't know how to find a place, but a waitress in the YWCA coffee shop told me about it, and when I saw it, I knew I had to have it.

It's in a neighborhood of spacious old homes and small unobtrusive apartment houses; quiet, dignified, and comfortably frayed around the edges. This house is quite old and weathered, with funny cupolas and old-fashioned bay windows. The front and side yards are small, but the back is large, pleasantly treed and flowered, and boasts a quaint goldfish pond.

My landlady is a widow who has lived here for over forty years, and she's converted every available space into an apartment. She lives on the first floor with several cats, and another elderly lady lives in the second apartment on that floor. Two young men of foreign extraction live in one apartment on the second floor, and I have yet to see the occupant of the other. I understand there's also a young male student living in part of the basement.

That leaves only the attic—the best for the last. It's perfect; I even have my own outside steps for private entry and exit. Because of the odd construction of the house, my walls and ceilings play tricks on me. My living room and kitchen are one large area and the ceiling, being under the steepest slope of the roof, is high. In the bedroom and bath the roof takes a suicidal plunge; as a result, the bedroom windows on one wall are scant inches off the floor and I must stoop to see out under the eaves, for the ceiling at that point is only four feet high. In the bath it is the same; one must enter and leave the tub in a bent position. Perhaps that's why I like it so much; it's funny and cozy, with a personality all its own.

The furnishings are old but comfortable. Everything in my living room area is overstuffed, and although the pieces don't match, they get along well together. The entire apartment is clean and freshly painted a soft green throughout. It's going to be a delight to live here.

I spent most of yesterday getting settled. Now I must close this and be off to the neighborhood market to stock my kitchen. I've even been giving some thought to a small television set. I've never had the pleasure of a television set. Maybe I'll use part of my first paycheck for that. Everything is going to be all right.

May 12: Today I had a visitor! The unseen occupant from the apartment below climbed my steps and knocked on my kitchen (and only) door just as I was finishing breakfast. I'm afraid I was awkward and ill at ease at first, but I invited her in and the visit ended pleasantly.

Her name is Sarah Cooley. She's a widow, small and stout, with gray hair and kind blue eyes. She'd noticed I don't have a car and offered the use of hers if I ever need it. She also invited me to attend church with her this morning. I handled it well, I think, thanking her politely for both offers, but declining. Of course I can never enter a car again, and she could not begin to understand my feelings toward the church. However, it was a grand experience, entertaining in my own home. I left her coffee cup sitting on the table all day just to remind myself she'd been there and that all had gone well. It's a good omen.

I must say a few words about starting my new job tomorrow. I try to be confident; everything else has worked out well. I'm the first to admit my getting a job at all is a bit of a miracle. I was not well prepared for that when I came here, but one trip to an employment agency convinced me that was pointless.

Something must have guided me to that particular street and that particular store with its little yellow sign in the window. Mr. Mazek was so kind. He was surprised that anyone could reach the age of thirty-two without ever having been employed, but I told him just enough of my life on the farm to satisfy him. He even explained how to get a Social Security card, the necessity of which I was not aware. He was so nice I regretted telling him I had a high-school diploma, but I'm sure he would never have considered someone with a mere eighth-grade education. Now my many years of surrepetitious reading come to my rescue. I actually have a normal job.

May 13: It went well. In fact, I'm so elated I'm unable to sleep.

I managed the bus complications and arrived exactly on time. Mr. Mazek seemed pleased to see me and started right off addressing me as Alice instead of Miss Whitehead. The day was over before I realized it.

The store is small and dark, a little neighborhood drugstore with two cramped aisles and comfortable clutter. Mr. Mazek is old-fashioned and won't have lunch counters or magazine displays to encourage loitering; he wants his customers to come in, conduct their business, and leave. He's been on that same corner for many years, so almost everyone who enters has a familiar face. I'm going to like being a part of that.

Most of the day I just watched Mr. Mazek and Gloria, the other clerk, but I'm convinced I can handle it. Toward the end of the day he let me ring up several sales on the cash register, and I didn't make one mistake. I'm sure I'll never know the names and positions of each item in the store, but Mr. Mazek says I'll have them memorized in no time and Gloria says if she can do it, I can.

I will do it! I feel safer as each day passes.

May 16: Three days have elapsed and I've neglected my journal. Time goes so quickly! How do I describe my feelings? I wake each morning in my own quiet apartment; I go to a pleasant job where I am needed and appreciated; and I come home to a peaceful evening of doing exactly as I wish. There are no restrictions and no watchful eyes. It's as I always dreamed it would be.

I'm learning the work quickly and am surprised it comes so easily. Gloria complains of boredom, but I find the days too short to savor.

Let me describe Gloria: She's a divorced woman near my own age, languid, slow-moving, with dyed red hair and thick black eyebrows. She's not fat, but gives the appearance of being so because she looks soft and pliable, like an old rubber doll. She has enormous long red fingernails that she fusses with constantly. She wears an abundance of pale makeup, giving her a somewhat startling appearance, but she's been quite nice to me and has worked for Mr. Mazek for several years, so she must be reliable.

I feel cowlike beside her with my great raw bones and awkward hands and feet. We're certainly not alike, but I'm hoping she becomes my first real friend. Yesterday we took our coffee break together, and during our conversation she stopped fiddling with her nails and said, "Gee, Alice, you know you talk just like a book?" At first I was taken aback, but she was smiling so I smiled too. I must listen more to other people and learn. Casual conversation does not come easily to me.

Mr. Mazek continues to be kind and patient, assuring me I am learning well. In many ways he reminds me of Daddy.

I've already made an impression of sorts. Today something was wrong with the pharmaceutical scales, so I asked to look at them and had them right again in no time. Mr. Mazek was amazed. I hadn't realized it was a unique achievement. Being Daddy's right hand on the farm for so many years, there's nothing about machinery I don't know. But I promised I wouldn't think about Daddy.

May 17: Today I received my first paycheck. Not a very exciting piece of paper, but it means everything to me. I hadn't done my figures before, but it's apparent now I won't be rich. And there'll be no television set for me. I can manage rent, food, and few extras. Fortunately I wear uniforms to work, so I won't need clothes soon.

Immediately after work I went to the bank and opened an account with my check and what remains of the other. I did that too without a mistake. And now it's safe. It looks as though I've really won; they would have come for me by now if she had found me. I'm too far away and too well hidden. Bless her for mistrusting banks; better I should have taken it than some itinerant thief. She's probably praying for my soul. Now, no more looking back.

May 18: I don't work on weekends; Mr. Mazek employs a part-time student. I would rather work since it disturbs me to have much leisure. It's then I think too much.

This morning I allowed myself the luxury of a few extra minutes in bed, and as I watched the sun rise I noticed an odd phenomenon beneath the eaves outside my window. Because of their extension and perhaps some quirk of temperature, the eaves must trap moisture. A definite mist was swirling softly against the top of the window all the while the sun shone brightly through the bottom. It was so interesting I went to the kitchen window to see if it was there, but it wasn't. It continued for several minutes before melting away, and nestled up here in my attic I felt almost as though I were inside a cloud.

This morning I cleaned and shopped. As I was carrying groceries up the steps, Sarah Cooley called me to come sit with her in the backyard. She introduced me to the other widow from the first floor, Mrs. Harmon. Once again Sarah offered her car for marketing, but I said I like the exercise.

It was unusually soft and warm for May, and quite pleasant sitting idly in the sun. A light breeze was sending tiny ripples across the fishpond, and although the fish are not yet back in it I became aware that some trick of light made it appear as though something were down there, a shadowy shape just below the surface. Neither of the ladies seemed to notice it, but I could not make myself look away. It became so obvious to me something was down there under the water that I became ill, having no choice but to excuse myself from pleasant company.

All day I was restless and apprehensive and finally went to bed early, but in the dark it came, my mind playing forbidden scenes. Over and over I heard the creaking pulleys and saw the placid surface of Jordan's pond splintered by the rising roof of Daddy's rusty old car. I heard tortured screams and saw her wild crazy eyes. I must not sit by the fishpond again.

May 19: I was strong again this morning. I lay and watched the little cloud. There is something strangely soothing about its silent drifting; I was almost sorry to see it go.

I ate well and tried to read the paper, but I kept being drawn to the kitchen window and its clear view of the fishpond. At last I gave up and went out for some fresh air. Sarah and Mrs. Harmon were preparing for a drive in the country as I went down my steps and Sarah invited me, but I declined.

Mr. Mazek was surprised to see me in the store on Sunday. They were quite busy and I offered to stay, but he said I should go and enjoy myself while I'm young. Gloria waggled her fingernails at me. I lingered awhile, but finally just bought some shampoo and left.

A bus was sitting at the corner, and not even noticing where it was going, I got on. Eventually it deposited me downtown and I spent the day wandering and watching people. I find the city has a vigorous pulse. Everyone seems to know exactly where he's going.

I must have left the shampoo somewhere. It doesn't matter. I already have plenty.

May 20: Today I arrived at the store early. Last week I noticed that the insides of the glass display cases were dirty, so I cleaned them. Mr. Mazek was delighted; he said Gloria never sees when things need cleaning.

Gloria suggested I should have my hair cut and styled, instead of letting it just hang straight; she told me where she has hers done. I'm sure she was trying to be friendly and I thanked her, but I have to laugh when I think of me wearing something like her dyed red frizz.

Mr. Mazek talked to me today about joining some sort of group to meet new people. He suggested a church group as a promising place to start. A church group, of all things! Perhaps he thought I came into the store yesterday because I was lonely and had nothing better to do.

Tonight my landlady, Mrs. Wright, inquired if I had made proper arrangements for mail delivery. Since I've received none, she thought there might have been an error. Again I regretted having to lie. Only the white coats and she would be interested in my whereabouts, and I have worked too hard to evade them.

I am restless and somewhat tense this evening.

May 24: My second week and second paycheck in the bank, and it still goes well.

I've realized with some regret that Gloria and I are not going to be friends. I try, but I'm not fond of her. For one thing, she's lazy; I find myself finishing half of her duties. She makes numerous errors in transactions, and although I've pointed them out to her, she doesn't do any better. I'm undecided whether to bring this to Mr. Mazek's attention. Surely he must be aware of it.

On several occasions this week I've experienced a slight blurring of vision, as though a mist were before my eyes. I'm concerned about the cost involved, but prices and labels have to be read accurately, so it seems essential that I have my eyes tested.

May 26: What an odd thing! The little cloud has moved from under the eaves in my bedroom to the kitchen window. Yesterday when I awoke it wasn't there, and as I was having breakfast, suddenly there it was outside the window, soft and friendly, rolling gently against the pane. Perhaps it's my imagination, but it seems larger. It was there again today, a most welcome sight.

Yesterday was an enjoyable day—the usual cleaning and shopping.

Today was not so enjoyable. Just as I was finishing lunch, I heard voices under my steps where Sarah parks her car. The ladies were getting ready for another Sunday drive and when I looked out, they were concerned over an ominous sound in the engine. Before I stopped to think, I heard myself offering to look at it. All the way down the steps I told myself it would be all right, but as soon as I raised the hood, the blackness and nausea came. I couldn't see and somewhere far away I heard a voice calling, "Allie! Allie, where are you?"

Somehow I managed to find the trouble and get back upstairs. Everything was shadows, threatening. I couldn't catch my breath and my hands wouldn't stop shaking. Suddenly I was at the kitchen window, straining to see down into the fishpond. I'm afraid I don't know what happened next.

But the worst is over. I'm all right now. I have drawn the shade over the kitchen window so I will never see the fishpond again. It's going to be all right.

I wish it were tomorrow and time to be with Mr. Mazek again.

May 30: Gloria takes advantage of him. I have watched her carefully this week and she is useless in that store. Mr. Mazek is so warm and gentle he tends to overlook her inadequacy, but it is wrong of her. I see now she's also a shameless flirt, teasing almost every man who comes in. Today she and a pharmaceutical salesman were in the back stockroom for over an hour, laughing and smoking. I could see that Mr. Mazek didn't like it, but he did nothing to stop it. I've been there long enough to see that he and I could manage that store quite nicely. We really don't need Gloria.

I have an appointment for my eyes. The mist occurs frequently now.

June 2: The cloud *is* getting bigger. Yesterday morning the sun shone brightly in my bedroom, but the kitchen was dim and there was a shadow on the shade. When I raised it a fraction, there were silky fringes resting on the sill. I stepped out on the landing and saw it pressed securely over the pane. It is warm, not damp to the touch— warm, soft, and soothing. I have raised the kitchen shade again—the cloud blots out the fishpond completely.

Yesterday I started down the steps to do my marketing, my eyes lowered to avoid sight of the fishpond, and through the steps I saw the top of Sarah's car. Something stirred across it like currents of water, and suddenly I was so weak and dizzy I had to grip the railing to keep from falling as I crept back up the stairs.

I have stayed in all day.

June 7: I have been in since Wednesday with the flu. I began feeling badly Tuesday, but I worked until Wednesday noon when Mr. Mazek insisted I go home. I'm sorry to leave him with no one but Gloria, but I am certainly not well enough to work.

I came home to bed, but the sun shining through my window made disturbing movements in the room. Everything is so green, and the pulsing shadows across the ceiling made it seem that I was underwater. Suddenly I was trapped, suffocating, my lungs bursting for air.

I've moved my bedding and fashioned a bed for myself on the living room couch. Here I can see and draw comfort from the cloud. I will sleep now.

June 10: I have been very ill. Sarah has come to my door twice, but I was too tired and weak to call out, so she went away. I am feverish; sometimes I am not sure if I'm awake or asleep and dreaming. I just realized today is special—the first month's anniversary of my new life. Somehow it seems longer.

June 11: I've just awakened and am watching the cloud. Little wisps are peeping playfully under my door. I think it wants to come inside.

June 12: I am better today. Mrs. Wright used her passkey to come in and was horrified to find I'd been so sick and no one knew. She and Sarah wanted to take me to a doctor, but I cannot get inside that car, so I convinced them I'm recovering. She brought hot soup and I managed to get some down.

The cloud pressed close behind her when she came in, but didn't enter. Perhaps it's waiting for an invitation. Poor Mrs. Wright was so concerned with me she didn't notice the cloud.

June 13: Today I felt well enough to go downstairs to Mrs. Wright's and call Mr. Mazek. I couldn't go until after noon—Sarah's car was down there. I became quite anxious, sure that he needed me in the store. He sounded glad to hear my voice and pleased that I am better, but insisted I not come in until Monday when I am stronger.

I am so ashamed. Suddenly wanting to be with him today, I heard myself pleading. Before I could stop, I told him my entire plan for letting Gloria go and having the store just to ourselves. He was silent so long that I came to my senses and realized my mistake, so I laughed and said something about the fever talking. After a moment he laughed too, and I said I would see him on Monday.

I have let the cloud come in. It sifts about me gently and seems to fill the room.

June 21: Didn't go to the bank today. Crowds and lines begin to annoy me. I will manage with the money and food I have on hand.

Mr. Mazek, bless him, is concerned about my health. I see him watching me with a grave expression, so I work harder to show him I am strong and fine.

I've started taking the cloud to work with me. It stays discreetly out of the way, piling gently in the dim corners, but it comforts me to know it's there, and I find myself smiling at it when no one's looking.

Yesterday afternoon I went to the back stockroom for something, and I'd forgotten Gloria and another one of her salesmen were in there. I stopped when I heard their voices, but not before I heard Gloria say my name and something about "stupid hick"; then they laughed together. Tears came to my eyes, but suddenly a mist was all around me and the cloud was there, smoothing, enfolding, shutting everything away.

A note from Mrs. Wright on my door tonight said that the eye doctor had called to remind me of my appointment. No need to keep it now.

June 23: Sarah's car was here all day yesterday, so I did not go out.

I don't even go into the bedroom now. I am still sleeping on the couch. Because it's old and lumpy, perhaps that's what's causing the dreams. Today I awoke suddenly, my heart pounding and my face wet with tears. I thought I was back there again and all the white coats stood leaning over me. "You can go home," they chorused in a nasty singsong. "You can go home at last to live with your mother." I lay there shaking, remembering. They really believed I would stay with *her!*

Marketed, but did not clean. I am so tired

June 27: You see? I function normally. I reason, so I am all right. It's that lumpy old couch. Last night the dream was about Daddy choking out his life at the bottom of Jordan's pond. I was out of control when I awoke, but the cloud came and took it all away. Today I fixed my blankets on the floor.

June 28: Dear Mr. Mazek continues to be solicitous of my health. Today he suggested I take a week off—get some rest or take a little vacation. He looked so troubled, but of course I couldn't leave him like that.

Sometimes I feel afraid, feel that everything is slipping away. I am trying so hard.

Maybe I should be more tolerant of Gloria.

July 5: After several hours inside my blessed cloud, I believe I am calm enough to think things through. I have been hurt and betrayed. I cannot conceive such betrayal!

Today I discovered that Gloria is—how shall I say it?—"carrying on" with Mr. Mazek and has evidently been doing so for years. Apparently they were supposed to spend the holiday yesterday together, but Gloria went off with someone else. I heard them through the closed door of Mr. Mazek's little office—their voices were very loud—and Gloria was laughing at him! The cloud came to me instantly and I don't remember the rest of the day.

Now I begin to understand. It explains so many things. At first I was terribly angry with Mr. Mazek. Now I realize Gloria tempted him and he was too weak to resist. The evil of that woman. Something must be done. This cannot be allowed to continue.

July 8: I found my opportunity today when we were working together in the stockroom. I began by telling her my finding out was an accident, but that now she must stop it at once. She just played with her fingernails, smiled, and said nothing until I reminded her he was a respected married man with grandchildren and she was ruining all their lives. Then she laughed out loud, said Mr. Mazek was a big boy, and why didn't I mind my own business.

July 11: I'm afraid it's hopeless. For three days I've pursued and pleaded with her to stop her heartless action. This afternoon she suddenly turned on me, screaming harsh cruel things I can't bring myself to repeat. I couldn't listen, so I took refuge in the cloud. Later I saw her speaking forcefully to Mr. Mazek; it looked almost as though she were threatening him. What shall I do now?

I am not sleeping well at all

July 12: I have been let out of my job. There is no less painful way to say it. This afternoon Mr. Mazek called me into his office and let me go as of today, but he will pay me for an extra week. I could say nothing, I was so stunned. He said something about his part-time student needing more money in the summer, but of course I know that's not the reason. He said he was sorry, and he looked so unhappy that I felt sorry for him. I know it isn't his fault. I know he would rather have me with him than Gloria. Even the cloud has not been able to save me today

July 16: I have not left here for four days. I know, because I have marked them on the wall the way I did when I was there. Tomorrow I will draw a crossbar over the four little straight sticks.

I think I have eaten. There are empty cans on the floor and bits of food in my blankets.

The cloud sustains me—whispering, shutting out the pain.

July 19: It is all arranged. Gloria was alone when I went in this morning for my last paycheck. She seemed nervous and a bit ashamed. We were both polite and she went back to Mr. Mazek's office for my pay.

I felt a great sadness. I love that little store. And I have memorized it so well in the time I was allowed to be a part of it. It is fortunate that I know precisely where everything is kept.

At first she refused my invitation to have lunch with me today. She said she begins her vacation tomorrow. But I was persistent, pleading how vital it is to me that we part with no hard feelings between us. Finally she agreed, and I am calm inside the cloud, and strong and confident again.

She came here to my apartment and it went well. Lunch was pleasant and Mr. Mazek's name was never mentioned. I even told her all about myself, and she seemed no more upset than could be expected . . .

Tonight I put a note on Mrs. Wright's door saying I'd been called away for a few weeks. I've moved my heavy furniture in front of the door. I must be very still and remember not to turn on lights. There is enough light from the street to write by and the cloud is here to protect and keep me. I have come a long way. This time it is right.

July: All goes back, goes back. The white coats were wrong. I can't do it.

I saw Daddy again. We stood under the lantern in the big old barn. He showed me all the parts of his old car and how each one of them worked. It felt so safe and good to be with him, and he told me again that I was his good right hand. I wanted

Bad. Oh bad. Everyone said you were crazy. Mean. Your Bible and your praying and church, over and over, your church every night, shouting and praying, never doing anything to help Daddy and me on the farm. Sitting at the kitchen table with your Bible, singing and praying, everything dirty and undone, then into the old car and off to church to shout and pray some more while Daddy and I did all the work.

Never soothed him, never loved him, just prayed at him and counted his sins. Couldn't go to school, made me stay home and work on the farm, no books, books are the devil's tools, had to hide my books in the barn high up under the eaves. Ugly, you're a big ugly child, girl, and you prayed for my soul, prayed for mine and Daddy's souls. Poor sad Daddy's soul.

Took it too hard they said, oh yes, took it too hard, so they sent me away for the white coats to fix and then they made me go back to you, your Bible, and your praying, and everyone said it was an accident, a tragic accident they said, but you knew, you never said but you knew, and you prayed and sang and quoted the Bible and you broke my daddy's life. In the clouds, girl's always got her head in the clouds, I loved my daddy and you prayed for souls and went to church every night and every night It is hot in here. It must be summer outside. All the windows are closed up tight and it is very hot here under the eaves. In the clouds

Today: I do not know what day it is. How many days I have been here. Markings on my walls, words and drawings I do not understand. I lie here on the floor and watch my cloud. It sighs and swirls and keeps me safe. I can't see outside it anymore. It is warm and soft and I will stay inside forever. No one can find me now.

Gloria is beginning to smell. Puffy Gloria and her long red claws. Silly foolish Gloria who didn't even complain when the coffee tasted strange. I have set my Daddy free.

I am in the barn. Night. I am supposed to be milking the cow. I am peaceful, serene. I have done it well and now life will be rich and good. The old car coughs and soon I hear it rattling toward the steep hill over Jordan's pond. It starts down. I listen. Content. The sound fades, a voice, the wrong voice, calling my name: "Allie! Allie, where are you?" The light goes out of the world.

Odaddydaddydaddy, where were you going in the car that night? Wasn't supposed to be you supposed to be her her her

THIS IS DEATH

by Donald E. Westlake

It's hard not to believe in ghosts when you are one. I hanged myself in a fit of truculence—stronger than pique, but not so dignified as despair—and regretted it before the thing was well begun. The instant I kicked the chair away I wanted it back, but gravity was turning my former wish to its present command; the chair would not right itself from where it lay on the floor, and my 193 pounds would not cease to urge downward from the rope thick around my neck.

There was pain, of course, quite horrible pain centered in my throat, but the most astounding thing was the way my cheeks seemed to swell. I could barely see over their round red hills, my eyes staring in agony at the door, *willing* someone to come in and rescue me, though I knew there was no one in the house, and in any event the door was carefully locked. My kicking legs caused me to twist and turn, so that sometimes I faced the door and sometimes the window, and my shivering hands struggled with the rope so deep in my flesh I could barely find it and most certainly not pull it loose.

I was frantic and terrified, yet at the same time my brain possessed a cold corner of aloof observation. I seemed now to be everywhere in the room at once, within my writhing body but also without, seeing my frenzied spasms, the thick rope, the heavy beam, the mismatched pair of lit bedside lamps throwing my convulsive double shadow on the walls, the closed locked door, the white-curtained window with

191

its shade drawn all the way down. *This is death,* I thought, and I no longer wanted it, now that the choice was gone forever.

My name is—was—Edward Thornburn, and my dates are 1938–1977. I killed myself just a month before my fortieth birthday, though I don't believe the well-known pangs of that milestone had much if anything to do with my action. I blame it all (as I blamed most of the errors and failures of my life) on my sterility. Had I been able to father children my marriage would have remained strong, Emily would not have been unfaithful to me, and I would not have taken my own life in a final fit of truculence.

The setting was the guestroom in our house in Barnstaple, Connecticut, and the time was just after seven P.M.; deep twilight, at this time of year. I had come home from the office—I was a realtor, a fairly lucrative occupation in Connecticut, though my income had been falling off recently—shortly before six, to find the note on the kitchen table: "Antiquing with Greg. Afraid you'll have to make your own dinner. Sorry. Love, Emily."

Greg was the one; Emily's lover. He owned an antique shop out on the main road toward New York, and Emily filled a part of her days as his ill-paid assistant. I knew what they did together in the back of the shop on those long midweek afternoons when there were no tourists, no antique collectors to disturb them. I knew, and I'd known for more than three years, but I had never decided how to deal with my knowledge. The fact was, I blamed myself, and therefore I had no way to *behave* if the ugly subject were ever to come into the open.

So I remained silent, but not content. I was discontent, unhappy, angry, resentful—truculent.

I'd tried to kill myself before. At first with the car, by steering it into an oncoming truck (I swerved at the last second, amid howling horns) and by driving it off a cliff into the Connecticut River (I slammed on the brakes at the very brink, and sat covered in perspiration for half an hour before backing away) and finally by stopping athwart one of the few level crossings left in this neighborhood. But no train came for twenty minutes, and my truculence wore off, and I drove home.

Later I tried to slit my wrists, but found it impossible to push sharp metal into my own skin. Impossible. The vision of my naked wrist and that shining steel so close together washed my truculence completely out of my mind. Until the next time.

With the rope; and then I succeeded. Oh, totally, oh, fully I succeeded. My legs kicked at air, my fingernails clawed at my throat, my bulging eyes stared out over my swollen purple cheeks, my tongue thickened and grew bulbous in my mouth, my body jigged and jangled like a toy at the end of a string, and the pain was excruciating, horrible, not to be endured. I can't endure it, I thought, it can't be endured. Much worse than knife slashings was the knotted strangled pain in my throat, and my head ballooned with pain, pressure outward, my face turning black, my eyes no longer human, the pressure in my head building and building as though I would explode. Endless horrible pain, not to be endured, but going on and on.

My legs kicked more feebly. My arms sagged, my hands dropped to my sides, my fingers twitched uselessly against my sopping trouser legs, my head hung at an angle from the rope, I turned more slowly in the air, like a broken windchime on a breezeless day. The pains lessened, in my throat and head, but never entirely stopped.

And now I saw that my distended eyes had become lusterless, gray. The moisture had dried on the eyeballs, they were as dead as stones. And yet I could see them, my own eyes, and when I widened my vision I could see my entire body, turning, hanging, no longer twitching, and with horror I realized I was dead.

But *present.* Dead, but still present, with the scraping ache still in my throat and the bulging pressure still in my head. Present, but no longer in that used-up clay, that hanging meat; I was suffused through the room, like indirect lighting, everywhere present but without a source. What happens now? I wondered, dulled by fear and strangeness and the continuing pains, and I waited, like a hovering mist, for whatever would happen next.

But nothing happened. I waited; the body became utterly still; the double shadow on the wall showed no vibration; the bedside lamps continued to burn; the door remained shut and the window shade drawn; and nothing happened.

What *now?* I craved to scream the question aloud, but I could not. My throat ached, but I had no throat. My mouth burned, but I had no mouth. Every final strain and struggle of my body remained imprinted in my mind, but I had no body and no brain and no *self,* no substance. No power to speak, no power to move myself, no power to *re*move myself from this room and this suspended corpse. I could only wait here, and wonder, and go on waiting.

There was a digital clock on the dresser opposite the bed, and when it first occurred to me to look at it the numbers were 7:21— perhaps twenty minutes after I'd kicked the chair away, perhaps fifteen minutes since I'd died. Shouldn't something happen, shouldn't some *change* take place?

The clock read 9:11 when I heard Emily's Volkswagen drive around to the back of the house. I had left no note, having nothing I wanted to say to anyone and in any event believing my own dead body would be eloquent enough, but I hadn't thought I would be *present* when Emily found me. I was justified in my action, however much I now regretted having taken it, I was justified, I knew I was justified, but I didn't want to see her face when she came through that door. She had wronged me, she was the cause of it, she would have to know that as well as I, but I didn't want to see her face.

The pains increased, in what had been my throat, in what had been my head. I heard the back door slam, far away downstairs, and I stirred like air currents in the room, but I didn't leave. I couldn't leave.

"Ed? Ed? It's me, hon!"

I know it's you. I must go away now, I can't stay here, I must go away. Is there a God? Is this my soul, this hovering presence? *Hell* would be better than this, take me away to Hell or wherever I'm to go, don't leave me here!

She came up the stairs, calling again, walking past the closed guestroom door. I heard her go into our bedroom, heard her call my name, heard the beginnings of apprehension in her voice. She went by again, out there in the hall, went downstairs, became quiet.

What was she doing? Searching for a note perhaps, some message from me. Looking out the window, seeing again my Chevrolet, knowing I must be home. Moving through the rooms of this old house, the original structure a barn nearly 200 years old, converted by some previous owner just after the Second World War, bought by me twelve years ago, furnished by Emily—and Greg—from their interminable, damnable, awful antiques. Shaker furniture, Colonial furniture, hooked rugs and quilts, the old yellow pine tables, the faint sense always of being in some slightly shabby minor museum, this house that I had bought but never loved. I'd bought it for Emily, I did everything for Emily, because I knew I could never do the one thing for Emily that mattered. I could never give her a child.

She was good about it, of course. Emily *is* good, I never blamed her, never completely blamed *her* instead of myself. In the early days of our marriage she made a few wistful references, but I suppose she saw the effect they had on me, and for a long time she has said nothing. But I have known.

The beam from which I had hanged myself was a part of the original building, a thick hand-hewed length of aged timber eleven inches square, chevroned with the marks of the hatchet that had shaped it. A strong beam, it would support my weight forever. It would support my weight until I was found and cut down. Until I was found.

The clock read 9:23 and Emily had been in the house twelve minutes when she came upstairs again, her steps quick and light on the old wood, approaching, pausing, stopping. "Ed?"

The doorknob turned.

The door was locked, of course, with the key on the inside. She'd have to break it down, have to call someone else to break it down, perhaps she wouldn't be the one to find me after all. Hope rose in me, and the pains receded.

"Ed? Are you in there?" She knocked at the door, rattled the knob, called my name several times more, then abruptly turned and ran away downstairs again, and after a moment I heard her voice, murmuring and unclear. She had called someone, on the phone.

Greg, I thought, and the throat-rasp filled me, and I wanted this to be the end. I wanted to be taken away, dead body and living soul, taken away. I wanted everything to be finished.

She stayed downstairs, waiting for him, and I stayed upstairs, waiting for them both. Perhaps she already knew what she'd find up here, and that's why she waited below.

I didn't mind about Greg, about being present when he came in. I didn't mind about *him.* It was Emily I minded.

The clock read 9:44 when I heard tires on the gravel at the side of the house. He entered, I heard them talking down there, the deeper male voice slow and reassuring, the lighter female voice quick and frightened, and then they came up together, neither speaking. The doorknob turned, jiggled, rattled, and Greg's voice called, "Ed?"

After a little silence Emily said, "He wouldn't— He wouldn't *do* anything, would he?"

"Do anything?" Greg sounded almost annoyed at the question. "What do you mean, do anything?"

"He's been so depressed, he's— Ed!" And forcibly the door was rattled, the door was shaken in its frame.

"Emily, don't. Take it easy."

"I shouldn't have called you," she said. "Ed, *please!*"

"Why not? For heaven's sake, Emily—"

"Ed, *please* come out, don't scare me like this!"

"Why *shouldn't* you call me, Emily?"

"Ed isn't stupid, Greg. He's—"

There was then a brief silence, pregnant with the hint of murmuring. They thought me still alive in here, they didn't want me to hear Emily say, "He *knows,* Greg, he knows about us."

The murmurings sifted and shifted, and then Greg spoke loudly, "That's ridiculous. Ed? Come out, Ed, let's talk this over." And the doorknob rattled and clattered, and he sounded annoyed when he said, "We must get in, that's all. Is there another key?"

"I think all the locks up here are the same. Just a minute."

They were. A simple skeleton key would open any interior door in the house. I waited, listening, knowing Emily had gone off to find another key, knowing they would soon come in together, and I felt such terror and revulsion for Emily's entrance that I could feel myself shimmer in the room, like a reflection in a warped mirror. Oh, can I at least stop seeing? In life I had eyes, but also eyelids, I could shut out the intolerable, but now I was only a presence, a total presence, I *could not* stop my awareness.

The rasp of key in lock was like rough metal edges in my throat; my memory of a throat. The pain flared in me, and through it I heard Emily asking what was wrong, and Greg answering, "The key's in it, on the other side."

"Oh, dear God! Oh, Greg, what has he done?"

"We'll have to take the door off its hinges," he told her. "Call Tony. Tell him to bring the toolbox."

"Can't you push the key through?"

Of course he could, but he said, quite determinedly, "Go *on*, Emily," and I realized then he had no intention of taking the door down. He simply wanted her away when the door was first opened. Oh, very good, *very* good!

"All right," she said doubtfully, and I heard her go away to phone Tony. A beetle-browed young man with great masses of black hair and an olive complexion, Tony lived in Greg's house and was a kind of handyman. He did work around the house and was also (according to Emily) very good at restoration of antique furniture; stripping paint, reassembling broken parts, that sort of thing.

There was now a renewed scraping and rasping at the lock, as Greg struggled to get the door open before Emily's return. I found myself feeling unexpected warmth and liking toward Greg. He wasn't a bad person; an opportunist with my wife, but not in general a bad person. Would he marry her now? They could live in this house, he'd had more to do with its furnishing than I. Or would this room hold too grim a memory, would Emily have to sell the house, live elsewhere? She might have to sell at a low price; as a realtor, I knew the difficulty in selling a house where a suicide has taken place. No matter how much they may joke about it, people are still afraid of the supernatural. Many of them would believe this room was haunted.

It was then I finally realized the room *was* haunted. With me! *I'm a ghost,* I thought, thinking the word for the first time, in utter blank astonishment. I'm a ghost.

Oh, how dismal! To hover here, to be a boneless fleshless aching *presence* here, to be a kind of ectoplasmic mildew seeping through the days and nights, alone, unending, a stupid pain-racked, misery-filled observer of the comings and goings of strangers—she *would* sell the house, she'd have to, I was sure of that. Was this my punishment? The punishment of the suicide, the solitary hell of him who takes his own life. To remain forever a sentient nothing, bound by a force greater than gravity itself to the place of one's finish.

I was distracted from this misery by a sudden agitation in the key on this side of the lock. I saw it quiver and jiggle like something alive, and then it popped out—it seemed to *leap* out, itself a suicide leaping from a cliff—and clattered to the floor, and an instant later the door was pushed open and Greg's ashen face stared at my own purple face, and after the astonishment and horror, his expression shifted to revulsion—and contempt?—and he backed out, slamming the door. Once more the key turned in the lock, and I heard him hurry away downstairs.

The clock read 9:58. *Now* he was telling her. *Now* he was giving her a drink to calm her. *Now* he was phoning the police. *Now* he was talking to her about whether or not to admit their affair to the police; what would they decide?

"Noooooooooo!"

The clock read 10:07. What had taken so long? Hadn't he even called the police yet?

She was coming up the stairs, stumbling and rushing, she was pounding on the door, screaming my name. I shrank into the corners of the room, I *felt* the thuds of her fists against the door, I cowered from her. She can't come in, dear God don't let her in! I don't care what she's done, I don't care about anything, just don't let her see me! *Don't let me see her!*

Greg joined her. She screamed at him, he persuaded her, she raved, he argued, she demanded, he denied. "Give me the key. Give me the key."

Surely he'll hold out, surely he'll take her away, surely he's stronger, more forceful.

He gave her the key.

No. *This* cannot be endured. *This* is the horror beyond all else. She came in, she walked into the room, and the sound she made will always live inside me. That cry wasn't human; it was the howl of every creature that has ever despaired. *Now* I know what despair is, and why I called my own state mere truculence.

Now that it was too late, Greg tried to restrain her, tried to hold her shoulders and draw her from the room, but she pulled away and crossed the room toward . . . not toward *me*. I was everywhere in the room, driven by pain and remorse, and Emily walked toward the carcass. She looked at it almost tenderly, she even reached up and touched its swollen cheek. "Oh, Ed," she murmured.

The pains were as violent now as in the moments before my death. The slashing torment in my throat, the awful distension in my head, they made me squirm in agony all over again; but I *could not* feel her hand on my cheek.

Greg followed her, touched her shoulder again, spoke her name, and immediately her face dissolved, she cried out once more and wrapped her arms around the corpse's legs and clung to it, weeping and gasping and uttering words too quick and broken to understand. Thank *God* they were too quick and broken to understand!

Greg, that fool, did finally force her away, though he had great trouble breaking her clasp on the body. But he succeeded, and pulled her out of the room, and slammed the door, and for a little while the body swayed and turned, until it became still once more.

That was the worst. Nothing could be worse than that. The long days and nights here—how long must a stupid creature like myself *haunt* his death-place before release?—would be horrible, I knew that, but not so bad as this. Emily would survive, would sell the house, would slowly forget. (Even I would slowly forget.) She and Greg could marry. She was only thirty-six, she could still be a mother.

For the rest of the night I heard her wailing, elsewhere in the house. The police did come at last, and a pair of grim silent white-coated men from the morgue entered the room to cut me—it—down. They bundled it like a broken toy into a large oval wicker basket with long wooden handles, and they carried it away.

I had thought I might be forced to stay with the body, I had feared the possibility of being buried with it, of spending eternity as a thinking nothingness in the black dark of a casket, but the body left the room and I remained behind.

A doctor was called. When the body was carried away the room door was left open, and now I could plainly hear the voices from downstairs. Tony was among them now, his characteristic surly monosyllable occasionally rumbling, but the main thing for a while was the doctor. He was trying to give Emily a sedative, but she kept wailing, she kept speaking high hurried frantic sentences as though she had too little time to say it all. "I did it!" she cried, over and over. "I did it! I'm to blame!"

Yes. That was the reaction I'd wanted, and expected, and here it was, and it was horrible. Everything I had desired in the last moments of my life had been granted to me, and they were all ghastly beyond belief. I *didn't* want to die! I *didn't* want to give Emily such misery! And more than all the rest I didn't want to be here, seeing and hearing it all.

They did quiet her at last, and then a policeman in a rumpled blue suit came into the room with Greg and listened while Greg described everything that had happened. While Greg talked, the policeman rather grumpily stared at the remaining length of rope still knotted around the beam, and when Greg had finished the policeman said, "You're a close friend of his?"

"More of his wife. She works for me. I own The Bibelot, an antique shop out on the New York road."

"Mm. Why on earth did you let her in here?"

Greg smiled; a sheepish embarrassed expression. "She's stronger than I am," he said. "A more forceful personality. That's always been true."

It was with some surprise I realized it *was* true. Greg was something of a weakling, and Emily was very strong. (*I* had been something of a weakling, hadn't I? Emily was the strongest of us all.)

The policeman was saying, "Any idea why he'd do it?"

"I think he suspected his wife was having an affair with me." Clearly Greg had rehearsed this sentence, he'd much earlier come to the decision to say it and had braced himself for the moment. He blinked all the way through the statement, as though standing in a harsh glare.

The policeman gave him a quick shrewd look. "Were you?"

"Yes."

"She was getting a divorce?"

"No. She doesn't love me, she loved her husband."

"Then why sleep around?"

"Emily wasn't sleeping *around*," Greg said, showing offense only with that emphasized word. "From time to time, and not very often, she was sleeping with me."

"Why?"

"For comfort." Greg too looked at the rope around the beam, as though it had become me and he was awkward speaking in its presence. "Ed wasn't an easy man to get along with," he said carefully. "He was moody. It was getting worse."

"Cheerful people don't kill themselves," the policeman said.

"Exactly. Ed was depressed most of the time, obscurely angry now and then. It was affecting his business, costing him clients. He made Emily miserable but she wouldn't leave him, she loved him. I don't know what she'll do now."

"You two won't marry?"

"Oh, no." Greg smiled, a bit sadly. "Do you think we murdered him, made it look like suicide so we could marry?"

"Not at all," the policeman said. "But what's the problem? You already married?"

"I am homosexual."

The policeman was no more astonished than I. He said, "I don't get it."

"I live with my friend; that young man downstairs. I am—capable—of a wider range, but my preferences are set. I am very fond of Emily, I felt sorry for her, the life she had with Ed. I told you our physical relationship was infrequent. And often not very successful."

Oh, Emily. Oh, poor Emily.

The policeman said, "Did Thornburn know you were, uh, that way?"

"I have no idea. I don't make a public point of it."

"All right." The policeman gave one more half-angry look around the room, then said, "Let's go."

They left. The door remained open, and I heard them continue to talk as they went downstairs, first the policeman asking, "Is there somebody to stay the night? Mrs. Thornburn shouldn't be alone."

"She has relatives in Great Barrington. I phoned them earlier. Somebody should be arriving within the hour."

"You'll stay until then? The doctor says she'll probably sleep, but just in case—"

"Of course."

That was all I heard. Male voices murmured a while longer from below, and then stopped. I heard cars drive away.

How complicated men and women are. How stupid are simple actions. I had never understood anyone, least of all myself.

The room was visited once more that night, by Greg, shortly after the police left. He entered, looking as offended and repelled as though the body were still here, stood the chair up on its legs, climbed on it, and with some difficulty untied the remnant of rope. This he stuffed partway into his pocket as he stepped down again to the floor, then returned the chair to its usual spot in the corner of the room, picked the key off the floor and put it in the lock, switched off both bedside lamps and left the room, shutting the door behind him.

Now I was in darkness, except for the faint line of light under the door, and the illuminated numerals of the clock. How long one minute is! That clock was my enemy, it dragged out every minute, it paused and waited and paused and waited till I could stand it no more, and then it waited longer, and *then* the next number dropped into place. Sixty times an hour, hour after hour, all night long. I couldn't stand one night of this, how could I stand eternity?

And how could I stand the torment and torture inside my brain? That was much worse now than the physical pain, which never entirely left me. I had been right about Emily and Greg, but at the same time I had been hopelessly brainlessly wrong. I had been right about my life, but wrong; right about my death, but wrong. How *much* I wanted to make amends, and how impossible it was to do anything anymore, anything at all. My actions had all tended to this, and ended with this: black remorse, the most dreadful pain of all.

I had all night to think, and to feel the pains, and to wait without knowing what I was waiting for or when—or if—my waiting would ever end. Faintly I heard the arrival of Emily's sister and brother-in-law, the murmured conversation, then the departure of Tony and Greg. Not long afterward the guestroom door opened, but almost immediately closed again, no one having entered, and a bit after that the hall light went out, and now only the illuminated clock broke the darkness.

When next would I see Emily? Would she ever enter this room

again? It wouldn't be as horrible as the first time, but it would surely be horror enough.

Dawn grayed the window shade, and gradually the room appeared out of the darkness, dim and silent and morose. Apparently it was a sunless day, which never got very bright. The day went on and on, featureless, each protracted minute marked by the clock. At times I dreaded someone's entering this room, at other times I prayed for something, anything—even the presence of Emily herself—to break this unending boring *absence*. But the day went on with no event, no sound, no activity anywhere—they must be keeping Emily sedated through this first day—and it wasn't until twilight, with the digital clock reading 6:52, that the door again opened and a person entered.

At first I didn't recognize him. An angry-looking man, blunt and determined, he came in with quick ragged steps, switched on both bedside lamps, then shut the door with rather more force than necessary and turned the key in the lock. Truculent, his manner was, and when he turned from the door I saw with incredulity that he was *me*. Me! I wasn't dead, I was alive! But how could that be?

And what was that he was carrying? He picked up the chair from the corner, carried it to the middle of the room, stood on it—

No! No!

He tied the rope around the beam. The noose was already in the other end, which he slipped over his head and tightened around his neck.

Good God, *don't!*

He kicked the chair away.

The instant I kicked the chair away I wanted it back, but gravity was turning my former wish to its present command; the chair would not right itself from where it lay on the floor, and my 193 pounds would not cease to urge downward from the rope thick around my neck.

There was pain, of course, quite horrible pain centered in my throat, but the most astounding thing was the way my cheeks seemed to swell. I could barely see over their round red hills, my eyes staring in agony at the door, *willing* someone to come in and rescue me, though I knew there was no one in the house, and in any event the door was carefully locked. My kicking legs caused me to twist and turn, so that sometimes I faced the door and sometimes the window, and my shivering hands struggled with the rope so deep in my flesh I could barely find it and most certainly could not pull it loose.

I was frantic and horrified, yet at the same time my brain possessed a cold corner of aloof observation. I seemed now to be everywhere in the room at once, within my writhing body but also without, seeing my frenzied spasms, the thick rope, the heavy beam, the mismatched pair of lit bedside lamps throwing my convulsive double shadow on the walls, the closed locked door, the white-curtained window with its shade drawn all the way down. *This is death.*

HORN MAN

by Clark Howard

When Dix stepped off the Greyhound bus in New Orleans, old Rainey was waiting for him near the terminal entrance. He looked just the same as Dix remembered him. Old Rainey had always looked old, since Dix had known him, ever since Dix had been a little boy. He had skin like black saddle leather and patches of cotton-white hair, and his shoulders were round and stooped. When he was contemplating something, he chewed on the inside of his cheeks, pushing his pursed lips in and out as if he were revving up for speech. He was doing that when Dix walked up to him.

"Hey, Rainey."

Rainey blinked surprise and then his face split into a wide smile of perfect, gleaming teeth. "Well, now. Well, well, well, now." He looked Dix up and down. "They give you that there suit of clothes?"

Dix nodded. "Everyone gets a suit of clothes if they done more than a year." Dix's eyes, the lightest blue possible without being gray, hardened just enough for Rainey to notice. "And I sure done more than a year," he added.

"That's the truth," Rainey said. He kept the smile on his face and changed the subject as quickly as possible. "I got you a room in the Quarter. Figured that's where you'd want to stay."

Dix shrugged. "It don't matter no more."

"It will," Rainey said with the confidence of years. "It will when you hear the music again."

Dix did not argue the point. He was confident that none of it mattered. Not the music, not the French Quarter, none of it. Only one thing mattered to Dix.

"Where is she, Rainey?" he asked. "Where's Madge?"

"I don't rightly know," Rainey said.

Dix studied him for a moment. He was sure Rainey was lying. But it didn't matter. There were others who would tell him.

They walked out of the terminal, the stooped old black man and the tall, prison-hard white man with a set to his mouth and a canvas zip-bag containing all his worldly possessions. It was late afternoon: The sun was almost gone and the evening coolness was coming in. They walked toward the Quarter, Dix keeping his long-legged pace slow to accommodate old Rainey.

Rainey glanced at Dix several times as they walked, chewing inside his mouth and working up to something. Finally he said, "You been playing at all while you was in?"

Dix shook his head. "Not for a long time. I did a little the first year. Used to dry play, just with my mouthpiece. After a while, though, I gave it up. They got a different kind of music over there in Texas. Stompin' music. Not my style." Dix forced a grin at old Rainey. "I ever kill a man again, I'll be sure I'm on *this* side of the Louisiana line."

Rainey scowled. "You know you ain't never killed nobody, boy," he said harshly. "You know it wudn't you that done it. It was *her.*"

Dix stopped walking and locked eyes with old Rainey. "How long have you knowed me?" he asked.

"Since you was eight months old," Rainey said. "You know that. Me and my sistuh, we worked for your grandmamma, Miz Jessie DuChatelier. She had the finest gentlemen's house in the Quarter. Me and my sistuh, we cleaned and cooked for Miz Jessie. And took care of you after your own poor mamma took sick with the consumption and died—"

"Anyway, you've knowed me since I was less than one, and now I'm *forty*-one."

Rainey's eyes widened. "Naw," he said, grinning again, "you ain't that old. Naw."

"Forty-one, Rainey. I been gone sixteen years. I got twenty-five, remember? And I done sixteen."

Sudden worry erased Rainey's grin. "Well, if you forty-one, how old that make *me?*"

"About two hundred. I don't know. You must be seventy or eighty. Anyway, listen to me now. In all the time you've knowed me, have I ever let anybody make a fool out of me?"

Rainey shook his head. "Never. No way."

"That's right. And I'm not about to start now. But if word got around that I done sixteen years for a killing that was somebody else's, I'd look like the biggest fool that ever walked the levee, wouldn't I?"

"I reckon so," Rainey allowed.

"Then don't ever say again that I didn't do it. Only one person alive knows for certain positive that I didn't do it. And I'll attend to her myself. Understand?"

Rainey chewed the inside of his cheeks for a moment, then asked, "What you fixin' to do about her?"

Dix's light blue eyes hardened again. "Whatever I have to do, Rainey," he replied.

Rainey shook his head in slow motion. "Lord, Lord, Lord," he whispered.

Old Rainey went to see Gaston that evening at Tradition Hall, the jazz emporium and restaurant that Gaston owned in the Quarter. Gaston was slick and dapper. For him, time had stopped in 1938. He still wore spats.

"How does he look?" Gaston asked old Rainey.

"He *look* good," Rainey said. "He *talk* bad." Rainey leaned close to the white club owner. "He fixin' to kill that woman. Sure as God made sundown."

Gaston stuck a sterling-silver toothpick in his mouth. "He know where she is?"

"I don't think so," said Rainey. "Not yet."

"*You* know where she is?"

"Lastest I heard, she was living over on Burgundy Street with some doper."

Gaston nodded his immaculately shaved and lotioned chin. "Correct. The doper's name is LeBeau. He's young. I think he keeps her around to take care of him when he's sick." Gaston examined his beautifully manicured nails. "Does Dix have a lip?"

Rainey shook his head. "He said he ain't played in a while. But a natural like him, he can get his lip back in no time a'tall."

"Maybe," said Gaston.

"He can," Rainey insisted.

"Has he got a horn?"

"Naw. I watched him unpack his bag and I didn't see no horn. So I axed him about it. He said after a few years of not playing, he just give it away. To some cowboy he was in the Texas pen with."

Gaston sighed. "He should have killed that fellow on this side of the state line. If he'd done the killing in Louisiana, he would have went to the pen at Angola. They play good jazz at Angola. Eddie Lumm is up there. You remember Eddie Lumm? Clarinetist. Learned to play from Frank Teschemacher and Jimmie Noone. Eddie killed his old lady. So now he blows at Angola. They play good jazz at Angola."

Rainey didn't say anything. He wasn't sure if Gaston thought Dix had really done the killing or not. Sometimes Gaston *played* like he didn't know a thing, just to see if somebody *else* knew it. Gaston was smart. Smart enough to help keep Dix out of trouble if he was a mind. Which was what old Rainey was hoping for.

Gaston drummed his fingertips silently on the table where they sat. "So. You think Dix can get his lip back with no problem, is that right?"

"Tha's right. He can."

"He planning to come around and see me?"

"I don't know. He probably set on finding that woman first. Then he might not be *able* to come see you."

"Well, see if you can get him to come see me first. Tell him I've got something for him. Something I've been saving for him. Will you do that?"

"You bet." Rainey got up from the table. "I'll go do it right now."

*   *   *

George Tennell was big and beefy and mean. Rumor had it that he had once killed two men by smashing their heads together with such force that he literally knocked their brains out. He had been a policeman for thirty years, first in the colored section, which was the only place he could work in the old days, and now in the *Vieux Carre*, the Quarter, where he was detailed to keep the peace to whatever extent it was possible. He had no family, claimed no friends. The Quarter was his home as well as his job. The only thing in the world he admitted to loving was jazz.

That was why, every night at seven, he sat at a small corner table in Tradition Hall and ate dinner while he listened to the band tune their instruments and warm up. Most nights, Gaston joined him later for a liqueur. Tonight he joined him before dinner.

"Dix got back today," he told the policeman. "Remember Dix?"

Tennell nodded. "Horn man. Killed a fellow in a motel room just across the Texas line. Over a woman named Madge Noble."

"That's the one. Only there's some around don't think he did it. There's some around think *she* did it."

"Too bad he couldn't have found twelve of those people for his jury."

"He didn't have no jury, George. Quit laying back on me. You remember it as well as I do. One thing you'd *never* forget is a good horn man."

Tennell's jaw shifted to the right a quarter of an inch, making his mouth go crooked. The band members were coming out of the back now and moving around on the bandstand, unsnapping instrument cases, inserting mouthpieces, straightening chairs. They were a mixed lot—black, white, and combinations; clean-shaven and goateed; balding and not; clear-eyed and strung out. None of them was under fifty—the oldest was the trumpet player, Luther Dodd, who was eighty-six. Like Louis Armstrong, he had learned to blow at the elbow of Joe "King" Oliver, the great cornetist. His Creole-style trumpet playing was unmatched in New Orleans. Watching him near the age when he would surely die was agony for the jazz purists who frequented Tradition Hall.

Gaston studied George Tennell as the policeman watched Luther

Dodd blow out the spit plug of his gleaming Balfour trumpet and loosen up his stick-brittle fingers on the valves. Gaston saw in Tennell's eyes that odd look of a man who truly worshipped traditional jazz music, who felt it down in the pit of himself just like the old men who played it, but who had never learned to play himself. It was a look that had the mix of love and sadness and years gone by. It was the only look that ever turned Tennell's eyes soft.

"You know how long I been looking for a horn man to take Luther's place?" Gaston asked. "A straight year. I've listened to a couple dozen guys from all over. Not a one of them could play traditional. Not a one." He bobbed his chin at Luther Dodd. "His fingers are like old wood, and so's his heart. He could go on me any night. And if he does, I'll have to shut down. Without a horn man, there's no Creole sound, no tradition at all. Without a horn, this place of mine, which is the last of the great jazz emporiums, will just give way to"—Gaston shrugged helplessly—"whatever. Disco music, I suppose."

A shudder circuited George Tennell's spine, but he gave no outward sign of it. His body was absolutely still, his hands resting motionlessly on the snow-white tablecloth, eyes steadily fixed on Luther Dodd. Momentarily the band went into its first number, "Lafayette," played Kansas City-style after the way of Bennie Moten. The music pulsed out like spurts of water, each burst overlapping the one before it to create an even wave of sound that flooded the big room. Because Kansas City style was so rhythmic and highly danceable, some of the early diners immediately moved onto the dance floor and fell in with the music.

Ordinarily, Tennell liked to watch people dance while he ate; the moving bodies lent emphasis to the music he loved so much, music he had first heard from the window of the St. Pierre Colored Orphanage on Decatur Street when he had been a boy; music he had grown up with and would have made his life a part of if he had not been so completely talentless, so inept that he could not even read sharps and flats. But tonight he paid no attention to the couples out in front of the bandstand. He concentrated only on Luther Dodd and the old horn man's breath intake as he played. It was clear to Tennell that Luther was struggling for breath, fighting for every note he blew, utilizing every cubic inch of lung power that his old body could marshal.

After watching Luther all the way through "Lafayette," and halfway through "Davenport Blues," Tennell looked across the table at Gaston and nodded.

"All right," he said simply. "All right."

For the first time ever Tennell left the club without eating dinner.

As Dix walked along with old Rainey toward Gaston's club, Rainey kept pointing out places to him that he had not exactly forgotten, but had not remembered in a long time.

"That house there," Rainey said, "was where Paul Mares was born back in nineteen-and-oh-one. He's the one formed the original New Orleans Rhythm Kings. He only lived to be forty-eight but he was one of the best horn men of all time."

Dix would remember, not necessarily the person himself but the house and the story of the person and how good he was. He had grown up on those stories, gone to sleep by them as a boy, lived the lives of the men in them many times over as he himself was being taught to blow trumpet by Rozell "The Lip" Page when Page was already past sixty and he, Dix, was only eight. Later, when Page died, Dix's education was taken over by Shepherd Norden and Blue Johnny Meadows, the two alternating as his teacher between their respective road tours. With Page, Norden, and Meadows in his background, it was no wonder that Dix could blow traditional.

"Right up the street there," Rainey said as they walked, "is where Wingy Manone was born in nineteen-and-oh-four. His given name was Joseph, but after his accident ever'body taken to calling him 'Wingy.' The accident was, he fell under a street car and lost his right arm. But that boy didn't let a little thing like that worry him none, no sir. He learned to play trumpet *left-handed,* and *one-handed.* And he was *good.* Lord, he was good."

They walked along Dauphin and Chartres and Royal. All around them were the French architecture and grillework and statuary and vines and moss that made the *Vieux Carre* a world unto itself, a place of subtle sights, sounds, and smells—black and white and fish and age—that no New Orleans tourist, no Superdome visitor, no casual observer, could ever experience, because to experience was to understand, and understanding of the Quarter could not be acquired, it had to be lived.

"Tommy Ladnier, he used to live right over there," Rainey said, "right up on the second floor. He lived there when he came here from his hometown of Mandeville, Loozey-ana. Poor Tommy, he had a short life too, only thirty-nine years. But it was a good life. He played with King Oliver and Fletcher Henderson and Sidney Bechet. Yessir, he got in some good licks."

When they got close enough to Tradition Hall to hear the music, at first faintly, then louder, clearer, Rainey stopped talking. He wanted Dix to hear the music, to *feel* the sound of it as it wafted out over Pirate's Alley and the Café du Monde and Congo Square (they called it Beauregard Square now, but Rainey refused to recognize the new name). Instinctively, Rainey knew that it was important for the music to get back into Dix, to saturate his mind and catch in his chest and tickle his stomach. There were some things in Dix that needed to be washed out, some bad things, and Rainey was certain that the music would help. A good purge was always healthy.

Rainey was grateful, as they got near enough to define melody, that "Sweet Georgia Brown" was being played. It was a good melody to come home to.

They walked on, listening, and after a while Dix asked, "Who's on horn?"

"Luther Dodd."

"Don't sound like Luther. What's the matter with him?"

Rainey waved one hand resignedly. "Old. Dying, I 'spect."

They arrived at the Hall and went inside. Gaston met them with a smile. "Dix," he said, genuinely pleased, "it's good to see you." His eyes flicked over Dix. "The years have been good to you. Trim. Lean. No gray hair. How's your lip?"

"I don't have a lip no more, Mr. Gaston," said Dix. "Haven't had for years."

"But he can get it back quick enough," Rainey put in. "He gots a natural lip."

"I don't play no more, Mr. Gaston," Dix told the club owner.

"That's too bad," Gaston said. He bobbed his head toward the stairs. "Come with me. I want to show you something."

Dix and Rainey followed Gaston upstairs to his private office. The office was furnished the way Gaston dressed—old-style, roaring twenties. There was even a wind-up Victrola in the corner.

Gaston worked the combination of a large, ornate floor vault and pulled its big-tiered door open. From somewhere in its dark recess he withdrew a battered trumpet case, one of the very old kind with heavy brass fittings on the corners and, one knew, real velvet, not felt, for a lining. Placing it gently in the center of his desk, Gaston carefully opened the snaplocks and lifted the top. Inside, indeed on real velvet, deep-purple real velvet, was a gleaming, silver, hand-etched trumpet. Dix and Rainey stared at it in unabashed awe.

"Know who it once belonged to?" Gaston asked.

Neither Dix nor Rainey replied. They were mesmerized by the instrument. Rainey had not seen one like it in fifty years. Dix had *never* seen one like it; he had only heard stories about the magnificent silver horns that the quadroons made of contraband silver carefully hidden away after the War Between the States. Because the silver cache had not, as it was supposed to, been given over to the Federal army as part of the reparations levied against the city, the quadroons, during the Union occupation, had to be very careful what they did with it. Selling it for value was out of the question. Using it for silver service, candlesticks, walking canes, or any other of the more obvious uses would have attracted the notice of a Union informer. But letting it lie dormant, even though it was safer as such, was intolerable to the quads, who refused to let a day go by without circumventing one law or another.

So they used the silver to plate trumpets and cornets and slide trombones that belonged to the tabernacle musicians who were just then beginning to experiment with the old *Sammsamounn* tribal music that would eventually mate with work songs and prison songs and gospels, and evolve into traditional blues, which would evolve into traditional, or Dixie-style, jazz.

"Look at the initials," Gaston said, pointing to the top of the bell.

Dix and Rainey peered down at three initials etched in the silver: BRB.

"Lord have mercy," Rainey whispered. Dix's lips parted as if he too intended to speak, but no words sounded.

"That's right," Gaston said. "Blind Ray Blount. The first, the best, the *only*. Nobody has ever touched the sounds he created. That man hit notes nobody ever heard before—or since. He was the master."

"Amen," Rainey said. He nodded his head toward Dix. "Can he touch it?"

"Go ahead," Gaston said to Dix.

Like a pilgrim to Mecca touching the holy shroud, Dix ever so lightly placed the tips of three fingers on the silver horn. As he did, he imagined he could feel the touch left there by the hands of the amazing blind horn man who had started the great blues evolution in a patch of town that later became Storyville. He imagined that—

"It's yours if you want it," Gaston said. "All you have to do is pick it up and go downstairs and start blowing."

Dix wet his suddenly dry lips. "Tomorrow I—"

"Not tomorrow," Gaston said. "Tonight. Now."

"Take it, boy," Rainey said urgently.

Dix frowned deeply, his eyes narrowing as if he felt physical pain. He swallowed, trying to push an image out of his mind; an image he had clung to for sixteen years. "I can't tonight—"

"Tonight or never," Gaston said firmly.

"For God's sake, boy, take it!" said old Rainey.

But Dix could not. The image of Madge would not let him.

Dix shook his head violently, as if to rid himself of devils, and hurried from the room.

Rainey ran after him and caught up with him a block from the Hall. "Don't do it," he pleaded. "Hear me now. I'm an old man and I know I ain't worth nothin' to nobody, but I'm begging you, boy, please, please, please don't do it. I ain't never axed you for nothing in my whole life, but I'm axing you for this: *please* don't do it."

"I got to," Dix said quietly. "It ain't that I want to; I *got* to."

"But why, boy? *Why?*"

"Because we made a promise to each other," Dix said. "That night in that Texas motel room, the man Madge was with had told her he was going to marry her. He'd been telling her that for a long time. But he was already married and kept putting off leaving his wife. Finally Madge had enough of it. She asked me to come to her room between sets. I knew she was just doing it to make him jealous, but it didn't matter none to me. I'd been crazy about her for so long that I'd do anything she asked me to, and she knew it.

"So between sets I slipped across the highway to where she had her room. But he was already there. I could hear through the transom that he was roughing her up some, but the door was locked and I couldn't get in. Then I heard a shot and everything got quiet. A minute later Madge opened the door and let me in. The man was laying across the bed dying. Madge started bawling and saying how they would put her in the pen and how she wouldn't be able to stand it, she'd go crazy and kill herself.

"It was then I asked her if she'd wait for me if I took the blame for her. She promised me she would. And I promised her I'd come back to her." Dix sighed quietly. "That's what I'm doing, Rainey—keeping my promise."

"And what going to happen if she ain't kept *hers?*" Rainey asked.

"Mamma Rulat asked me the same thing this afternoon when I asked her where Madge was at." Mamma Rulat was an octaroon fortune-teller who always knew where everyone in the Quarter lived.

"What did you tell her?"

"I told her I'd do what I had to do. That's all a man *can* do, Rainey." Dix walked away, up a dark side street. Rainey, watching him go, shook his head in the anguish of the aged and helpless.

"Lord, Lord, Lord—"

The house on Burgundy Street had once been a grand mansion with thirty rooms and a tiled French courtyard with a marble fountain in its center. It had seen nobility and aristocracy and great generals come and go with elegant, genteel ladies on their arms. Now the thirty rooms were rented individually with hot-plate burners for light cooking, and the only ladies who crossed the courtyard were those of the New Orleans night.

A red light was flashing atop a police car when Dix got there, and uniformed policemen were blocking the gate into the courtyard. There was a small curious crowd talking about what happened.

"A doper named LeBeau," someone said. "He's been shot."

"I heared it," an old man announced. "I heared the shot."

"There's where it happened, that window right up there—"

Dix looked up, but as he did another voice said, "They're bringing him out now!"

Two morgue attendants wheeled a sheet-covered gurney across the courtyard and lifted it into the back of a black panel truck. Several policemen, led by big beefy George Tennell, brought a woman out and escorted her to the car with the flashing red light. Dix squinted, focusing on her in the inadequate courtyard light. He frowned. Madge's mother, he thought, his mind going back two decades. What's Madge's mother got to do with this?

Then he remembered. Madge's mother was dead. She had died five years after he had gone to the pen.

Then who—?

Madge?

Yes, it *was* her. It was Madge. Older, as he was. Not a girl anymore, as he was not a boy anymore. For a moment he found it difficult to equate the woman in the courtyard with the memory in his mind. But it was Madge, all right.

Dix tried to push forward, to get past the gate into the courtyard, but two policemen held him back. George Tennell saw the altercation and came over.

"She's under arrest, mister," Tennell told Dix. "Can't nobody talk to her but a lawyer right now."

"What's she done anyhow?" Dix asked.

"Killed her boyfriend," said Tennell. "Shot him with this."

He showed Dix a pearl-handled over-and-under Derringer two-shot.

"Her boyfriend?"

Tennell nodded. "Young feller. 'Bout twenty-five. Neighbors say she was partial to young fellers. Some women are like that."

"Who says she shot him?"

"I do. I was in the building at the time, on another matter. I heard the shot. Matter of fact, I was the first one to reach the body. Few minutes later she come waltzing in. Oh, she put on a good act, all right, like she didn't even know what happened. But I found the gun in her purse myself."

By now the other officers had Madge Noble in the police car and were waiting for Tennell. He slipped the Derringer into his coat pocket and hitched up his trousers. Jutting his big jaw out an inch, he fixed Dix in a steady gaze.

"If she's a friend of yours, don't count on her being around for a spell. She'll do a long time for this."

Tennell walked away, leaving Dix still outside the gate. Dix waited there, watching, as the police car came through to the street. He tried to catch a glimpse of Madge as it passed, but there was not enough light in the backseat where they had her. As soon as the car left, the people who had gathered around began to leave too.

Soon Dix was the only one standing there.

At midnight George Tennell was back at his usual table in Tradition Hall for the dinner he had missed earlier. Gaston came over and joined him. For a few minutes they sat in silence, watching Dix up on the bandstand. He was blowing the silver trumpet that had once belonged to Blind Ray Blount; sitting next to the aging Luther Dodd; jumping in whenever he could as they played "Tailspin Blues," then "Tank Town Bump," then "Everybody Loves My Baby."

"Sounds like he'll be able to get his lip back pretty quick," Tennell observed.

"Sure," said Gaston. "He's a natural. Rozell Page was his first teacher, you know."

"No, I didn't know that."

"Sure." Gaston adjusted the celluloid collar he wore, and turned the diamond stickpin in his tie. "What about the woman?" he asked.

Tennell shrugged. "She'll get twenty years. Probably do ten or eleven."

Gaston thought for a moment, then said, "That should be time enough. After ten or eleven years nothing will matter to him except the music. Don't you think?"

"It won't even take that long," Tennell guessed. "Not for him."

Up on the bandstand the men who played traditional went into "Just a Closer Walk with Thee."

And sitting on the sawdust floor behind the bandstand, old Rainey listened with happy tears in his eyes.

THE ABSENCE OF EMILY

by Jack Ritchie

The phone rang and I picked up the receiver. "Yes?"

"Hello, darling, this is Emily."

I hesitated. "Emily who?"

She laughed lightly. "Oh, come now, darling. Emily, your wife."

"I'm sorry, you must have a wrong number." I hung up, fumbling a bit as I cradled the phone.

Millicent, Emily's cousin, had been watching me. "You look white as a sheet."

I glanced covertly at a mirror.

"I don't mean in actual *color,* Albert. I mean figuratively. In attitude. You seem frightened. Shocked."

"Nonsense."

"Who phoned?"

"It was a wrong number."

Millicent sipped her coffee. "By the way, Albert, I thought I saw Emily in town yesterday, but, of course, that was impossible."

"Of course it was impossible. Emily is in San Francisco."

"Yes, but *where* in San Francisco?"

"She didn't say. Just visiting friends."

"I've known Emily all her life. She has very few secrets from me. She doesn't *know* anybody in San Francisco. When will she be back?"

219

"She might be gone a rather long time."

"How long?"

"She didn't know."

Millicent smiled. "You have been married before, haven't you, Albert?"

"Yes."

"As a matter of fact, you were a widower when you met Emily?"

"I didn't try to keep that fact a secret."

"Your first wife met her death in a boating accident five years ago? She fell overboard and drowned?"

"I'm afraid so. She couldn't swim a stroke."

"Wasn't she wearing a life preserver?"

"No. She claimed they hindered her movements."

"It appears that you were the only witness to the accident."

"I believe so. At least no one else ever came forward."

"Did she leave you any money, Albert?"

"That's none of your business, Millicent."

Cynthia's estate had consisted of a fifty-thousand-dollar life-insurance policy, of which I was the sole beneficiary, some forty-thousand dollars in sundry stocks and bonds, and one small sailboat.

I stirred my coffee. "Millicent, I thought I'd give you first crack at the house."

"First crack?"

"Yes. We've decided to sell this place. It's really too big for just the two of us. We'll get something smaller. Perhaps even an apartment. I thought you might like to pick up a bargain. I'm certain we can come to satisfactory terms."

She blinked. "Emily would never sell this place. It's her home. I'd have to hear the words from her in person."

"There's no need for that. I have her power of attorney. She has no head for business, you know, but she trusts me implicitly. It's all quite legal and aboveboard."

"I'll think it over." She put down her cup. "Albert, what did you do for a living before you met Emily? Or Cynthia, for that matter?"

"I managed."

When Millicent was gone, I went for my walk on the back grounds of the estate. I went once again to the dell and sat down on the fallen log. How peaceful it was here. Quiet. A place to rest. I had been coming here often in the last few days.

Millicent and Emily. Cousins. They occupied almost identical large homes on spacious grounds next to each other. And, considering that fact, one might reasonably have supposed that they were equally wealthy. Such, however, was not the case, as I discovered after my marriage to Emily.

Millicent's holdings must certainly reach far into seven figures, since they require the full-time administrative services of Amos Eberly, her attorney and financial advisor.

Emily, on the other hand, owned very little more than the house and the grounds themselves and she had borrowed heavily to keep them going. She had been reduced to two servants, the Brewsters. Mrs. Brewster, a surly creature, did the cooking and desultory dusting, while her husband, formerly the butler, had been reduced to a man-of-all-work, who pottered inadequately about the grounds. The place really required the services of two gardeners.

Millicent and Emily. Cousins. Yet it was difficult to imagine two people more dissimilar in either appearance or nature.

Millicent is rather tall, spare, and determined. She fancies herself an intellect and she has the tendency to rule and dominate all those about her, and that had certainly included Emily. It is obvious to me that Millicent deeply resents the fact that I removed Emily from under her thumb.

Emily. Shorter than average. Perhaps twenty-five pounds overweight. An amiable disposition. No claim to blazing intelligence. Easily dominated, yes, though she had a surprising stubborn streak when she set her mind to something.

When I returned to the house, I found Amos Eberly waiting. He is a man in his fifties and partial to gray suits.

"Where is Emily?" he asked.

"In Oakland." He gave that thought.

"I meant San Francisco. Oakland is just across the bay, isn't it? I usually think of them as one, which, I suppose, is unfair to both."

He frowned. "San Francisco? But I saw her in town just this morning. She was looking quite well."

"Impossible."

"Impossible for her to be looking well?"

"Impossible for you to have seen her. She is still in San Francisco."

He sipped his drink. "I know Emily when I see her. She wore a lilac dress with a belt. And a sort of gauzy light-blue scarf."

"You were mistaken. Besides, women don't wear gauzy light-blue scarves these days."

"Emily did. Couldn't she have come back without letting you know?"

"No."

Eberly studied me. "Are you ill or something, Albert? Your hands seem to be shaking."

"Touch of the flu," I said quickly. "Brings out the jitters in me. What brings you here anyway, Amos?"

"Nothing in particular, Albert. I just happened to be in the neighborhood and thought I'd drop in and see Emily."

"Damn it, I told you she isn't here."

"All right, Albert," he said soothingly. "Why should I doubt you? If you say she isn't here, she isn't here."

It has become my habit on Tuesday and Thursday afternoons to do the household food shopping, a task which I preempted from Mrs. Brewster when I began to suspect her arithmetic.

As usual, I parked in the supermarket lot and locked the car. When I looked up, I saw a small, slightly stout woman across the street walking toward the farther end of the block. She wore a lilac dress and a light-blue scarf. It was the fourth time I'd seen her in the last ten days.

I hurried across the street. I was still some seventy-five yards behind her when she turned the corner.

Resisting the temptation to shout at her to stop, I broke into a trot.

When I reached the corner, she was nowhere in sight. She could have disappeared into any one of a dozen shop fronts.

I stood there, trying to regain my breath, when a car pulled to the curb.

It was Millicent. "Is that you, Albert?"

I regarded her without enthusiasm. "Yes."

"What in the world are you doing? I saw you running and I've never seen you run before."

"I was *not* running. I was merely trotting to get my blood circulating. A bit of jogging is supposed to be healthy, you know."

I volunteered my adieu and strode back to the supermarket.

The next morning when I returned from my walk to the dell, I found Millicent in the drawing room, pouring herself coffee and otherwise making herself at home—a habit from the days when only Emily occupied the house.

"I've been upstairs looking over Emily's wardrobe," Millicent said. "I didn't see anything missing."

"Why should anything be missing? Has there been a thief in the house? I suppose you know every bit and parcel of her wardrobe?"

"Not every bit and parcel, but almost. Almost. And very little, if anything, seems to be missing. Don't tell me that Emily went off to San Francisco without any luggage."

"She had luggage. Though not very much."

"What was she wearing when she left?"

Millicent had asked that question before. This time I said, "I don't remember."

Millicent raised an eyebrow. "You don't remember?" She put down her cup. "Albert, I'm holding a seance at my place tonight. I thought perhaps you'd like to come."

"I will not go to any damn seance."

"Don't you want to communicate with any of your beloved dead?"

"I believe in letting the dead rest. Why bother them with every trifling matter back here."

"Wouldn't you want to speak to your first wife?"

"Why the devil would I want to communicate with Cynthia? I have absolutely nothing to say to her anyway."

"But perhaps she has something to say to you."

I wiped my forehead. "I'm not going to your stupid seance and that's final."

That evening, as I prepared for bed, I surveyed the contents of Emily's closet. How would I dispose of her clothes? Probably donate them to some worthy charity, I thought.

*　　*　　*

I was awakened at two A.M. by the sound of music.

I listened. Yes, it was plainly Emily's favorite sonata being played on the piano downstairs.

I stepped into my slippers and donned my dressing robe. In the hall, I snapped on the lights.

I was halfway down the stairs when the piano playing ceased. I completed my descent and stopped at the music-room doors. I put my ear to one of them. Nothing. I slowly opened the door and peered inside.

There was no one at the piano. However, two candles in holders flickered on its top: The room seemed chilly. Quite chilly.

I found the source of the draft behind some drapes and closed the French doors to the terrace. I snuffed out the candles and left the room.

I met Brewster at the head of the stairs.

"I thought I heard a piano being played, sir," he said. "Was that you?"

I wiped the palms of my hands on my robe. "Of course."

"I didn't know you played the piano, sir."

"Brewster, there are a lot of things you don't know about me and never will."

I went back to my room, waited half an hour, and then dressed. In the bright moonlight outside, I made my way to the garden shed. I unbolted its door, switched on the lights, and surveyed the gardening equipment. My eyes went to the tools in the wall racks.

I pulled down a long-handled irrigating shovel and knocked a bit of dried mud from its tip. I slung the implement over my shoulder and began walking toward the dell.

I was nearly there when I stopped and sighed heavily. I shook my head and returned to the shed. I put the shovel back into its place on the rack, switched off the lights, and returned to bed.

The next morning, Millicent dropped in as I was having breakfast.

"How are you this morning, Albert?"

"I have felt better."

Millicent sat down at the table and waited for Mrs. Brewster to bring her a cup.

Mrs. Brewster also brought the morning mail. It included a number of advertising fliers, a few bills, and one small blue envelope addressed to me.

I examined it. The handwriting seemed familiar and so did the scent. The postmark was town.

I slit open the envelope and pulled out a single sheet of notepaper.

Dear Albert:

You have no idea how much I miss you. I shall return home soon, Albert. Soon.

Emily

I put the note back into the envelope and slipped both into my pocket.

"Well?" Millicent asked.

"Well, what?"

"I thought I recognized Emily's handwriting on the envelope. Did she say when she'd be back?"

"That is *not* Emily's handwriting. It is a note from my aunt in Chicago."

"I didn't know you had an aunt in Chicago."

"Millicent, rest assured. I *do* have an aunt in Chicago."

That night I was in bed, but awake, when the phone on my night table rang. I picked up the receiver.

"Hello, darling. This is Emily."

I let five seconds pass. "You are *not* Emily. You are an impostor."

"Now, Albert, why are you being so stubborn? Of course this is me. Emily."

"You couldn't be."

"Why couldn't I be?"

"Because."

"Because why?"

"Where are you calling from?"

She laughed. "I think you'd be surprised."

"You couldn't be Emily. I *know* where she is and she couldn't—*wouldn't*—make a phone call at this hour of the night just to say hello. It's well past midnight."

"You think you know where I am, Albert? No, I'm not there anymore. It was so uncomfortable, so dreadfully uncomfortable. And so I left, Albert. I left."

I raised my voice. "Damn you, I can *prove* you're still there."

She laughed. "Prove? How can you prove anything like that, Albert? Good night." She hung up.

I got out of bed and dressed. I made my way downstairs and detoured into the study. I made myself a drink, consumed it slowly, and then made another.

When I consulted my watch for the last time it was nearly one A.M. I put on a light jacket against the chill of the night and made my way to the garden shed. I opened the doors, turned on the lights, and pulled the long-handled shovel from the rack.

This time I went all the way to the dell. I paused beside a huge oak and stared at the moonlit clearing.

I counted as I began pacing. "One, two, three, four—" I stopped at sixteen, turned ninety degrees, and then paced off eighteen more steps.

I began digging.

I had been at it for nearly five minutes when suddenly I heard the piercing blast of a whistle and immediately I became the focus of perhaps a dozen flashlight beams and approaching voices.

I shielded my eyes against the glare and recognized Millicent. "What the devil is this?"

She showed cruel teeth. "You had to make sure she was really dead, didn't you, Albert? And the only way you could do that was to return to her grave."

I drew myself up. "I am looking for Indian arrowheads. There's an ancient superstition that if one is found under the light of the moon it will bring luck for the finder for several weeks."

Millicent introduced the people gathered about me. "Ever since I began suspecting what really has happened to Emily you've been under twenty-four-hour surveillance by private detectives."

She indicated the others. "Miss Peters. She is quite a clever mimic and was the voice of Emily you heard over the phone. She also plays piano. And Mrs. McMillan. She reproduced Emily's handwriting and was the woman in the lilac dress and the blue scarf."

Millicent's entire household staff seemed to be present. I also recognized Amos Eberly and the Brewsters. I would fire them tomorrow.

The detectives had brought along their own shovels and spades, and two of them superseded me in my shallow depression. They began digging.

"See here," I said, exhibiting indignation. "You have no right to do that. This is *my* property. At the very least you need a search warrant."

Millicent found that amusing. "This is *not* your property, Albert. It is *mine*. You stepped over the dividing line six paces back."

I wiped my forehead. "I'm going back to the house."

"You are under arrest, Albert."

"Nonsense, Millicent. I do not see a *proper* uniformed policeman among these people. And in this state private detectives do not have the right to arrest anyone at all."

For a moment she seemed stymied, but then saw light. "You are under *citizen's* arrest, Albert. Any citizen has the power to make a citizen's arrest and I am a citizen."

Millicent twirled the whistle on its chain. "We knew we were getting to you, Albert. You almost dug her up last night, didn't you? But then you changed your mind. But that was just as well. Last night I couldn't have produced as many witnesses. Tonight we were ready and waiting."

The detectives dug for some fifteen minutes and then paused for a rest. One of them frowned. "You'd think the digging would be easier. This ground looks like it's never been dug up before."

They resumed their work and eventually reached a depth of six feet before they gave up. The spade man climbed out of the excavation. "Hell, nothing's been buried here. The only thing we found was an Indian arrowhead."

Millicent had been glaring at me for the last half-hour.

I smiled. "Millicent, what makes you think that I *buried* Emily?"

With that I left them and returned to the house.

When had I first become aware of Millicent's magnificent maneuverings and the twenty-four-hour surveillance? Almost from the very beginning, I suspect. I'm rather quick on the uptake.

What had been Millicent's objective? I suppose she envisioned reducing me to such a state of fear that eventually I'd break down and confess to the murder of Emily.

Frankly, I would have regarded the success of such a scheme as farfetched, to say the least. However, once I was aware of what Millicent was attempting, I got into the spirit of the venture.

Millicent may have initiated the enterprise, the play, but it is I who led her to the dell.

There were times when I thought I overdid it just a bit—wiping at nonexistent perspiration, trotting after the elusive woman in the lilac dress, that sort of thing—but on the other hand I suppose these reactions were rather expected of me and I didn't want to disappoint any eager watchers.

Those brooding trips to the dell had been quite a good touch, I thought. And the previous night's halfway journey there, with the shovel over my shoulder, had been intended to assure a large audience at the finale twenty-four hours later.

I had counted eighteen witnesses, excluding Millicent.

I pondered. Defamation of character? Slander? Conspiracy? False arrest? Probably a good deal more.

I would threaten to sue for a large and unrealistic amount. That was the fashion nowadays, wasn't it? Twenty million? It didn't really matter, of course, because I doubted very much if the matter would ever reach court.

No, Millicent wouldn't be able to endure the publicity. She couldn't let the world know what a total fool she'd made of herself. She couldn't bear to be the laughingstock of her circle, her peers.

She would, of course, attempt to hush it up as best she could. A few dollars here and a few there to buy the silence of the witnesses. But could one seriously hope to buy the total silence of eighteen individual people? Probably not. However, when the whispers began to circulate, it would be a considerable help to Millicent if the principal player involved would join her in vehemently denying that any such ridiculous event had ever taken place at all.

And I would do that for Millicent. For a consideration. A *large* consideration.

At the end of the week, my phone rang.

"This is Emily. I'm coming home now, dear."

"Wonderful."

"Did anyone miss me?"

"You have no idea."

"You haven't told anyone where I've been these last four weeks, have you, Albert? Especially not Millicent?"

"Especially not Millicent."

"What *did* you tell her?"

"I said you were visiting friends in San Francisco."

"Oh, dear. I don't *know* anybody in San Francisco. Do you suppose she got suspicious?"

"Well, maybe just a little bit."

"She thinks I have absolutely no will power, but I really have. But just the same, I didn't want her laughing at me if I didn't stick it out. Oh, I suppose going to a health farm is cheating, in a way. I mean you can't be tempted because they control all of the food. But I really stuck it out. I could have come home anytime I wanted to."

"You have marvelous will power, Emily."

"I've lost *thirty* pounds, Albert! And it's going to *stay* off. I'll bet I'm every bit as slim now as Cynthia ever was."

I sighed. There was absolutely no reason for Emily to keep comparing herself to my first wife. The two of them are separate entities and each has her secure compartment in my affections.

Poor Cynthia. She had insisted on going off by herself in that small craft. I had been at the yacht-club window sipping a martini and watching the cold gray harbor.

Cynthia's boat seemed to have been the only one on the water on that inhospitable day and there had apparently been an unexpected gust of wind. I had seen the boat heel over sharply and Cynthia thrown overboard. I'd raised the alarm immediately, but by the time we got out there it had been too late.

Emily sighed too. "I suppose I'll have to get an entire new wardrobe. Do you think we can really afford one, Albert?"

We could now. And then some.

THE NEW
GIRL FRIEND

by Ruth Rendell

"You know what we did last time?" he said.

She had waited for this for weeks. "Yes?"

"I wondered if you'd like to do it again."

She longed to but she didn't want to sound too keen. "Why not?"

"How about Friday afternoon then? I've got the day off and Angie always goes to her sister's on Friday."

"Not *always,* David." She giggled.

He also laughed a little. "She will this week. Do you think we could use your car? Angie'll take ours."

"Of course. I'll come for you about two, shall I?"

"I'll open the garage doors and you can drive straight in. Oh, and Chris, could you fix it to get back a bit later? I'd love it if we could have the whole evening together."

"I'll try," she said, and then, "I'm sure I can fix it. I'll tell Graham I'm going out with my new girl friend."

He said goodbye and that he would see her on Friday. Christine put the receiver back. She had almost given up expecting a call from him. But there must have been a grain of hope still, for she had never left the receiver off the way she used to.

The last time she had done that was on a Thursday three weeks before, the day she had gone round to Angie's and found David there alone. Christine had got into the habit of taking the phone off the hook during the middle part of the day to avoid getting calls for the Midland Bank. Her number and the Midland Bank's differed by only one digit. Most days she took the receiver off at nine-thirty and put it back at three-thirty. On Thursday afternoons she nearly always went round to see Angie and never bothered to phone first.

Christine knew Angie's husband quite well. If she stayed a bit later on Thursdays she saw him when he came home from work. Sometimes she and Graham and Angie and David went out together as a foursome. She knew that David, like Graham, was a salesman, or sales executive, as Graham always described himself, and she guessed from her friend's lifestyle that David was rather more successful at it. She had never found him particularly attractive, for, although he was quite tall, he had something of a girlish look and very fair wavy hair.

Graham was a heavily built, very dark man with a swarthy skin. He had to shave twice a day. Christine had started going out with him when she was fifteen and they had got married on her eighteenth birthday. She had never really known any other man at all intimately and now if she ever found herself alone with a man she felt awkward and apprehensive. The truth was that she was afraid a man might make an advance to her and the thought of that frightened her very much. For a long while she carried a penknife in her handbag in case she should need to defend herself. One evening, after they had been out with a colleague of Graham's and had had a few drinks, she told Graham about this fear of hers.

He said she was silly but he seemed rather pleased.

"When you went off to talk to those people and I was left with John I felt like that. I felt terribly nervous. I didn't know how to talk to him."

Graham roared with laughter. "You don't mean you thought old John was going to make a pass at you in the middle of a crowded restaurant?"

"I don't know," Christine said. "I never know what they'll do."

"So long as you're not afraid of what I'll do," said Graham, beginning to kiss her, "that's all that matters."

There was no point in telling him now, ten years too late, that she was afraid of what he did and always had been. Of course she had got used to it, she wasn't actually terrified, she was resigned and sometimes even quite cheerful about it. David was the only man she had ever been alone with when it felt all right.

That first time, that Thursday when Angie had gone to her sister's and hadn't been able to get through on the phone and tell Christine not to come, that time it had been fine. And afterwards she had felt happy and carefree, though what had happened with David took on the coloring of a dream next day. It wasn't really believable. Early on he had said:

"Will you tell Angie?"

"Not if you don't want me to."

"I think it would upset her, Chris. It might even wreck our marriage. You see—" He had hesitated. "You see, that was the first time I—I mean, anyone ever—" And he had looked into her eyes. "Thank God it was you."

The following Thursday she had gone round to see Angie as usual. In the meantime there had been no word from David. She stayed late in order to see him, beginning to feel a little sick with apprehension, her heart beating hard when he came in.

He looked quite different from how he had when she had found him sitting at the table reading, the radio on. He was wearing a grey flannel suit and a grey striped tie. When Angie went out of the room and for a minute she was alone with him, she felt a flicker of that old wariness that was the forerunner of her fear. He was getting her a drink. She looked up and met his eyes and it was all right again. He gave her a conspiratorial smile, laying a finger on his lips.

"I'll give you a ring," he had whispered.

She had to wait two more weeks. During that time she went twice to Angie's and twice Angie came to her. She and Graham and Angie and David went out as a foursome and while Graham was fetching drinks and Angie was in the Ladies, David looked at her and smiled and lightly touched her foot with his foot under the table.

"I'll phone you. I haven't forgotten."

It was a Wednesday when he finally did phone. Next day Christine told Graham she had made a new friend, a girl she had met at work. She would be going out somewhere with this new friend on Friday and she wouldn't be back till eleven. She was desperately afraid he would want the car—it was *his* car, or his firm's—but it so happened he would be in the office that day and would go by train. Telling him these lies didn't make her feel guilty. It wasn't as if this were some sordid affair, it was quite different.

When Friday came she dressed with great care. Normally, to go round to Angie's, she would have worn jeans and a T-shirt with a sweater over it. That was what she had on the first time she found herself alone with David. She put on a skirt and blouse and her black velvet jacket. She took the heated rollers out of her hair and brushed it into curls down on her shoulders. There was never much money to spend on clothes. The mortgage on the house took up a third of what Graham earned and half what she earned at her part-time job. But she could run to a pair of sheer black tights to go with the highest-heeled shoes she'd got, her black pumps.

The doors of Angie and David's garage were wide open and their car was gone. Christine turned into their driveway, drove into the garage, and closed the doors behind her. A door at the back of the garage led into the yard and garden. The kitchen door was unlocked as it had been that Thursday three weeks before and always was on Thursday afternoons. She opened the door and walked in.

"Is that you, Chris?"

The voice sounded very male. She needed to be reassured by the sight of him. She went into the hall as he came down the stairs.

"You look lovely," he said.

"So do you."

He was wearing a suit. It was of navy silk with a pattern of pink-and-white flowers. The skirt was very short, the jacket clinched into his waist with a wide navy patent-leather belt. The long golden hair fell to his shoulders. He was heavily made-up and this time he had painted his fingernails. He looked far more beautiful than he had that first time.

Then, that first time, three weeks before, the sound of her entry drowned in loud music from the radio, she had come upon this girl sitting at the table reading *Vogue*. For a moment she had thought it must be David's sister. She had forgotten Angie had said David was an only child. The girl had long fair hair and was wearing a red summer dress with white spots on it, white sandals, and around her neck a string of white beads. When Christine saw that it was not a girl but David himself she didn't know what to do.

He stared at her in silence and without moving, and then he switched off the radio. Christine said the silliest and least relevant thing. "What are you doing home at this time?"

That made him smile. "I'd finished, so I took the rest of the day off. I should have locked the back door. Now you're here you may as well sit down."

She sat down. She couldn't take her eyes off him. He didn't look like a man dressed up as a girl, he looked like a girl—and a much prettier one than she or Angie. "Does Angie know?"

He shook his head.

"But why do you do it?" she burst out and she looked about the room, Angie's small, rather untidy living room, at the radio, the *Vogue* magazine. "What do you get out of it?" Something came back to her from an article she had read. "Did your mother dress you as a girl when you were little?"

"I don't know," he said. "Maybe. I don't remember. I don't want to *be* a girl. I just want to dress up as one sometimes."

The first shock of it was past and she began to feel easier with him. It wasn't as if there was anything grotesque about the way he looked. The very last thing he reminded her of was one of those female impersonators. A curious thought came into her head—that it was *nicer,* somehow more civilized, to be a woman and that if only all men were more like women— That was silly, of course, it couldn't be.

"And it's enough for you just to dress up and be here on your own?"

He was silent for a moment. "Since you ask, what I'd really like would be to go out like this and—" he paused, looking at her "— and be seen by lots of people, that's what I'd like. I've never had the nerve for that."

The bold idea expressed itself without her having to give it a moment's thought. She wanted to do it. She was beginning to tremble with excitement.

"Let's go out then, you and I. Let's go out now. I'll put my car in

your garage and you can get into it so the people next door don't see
and then we'll go somewhere. Let's do that, David, shall we?"

She wondered afterwards why she had enjoyed it so much. What had
it been, after all, as far as anyone else knew but two girls walking on
Hampstead Heath? If Angie had suggested that the two of them do it
she would have thought it a poor way of spending the afternoon. But
with David— She hadn't even minded that of the two of them he was
infinitely the better dressed, taller, better-looking, more graceful. She
didn't mind now as he came down the stairs and stood in front of her.

"Where shall we go?"

"Not the Heath this time," he said. "Let's go shopping."

He bought a blouse in one of the big stores. Christine went into
the changing room with him when he tried it on. They walked about
in Hyde Park. Later on they had dinner and Christine noted that they
were the only two women in the restaurant dining together.

"I'm grateful to you," David said. He put his hand over hers on
the table.

"I enjoy it," she said. "It's so—crazy. I really love it. You'd better
not do that, had you? There's a man over there giving a funny look."

"Women hold hands," he said.

"Only *those* sort of women. David, we could do this every Friday
you don't have to work."

"Why not?" he said.

There was nothing to feel guilty about. She wasn't harming Angie
and she wasn't being disloyal to Graham. All she was doing was going
on innocent outings with another girl. Graham wasn't interested in
her new friend, he didn't even ask her name. Christine came to long
for Fridays, especially for the moment when she let herself into Angie's house and saw David coming down the stairs, and for the moment when they stepped out of the car in some public place and the
first eyes were turned on him. They went to Holland Park, they went
to the zoo, to Kew Gardens. They went to the cinema and a man
sitting next to David put his hand on his knee. David loved that, it
was a triumph for him, but Christine whispered they must change
their seats and they did.

When they parted at the end of an evening he kissed her gently on the lips. He smelt of Alliage or Je Reviens or Opium. During the afternoon they usually went into one of the big stores and sprayed themselves out of the tester bottles.

Angie's mother lived in the north of England. When she had to convalesce after an operation Angie went up there to look after her. She expected to be away two weeks and the second weekend of her absence Graham had to go to Brussels with the sales manager.

"We could go away somewhere for the weekend," David said.

"Graham's sure to phone," Christine said.

"One night then. Just for the Saturday night. You can tell him you're going out with your new girl friend and you're going to be late."

"All right."

It worried her that she had no nice clothes to wear. David had a small but exquisite wardrobe of suits and dresses, shoes and scarves and beautiful underclothes. He kept them in a cupboard in his office to which only he had a key and he secreted items home and back again in his briefcase. Christine hated the idea of going away for the night in her grey flannel skirt and white silk blouse and that velvet jacket while David wore his Zandra Rhodes dress. In a burst of recklessness she spent all of two weeks' wages on a linen suit.

They went in David's car. He had made the arrangements and Christine had expected they would be going to a motel twenty miles outside London. She hadn't thought it would matter much to David where they went. But he surprised her by his choice of a hotel that was a three-hundred-year-old house on the Suffolk coast.

"If we're going to do it," he said, "we may as well do it in style."

She felt very comfortable with him, very happy. She tried to imagine what it would have felt like going to spend a night in a hotel with a man, a lover. If the person sitting next to her were dressed not in a black-and-white printed silk dress and scarlet jacket but in a man's suit with shirt and tie. If the face it gave her so much pleasure to look at were not powdered and rouged and mascara'd but rough and already showing beard growth. She couldn't imagine it. Or, rather, she could think only how in that case she would have jumped out of the car at the first red traffic lights.

They had single rooms next door to each other. The rooms were very small, but Christine could see that a double might have been awkward for David, who must at some point—though she didn't care to think of this—have to shave and strip down to being what he really was.

He came in and sat on her bed while she unpacked her nightdress and spare pair of shoes.

"This is fun, isn't it?"

She nodded, squinting into the mirror, working on her eyelids with a little brush. David always did his eyes beautifully. She turned round and smiled at him. "Let's go down and have a drink."

The dining room, the bar, the lounge were all low-ceilinged timbered rooms with carved wood on the walls David said was called linenfold paneling. There were old maps and pictures of men hunting in gilt frames and copper bowls full of roses. Long windows were thrown open onto a terrace. The sun was still high in the sky and it was very warm. While Christine sat on the terrace in the sunshine David went off to get their drinks. When he came back to their table he had a man with him, a thick-set paunchy man of about forty who was carrying a tray with four glasses on it.

"This is Ted," David said.

"Delighted to meet you," Ted said. "I've asked my friend to join us. I hope you don't mind."

She had to say she didn't. David looked at her and from his look she could tell he had deliberately picked Ted up.

"But why did you?" she said to him afterward. "Why did you want to? You told me you didn't really like it when that man put his hand on you in the cinema."

"That was so physical. This is just a laugh. You don't suppose I'd let them touch me, do you?"

Ted and Peter had the next table to theirs at dinner. Christine was silent and standoffish but David flirted with them. Ted kept leaning across and whispering to him and David giggled and smiled. You could see he was enjoying himself tremendously. Christine knew they would ask her and David to go out with them after dinner and she began to be afraid. Suppose David got carried away by the excitement of it, the "fun," and went off somewhere with Ted, leaving her and Peter alone together? Peter had a red face and a black moustache and beard and a wart with black hairs growing out of it on his left cheek. She and David were eating steak and the waiter had brought them sharp pointed steak knives. She hadn't used hers. The steak was very tender. When no one was looking she slipped the steak knife into her bag.

Ted and Peter were still drinking coffee and brandies when David got up quite abruptly and said, "Coming?" to Christine.

"I suppose you've arranged to meet them later?" Christine said as soon as they were out of the dining room.

David looked at her. His scarlet-painted lips parted into a wide smile. He laughed.

"I turned them down."

"Did you *really?*"

"I could tell you hated the idea. Besides, we want to be alone, don't we? I know I want to be alone with you."

She nearly shouted his name so that everyone could hear, the relief was so great. She controlled herself but she was trembling. "Of course I want to be alone with you," she said.

She put her arm in his. It wasn't uncommon, after all, for girls to walk along with linked arms. Men turned to look at David and one of them whistled. She knew it must be David the whistle was directed at because he looked so beautiful with his long golden hair and high-heeled red sandals. They walked along the sea front, along the little low promenade. It was too warm even at eight-thirty to wear a coat. There were a lot of people about but not crowds. The place was too select to attract crowds. They walked to the end of the pier. They had a drink in the Ship Inn and another in the Fishermen's Arms. A man tried to pick David up in the Fishermen's Arms but this time he was cold and distant.

"I'd like to put my arm round you," he said as they were walking back, "but I suppose that wouldn't do, though it is dark."

"Better not," said Christine. She said suddenly, "This has been the best evening of my life."

He looked at her. "You really mean that?"

She nodded. "Absolutely the best."

They came into the hotel. "I'm going to get them to send us up a couple of drinks. To my room. Is that okay?"

She sat on the bed. David went into the bathroom. To do his face, she thought, maybe to shave before he let the man with the drinks see him. There was a knock at the door and a waiter came in with a tray on which were two long glasses of something or other with fruit and leaves floating in it, two pink table napkins, two olives on sticks, and two peppermint creams wrapped up in green paper.

Christine tasted one of the drinks. She ate an olive. She opened her handbag and took out a mirror and a lipstick and painted her lips. David came out of the bathroom. He had taken off the golden wig and washed his face. He hadn't shaved. There was a pale stubble showing on his chin and cheeks. His legs and feet were bare and he was wearing a very masculine robe made of navy blue toweling. She tried to hide her disappointment.

"You've changed," she said brightly.

He shrugged. "There are limits."

He raised his glass and she raised her glass and he said: "To us!"

The beginnings of a feeling of panic came over her. Suddenly he was so evidently a man. She edged a little way along the mattress.

"I wish we had the whole weekend."

She nodded nervously. She was aware her body had started a faint trembling. He had noticed it, too. Sometimes before he had noticed how emotion made her tremble.

"Chris," he said.

She sat passive and afraid.

"I'm not really like a woman, Chris. I just play at that sometimes for fun. You know that, don't you?" The hand that touched her smelt of nail-varnish remover. There were hairs on the wrist she had never noticed before. "I'm falling in love with you," he said. "And you feel the same, don't you?"

She couldn't speak. He took her by the shoulders. He brought his mouth up to hers and put his arms round her and began kissing her. His skin felt abrasive and a smell as male as Graham's came off his body. She shook and shuddered. He pushed her down on the bed and his hands began undressing her, his mouth still on hers and his body heavy on top of her.

She felt behind her, put her hand into the open handbag, and pulled out the knife. Because she could feel his heart beating steadily against her right breast she knew where to stab and she stabbed again and again. The bright red heart's blood spurted over her clothes and the bed and the two peppermint creams on the tray.

THE ANDERSON BOY

by Joseph Hansen

Prothero, fastening the pegs of his car coat, pushed out through the heavy doors of the Liberal Arts Building, and saw the Anderson boy. The boy loped along in an Army surplus jacket and Army surplus combat boots, a satchel of books on his back. His hair, as white and shaggy as when he was five, blew in the cold wind.

He was a long way off. Crowds of students hurried along the paths under the naked trees between lawns brown and patched with last week's snow. But Prothero picked out the Anderson boy at once and with sickening certainty.

Prothero almost ran for his car. When he reached it, in the grey-cement vastness of Parking Building B, his hands shook so that he couldn't at first fit the key into the door. Seated inside, he shuddered. His sheepskin collar was icy with sweat crystals. He shut his eyes, gripped the wheel, leaned his head against it.

This was not possible. The trip to promote his book—those staring airport waiting rooms, this plane at midnight, that at four A.M., snatches of sleep in this and that hotel room, this bookseller luncheon, that radio call-in program, dawns for the *Today Show* and *Good Morning America*, yawns for Johnny Carson. Los Angeles in ninety-degree heat, Denver in snow, Chicago in wind, New York in rain; pills to make him sleep, pills to wake him up; martinis, wine, and scotch poured down him like water. Three weeks of it had been too much. His nerves were frayed. He was seeing things. The very worst things.

He drove off campus. By the shopping center, he halted for a red light. He thought about his lecture. It had gone well, which was surprising, tired as he was. But he'd been happy to be back where he belonged, earning an honest living, doing what he loved. Promotion tours? Never again. His publisher was pleased. The book was selling well. But Donald Prothero was a wreck.

The Anderson boy loped across in front of him. He shut his eyes, drew a deep breath, opened his eyes, and looked again. He was still sure. Yet how could it be? It was thirteen years since he'd last seen him, and more than a thousand miles from here. On that night, the boy had been a pale little figure in pajamas, standing wide-eyed in the dark breezeway outside the sliding glass wall of his bedroom, hugging a stuffed toy kangaroo. Prothero, in his panicked flight, naked, clutching his clothes, had almost run him over.

The boy had to have recognized him. Prothero was always around. He'd taught the boy to catch a ball, to name birds, lizards, cacti, to swim in the bright blue pool just beyond that breezeway. Prothero had given him the toy kangaroo. He should have stopped. Instead, he'd kept running. He was only eighteen. Nothing bad had ever happened to him. Sick and sweating, he'd driven far into the desert. On some lost, moonlit road, half overgrown by chaparral, he'd jerked into his clothes, hating his body.

He'd known what he had to do—go to the sheriff. He'd started the car again, but he couldn't make himself do it. He couldn't accept what had happened. Things like that took place in cheap books and bad movies, or they happened to sleazy people on the TV news. Not to people like the Andersons. Not to people like him. It could wreck his whole life. He went home. To his room. As always. But he couldn't sleep. All he could do was vomit. His father, bathrobe, hair rumpled, peered at him in the dusky hall when Prothero came out of the bathroom for the third time.

"Have you been drinking?"

"You know better than that."

"Shall we call the doctor?"

"No, I'm all right now."

But he would never be all right again. Next morning, when he stripped to shower, he nearly fainted. His skin was caked with dried blood. He nearly scalded himself, washing it off. He trembled and felt weak, dressing, but he dressed neat and fresh as always. He kissed his mother and sat on his stool at the breakfast bar, smiling as always. He was a boy who smiled. He'd been senior class president in high school, captain of the basketball team, editor of the yearbook. These things had been handed him, and he'd accepted them without question. As he'd accepted scholarships to University for the coming fall. As he'd accepted his role as Jean Anderson's lover.

His mother set orange juice in front of him, and his mug with his initial on it, filled with creamy coffee. He knew what she would do next. He wanted to shout at her not to do it. He didn't shout. They would think he was crazy. She snapped on the little red-shelled TV set that hung where she could watch it as she cooked at the burner deck, where his father and he could watch it while they ate. He wanted to get off the stool and go hide. But they would ask questions. He stayed.

And there on the screen, in black and white, was the Anderson house with its rock roof and handsome plantings, its glass slide doors, the pool with outdoor furniture beside it, the white rail fence. There in some ugly office sat the Anderson boy in his pajamas on a molded plastic chair under a bulletin board tacked with papers. The toy kangaroo lay on a floor of vinyl tile among cigarette butts. A pimply-faced deputy bent over the boy, trying to get him to drink from a striped wax-paper cup. The boy didn't cry. He didn't even blink. He sat still and stared at nothing. There were dim, tilted pictures, for a few seconds, of a bedroom, dark blotches on crumpled sheets, dark blotches on pale carpeting. Bodies strapped down under the blankets were wheeled on gurneys to an ambulance whose rear doors gaped. The sheriff's face filled the screen—thick, wrinkled eyelids, nose with big pores, cracked lips. He spoke. Then a cartoon tiger ate cereal from a spoon.

"People shouldn't isolate themselves miles from town." Prothero's father buttered toast. "Husband away traveling half the time. Wife and child alone. Asking for trouble."

"He came home." Prothero's mother set plates of scrambled eggs and bacon on the counter. "It didn't help."

"All sorts of maniacs running loose these days," Prothero's father said. "Evidently no motive. They'll probably never find who did it."

His father went to his office. His mother went to a meeting of the Episcopal Church altar guild. He drove to the sheriff's station. He parked on a side street, but he couldn't get out of the car. He sat and stared at the flat-roofed, sand-colored building with the flagpole in front. He ran the radio. At noon, it said the sheriff had ruled out the possibility of an intruder. The gun had belonged to Anderson. His were the only fingerprints on it. Plainly, there had been a quarrel and Anderson had shot first his wife and then himself. The Anderson boy appeared to be in a state of shock and had said nothing. A grandmother had flown in from San Diego to look after him. Prothero went home to the empty house and cried.

Now, at the intersection, he watched from his car as the boy pushed through glass doors into McDonald's. He had to be mistaken. This wasn't rational. Horns blared behind him. The light had turned green. He pressed the throttle. The engine coughed and died. Damn. He twisted the key, the engine started, the car bucked ahead half its length and quit again. The light turned orange. On the third try, he made it across the intersection, but the cars he'd kept from crossing honked angrily after him.

The Anderson boy? What made him think that? He'd known a runty little kid. This boy was over six feet tall. A towhead, yes, but how uncommon was that? He swung the car into the street that would take him home beneath an over-arch of bare tree limbs. The boy looked like his father—but that skull shape, those big long bones, were simply North European characteristics. Millions of people shared those. The odds were out of the question. It was his nerves. It couldn't be the Anderson boy.

He went from the garage straight to the den, shed the car coat, and poured himself a drink. He gulped down half of it and shivered. The den was cold and smelled shut up. He hadn't come into it yesterday when he got home from the airport. The curtains were drawn. He touched a switch that opened them. Outside, dead leaves stuck to flagging. Winter-brown lawn with neat plantings of birches sloped to a little stream. Woods were grey beyond the stream.

"Ah," Barbara said, "it is you."

"Who else would it be?" He didn't turn to her.

"How did the lecture go?"

"Who built the footbridge?" he said.

"The nicest boy," she said. "A friend of yours from California. Wayne Anderson. Do you remember him?"

"I was going to build it," he said.

"I thought it would be a pleasant surprise for you when you got home. I was saving it." She stepped around stacks of books on the floor and touched him. "You all right?"

"It would have been good therapy for me. Outdoors. Physical labor. Sense of accomplishment."

"He said you'd been so nice to him when he was a little boy. When he saw the lumber piled up down there, and I told him what you had in mind, he said he'd like to do it. And he meant it. He was very quick and handy. Came faithfully each day for a whole week. He's an absolute darling."

Prothero finished his drink. "How much did you have to pay him?"

"He wouldn't let me pay him," she said. "So I fed him. That seemed acceptable. He eats with gusto."

Flakes of snow began to fall. Prothero said, "It's hard to believe."

"He saw you on television in San Diego, but it was tape, and when he phoned the station, you'd gone. He thought you'd come back here. He got on a plane that night." She laughed. "Isn't it wonderful how these children just leap a thousand miles on impulse? Could we even have imagined it at his age? He got our address from Administration and came here without even stopping to unpack. Not that he brought much luggage. A duffel bag is all."

"You didn't invite him to stay."

"I thought of it," she said.

He worked the switch to close the curtains. He didn't want to see the bridge. It was dim in the den and she switched on the desk lamp. He was pouring more whiskey into his glass. He said, "I didn't ask you about Cora last night. How's she doing?"

"It's a miracle. You'd never know she'd had a stroke." He knew from her voice that she was watching him and worried. His hands shook. He spilled whiskey. "You're not all right," she said. "I've never seen you so pale. Don, don't let them talk you into any more book peddling. Please?"

"Is he coming here again?"

"Yes. This afternoon." She frowned. "What's wrong? Don't you want to see him? He's very keen to see you. I'd say he worships you—exactly as if he were still five years old."

"They don't mature evenly," Prothero said.

"He hasn't forgotten a thing," she said.

In thickly falling snow, the Anderson boy jumped up and down on the little bridge and showed his teeth. He was still in the floppy Army surplus jacket. The clumsy Army surplus boots thudded on the planks. He took hold of the raw two-by-fours that were the railings of the bridge and tried to shake them with his big, clean hands. They didn't shake. Clumps of snow drifted under the bridge on the cold slow surface of the stream. Prothero stood on the bank, hands pushed into the pockets of the car coat. His ears were cold.

"It would hold a car." The Anderson boy came off the bridge. "If it was that wide. Not a nail in it. Only bolts and screws. No props in the streambed to wash out. Cantilevered."

Prothero nodded. "Good job," he said. "Your major will be engineering, then, right?"

"No." Half a head taller than Prothero, and very strong, the boy took Prothero's arm as if Prothero were old and frail, or as if he were a woman, and walked him back up the slope. "No, my grandfather's a contractor. I started working for him summers when I was fourteen. I got my growth early." He stopped on the flags and pawed at his hair to get the snow out of it. His hair was so white it looked as if he were shedding.

"So you learned carpentry by doing?" Prothero reached for the latch of the sliding door to the den.

But the Anderson boy's arm was longer. He rolled the door back and with a hand between Prothero's shoulderblades pushed the man inside ahead of him. "It's like breathing or walking to me." He shut the door and helped Prothero off with his coat. "And just about as interesting." He took the coat to the bathroom off the den. He knew right where it was. Prothero watched him shed his own jacket there and hang both coats over the bathtub to drip. He sat on the edge of the tub to take off his boots. "I wouldn't do it for a living."

"What about coffee?" Barbara came into the den. Prothero thought she looked younger. Maybe it was the new way she'd had her hair done. "It will be half an hour till dinner."

"I'll have coffee." the Anderson boy set his boots in the tub. He came out in a very white sweater and very white gym socks. His blue jeans were damp from the snow. He lifted bottles off the liquor cabinet and waved them at Barbara while he looked at Prothero with eyes clear as water, empty of intent as water. "Don will have a stiff drink."

"I'll have coffee," Prothero said, "thanks."

The Anderson boy raised his eyebrows, shrugged, and set the bottles down. Barbara went away. The Anderson boy dropped into Prothero's leather easy chair, stretched out his long legs, clasped his hands behind his head, and said, "No, my major will be psychology."

"That's a contrast," Prothero said. "Why?"

"I had a strange childhood," the Anderson boy said. "My parents were murdered when I was five. But you knew that, right?"

Prothero knelt to set a match to crumpled newspaper and kindling in the fireplace. "Yes," he said.

"I didn't. Not till I was sixteen. My grandparents always claimed they'd been killed in a highway accident. Finally they thought I was old enough to be told what really happened. They were murdered. Somebody broke in at night. Into their bedroom. I was there—in the house, I mean. I must have heard it. Shouts. Screams. Gunshots. Only I blacked it all out."

"They said you went into shock." The kindling flared up. Prothero reached for a log and dropped it. His fingers had no strength. The Anderson boy jumped out of the chair, picked up the log, laid it on the fire. Sparks went up the chimney. He rattled the firescreen into place and brushed his hands.

"I stayed in shock," he said. "I couldn't remember it even after they told me. They showed me old snapshots—the house, my parents, myself. It still didn't mean anything. It was as if it was somebody else, not me."

"You wouldn't even talk." Prothero wanted not to have said that. He went to the liquor cabinet and poured himself a stiff drink. "It was on television. On the radio."

"Oh," Barbara said, coming in with mugs of coffee.

"I told you, didn't I?" the Anderson boy asked her.

"He's going to be a psychologist," Prothero said.

"I should think so," Barbara said, and took one of the mugs back to the kitchen with her.

The Anderson boy clutched the other one in both hands and blew steam off it. He was in the easy chair again. "I didn't utter a sound for weeks. Then they took me to a swim school. I was afraid of the water. I screamed. They had to call a doctor with a needle to make me stop."

Prothero blurted, "You could swim. I taught you."

The Anderson boy frowned. Cautiously he tried the coffee. He sucked in air with it, making a noise. He said, "Hey, that's true. Yeah, I remember now."

Prothero felt hollow. He drank. "Just like that?"

"Really. The pool—one of those little oval-shape ones. How the sun beat down out there—it made you squint." He closed his eyes. "I can see you. What were you then—seventeen? Bright red swim trunks, no?"

Jean had given them to him. He'd been wearing floppy Hawaiian ones. The red ones were tight and skimpy. They'd made him shy but she teased him into wearing them. He felt her trembling hands on him now, peeling them off him in the that glass-walled bedroom where the sun stung speckled through the loose weave of the curtains, and her son napped across the breezeway. Prothero finished his drink.

The Anderson boy said, "And there was a big striped beach ball. Yeah." He opened his eyes. "It's really fantastic, man. I mean, I can feel myself bobbing around in that water. I can taste the chlorine. And I won't go near a pool. They scare me to death."

"Every pool has chlorine and a beach ball." Prothero poured more whiskey on ice cubes that hadn't even begun to melt. "My trunks had to be some color."

"No, I swear, I remember. And that's why I came. When I saw you on TV, it began to happen. I began to remember—the house, the desert, my parents."

"The shouts?" Prothero asked numbly. "The screams? The gunshots?"

"Not that." The Anderson boy set down his mug. "I've read enough to know I'll probably never remember that." He pushed out of the chair and went to stand at the window. The light had gone murky. Only the snow fell white. "You can help me with the rest but you can't help me with that." He turned with a wan smile. "I mean, you weren't there. Were you?"

A shiny red moped stood under the thrust of roof above the front door. With the sunlight on the snow, it made the house look like a scene on Christmas morning. When the motor that let down the garage door stopped whining, Prothero heard the whine of a power saw from inside the house. The saw was missing from its hangers on the garage wall. He went indoors and smelled sawdust.

The Anderson boy was working in the den. He wasn't wearing a shirt. Barbara was watching him from the hall doorway. She smiled at Prothero. The noise of the saw was loud and she mouthed words to him and went off, probably to the kitchen. The Anderson boy switched off the saw, laid it on the carpet, rubbed a hand along the end of the eight-inch board he'd cut, and carried it to the paneled wall where pictures had hung this morning. He leaned it there with others of its kind and turned back and saw Prothero and smiled.

"Don't you ever have classes?" Prothero asked.

"I didn't get here in time to register," the Anderson boy said. "I'm auditing a little. I'll enroll for fall." He nudged one of the stacks of books on the floor. He was barefoot. "You need more shelves."

"I work in here, you know." The pictures were piled on the desk. He lifted one and laid it down. "I have lectures to prepare, papers to read, critiques to write."

"And books?" the Anderson boy said.

"No," Prothero said, "no more books."

"It was your book that led me to you," the Anderson boy said. "I owe a lot to that book."

Prothero looked at a photo of himself on a horse.

"I won't get in your way," the Anderson boy said. "I'll only be here when you're not." He looked over Prothero's shoulder. "Hey, you took me riding once, held me in front of you on the saddle. Remember?"

Barbara called something from the kitchen.

"That's lunch," the Anderson boy said, and flapped into his shirt. "Come on. Grilled ham-and-cheese on Swedish rye." He went down the hall on his big clean bare feet. He called back over his shoulder, "Guess whose favorite that is."

In the dark, Prothero said, "I'm sorry."

"You're still exhausted from that wretched tour." Barbara kissed him tenderly, stroked his face. "It's all right, darling. Don't brood. You need rest, that's all." She slipped out of bed and in the snow-lit room there was the ghostly flutter of a white nightgown. She came to him and laid folded pajamas in his hands. They were soft and smelled of some laundry product. "Sleep and don't worry. Worry's the worst thing for it."

He sat up and got into the pajamas. Buttoning them, he stared at the vague shape of the window. He was listening for the sound of the moped. It seemed always to be arriving or departing. The bed moved as Barbara slipped into it again. He lay down beside her softness and warmth and stared up into the darkness.

She said, "It's what all the magazine articles say."

"Who paid for the shelving?" he asked.

"You did," she said. "Naturally."

He said, "It's you I'm worried about."

"I'll be all right," she said. "I'll be fine."

The sound of the moped woke him. The red numerals of the clock read 5:18. It would be the man delivering the newspaper. He went back to sleep. But when he went out in his robe and pajamas to pick up the newspaper, he walked to the garage door. The moped had sheltered there, the new one, the Anderson boy's—the marks of the tire treads were crisp in the snow. There were the tracks of boots. He followed them along the side of the house. At the corner he stopped. He was terribly cold. The tracks went out to and came back from one of the clumps of birches on the lawn. Prothero went there, snow leaking into his slippers, numbing his feet. The snow was trampled under the birches. He stood on the trampled snow and looked at the house. Up there was the bedroom window.

In the new University Medical Center, he spent three hours naked in a paper garment that kept slipping off one shoulder and did nothing to keep from him the cold of the plastic chairs on which he spent so much of the time waiting. They were the same chairs in all the shiny rooms, bright-colored, ruthlessly cheerful, hard and sterile like the walls, counters, cabinets, tables.

Needles fed from the veins in his arms. He urinated into rows of bottles. A bald man sat in front of him on a stool and handled his genitals while he gazed out the wide and staring tenth-floor window at the city under snow. The paper of his garment whispered to and mated with the paper on the examination table while his rectum was probed with indifferent ferocity. The X-ray table was high and hard, a steel catafalque. He feared the blocky baby-blue machine above it would snap the thick armatures that held it and drop on him. The nurse need not have asked him to lie rigid. When he breathed in at her request, the sterilized air hissed at his clenched teeth. They told him there was nothing wrong with him.

"Do you remember the rattlesnake?" the Anderson boy asked. He had cut channels in the uprights and fitted the shelves into them. The workmanship was neat. Horizontals and verticals were perfect. He was staining the shelves dark walnut to match the others already in the den. The stain had a peculiar smell. Prothero thought it was hateful. The big blond boy squatted to tilt up the can of stain and soak the rag he was using. "We were always out there taking hikes, weren't we? And one day there was this little fat snake."

"Sidewinder," Prothero said. "I thought you weren't going to be here when I was here."

"Sorry," the Anderson boy said. "I loused up the timing on this. Can't stop it in the middle. I'll be as fast about it as I can." He stood up and made the white of the raw fir plank vanish in darkness. "If you want to work, let me finish this half and I'll clear out."

"I was trying to teach you the names of the wildflowers. It would have been February. That's when they come out. Sidewinders don't grow big."

"It's a rattlesnake, though. Poisonous. I mean, you let me handle a nonpoisonous snake once. I can still feel how dry it was. Yellow and brown."

"Boyle's king snake." Prothero took off his coat.

"You remember what you did?" the Anderson boy said.

"About the sidewinder?" Prothero poured a drink.

"Caught it. Pinned it down with a forked stick back of its head. It was mad. It thrashed around. I can shut my eyes and see that. Like a film."

"I didn't want it sliding around with you out there. You could stumble on it again. If I'd been alone or with grownups I'd have just waited for it to go away."

The Anderson boy knelt again to soak the rag. "You had me empty your knapsack. You got it behind the head with your fist and dropped it in the sack. We took it to the little desert museum in town."

"There was nothing else to do," Prothero said.

"You could have killed it," the Anderson boy said.

"I can't kill anything," Prothero said.

"That's no longer accepted," the Anderson boy said. "Anybody can kill. We know that now. It just depends on the circumstances."

Kessler was on the University faculty, but he had a private practice. His office, in a new one-story medical center built around an atrium, smelled of leather. It was paneled in dark woods. A Monet hung on one wall. Outside a window of diamond-shaped panes, pine branches held snow. From beyond a broad, glossy desk, Kessler studied Prothero with large, pained eyes in the face of a starved child.

"Has it ever happened to you before? I don't mean isolated instances—every man has those—I mean for prolonged periods, months, years."

"From the summer I turned eighteen until nearly the end of my senior year in college."

Kessler's eyebrows moved. "Those are normally the years of permanent erection. What happened?"

"I was having a crazy affair with, well, an older woman. In my hometown. Older? What am I saying? She was probably about the age I am now."

"Married?" Kessler asked.

"Her husband traveled all the time."

"Except that once, when you thought he was traveling, he wasn't— right?"

"He caught us," Prothero said. "In bed together."

"Did you have a lot of girls before her?"

"None. Sexually, you mean? None."

There were netsuke on the desk, little ivory carvings of deer, monkeys, dwarfish humans. Prothero thought that if it were his desk, he'd be fingering them while he listened, while he talked. Kessler sat still. He said:

"Then she did the seducing, right?"

"We were on a charity fund-raising committee." Prothero made a face. "I mean, I was a token member, the high school's fair-haired boy. The rest were adults. She kept arranging for her and me to work together."

"And after her husband caught you, you were impotent?"

"For a long while I didn't know it. I didn't care. I didn't want to think about sex." He smiled thinly. "To put it in today's parlance—I was turned off."

"Did the man beat you? Did he beat her?"

Prothero asked, "Why has it started again?"

"It's never happened in your married life?"

Prothero shook his head.

"How did you come to marry your wife? Let me guess—she was the seducer, right?"

"That's quite a word," Prothero said.

"Never mind the word," Kessler said. "You know what I mean. The aggressor, sexually. She took the initiative, she made the advances." His smile reminded Prothero of the high suicide rate among psychiatrists. Kessler said, "What do you want from me?"

"Yes," Prothero said. "She was the seducer."

"Has she lost interest in you sexually?"

"There's nothing to be interested in," Prothero said.

"Do you get letters from the woman?"

"What woman? Oh. No. No, she's—she's dead."

"On this book-promotion tour of yours," Kessler said, "did you see the man somewhere?"

Prothero said, "I wonder if I could have a drink."

"Certainly." Kessler opened a cabinet under the Monet. Bottles glinted. He poured fingers of whiskey into squat glasses and handed one to Prothero. "Been drinking more than usual over this?"

Prothero nodded and swallowed the whiskey. It was expensive and strong. He thought that in a minute it would make him stop trembling. "They had a child," he said, "a little boy. I liked him. We spent a lot of time together. Lately, he saw me on television. And now he's here."

Kessler didn't drink. He held his glass. "What's your sexual drive like?" he asked. "How often do you and your wife have sexual relations?"

"Four times a week, five." Prothero stood up, looking at the cabinet. "Did."

"Help yourself," Kessler said. "How old is he?"

The trembling hadn't stopped. The bottle neck rattled on the glass. "Eighteen, I suppose. With his father away most of the time, he took to me."

"Does he look like his father?"

"It's not just that." Prothero drank. "He keeps hanging around. He's always at the house." He told Kessler about the footbridge, about the bookshelves. "But there's more. Now he comes at night on that damn motorbike and stands in the dark, staring up at our bedroom. While we're asleep."

"Maybe he's homosexual," Kessler said.

"No." Prothero poured whiskey into his glass again.

"How can you be sure?" Kessler gently took the bottle from him, capped it, set it back in place, and closed the cabinet. "It fits a common pattern."

"He's too easy with women—Barbara, anyway, my wife." Prothero stared gloomily into his whiskey. "Like it was her he'd known forever. They've even developed private jokes."

"Why not just tell him to go away?" Kessler asked.

"How can I?" Prothero swallowed the third drink. "What excuse can I give? I mean, he keeps doing me these kindnesses." Kessler didn't answer. He waited. Prothero felt his face grow hot. "Well, hell, I told him to keep out from under my feet. So what happens? He's there all the time I'm not. He's got changes of clothes in my closet. His shaving stuff is there. My bathroom stinks of his deodorant."

Kessler said, "Are they sleeping together?"

"Barbara and that child?"

"Why so appalled?" Kessler said mildly. "Weren't you a child when you slept with his mother?"

Prothero stood up.

"Don't go away mad," Kessler said. "You're going to get a bill for this visit, so you may as well listen to me. You're afraid of this boy. Now, why? Because he looks like his father—right? So what happened in that bedroom?"

"That was a long time ago." Prothero read his watch.

"Not so long ago it can't still make you impotent," Kessler said. "Thirty years old, perfect health, better than average sexual drive. It wasn't a beating, was it? It was something worse."

"It was embarrassing," Prothero said. "It was comic. Isn't that what those scenes always are? Funny?"

"You tell me," Kessler said.

Prothero set down the glass. "I have to go," he said.

When he stepped into the courtyard with its big Japanese pine, the Anderson boy was walking ahead of him out to the street. Prothero ran after him, caught his shoulder, turned him. "What are you doing here? Following me?"

The boy blinked, started to smile, then didn't. "I dropped a paper off on Dr. Lawrence. I've been sitting in on his lectures. He said he'd like to read what I've written about my case—the memory loss."

Prothero drew breath. "Do you want a cup of coffee?"

"Why would you think I was following you?" The Anderson boy frowned at the hollow square of offices, the doors lettered with the names of specialists. "Are you feeling okay?"

"Nothing serious." Prothero smiled and clapped the boy's shoulder. "Come on. Coffee will warm us up."

"I have to get home. My grandparents will be phoning from Cali-

fornia." He eyed the icy street. "I sure do miss that sunshine." His
red moped was at the curb. He straddled it. Prothero couldn't seem
to move. The boy called, "The shelves are finished. I'm going to lay
down insulation in your attic next." He began to move off, rowing
with his feet in clumsy boots. "You're losing expensive heat, wasting
energy." The moped sputtered. If Prothero had been able to answer,
he wouldn't have been heard. The Anderson boy lifted a goodbye
hand, and the little machine wobbled off with him.

Prothero ran to his car and followed. The boy drove to the edge of
town away from the campus and turned in at an old motel, blue paint
flaking off white stucco. Prothero circled the block and drove into an
abandoned filling station opposite. The boy was awkwardly pushing
the moped into a unit of the motel. The door closed. On it was the
number nine. Prothero checked his watch and waited. It grew cold
in the car, but it was past noon. The boy liked his meals. He would
come out in search of food. He did. He drove off on the moped.

The woman behind the motel office counter was heavy-breasted,
middle-aged, wore rimless glasses, and reminded Prothero of his own
mother. He showed the woman his University ID and said that an
emergency had arisen: He needed to get from Wayne Anderson's
room telephone numbers for his family on the West Coast. The woman
got a key and moved to come with him. But a grey, rumpled-faced
man in a grey, rumpled suit arrived, wanting a room, and she put
into Prothero's hand the key to unit nine.

It needed new wallpaper, carpet, and curtains, but the boy kept it
neat. Except for the desk. The desk was strewn with notebook pages,
scrawled with loose handwriting in ballpoint pen with typewritten
pages with Xerox copies of newspaper clippings.

Dry-mouthed, he went through the clippings. They all reported the
shootings and the aftermath of the shootings. The Anderson boy's
mother had lain naked in the bed. The man had lain clothed on the
floor beside the bed, gun in his hand. Both shot dead. The child had
wandered dazedly in and out of the desert house in sleepers, clutching a stuffed toy kangaroo and unable to speak. Prothero shivered
and pushed the clippings into a manila envelope on which the boy
had printed CLIPPINGS. He picked up the notebook pages and tried

to read. It wasn't clear to him what the boy had tried to do here. Events were broken down under headings with numbers and letters. It looked intricate and mad.

Prothero tried the typewritten pages. Neater, easier to read, they still seemed to go over and over the same obsessive points. No page was complete. These must be drafts of the pages the boy had taken to Dr. Lawrence. A red plastic wastebasket overflowed with crumpled pages. He took some of these out, flattened them, tried to read them, looking again and again at his watch. For an instant, the room darkened. He looked in alarm at the window. The woman from the motel office passed. Not the boy. Prothero would hear the moped. Anyway, he had plenty of time. But the crumpled pages told him nothing. He pushed them back into the wastebasket. Then he noticed the page sticking out of the typewriter. It read:

Don Prothero seems to have been a good friend to me, even though he was much older. My interviews with him have revealed that we spent much time together. He taught me to swim, though I afterward forgot how. He took me on nature walks in the desert, which I also had forgotten until meeting him again. He bought me gifts. The shock of my parents' death made me forget what I witnessed that night—if I witnessed anything. But why didn't Don come to see me or try to help me when he learned what had happened? He admits he didn't. And this isn't consistent with his previous behavior. My grandmother says he didn't attend the funeral. A friendship between a small boy and a teenage boy is uncommon. Perhaps there never was such a friendship. Maybe it wasn't me Don came to see at all. Maybe he came—

Prothero turned the typewriter platen, but the rest of the page was blank. He laid the key with a clatter on the motel-office counter, muttered thanks to the woman, and fled. His hands shook and were slippery with sweat as he drove. He had a lecture at two. How he would manage to deliver it, he didn't know, but he drove to the campus. Habit got him there. Habit would get him through the lecture.

Barbara's car was in the garage. He parked beside it, closed the garage, went into the den, poured a drink, and called her name. He wondered at the stillness of the house. Snow began to fall outside. "Barbara?" He searched for her downstairs. Nowhere. She was never away at this hour. She would have left a note. In the kitchen. Why, when she was gone, did the kitchen always seem the emptiest of rooms? He peered at the cross-stitched flowers of the bulletin board by the kitchen door. There was no note. He frowned. He used the yellow kitchen wall-phone. Cora answered, sounding perky.

He said, "Are you all right? Is Barbara there?"

"I'm fine. No—did she say she was coming here?"

"I thought there might have been an emergency."

"No emergency, Don. Every day, in every way, I'm—"

"I wonder where the hell she is," he said and hung up. Of course she wouldn't have been at her mother's. Her car was still here, and Cora wouldn't have picked her up—Cora no longer drove.

Had Barbara been taken ill herself? He ran up the stairs. She wasn't in the bathroom. She wasn't in the bedroom. What was in the bedroom was a toy kangaroo. The bedclothes were neatly folded back and the toy kangaroo sat propped against a pillow, looking at him with empty glass eyes. Its grey cloth was soiled and faded, its stitching had come loose, one of the eyes hung by a thread. But it was the same one. He would know it anywhere. As he had known the boy.

He set the drink on the dresser and rolled open the closet. It echoed hollowly. Her clothes were gone. A set of matched luggage she had bought for their trip to Europe two years ago had stood on the shelf above. It didn't stand there now. Involuntarily, he sat on the bed. "But it wasn't my fault," he said. He fumbled with the bedside phone, whimpering, "It wasn't my fault, it wasn't my fault." From directory assistance he got the number of the motel. He had to dial twice before he got it right.

The motherly woman said, "He checked out. When I told him you'd been here, going through his papers, he packed up, paid his bill, asked where the nearest place was he could rent a car, and cleared right off."

"Car?" Prothero felt stupid. "What about his moped?"

"He asked me to hold it. He'll arrange for a college friend to sell it for him—some boy. Goldberg?"

"Where's the nearest place to rent a car?"

"Econo. On Locust Street. It's only two blocks."

                        *   *   *

The directory-assistance operator didn't answer this time. Prothero
ran down to the den. He used the phonebook. The snow fell thicker
outside the glass doors. He longed for it to cover the footbridge. Econo
Car Rentals was slow in answering, too. And when at last a dim
female voice came on, he could not get it to tell him what he wanted
to know.

"This is the college calling, don't you understand? He wasn't supposed to leave. His family are going to be very upset. There's been
a little confusion, that's all. He can't be allowed to go off this way.
Now, please—"

A man spoke. "What's this about Wayne Anderson?"

"He's just a student," Prothero said. "Do you realize he'll take that
car clear out to California?"

"That information goes on the form. Routinely," the man said. "Are
you a relative of this Wayne Anderson?"

"Ah," Prothero said, "you did rent him a car, then?"

"I never said that. I can't give out that kind of information. On the
phone? What kind of company policy would that be?"

"If this turns out to be a kidnapping," Prothero said recklessly,
"your company policy is going to get you into a lot of trouble. Now—
what kind of car was it? What's the license number?"

"If it's a kidnapping," the man said, "the people to call are the
police." His mouth left the phone. In an echoing room, he said to
somebody, "It's some stupid college-kid joker. Hang it up." And the
phone hummed in Prothero's hand.

He was backing the car down the driveway when Helen Moore's new
blue Subaru hatchback pulled into the driveway next door. He
stopped and honked. She stopped, too. The door of her garage opened.
She didn't drive in. She got out of the car, wearing boots and a Rus-
sian fur hat. Before she closed the door behind her, Prothero glimpsed
supermarket sacks on the seat. With a gloved hand, she held the dark
fur collar of her coat closed at the throat. The door of her garage
closed again. She came toward the snow-covered hedge. Snowflakes
were on her lashes. "Something wrong?"

"I'm missing one wife. Any suggestions?"

"Are you serious?" She tilted her head, worry lines between her brows. "You are. Don, dear—she left for the airport." Helen struggled to read her wristwatch, muffled in a fur coat cuff, the fur lining of a glove. "Oh, when? An hour ago? You mean you didn't know? What have we here? Scandal in academe?"

Prothero felt his face redden. "No, no, of course not. I forgot, that's all. Wayne Anderson came for her, right?"

"Yes. Brought her luggage out, put it in the trunk. Nice boy, that."

Prothero felt sick. "Did you talk with Barbara?"

"She looked preoccupied. She was already in the car." She winced upward. "Can they really fly in this weather?"

"There'll be a delay," Prothero said. "So maybe I can catch them. She's taking this trip for me. There are things I forgot to tell her. Did you notice the car?"

"Japanese. Like mine. Darling, I'm freezing." She hurried back to the Subaru and opened the door. "Only not blue, of course—I've got an exclusive on blue." Her voice came back to him, cheerful as a child's at play in the falling snow. "White. White as a bridal gown." She got into the car and slammed the door. Her garage yawned again, and she drove inside.

Defroster and windshield wipers were no match for the snow. The snowplows hadn't got out here yet. He hadn't put on chains, and the car kept slurring. So did others. Not many. Few drivers had been foolhardy enough to venture out of town. Those who had must have had life or death reasons. But life and death were no match for the snow, either. Their cars rested at angles in ditches, nosed in, backed in. The snow was so dense in its falling that it made blurs of the drivers' bundled shapes. They moved about their stranded machines like discoverers from some future ice age come upon the wreckage of our own.

A giant eighteen-wheeler loomed through the whiteness. Prothero was on the wrong side of the road. He hadn't realized this. The truck came directly at him. He twisted the wheel, slammed down on the brake pedal. The car spun out of control—but also out of the path of the truck. He ended up, joltingly, against the trunk of a winter-

stripped tree. He tried for a while to make the car back up, but the
wheels only spun.

He turned off the engine and leaned on the horn. Its sound was
frail in the falling snow. He doubted anyone would hear it up on the
empty road. And if the crews didn't find him before dark they would
stop searching. By morning, when they came out again, he might be
frozen to death. There was a heater in the car, but it wouldn't run
forever. He left the car, waded up to the road. He saw nothing—not
the road itself, now, let alone a car, a human being. He shouted, but
the thickly falling snow seemed to swallow up the sound. It was too
far to try to walk back to town. Too cold. No visibility. He returned
to the car. If he froze to death, did he care?

They found him before dark and delivered him, though not his car,
back home. For a long time he sat dumbly in the den, staring at his
reflection in the glass doors. Night fell. The doors became black
mirrors. He switched on the desk lamp, reached for the telephone,
drew his hand back. He couldn't call the police. Not now, any more
than on that desert night twelve years ago. He got up and poured
himself a drink. And remembered Goldberg. He got Goldberg's telephone number from Admissions, rang it, left a message. He sat drinking, waiting for Goldberg to call. *Barbara*, he kept thinking, *Barbara*.

He heard the Anderson boy's moped. He had been asleep and the
sound confused him. He got up stiffly and stumbled to the front door.
The snow had stopped falling. The crystalline look of the night made
him think it must be late. He read his watch. Eleven. He'd slept, all
right. Even the snowplow passing hadn't wakened him. The street, in
its spaced circles of lamplight, was cleared. He switched on the front-
door lamp. Goldberg came wading up the walk in a bulky wind-
breaker with a fake-fur hood, his round, steel-rimmed glasses frosted
over. He took them off when he stepped into the house. He had a
round, innocent, freckled face. Prothero shut the door.

"Why didn't you phone?" he said.

The boy cast him a wretched purblind look and shook his head.
"I couldn't tell you like that."

"Where is Anderson? Where did he tell you to send the money
when you sold his moped?"

"Home. San Diego," Goldberg said. "Is that whiskey? Could I have some, please? I'm frozen stiff."

"Here." Prothero thrust out the glass. Goldberg pulled off a tattered driving glove and took the glass. His teeth chattered on the rim. Prothero said, "What was his reason for leaving? Did he tell you?"

Miserably, Goldberg nodded. He gulped the whiskey, shut his eyes, shuddered. "Oh God," he said softly, and rubbed the fragile-looking spectacles awkwardly on a jacket sleeve, and hooked them in place. He looked at the door, the floor, the staircase—everywhere but at Prothero. Then he gulped the rest of the whiskey and blurted, "He ran off with your wife. Didn't he? I laughed when he said it, but it's true, isn't it? That's why you phoned me."

Prothero said, "My wife is in Mankato. Celebrating the birthday of an ancient aunt. I called you because I'm worried about Anderson."

"Oh, wow. What a relief." Goldberg's face cleared of its worry and guilt. "I knew he was a flake. I mean—I'm sorry, sir, but I mean, a little weird, right? I was a wimp to believe him. Forgive me?"

"Anything's possible," Prothero said.

"He really sold me." Goldberg set the empty whiskey glass on one of a pair of little gilt Venetian chairs beside the door. "See, I said if he did it I'd have to tell you. And he said I didn't need to bother—you'd already know." Goldberg pushed the freckled fat hand into its glove again. His child's face pursed in puzzlement. "That was kinky enough, but then he said something really spacey, okay? He said you wouldn't do anything about it. You wouldn't dare. What did he mean by that?"

"Some complicated private fantasy. Don't worry about it." Prothero opened the door, laid a hand on the boy's shoulder. "As you say, he's a little weird. Disturbed. And my wife's been kind to him."

"Right. He had a traumatic childhood. His parents were murdered. He told you, right?" Goldberg stepped out onto the snowy doorstep. "He said he liked coming here." Halfway down the path, Goldberg turned back. "You know, I read your book. It helped me. I mean, this is a killer world. Sometimes you don't think there's any future for it. Your book made me feel better." And he trudged bulkily away through the snow toward the moped that twinkled dimly in the lamplight at the curb.

*   *   *

Prothero shut the door and the telephone rang. He ran for the den, snatched up the receiver, shouted hello. For a moment, the sounds from the other end of the wire made no sense. Had some drunk at a party dialed a wrong number? No. He recognized Barbara's voice.

"Don't come!" she shouted. "Don't come, Don!"

And the Anderson boy's voice. "Apple Creek," he said. "You know where that is? The Restwell Motel." Prothero knew where Apple Creek was. West and south, maybe a hundred miles—surely no more. Why had he stopped there? The snow? But the roads would have been cleared by now. "We'll expect you in two hours."

"Let her go, Wayne. She had nothing to do with it."

"She has now. Don't worry. She's all right."

She didn't sound all right. In the background, she was screaming. Most of her words got lost. But some Prothero was able to make out. "He's got a gun! Don't come, Don! He'll kill you if you come!"

"I'll be there, Wayne," Prothero said. "We'll talk. You've got it wrong. I'll explain everything. Don't hurt Barbara. She was always good to you."

"Not the way my mother was good to you."

Prothero felt cold. "You keep your hands off her."

"We're going to bed now, Don," the Anderson boy said. "But it's all right. You just knock when you get here. Room eighteen. We won't be sleeping."

"Don't do this!" Prothero shouted. "It was an accident, Wayne— I didn't kill them! I was only a kid!"

But the Anderson boy had hung up.

The keys to Barbara's car ordinarily hung from a cup hook on the underside of a kitchen cupboard, but they weren't there now. He ran upstairs. He was the professor, but she was the absent-minded one in the family. She sometimes locked the keys inside her car—so she kept an extra set of keys. He fumbled through drawers with shaking hands, tossing flimsy garments out onto the floor in his panic.

He found the keys, started out of the bedroom, and saw the tattered toy kangaroo staring at him from the bed with its lopsided glass eyes that had seen everything. He snatched it up and flung it into a corner.

He ran to it and drew back his foot to kick it. Instead, he dropped to his knees, picked it up, and hugged it hard against his chest and began to cry, inconsolably. *Dear God, dear God!*

Blind with tears, he stumbled from the room, down the stairs, blundered into his warm coat, burst into the garage. When he backed down the drive, the car hard to control in the snow, twice wheeling stupidly backward into the hedge, the kangaroo lay facedown on the seat beside him.

He passed the town square where the old courthouse loomed up dark beyond its tall, reaching, leafless trees, the cannon on the snow-covered lawn hunching like some shadow beast in a child's nightmare. No—the building wasn't entirely dark. Lights shone beyond windows at a corner where narrow stone steps went up to glass-paned doors gold-lettered POLICE. He halted the car at the night-empty intersection and stared long at those doors—as he had sat in his car staring at the sunny desert police station on that long-ago morning. *I was only a kid!* He gave a shudder, wiped his nose on his sleeve, and drove on.

The little towns were out there in the frozen night that curved over the snowy miles and miles of sleeping prairie, curved like a black ice dome in which the stars were frozen. Only the neon embroidery on their margins showed that the towns were there. At their hearts they were darkly asleep, except for here and there a streetlight, now and then a traffic signal winking orange. He had never felt so lonely in his life. He drove fast. The reflector signs bearing the names of the little lost towns went past in flickers too brief to read.

But there was no mistaking Apple Creek, no mistaking that this was the place he had headed for in the icy night, the end of his errand, the end of Don Prothero, the end so long postponed. The Restwell Motel stretched along the side of the highway behind a neat white rail fence and snow-covered shrubs, the eaves of its snow-heaped roof outlined in red neon tubing.

And on its blacktop drive, not parked neatly on the bias in the painted slots provided by the management but jammed in at random angles, stood cars with official seals on their doors and amber lights that winked and swiveled on their rooftops. Uniformed men in bulky leather coats, crash helmets, stetsons, and boots stood around, guns on their thighs in holsters, rifles in their gloved hands.

Prothero left his car and ran toward the men. The one he chose to speak to had a paunch. His face was red under a ten-gallon hat. He was holding brown sheepskin gauntlets over his ears. He lowered them when he saw Prothero, but his expression was not welcoming.

Prothero asked, "What's happening here?"

"You want a room? Ask in the office." The officer pointed at a faroff door, red neon spelling out OFFICE. But at that instant a clutch of officers on the far side of the bunched cars moved apart and Prothero saw another door, the door they all seemed interested in. Without needing to, he read the numbers on the door. 18.

"My wife's in there!" he said.

The heavy man had turned away, hands to his cold ears again. But the brown wool hadn't deafened him. He turned back, saying, "What!" It was not a question.

"Barbara Prothero." He dug out his wallet to show identification cards. "I'm Donald Prothero."

"Hasenbein!" It was a name. The bulky man shouted it. "Hasenbein!" And Hasenbein separated himself from the other officers. He was at least twenty years younger than the bulky man. "This here's Lieutenant Hasenbein. You better tell him. He's in charge."

Hasenbein, blue-eyed, rosy-cheeked, looked too young to be in charge of anything. Prothero told him what seemed safe to tell. "He became a friend. He's disturbed."

"You better believe it," Hasenbein said. He dug from a jacket pocket a small black-and-white tube, uncapped it, rubbed it on his mouth like lipstick. "See that broken window?" He capped the tube and pushed it back into the pocket. "He fired a gun through that window." Hasenbein studied him. "Why did he stop here? Why did he telephone you? What does he want? Money?"

"There's something wrong with his mind," Prothero said. "He's got it into his head that I harmed him. He's trying to avenge himself. He phoned to tell me to come here. No, he doesn't want money. I don't know what he wants. To kill me, I guess. What brought you here?"

"The manager. He came out to turn off the signs. The switch box is down at this end. And he heard this woman screaming in unit eighteen—your wife, right? He banged on the window and told them to quiet down or he'd call the sheriff. And the kid shot at him. Luckily, he missed."

Prothero's knees gave. Hasenbein steadied him. "Is my wife all right?"

"There was only the one shot."

"There are so many of you," Prothero said. "Can't you go in there and get her out?" He waved his arms. "What's the good of standing around like this?"

"It's a question of nobody getting hurt needlessly."

"Needlessly! He could be doing anything in there—he could be doing anything to her!" Hasenbein didn't respond. He was too young. He was in way over his head.

Prothero ran forward between the cars. "Barbara!" he shouted. "Barbara? It's Don. I'm here! Wayne? Wayne!" Two officers jumped him, held his arms. He struggled, shouting at the broken window, "Let her go, now! I'll come in and we'll talk—I said I'd come, and I came!"

No light showed beyond the broken window, but in the eerie, darting beams of the amber lights atop the patrol cars Prothero saw for a moment what he took to be a face peering out. The Anderson boy said, "Tell them to let you go." Prothero looked at the officers holding him. They didn't loosen their grip on his arms. Hasenbein appeared. He twitched the corners of his boyish mouth in what was meant for a reassuring smile and turned away.

"Anderson?" he shouted. "We can't do that! We can't let him come in there—we can't take a chance on what will happen to him! Why don't you calm down now, and just toss that gun out here and come out the door nice and quiet with your hands in the air? We're not going to hurt you—that's a promise! It's a cold night, Anderson, let's get this over with!"

"Where's Barbara?" Prothero shouted. "What have you done with her? If you've hurt her, I'll kill you!"

"Sure!" the Anderson boy shouted. Now his face was plain to see at the window. Prothero wondered why nobody shot him. "You killed my father and my mother, why not me? Why not finish off the whole family? Why didn't you kill *me* that night? Then there wouldn't have been any witnesses!"

"I didn't kill them!" Prothero gave his body a sudden twist. It surprised the men holding him. It surprised him too. He fell forward. The cold blacktop stung his hands. He scrambled to his feet and lunged at the broken window. He put his hands on the window frame and leaned into the dark room.

"Your father came in from the breezeway—he was supposed to be out of town." Prothero heard his own voice as if it were someone else's voice. He had cut his hands on the splinters of glass in the window frame and could feel the warm blood. "He had a gun, and he stood there in the doorway and shot at us." Prothero wondered why the boy didn't shoot him now. He wondered what had happened to the officers. But the words kept coming.

"It was dark, but he knew where to shoot. I heard the bullet hit her. I've heard it in my nightmares for years. I rolled off the bed. He came at me, and I kicked him. He bent over and I tried to get past him, but he grabbed me. I fought to get away and the gun went off. You hear me, Wayne? He had the gun—not me. He shot himself! His blood got all over me, but I didn't kill him, I didn't kill him, I—"

"All right, sir." Hasenbein spoke almost tenderly. He took Prothero gently and turned him. He frowned at Prothero's hands and swung toward the officers standing by the cars, the vapor of their breath gold in the flickering lights. "We need a first-aid kit here." Hasenbein bent slightly toward the window. "Okay, Thomas—you can bring him out now."

"My wife," Prothero said. "Where's my wife?"

"Down at the substation where it's warm," Hasenbein said. "She's all right."

A frail-looking officer with a moustache brought a white metal box with a red cross pasted to it. He knelt on the drive and opened the box.

Carefully, he took Prothero's bleeding hands. Prothero scarcely noticed. He stared at the door of unit eighteen. It opened and a police officer stepped out, followed by the Anderson boy in his shapeless Army fatigues and combat boots. He was handcuffed. Under his arm, a worn manila envelope trailed untidy strips of Xeroxed newspaper clippings. He looked peacefully at Prothero.

"What did you do to Barbara?" Prothero said.

"Nothing. You put her through this—not me. You could have told me anytime." With his big, clean, carpenter's hands made awkward by the manacles, he gestured at the officers and cars. "Look at all the trouble you caused."

ELVIS LIVES

by Lynne Barrett

"Vegas ahead—see that glow?" said Mr. Page. "That's the glow of money, babes."

Lee looked up. All the way from Phoenix he'd ignored the others in the car and watched the desert as it turned purple and disappeared, left them rolling through big nothingness. Now lights filled his eyes as they drove into town. Lights zipped and jiggled in the night. Ain't it just like humans, he thought, to set up all this neon, like waving fire in the dark to scare away the beasts, to get rid of your own fear. Lights ascended, filling in a tremendous pink flamingo. There was something silly about Las Vegas—he laughed out loud. "What's so funny, man?" the kid, Jango, asked with that flicker in the upper lip he'd been hired for, that perfect snarl.

Lee shrugged and leaned his cheek against the car window, studying the lights.

"He's just happy 'cause we're finally here," said Baxter. "Here where the big bucks grow and we can pick some, right?" Baxter was a good sort, always carrying Lee and the kid. A pro.

"Just you remember, babes, we're here to collect the bucks, not throw 'em down the slots." Mr. Page pulled into the parking lot of the Golden Pyramid Hotel and Casino. On a huge marquee, yellow on purple spelled out E L V I S, then the letters danced around till they said L I V E S. The lights switched to a display of Elvis's face. "They do that with a computer," said Mr. Page.

Lee, Baxter, and Jango were silent, staring up. The same look came over them, a look that spoke of steamy dreams and sadness women wanted to console. The face—they all three had it. Three Elvises.

It was surely a strange way to make a living, imitating another man. Sometimes Lee thought he was the only one of them who felt its full weirdness. As they moved their gear into the suite of the hotel provided for Talent, the others seemed to take it all for granted. Of course, Baxter had been doing Elvis for ten years. And the kid thought this was just a temporary gig that would bankroll a new band, a new album, where he'd be his punk-rock self, Jango. But Lee had never been in show business before. Maybe that was why it kept striking him as something horrifying, bringing the dead to life.

He threw his suitcase on a bed and went out to the living room where the bar was stocked for Talent. He poured himself a whiskey and carried it back to sip while he unpacked. Or maybe, Lee thought, he was just getting into the role, like Mr. Page said to, understanding Elvis Presley's own hollow feeling. He played the sad, sick Elvis, after all. Maybe his horror was something the man had had himself in his later years as he echoed his own fame.

Lee snapped open his old leather suitcase, the same valise his mamma had forty years ago when she was on her honeymoon and getting pregnant with him. "Why buy something new?" he'd said when Cherry pestered him before their trip to New York that started all the trouble. "This is leather, the real thing—you can't get that anymore."

Cherry admired fresh vinyl, though. Her wish for new things was so strong it tore her up, he could see. Game shows made her cry. She entered sweepstakes, stayed up late at night thinking of new ways to say why she should win in twenty-five words or less. There was so little he could give her, he *had* to let her enter him in the contest the Bragg *Vindicator* ran. New York wanted, as part of its Statue of Liberty extravaganza, dozens of Elvis Presley imitators, and Bragg, Tennessee, was going to send one. Cherry had always fancied he resembled Elvis—she used to roll around with delight when he'd sing "hunka hunka burnin' love" to her in bed. She borrowed a cassette deck and sent a tape of him in, along with a Polaroid taken once at a Halloween party.

When he won, Lee said he didn't have the voice for it, that great voice, but they said no one would notice, there'd be so many others up there, he could mouth the words. He could too sing, Cherry said— oh, she still loved him then—he sang just beautifully in church. There was little enough Cherry was proud of him for anymore. They still lived in the trailer on his mamma's land, and now that he'd put it on a cement foundation and built on a porch it seemed all the more permanently true that they were never going to have it any better. He was picking up what jobs he could as an electrician since the profit went out of farming and their part of the country got depressed. A free trip to the Big Apple was maybe what they needed.

And it was fun. Lee liked the pure-dee craziness of the celebration, a whole city in love with itself. Cherry bought one of those Lady Liberty crowns and wore it with a sexy white dress she'd made with just one shoulder to it. When they were riding on the ferry he heard a man say, looking at them, "Duplication is America's fondest dream," and the man's friend laughed and answered, "Such is identity in a manufacturing nation." Lee glared at them, *I ain't a duplicate*, and anyway, he noticed, they both had the same fifties sunglasses and wrinkled jackets as everyone in soda-pop commercials. But when he got to rehearsal with all the other Elvises, he knew that, yes, it was hard to see them as real men instead of poor copies.

Because he had some age and gut on him, they put him toward the back, which was just fine. He didn't even feel too embarrassed during the show. After, he and Cherry were partying away when a white-haired man, very sharp in his western-tailored suit, came up and said Lee was just what he needed. Lee laughed loudly and said, "Oh, go on," but Cherry put Mr. Page's card inside her one-strap bra.

And when they were back home and Cherry sighing worse than ever over the slimy thin blond people on *Knots Landing*, Mr. Page showed up, standing on their porch with a big smile. Cherry had called him, but Lee couldn't be mad—it meant she thought he was good for something.

Mr. Page's plan was a show like a biography of Elvis in songs. And

he wanted three impersonators. For the kid Elvis, who drove a truck
and struggled and did those first Sun sessions and Ed Sullivan, he'd
found Jango, a California boy with the right hips and snarl. He had
Baxter, who had experience doing Elvis at his peak, the movie star,
the sixties Elvis. And he wanted Lee to be late Elvis, Elvis in gar-
gantuan glittery costumes, Elvis on the road, Elvis taking drugs, Elvis
strange, Elvis dying. "It's a great part, a tragic role," said Mr. Page.
"The King—unable to trust anyone, losing Priscilla, trapped by his
own fame—lonely, yes, tormented, yes, but always singing."

"Have you heard me sing?" Lee asked. He was leaning against the
fridge in the trailer, drinking a beer.

Mr. Page beamed at his pose, at his belly. "Why, yes," he said. "I
listened to the tape your lovely wife sent. You have a fine voice, big
whatchacallit, baritone. So you break up a bit now and then or miss
a note—that's great, babes, don't you see, it's his emotion, it's his
ruin. You'll be beautiful."

And Cherry's eyes were shining and Mr. Page signed Lee up.

"Check, check, one two three," Baxter said into the mike. His dark
Presley tones filled the Pharaoh's Lounge, where they'd spent the
morning setting up.

"Man, what a system," Jango said to Lee. "If they'd let me do my
stuff, my real stuff, on a system like this, I'd be starsville in a minute."

Lee looked over at the kid, who was leaning against an amp in the
black leather suit he'd had made after they played Indianapolis.
Jango wasn't saving a penny, really—he kept buying star gear.

"Yeah, one of these nights," Jango said, "when I'm in the middle
of a number—'All Shook Up,' I think—I'm just gonna switch right
into my own material. You remember that song I played you, 'Love's
a Tumor'?"

Lee grinned and finished his can of beer. Worst song he'd ever
heard in his life.

"Yeah, they'd be shook up then, all right," said Jango.

Mr. Page came over to them. "Go hit some high notes on there,
kid," he said, "let's check out the treble." While Jango went over to
the mike, Mr. Page said to Lee, "How you doing?"

Lee squatted down by the Styrofoam cooler they always stashed behind the drummer's platform, fished out a Coors, popped it open, stood drinking.

"You seem a little down, babes. Can I do something?"

"You can let me out of the contract so I can go on home," Lee said.

"Now, why should I do that? I could never find somebody else as good as you are. Why, you're the bleakest, saddest Elvis I've ever seen. Anyway, what home? But let me fix you up with a little something—some instant cheer, you know?" Mr. Page leaned over and put some capsules into the pocket of Lee's western shirt.

"What home" is right, Lee thought. He dug out one of the pills and washed it down with beer. Why not?

"Yeah, babes," said Mr. Page, "party. Here." He gave Lee a twenty. "After you get through here, go take a shot at the slot machines. But don't bet any more than that, right? We don't want you to lose anything serious."

"Oh, right," said Lee. He moved downstage to where Jango and Baxter were hacking around, singing "Check, Baby, Check" and dancing obscenely.

"My turn," said Lee and they went off so he could do his sound check.

He looked out into the theater filled with little tables set up in semicircles. Looks like a wedding reception, he thought, and laughed and then jumped back—he was always startled when he first heard his voice coming out through the speakers, it sounded so swollen and separate from him. It made him feel shy. He'd been so shy and frightened, he'd had to get drunk as hell the first time they did the show, and he'd been more or less drunk ever since. He started sweating as the men up on the catwalk aimed spots at him. They always had different lighting for him because he was bigger than the others. He squinted and went through his poses, singing lines for the sound check. The band took their places and swung in with him for a few bars of "Suspicious Minds," and then he was done and they started working on the band's levels.

He toured around the theater a bit, nodding to the technicians. Everywhere they went, Mr. Page hired local crews and Lee had found they were the only people he felt comfortable with. He'd always been good at electronics, ever since they trained him in the service, and hanging out with those crews the last few months he'd learned a lot. The Golden Pyramid had the most complicated system he'd seen. Up in the control booth, a fellow showed him the setup, talking about pre-sets and digital display. The show always had the backdrop with pictures suggesting what was happening in Elvis's life. Up until now they'd done this with slide projections, but here it would be computerized, same as the sign outside. Lee looked out at the stage and the fellow tapped into a keyboard and showed him Graceland all made of bits of light and then the blazing THE KING LIVES! that would come on with his finale.

He said thanks and made his way back down behind the set. Might be computers that were the brains of it, but there was a whole lot of juice powering the thing back here. Usually, he could stand behind the scrim backstage and follow what was going on, but now he faced a humming wall of wires. He knelt down by a metal box with power cables running out of it and held out his hands. Seemed like he could feel the electricity buzzing right through the air. Or Mr. Page's party pills, maybe.

Lee went through the backstage door and found his way into the casino. Bright? The place made his head whirl. He changed his twenty and the cashier gave him a chit. If he stayed in the casino an hour, he got a free three-minute call anywhere in the country.

He got a waitress to bring him a drink and started feeding quarters into a slot machine. He had a hard time focusing on the figures as they spun. He was buzzed, all right. He tried to go slow. If he made his money last an hour, who would he call?

When they began rehearsing in Nashville, he called Cherry every Saturday. Cherry would put on the egg timer so they'd keep track of the long distance. Mr. Page was giving a stipend, but he said the real bucks would have to wait till they were on the road. Lee, Baxter, and Jango shared a room, twin beds with a pull-out cot, in a motel. Mr. Page drilled them every minute, made them walk and dance and smile like Elvis. They practiced their numbers all day and studied Elvis footage at night. To Lee, it was a lot like the service, being apart from Cherry and having all his time accounted for. In '68, when

Lee was drafted, Cherry was still in high school—too young, her daddy said, to be engaged. He remembered calling her from boot camp, yearning for the sound of her but terrified when they did talk because she seemed so quiet and faraway. Just like she sounded now.

They'd barely started on the road, trying out in Arkansas and Missouri, when Cherry gave him the axe. She'd filed papers, she said when she called. She was charging him with desertion—gone four months now, she said.

"I'll come right back tonight," said Lee.

"I won't be here. You can send the support money through my lawyer." She said she'd hired Shep Stanwix, a fellow Lee knew in high school and never did like. He'd grown up to play golf and politics.

Cherry was still talking about money, how they wanted compensatory damages. "I gave up my career for you, Lee Whitney," she said.

She'd gotten her cosmetology license when they were first married, but she'd never gone past shampoo girl. She always said it was hopeless building up a clientele out there in the country, anyway—everybody already had their regular. Only hair she ever cut was his. She said she liked its darkness and the way it waved up in the front, like Elvis's.

"You can come along with us," Lee said, his voice breaking. "I'll get Mr. Page to hire you on as our hairdresser—he's spending money on that, anyway, dyeing us all blue-black and training our sideburns."

"There's no use talking. It's desertion and that's that."

"But, Cherry, this was all your idea."

"Oops, there's the timer," Cherry said. "Gotta go now."

"Wait—we can keep talking, can't we?"

"Save your money," Cherry said. "I need it." She hung up.

When he called back, he got no answer, then or all night. In the morning he called his mamma and she said Cherry'd been going into town till all hours since the day he left and now she'd taken everything out of the trailer that wasn't attached and moved into Bragg.

Lee went to Mr. Page—they were playing the Holiday House in Joplin, Missouri—and said he quit. That was when Mr. Page explained that Lee'd signed a personal-service contract for two years with options to renew and no way out. "Anyway," said Mr. Page, "what's one woman more or less? There's plenty of them interested in you—didn't you hear the sobbing over you last night? You were sad, babes, you were moving."

"Ain't the right woman," said Lee.

The women who came to the show only depressed him. Every night, die-hard Elvis Presley fans, women with their hair permed big and their clothes too girlish, were out there sighing, screeching, whimpering over Jango and Baxter and him. They'd come back after the show and flirt—hoping to get back their young dreams, it seemed to Lee, trying to revive what was in truth as lost as Elvis. Baxter took a pretty one to bed now and then—he considered it a right after so much time in the role. But then sometimes Lee wasn't sure Baxter fully realized he wasn't Elvis. Jango confided he found these women "too country." He waited for the big towns and went out in his punk clothes to find teenage girls who'd want him as himself. Lee slept alone, when he could get drunk enough to sleep.

When they were in Oklahoma, he got the forms from Shep Stanwix. He sent Cherry monthly checks. He had more money now than ever in his life and less to spend it on that mattered. Now and then he bought things he thought were pretty—a lapis lazuli pin, a silver bracelet made by Indians—and sent them to Cherry, care of Shep. No message—no words he could think of would change her mind.

One night in Abilene, Jango said he was going crazy so far from civilization and good radio and tried to quit. When he understood his contract, he went for Mr. Page in the hotel bar but Lee and Baxter pulled him off. Why? Lee wondered now. They dragged Jango up to his room and Baxter produced some marijuana and the three of them smoked it and discussed their situation.

"It's two years' steady work," Baxter said. "That's hard enough to find."

Lee nodded. He lay back across the bed. The dope made him feel like he was floating.

"Two years!" Jango stood looking at himself in the big mirror. "When two years are up I'll be twenty-three. Man, I'll be *old*."

Lee and Baxter had to laugh at him.

"Thing is," Lee said, "he tricked us."

"Not me," said Baxter. "I read the contract. Why didn't you?"

Lee remembered Cherry's hand on his shoulder as he signed. Remembered Mr. Page saying what a sweet Miss Liberty she made. And he felt Bax was right, a man's got to take responsibility for his mistakes.

Baxter passed the joint to Jango, who sucked on it and squinted at himself in the mirror.

"Mr. Page is building something up here," Baxter said. "What if we were quitting on him all the time and he had to keep training replacements? As it is—do you know he's hiring on a steady band? They'll travel in a van with the equipment while we go in the car. And he's upgrading the costumes. Not long, he says, till we'll be ready for Vegas. It's like what Colonel Parker did for Elvis."

Jango swiveled his hips slow motion in front of the mirror. " 'Colonel Tom Parker was a show-biz wizard,' " he quoted from his part of the show. He laughed. "Page wrote that. 'He guided me. And I—' " Jango's voice deepened into Memphis throb. " '—I came to look upon him as a second father.' Shit. Isn't one enough?"

"My daddy died when I was a boy," said Lee dreamily.

"Mine's a money-grubbing creep," said Jango. "Just like Page."

" 'Course, Elvis should have broken with him in the sixties," Baxter said. "That was his big mistake—he kept doing all those movies exactly alike because the colonel was afraid to change the formula. No, at the right moment, you've got to make your break."

Jango snarled at the mirror. "I'm gonna save every dollar, and when I've got enough I'm going to rent the best recording studio in L.A. and sing till I get Elvis out of my throat forever."

Lee circled quarters through the machine till they were gone. He hailed a waitress and while buying a drink asked her the time. Four o'clock here. It would be suppertime in Tennessee and darkness falling. Darkness never reached inside the casino, though—there were no windows, no natural light. Could you spend your life here and never feel it? He went and turned in his chit and they let him into a golden mummy case that was a phone booth.

He dialed his mamma. When she heard it was him, she went to turn down the pots on the stove and he was filled with longing for her kitchen. So far off. She exclaimed all right when he told her he was calling from a Las Vegas casino where he was to perform that night, but he could tell it didn't mean much to her, it was too strange.

The telephone glittered with gold spray paint.

"I only have a minute here, Mamma," he said, "so tell me straight—how's Cherry?"

"She was out here the other day. Kind of surprised me. Listen, Lee, you coming back soon?"

"I don't see how I can. Is something wrong?"

"It's Cherry. I know you're legally separate and all, but I don't think she's as hot on this divorce as she was. I was talking to my friend at the grocery, Maylene, she said to say hey to you—"

"Thirty seconds," said the casino operator.

"Mamma—" Lee's heart was pounding.

"Well, I mentioned Cherry stopping by for no good reason and Maylene said it's all over Bragg that Shep Stanwix dropped her to chase some country-club girl and—not that she deserves you, honey, after how she's acted—but maybe if you get back here right now, before she takes up with anyone else—"

Lee fell into a night with stars in it. When he came to, he was slumped in the golden mummy case and the line was dead. A lady from the casino leaned over him. "I'm fine," he said, "I just forgot my medicine." And he took a pill out of his pocket and washed it down with the last of his whiskey.

The lady was tall and half naked and concerned. "Is it heart trouble?"

"That's right, ma'am," said Lee. "My heart."

They ate dinner in their suite, at a table that rolled into the living room. The hotel sent up champagne in a bucket, for Talent on Opening Night. After they knocked it off, they ordered up some more to have while they got into costume in the mirrored dressing room off Jango's bedroom. Jango was ready first, in black jeans and a silky red shirt.

"Uhwelluh it's one fo' the moneyuh," he sang into the mirror, warming up. "Uhwelluh it's one," he sipped champagne, "one fo' the moneehah." He looked sulkier every day, Lee thought.

Baxter leaned into the mirror opposite, turning his head to check

the length of his sideburns, which weren't quite even. He plucked
out a single hair with tweezers. Beside him on the dressing table was
a tabloid he'd picked up that had a cover story about how the ghost
of Elvis got into a cab and had himself driven out past Graceland,
then disappeared. Baxter read all this stuff for research.

"Uhwelluh it's two fo' the show, damn it, fo' the showowhuh," sang
Jango.

Lee, who was drunk but not yet drunk enough to perform, confronted his costume. Hung up on wooden hangers, it looked like a
man he didn't want to be—the vast bell-bottoms, the jacket with
shoulders padded like a linebacker's, the belt five inches wide and
jewel-encrusted. The whole deal heavy as sin. Lee sighed, took off
his shirt and jeans, and stepped into the pants. The satin chilled his
legs. He wrapped a dozen scarves around his neck to toss out during
the show. He held out his arms and the others lifted the jacket onto
him. The top of the sequined collar scratched his ears. He sucked in
his stomach so they could fasten the belt on him, but just then Mr.
Page breezed in, all snappy and excited.

"You know who we got in the audience tonight, babes? You know
who?"

They all just looked at him.

"Alan Spahr!" he crowed. "I'm telling you, Alan *Spahr*. The Deal-
maker!"

Baxter said, "What kind of deals?"

"Hollywood deals, babes. Hollywood. The Emerald City. We're
talking moolah, we're talking fame, we're talking TV movie. What's
this, champagne? Yeah, let's have a toast here." He filled their
glasses. "Las Vegas to Hollywood—westward ho, babes, westward
ho!"

"The Emerald City," said Lee.

The champagne was cool and sour. He poured some more and
flexed his shoulders.

"Listen, man," Jango said. He still held Lee's belt in his hands. It
flashed in all the mirrors. "I am not going to Hollywood. There's no
way I'm going to play Elvis where anyone I know might see me."

"You won't be playing *in* Hollywood," said Mr. Page. "In fact, if
we make this deal I'm going to see to it that the script is expanded—

you know, do the whole life, filmed on location. Might even find a child, you know, to play Elvis at six, seven."

The poor kid, thought Lee.

"But a TV movie is on everywhere," said Jango.

"You betcha." Page drank champagne.

"I won't do it." Jango sneered. "Sue me—I don't have anything to lose."

Page leaned close to him. "Oh no? A lawsuit lasts a long, long time, babes, and I would own all your future work if you quit me. Any albums, any concert tours, I would own your damn poster sales, babes, get it?"

"Mr. Page," Lee said, "you don't need me and Jango for a TV movie. Baxter is the real talent here. On film they can do everything with light and makeup—Baxter can go from twenty to forty, can't you, Bax?"

Baxter looked up from his tabloid and said, "I know I could do it. It'd be my big break, sir."

"Babes, I can see you wouldn't be anywhere without me," said Mr. Page. "That there's three of you—" and he gestured at the mirrors where, small in his white suit, he was surrounded by ominous Elvises "—that's the whole gimmick. The three stages of the King. And with a TV movie behind us, babes, this show could run forever."

The show was on downstairs. Lee had finished the champagne and switched to whiskey. He had to find the right drunk place to be. The place without thought. Like in the Army. Which he never thought about. Stay stoned, don't think. He checked the clock—lots of time yet. He was in full costume, ready to go. Lee avoided the mirrors. He knew he looked bad. When he was young, he was dark and slim— like an Indian, Cherry used to say. Cherry had loved him. Cherry— better not think about Cherry. Where were his pills? In his shirt, on the floor of the dressing room. He tried to bend, but the belt cut into him, stopped him. He had to kneel, carefully, and then, as he threw back his head to wash down the pill, he saw. Who was that? Down on one knee, huge and glittery, his hair dark blue, his chest pale and puffy, his nose and eyes lost in the weight of his face. He looked like nothing human.

He had to get away. He took the service elevator down. It was smothering in there, but cold in the corridor, cold backstage. Sweat froze on his chest. Jango was on, near the end of his act. Off stage left, Lee saw Baxter talking to Mr. Page. He started toward them, then stopped.

Baxter had Mr. Page by his bolo tie. He pulled him close, shook him, then shoved him onto the floor. Baxter moved through the curtains, going on just as Jango came off with a leap, all hyped with performing and sparkling with sweat. Mr. Page was on his hands and knees, groggy. Jango did a swiveling dance step behind him and kicked out, sending him sprawling again. Then Jango saw Lee, shrugged, snarled, and flashed past.

Lee came forward and Mr. Page grabbed onto him and helped himself up. The old man was flushed—his red scalp glowed through his puffed white hair. He pulled at the big turquoise clasp of his tie and squawked. Baxter was singing "Love Me Tender." Lee shushed Mr. Page and led him behind the back wall, where the music was muffled. Page kept shaking his head and squinting. He looked dizzy and mean.

"I got contracts," he said. "There's nothing they can do." He started brushing his suit—dust smeared the white cloth.

Lee held out his shaking hands. "Look—I can't go on."

"Oh, babes, you're a young man still," said Page. "You just gotta cut down on the booze some. Listen, I'll get you something that'll make you feel like a newborn child."

"When I get too old and sick to do this, will you let me free?"

"At that point Baxter'll be ready for your job. And Jango for Baxter's." Page patted his hair.

"And you'll find a new kid."

"That's the way this business goes, babes. You can always find a new kid."

Lee's heart was pounding, pounding. He had to look away from Mr. Page, at the wall of wires, lights, power.

"Yeah, kids are a dime a dozen. But I'll tell you what, babes," said Mr. Page, "you were my greatest find. A magnificent Elvis. So courtly and screwed-up. A dead ringer."

Lee looked away, listening to the noise of his punished heart.

"A dead ringer?" He remembered the first pills Mr. Page handed him, just after Cherry—don't think about Cherry—and Lee knew he would die, would die as Elvis had and never again see his wife, his mother, Tennessee.

"Magnificent," said Mr. Page, "we gotta get that look on film! It's gorgeous, it's ruinous—I tell you, babes, it's practically tragic."

And Lee struck him, with all his weight and rage. Mr. Page fell onto the metal box where the power cables met. Lee bent over him, working fast. Green sparks sizzled around them.

Onstage, Lee was doing the talk section of his last song, "Are You Lonesome Tonight?" He was supposed to get lost, say what he liked, then come back into the lyric with a roar. "Tell me, dear—" he murmured into the mike and remembered Cherry when she was just out of high school. "You were so lovely." Wrapping a towel around him with a hug before she cut his hair. "And I know, I know you cared—but the—" Oh, what went wrong? "What went wrong? You sent me away—"

He stood still and looked out at the people sitting at little tables like they were in a nightclub. Well, it is a nightclub, he remembered, a hot spot. And he laughed. "Watch out." He shook his head. "Gotta get straight," he muttered and, looking out, saw tears on faces. "Don't cry for me," he said, "she's waiting." And then the song came back to him as it always returned, the band caught it up, and behind him the wall of light blazed and then ripped open with a force that cast him out into the screaming audience.

Breakfast was cheap here. Even in the diners they had slot machines. Lee drank black coffee and scanned the newspaper. He read how Liberace's ex-chauffeur had plastic surgery to look more like Liberace and about the tragic accident backstage at the Golden Pyramid. The manager of the ELVIS LIVES show had been caught in the electrical fire caused by the new computer system. Now, days after the accident, the newspaper was running follow-up stories about past casino fires.

The first day or so, there had been investigators around, in and out of their suite, but they mostly left Lee alone. He'd been onstage during the fire, when the finale display overburdened the wires, causing a short and an explosion. And there'd been so much emphasis on how complex the system was, digital this and that, no one imagined a hick like Lee could understand it. Even to him, his own quick work seemed now beyond himself, like something done by someone else. Lee supposed the other two thought they'd contributed to Page's death—left him woozy so he passed out backstage and got caught in the fire. But they accepted the explosion as the dazzling act of some god of electricity looking out for them. The second night, when Baxter came in with their contracts, they ripped them up without a word.

A new three-Elvis act was opening soon—Mr. Page had owned *them,* but anyone could use his gimmick. Baxter was staying on in Vegas—he'd pitched himself to Alan Spahr and they were talking about cable. This morning Jango was heading west, Lee east. Wasn't everyone better off? Except Page—better not think about Page. Already he seemed far back in time, almost as far back as things Lee'd done in the Army. Anyway, Lee blamed the pills. He'd sweated himself straight in the hotel sauna and meant to stay that way.

Lee paid for breakfast, picked up his old leather valise, and went outside. This early, you could smell the desert. The sun showed up the smallness of the buildings, their ordinariness squatted beneath their flamboyant signs. Lee stuck out his thumb and began walking backward.

The trucker who picked him up was heading for Albuquerque. At the truck stop there, Lee drank some beers and hung around till he found a ride through to Memphis. He had resolved to cut back to beer only until he saw Cherry again, but in the middle of the night in Texas he felt so good, heading home, home, home, he wanted to stay up the whole way and bought some speed for himself and the guys who were driving him, and knocked it back with some whiskey the driver had. Home, home, home, they tore along Route 40, through the darkness, listening to the radio. When Elvis came on, they all sang along.

"Hey, Lee, you sound like Elvis. Look a little like him, too," the driver said. He nudged his buddy. "What do you think? Have we picked up Presley's ghost?"

"Naw," said Lee. "He's dead and I'm alive and going home." Sipping whiskey through the night, song after song, he felt so happy he just sang his heart out.

CANDLES IN THE RAIN

by Doug Allyn

From a distance it looked like a modern-day siege of Rome. A small army of tents and campers were arrayed in a field across from the air-base entrance, and a ragged line of demonstrators were pacing along the shoulder of the road. But as I threaded my battered Chevy van past haphazardly parked cars and strolling protesters, the sense of conflict waned a bit.

The marchers were a mix of scruffy college kids and only slightly less scruffy adults in fashionably frayed denims, working-class duds à la Ralph Lauren. I gave them points for tenacity though. It was a chill, drizzly day but their spirits seemed high and dry.

Their placards were straightforward: No Nukes, No Incinerator. Ban Bombs and Toxic Waste. And on a less enlightened note: Don't Give America Back to the Redskins.

The airfield looked secure enough, protected by a fifteen-foot chain-link fence crowned with coils of bayonet wire. There were air police on duty at the gate, and a county sheriff's black-and-white parked on the shoulder of the road, flashers swirling slowly in the rain. The billboard beside the entrance was as formidable as the fence: lightning bolts clenched in an armored fist. Bullock Air Force Base, Strategic Air Command, Crater Creek, Michigan.

The air-police gate guard, starched and immaculate in white gloves

287

and cap, snapped to attention as I pulled up and gave me a smart salute. I returned it on reflex. Old habits die hard.

"Good afternoon, sir, welcome to Bullock. Can I help you?"

"My name's Delacroix. I have an appointment to see the base Commander, Colonel Webber."

"Yes, sir," the sergeant said. "Could I see some identification, please?" He gave my driver's license a quick onceover, then peered into an empty van. "Are you alone, Mr. Delacroix? It was my understanding that the Ojibwa Council was sending a delegation."

"They have," I said. "I'm it."

"I see," he said doubtfully. "A delegation of one?"

"You just have the one air base to give away, right?"

"Yessir," he said, frowning. "Still . . ." A bottle arched high in the air from behind the county black-and-white and smashed in the middle of the road, an explosion of beer foam and splintered glass.

"What's going on across the road, Sergeant?"

"The usual weekend demonstration," he said sourly, handing me a plastic visitor's card. "The local peaceniks have been picketing Bullock for years. Now that it's closing, they're griping about the base incinerator staying open. No pleasing 'em, I guess."

"At least they care enough to get wet," I said.

"Or they ain't got sense enough to get outa the rain," the sergeant said. "You'll find Colonel Webber at the base reception center just up the road. Please keep your pass with you at all times. Enjoy your visit, Mr. Delacroix." He waved me past and saluted. This time I didn't return it.

The base reception center was easy to find. It was the only building with cars parked in front of it. The others I passed were all closed and padlocked. On a field that once supported an entire wing of B-52s, only one solitary plane remained on the tarmac, a transport of some kind, with USAF markings. Beyond it, the runway stretched away endlessly into the silvery drizzle, silent and empty as a parking lot on the moon.

The portico in front of the entrance was draped with a red-white-and-blue banner. Welcome Michigan Ojibwa Council. I brushed the road dust off my corduroy sportcoat, straightened my tie, and walked in.

The reception room was jammed, a cocktail conclave in full swing, mostly civilians, men in suits, women in spring dresses, with a smattering of men in USAF blue uniforms scattered through the crowd. A gaggle of reporters and cameramen were clustered near the door and a refreshment table piled with sandwiches and hors d'oeuvres. Conversation died a slow death as I entered. I had a momentary flash of a half-forgotten dream, walking into high school minus my trousers.

A mid-thirtyish Native American woman in a stylish umber suit, her dark hair cropped boyishly short, left her companions and walked over. She had an open, honest face, and an eager smile. "Hello, I'm Eva Redfern. Are you with the delegation?"

"Not exactly," I said. "I am the delegation. My name's Delacroix, tribal constable from Algoma County. Can we talk somewhere for a moment? Privately?"

"I think we'd better," she said, her smile fading. A pity. I followed her back out under the portico. "Now, what's going on? When are the others arriving? We're running late already."

"We're going to run a little later, I'm afraid. The council voted last night to send me down to inspect the facility. If everything checks out, I've been authorized to accept the base on their behalf. Tomorrow."

"Tomorrow?" she echoed, stunned. "Are they out of their minds? I've spent weeks negotiating this arrangement. The transfer is set for this afternoon, and this is *not* a done deal, Delacroix. Not until the papers are signed. If we stall—"

"No one's stalling. Anytime somebody wants to cede land back to the tribes we'll take it. They just want me to take a last hard look at it."

"No offense, Mr. Delacroix, but this is hardly a police matter. Why did they send a constable?"

"Because I know a little about military bases. I served on a few. Look, I'm not your enemy, Miss Redfern, but I have my instructions. The sooner I carry them out, the sooner we'll get things back on schedule. Unfortunately, since they only called me in on this last night, I barely had time to scan the paperwork involved. Would you be kind enough to brief me? Please?"

Irritation and professionalism skirmished in her dark eyes for a moment. Professionalism won.

"All right. In a nutshell, Bullock is being closed. There was a government auction, and Kanelos Waste Disposal won the bidding. But since all Mr. Kanelos really wants is the base waste incinerator and a few hundred acres of runway for parking, he's offered to cede the base to the Ojibwa Council in return for a permanent lease on the incinerator and parking area."

"Which sounds almost too good to be true. Why should he give us the base?"

"To avoid taxes," she said simply. "Since the state can't tax tribal land, Mr. Kanelos can operate the waste facility tax free, and we get roughly five thousand acres of land, *gratis.*"

"Most of which is covered with concrete," I said.

"Dammit, it's still a good deal for us, Delacroix. Have you ever heard the old saying about looking a gift horse in the mouth?"

"Yes, ma'am. I also remember one about Greeks bearing gifts. Shall we get on with this?"

"I guess we haven't much choice. But by God, you'd better not blow this deal."

Redfern led me through the crush to a corner where the base commander was holding court. There was no other word for it. In his impeccably tailored blue uniform, close-cropped sandy hair, with just a trace of silver at the temples, Webber cut a striking military figure. The granite-faced black master sergeant standing half a pace behind him added to the effect. Webber was chatting with a gaunt vampire of a man, fortyish, with blue jowls, and fluid-filled pouches under his eyes. He was wearing a dark suit and shirt, a single strand of gold chain nestling in the hollow of his throat.

"Colonel Webber, Mr. Kanelos," Redfern said, "I'd like to introduce Mr. Delacroix, of the Ojibwa Council." She gave them a quick briefing on the situation. I expected annoyance, and got it.

"Mr. Delacroix," Webber said coolly, not bothering to offer his hand, "what's the problem? I was under the impression everything was arranged. Some members of the council having . . . reservations, so to speak?"

"As far as I know, everything's a go, Colonel," I said. "Or it will be as soon as I complete my inspection."

"But what kind of a survey can you do in a few hours?" Kanelos said heatedly. "The base is six thousand acres. Look, I've put myself on the line for you people. I stretched myself to my financial limits to win the bidding and I'm even giving hiring preference to Indians at the incinerator facility. Hell, I should think you people might show a bit more gratitude—"

"Easy, Frank," Webber interrupted, "the constable's just following orders, and as a soldier I can relate to that. Sergeant Jenkins, why don't you give Delacroix a tour of the base, show him whatever he wants to see. Frank, we'd better talk to the newspeople. I don't want any bad press over this." He stalked off without a backward glance, sweeping Kanelos along in his wake.

The sergeant shrugged. "Don't mind the boss. He's used to having people jump when he says frog. What do you want to see, Mr. Delacroix?"

"The major facilities, PX, hangars. As much as I can in the time we have," I said, watching the colonel and Kanelos disappear into the mob scene.

"I'm coming too," Redfern said.

"Then we'd better get started," Jenkins said. "The power's already been shut off to the perimeter lighting. When it gets dark out on the field these days, it really gets dark."

"What happened to the command and electronics bunkers?" I asked. We were in a closed Jeep, humming down a rain-slick runway toward the shadowy mountains of a hangar, Jenkins driving, me riding shotgun, Redfern in the back seat.

"All strategic or classified equipment was dismantled and shipped back to SAC headquarters, or destroyed on site," Jenkins said. "We blew the bunkers, filled 'em in, and laid sod on the graves. How do you know about bunkers? You serve on a base?"

"A few," I said. "U Bon, Thailand, and Tan Son Nhut."

"No kidding? I was U Bon during the war. When were you there?"

"When I was too young to know better."

"I know the feeling." Jenkins smiled, relaxing a little. "Okay, if you know bases, then you know there ain't all that much more I can show you. You've seen most of the buildings, there's really nothin' else to see but a lotta open concrete."

"And trucks," I said. "What are all those trucks doing on the far end of the runway?"

"Toxic waste tankers, waitin' their turn at the incinerator. Must be twenty of 'em down there at any given time. They come from all over the state. It's big business, waste disposal. It's closed for the weekend now, but come Monday they'll be humpin'. Pardon my French, ma'am. Sometimes when the wind's right, it smells a little funky, but mostly you can't hardly tell it's there. You want to drive over, take a closer look?"

"No, what Kanelos does with his end of the base in his business. I think I've seen enough. Let's head back."

"Fine by me," Jenkins said, wheeling the Jeep in a quick U-turn. "I served three tours on Bullock. Hate to see it like this. It's like attendin' your own funeral."

"I should think you'd be happy," Eva said. "No more wars, or at least no big ones."

"Oh, I don't miss war, ma'am. Nobody hates fightin' more'n the people who might have to bleed. But soldierin's an honest trade, and not such a bad life. How 'bout you, Delacroix? You ever miss the life?"

"The people sometimes," I said. "Never the life. What's all the hubbub over by the entrance?"

"Antinuke parade." Jenkins grinned, checking his watch. "Right on time, as usual. Wanna check it out? Way the world's goin', it may be the last one."

Redfern sighed. "I certainly hope so."

"Yes ma'am," Jenkins said, his smile fading, "me too."

Jenkins parked the Jeep in the reception-center lot and the three of us trotted briskly to the portico. The rain had started again, a steady, chilly drizzle, driven by the wind. The media people and some of the party-goers had wandered out to watch, but except for the cameramen filming the march through the fence, no one strayed from shelter. There was no reason to do so.

The local peace movement seemed to be winding down with a whimper, not a bang. A line of demonstrators formed a lopsided ring in the road opposite the gate. They were carrying candles, but except for a few who had umbrellas as well, most of the flames guttered in the first few moments. Still, I had to admire their persistence. They marched in a circle in the blustery dusk and drizzle for ten minutes or so, singing "Give Peace a Chance," out of tune, and out of step with each other. And with the times.

"Not much of a show, is it?" Colonel Webber said, moving up beside me. "Not like the old days. A few years ago there were a couple of hundred every weekend, blocking the entrance, chaining themselves to the fence, and being a general nuisance. Arrogant fools, the lot of them. They simply didn't see the big picture."

"I served a dozen years, in two wars, and I'm not sure I ever saw it either," I said mildly. "Maybe the picture seems clearer up at forty thousand feet."

"Perhaps it does," Webber said. "Sergeant Jenkins tells me you've finished your tour. I take it you're satisfied?"

"Yes, sir. As far as I'm concerned we can finalize the transfer tomorrow. I'll phone the council tonight, and—"

But Webber wasn't listening. He'd turned, frowning, peering into the drizzle. Even the marchers gradually stumbled to a halt, listening. Out on the tarmac, behind the curtain of rain, there was the sound of drumming. Tom-toms. And the chanting of many voices, instantly recognizable as Native Americans. But not a tribe I knew. Not Ojibwa.

"Sergeant," Webber snapped, "get out there and secure that aircraft. I don't know what's—"

WHOOOMP! Suddenly, far out on the runway, a pillar of fire erupted, a hundred-foot geyser of flame. And then there was an unearthly wail, louder than the drums and chanting. And a figure came running toward us out of the rain, a human being, ablaze, engulfed in fire, howling like a beast. He staggered, then fell to his knees, crawling like a smashed insect, screaming.

Jenkins was the first to react, sprinting for the Jeep. I followed, scrambling into the passenger's seat as he gunned the Jeep out of the lot and raced down the runway toward the burning man.

He jammed on the brakes a few yards short of the figure on the tarmac, and I banged headfirst into the windshield, hard. Jenkins yanked a portable fire extinguisher from its dash clip and ran to the figure cowering on the concrete. I followed on shaky legs. He quickly fogged the man down, then trotted beyond him and killed two smaller fires as well.

I knelt beside the blackened man, dazed, uncertain. His clothes were still smoldering, and he was moaning, in soul-deep agony. And I didn't know what to do. He smelled smoky sweet, almost . . . I recoiled mentally from the thought.

"Mister," I pleaded softly, "please, just hang on, okay? Help's coming. . . ."

The moaning stopped. And the breathing. My God. I tried to roll him onto his back to give mouth-to-mouth, but his body was rigid. His arms were locked over his face as though they were welded to it and I couldn't pull them away. And then a piece of seared flesh peeled off in my hand, and I lurched to my feet, gagging, and stumbled off down the runway, staggering like a gut-shot bear. Fleeing the smoking body. And the horror.

Jenkins caught me after twenty yards or so, grasping my shoulders, steadying me down to a walk, then stopping me. We stood there for a long time in silence, in the rain.

Behind us, the sheriff's patrol car screeched to a halt beside the Jeep. Doors slammed. People were shouting. And still Jenkins and I stood there. Holding each other. Like family at a funeral.

"Are you all right?" he asked at last.

"Yeah," I managed. My voice sounded as weak and shaky as I felt. "Is he . . . ?"

"He was dead before we got there," Jenkins said, releasing me cautiously, as if afraid I might fall. "He just didn't know it. There was nothing you could do. Nothing anyone could do."

He turned and trudged slowly back to the crowd gathered around the figure on the field, shrouded now by a blanket.

The sheriff rose slowly from beside the body, carefully unfolding the charred remains of a wallet.

"Buck," he read softly, "Geronimo G. My God, it's Jerry Buck." Eva Redfern paled and turned away, her eyes swimming. I touched her arm.

"You know him?" I said.

"I, ahm, no," she said, swallowing. "Not really. He's Native American but he's not Ojibwa. He's just a side—he came up from Detroit a year or so ago."

"A sidewalk Indian," I said.

"Yes," she nodded. "Lakota, I think. From out West somewhere. Montana maybe. Drank his way out of a line job at Ford. Moved up here, did odd jobs. He was an alcoholic."

"Why would he do this?"

"I . . . don't know. I didn't really know him well."

"When you got to him, did he say anything to you?" the sheriff asked me.

"No, he . . . didn't speak. He couldn't."

"Well, it's apparently a suicide," the sheriff said, glancing around. "Had to be. Nobody else could have been near him out here. Found a gas can back on the tarmac maybe sixty yards away. And what's left of a pile of rags. And a boom box. That's what the Indian music was. Apparently he just turned on the tape, doused himself with gas, and, ahm . . . set himself afire. Crazy. Had to be crazy."

"Maybe not," I said slowly.

"Why not?" Jenkins asked. "You know him?"

"No. But even a crazy wouldn't choose to die like this. It's too . . . horrible."

"But what makes you think—?"

"Dammit, I've seen this before! My first tour in 'Nam, the monks were burning themselves in the damn streets! And people said they were crazy. And nobody listened to them!"

"Easy, bro," Jenkins said quietly. "This ain't no Vietnamese police state. We're in backwoods freakin' Michigan. If the man had a point to make, he didn't have to smoke himself to do it. All he had to do was walk up and speak his piece, right? Nobody woulda stopped him."

"I don't know," I said, swallowing, trying to clear my head. "All I know is, the base was supposed to be transferred to the Ojibwa today. He must have been trying to stop it for some reason."

"You can't be sure of that," Jenkins said.

"You're right, I'm not. But I'm not going to go ahead with the transfer until we know."

"Look, Mr. Delacroix," Colonel Webber said, stiffening, "I know this has been a shock, to all of us. But surely the act of the demented individual—"

"You don't know he was demented," I said.

"But he *was* crazy, or nearly so," Redfern said. "He was borderline retarded and an alcoholic as well. Who knows what was in his mind? Delacroix, the colonel's right, this is too important to our people to stop now. He was just—"

"A drunk," I finished. "And not even Ojibwa. So forget it? Business as usual?"

"That isn't what I meant," she said, flushing. "It's just that—"

"Mr. Delacroix, I've tried to be patient, but I have my orders," Webber interrupted. "I agreed to delay the proceedings until tomorrow, but that's the best I can do. I must have your decision then, or I'll have to withdraw from our agreement. Since the man's death occurred on the base, it's technically a military matter, so if you wish to make inquiries, I can loan you Sergeant Jenkins to give you some official standing. I assume you'd have no objections, Sheriff Brandon?"

Brandon shrugged. "No, sir. It's a straightforward suicide. The decedent's state of mind isn't really a police matter, and frankly I've got my hands full as it is. As long as you don't harass anybody, make all the inquiries you like."

"You don't seem too happy about this," I said to Jenkins. We were in his Jeep, headed toward the main gate. Eva Redfern had stayed behind to try to pacify the colonel and Kanelos.

"I'm not," Jenkins said bluntly, keeping his eyes on the road. "I put up with these peacenik crazies every weekend for years, picketing the base, blockin' the gate to get themselves arrested. Now I'm one day away from gettin' outa here and . . . I got my own job to do, you know?"

"Maybe if you'd done it better we wouldn't be in this mess."

"What's that supposed to mean?"

"You're in charge of base security, right? So how did this guy manage to get out in the middle of the runway?"

"Wouldn't be hard. He couldn't have climbed the fence carrying the boom box and a gas can, so I'm guessin' he just cut the fence and walked in. The electronic barriers were disconnected last month when the last of the classified equipment was shipped out."

"And the fence isn't patrolled?"

"We inspect the perimeter once a shift, about every eight hours. I've only got six men and I need 'em at the gate."

"What about guard dogs? Most bases use them on the perimeter."

"We, ahm, we haven't used the dogs in a while. To be honest, I haven't worried much about security. Hell, there's nothin' left on Bullock worth stealin'."

"Maybe not," I said grimly, "but apparently there was something worth dying for."

Jenkins eased the Jeep cautiously down the lane between the demonstrators' tents and campers. There were only a few dozen left. He parked beside a battered trailer, covered with bumper stickers: No Nukes, Peace Now. The usual.

"This is Doc Klein's trailer," Jenkins said, switching off the Jeep. "He's been organizing peace marches since the sixties, and bugging me for at least ten years. If anybody knows anything about your guy, the doc will."

"Will he talk to me? With you there I mean?"

"No sweat," Jenkins said drily. "Gettin' the doc to talk isn't a problem. It's gettin' him to shut up. Come on."

We jogged through the downpour to the trailer door. Jenkins rapped and after a moment the door swung open, revealing a squat stump of a man, fiftyish, balding, with a fringe of shoulder-length, baby-fine blond hair, and a neatly trimmed blond beard. A bulldog pipe was clamped in the corner of his jaw. "Well, well," he said evenly, "if it isn't my favorite arresting officer."

"Doc," Jenkins said, "can we see you a minute?"

"Of course, come in, come in. I wouldn't leave a dog out on a night like this. Or a sergeant."

Jenkins introduced me to Klein, and we shook hands. The three of us filled the postage-stamp camper like pickles in a jar. I sat on the narrow cot that stretched across one end of the room, Jenkins leaned against the door, while Klein sat in the lone chair at the tiny table for one. A pot was burbling on the small camp stove. The aroma of chili and cherry-blend pipe smoke filled the room like incense in a bazaar.

"Mr. Delacroix, I can't tell you how sorry I am about what happened today," Dr. Klein said earnestly. "We're on opposite sides of this matter politically but, well, I'm sorry. It's a terrible irony that after a dozen years of peaceful demonstrations, such a thing would happen on the last day."

"Did you know the man who died, Doctor?" I asked.

He nodded. "A little. As well as anyone, I suppose. He, ahm, he drank, you know."

"So I understand. You said we're on opposite sides. Why? What have you got against us?"

"Against the Ojibwa? Nothing. My goodness, your people have been my life's work."

"The doc's an archaeologist, specializin' in Native American culture," Jenkins said. "When he's not playin' rabblerouser, that is."

"I see," I said. "Then why is your group opposed to our taking over the base?"

"Because of the way it was arranged. We believe you're being used."

"Used by whom?"

"By Kanelos, and Webber as well. Kanelos didn't win the bidding, you know. The high bidder was a salvage company that intended to dismantle the buildings and tear up the runway for the scrap concrete. Colonel Webber awarded the bid to Mr. Kanelos as being least disruptive to the community."

"Hey, he was right," Jenkins put in. "It'd take a helluva lot of blasting to break up the runway. It's a foot thick, most places."

"More disruptive than flying B-52s loaded with nuclear weapons out of there twenty-four hours a day?" Klein countered. "At least when the blasting was finished, we'd have the land back. As it is, we're trading one hazardous nuisance for another."

"But the incinerator isn't new, is it?" I asked.

"No," Klein said, "but it's never been operated on the scale it is now. And by trading you the land in return for a lifetime lease, Kanelos not only avoids paying taxes, he also avoids federal EPA inspections. Did you know that?"

"No," I said, glancing at Jenkins. "I didn't. And Jerry Buck? Was he strongly against the transfer too?"

"Jerry? No, not that I know of," Klein said, puzzled. "He was hardly the political type."

"You mean he wasn't part of your—group?"

"No. Not at all."

"But you said you knew him."

"I did, but not from the movement. We're doing an archaeological dig at an old Anishnabeg burial ground just west of the base. Jerry worked for me there, doing manual labor, catch as catch can. For beer money, really."

"Look, I don't understand, Doctor," I said. "If he wasn't political, why on earth would he have done what he did?"

"I honestly don't know. I've been asking myself the same thing since they told me it was Jerry. Joe Gesh might be able to tell you more."

"Joe Gesh?" I noticed that Jenkins stiffened at the mention of the name.

"He's a local character, an Ojibwa, lives in a shack on the edge of Bullock swamp near the burial ground. Jerry was staying with him out there, learning what he could."

"About what?"

"How to live in the past." Klein smiled. "Old Joe's an atavism, a throwback, the last of the wild Indians. He helps me at the dig occasionally, identifying tufts of decorative fur or animal tracks. He's incredibly knowledgeable."

"Oughta be," Jenkins said. "He eats most anything that walks or crawls back there."

"I guess we'd better talk to him," I said, rising. "One last question, Dr. Klein, could Buck's death have anything to do with this burial-ground dig you're doing? Will the transfer affect it in any way?"

"Nothin' to affect," Jenkins snorted. "I been back there, ain't nothin' *to* see."

"He's right on both counts," Klein said, smiling. "There is very little to see. Cracked stones from fire pits, a few pottery shards, discarded tools. The Anishnabeg lived on this land for nearly fifteen hundred years, and left almost no traces. I wish we could say the same. But the dig won't be affected by the closing of the base. And I doubt that it mattered much to Jerry anyway. He wasn't really serious about the work."

"Maybe not," I said, "but he was damn serious about something."

"Yes," Klein nodded soberly, "I guess he must have been."

"You know this Gesh character, don't you?" I asked. We were in the Jeep, following the narrow track along the outside of the perimeter fence.

"I know him," Jenkins said grimly. "Tangled with him more'n once. And if Buck was livin' with that ol' man, it might explain a lot about him goin' off the deep end."

"Why?"

" 'Cause Gesh is nuts, that's why. Lives back in the swamp like the last damn Apache or somethin'."

"Or Ojibwa," I said. "Why did you tangle with him?"

"Because base security is my job, and every now and then we hear gunfire back in that swamp. And we have to check it out. And that old man ain't heavy into hospitality, I'll tell ya."

"Maybe he was poaching, thought you might be the law."

"No," Jenkins said positively, "it wasn't that. He knew damn well we were air force. Even recognized my rank. Kept his gun on me the whole time anyway."

"And you just—let that pass?"

"Yeah, well, maybe I shouldn't have." Jenkins sighed, peering past the wipers into the downpour. "But I didn't figure it was worth gettin' anybody killed over, and that's what would've happened if we'd tried to disarm him. He was scared to death of us, and crazy as a loon."

"Why do you say he was crazy?"

"He was talkin' crazy. And he kept throwin' tobacco at me."

"Tobacco?"

"That's right. Held his rifle in one hand, aimed at my belly, and kept tossin' bits of loose tobacco at me, little pinches out of a can. Prince Albert, I think it was. And talkin' right out of his head."

"About what?"

"Ghosts," Jenkins said, glancing over at me with a fox's grin. "You know, I'm a black man in a white man's country, and I been called a lotta things in my time, but never a ghost. He kept callin' me a ghost. You sure you want to talk to him?"

"No." I sighed. "But I guess I have to. And maybe I'd better see him alone, if you don't mind."

"Hell no, I don't mind. Best news I've had all day," Jenkins said, easing the Jeep to a halt. He shrugged out of his raincoat and gave it to me. "There's a flashlight in the glove box. See that path up ahead to the left? It'll take you back to old Joe's shack, half a mile or so back in the swamp. Seems like it goes forever, but stay on it. And bro? You watch your ass, hear? If that ol' man wastes you, I'm gonna have to fill out a godawful stack of paperwork."

I didn't bother to reply. The rain was on me in an icy torrent the moment I stepped out of the Jeep, like standing under a waterfall. Jenkins's raincoat was little help. I was soaked to the bone before I'd stumbled fifty yards down the muddy track.

I've hunted all my life, so the trail wasn't all that hard to follow. Rough going though, sodden, slippery with uncertain footing. Tag alders and cedar saplings clawed at me out of the darkness, as if asking me to bide awhile, to share their loneliness. I spotted the faint glow of a lamp ahead.

Gesh's shack wasn't a shack exactly. It was a hogan, a rectangular log hut roofed with sod. It was crude, but not totally primitive. It had glass windows, and tarpaper had been tacked over a patch where the sod had washed away.

"Hello," I shouted. "Mr. Gesh?"

No answer. The lamp in the cabin winked out. "Mr. Gesh, my name's Delacroix. I'd like to talk to you."

"What do you want?" The voice was a low rasp, barely louder than a whisper.

"For openers, to come in out of the rain. I have news for you."

After what seemed like a month, a match flickered in the cabin and the lamp glowed to life. The door swung slowly open on leather hinges. "Come ahead. But move slow."

Even after the darkness of the forest, the hogan was dim, lit by a single kerosene lamp hanging from a sapling rafter. The air was thick with the stench of tallow and rancid suet from the hides stretched over ash hoops hanging on the walls, raccoon, lynx, muskrat. Gesh watched me from the shadows in the far corner of the room. He was smaller than I expected, a wiry little gnome of a man, grey hair tied back in a ratty ponytail, a brown, seamed face, carved from mahogany. He was wearing a green-and-black plaid flannel coat, faded jeans, worn moccasins. Even his rifle was small. A bolt-action Marlin .22. A trapper's gun. After a moment he lowered it, and leaned it in the corner.

"You're from up north someplace, aren't ya?" he said.

"Yes, sir. From Algoma. Bear Clan. How did you know?"

"Because your eyes don't get big. The young ones come out here from town, they always look around like my house is a museum or somethin'. But you know what things are," he said, gesturing at the hides, the hogan.

"I trapped for a few years, after I got out of the army," I said. "Lived with the Cree, up in Ontario."

"What was it like, that country?"

"Empty," I said. "And hungry. Winters last a hundred years."

"Here too, sometimes." He nodded. "Sit. Sorry it's cold in here, I'm outa kerosene for the stove. Here, wrap up in this, you'll be warm after a while." He handed me a frayed army blanket. I draped it over my shoulders and sat on a tree-stump stool that obviously doubled as a chopping block.

"You bring anything to drink?" Gesh asked.

"No," I said. "Sorry. I didn't know I was coming."

"It's okay." He shrugged. "You said you had news. Bad, right?"

"I'm afraid so. They tell me Jerry Buck was staying with you."

"A few months. Tried to dry him out, straighten him out. Didn't work. What happened to him?"

"He, ah, he's dead, Mr. Gesh. Soaked himself with gasoline, and . . . he burned."

"On the base," the old man said. It wasn't a question.

"Yes."

"Sweet Jesus," Gesh said, swallowing hard. "I told him. Stupid bastard."

"What did you tell him?"

"To stay off there. That they'd kill him."

"Who would?"

"The dead pilots, or whatever they are. The ghosts. They kill everything out there. All them planes, loaded with bombs. With death. Death is all they know. They killed themselves, now they kill everything else."

"I don't understand," I said.

"Maybe you can't," he said. "Do you know about ghosts?"

"I'm—not sure. I've never seen one."

"You won't see these either," the old man snorted. "They're dead. A long time ago. Fifteen, twenty years maybe. They died in the spring, in the rain. Now when it rains, they come back."

"Who comes back?" I asked.

"The dead flyers. The ones who died in the plane. Big one. I heard it fall in the night. Shook the ground. Thought it was the end of the damn world. I snuck over by the field, watched from the woods. There were a lotta bodies around, in them rubber bags, you know? Maybe a dozen. Maybe more. Nothing left of the damn plane. Junk. Pieces of it scattered half a mile. It was all gone the next day. The other airmen picked everything up, made it look like nothing happened. Like it had all been a dream. But it wasn't. I saw the dead men all right. And a few years later, their ghosts came back. They killed the dogs first, the ones that guarded the fence. Other animals too sometimes, coons, possums."

"Why do you think ghosts killed them?"

"Because they wasn't touched. No wounds, no blood. They just— take their souls. Leave the bodies behind. Dead all the same. Maybe the flyers weren't buried right. Maybe their souls are trapped out there and need food. I don't know. All I know is, they come back in the rain. And hunt."

"But Jerry Buck didn't just die. He was burned to death."

"Jerry was a man." Gesh shrugged. "Maybe he was harder to kill than the dogs."

"Maybe." I nodded, glancing around the hogan, inhaling the aroma of curing hides, and tobacco, and blood. A primeval scent that evoked a hazy memory of other lodges, in other places, long ago. Before I was born.

"Do you know what Jerry was doing out there?" I asked.

"Celebrating," the old man said. "Someone told him the air force is giving the base to the Ojibwa. Is that true?"

"Something like that," I said.

"But why? We don't have no planes."

"We'll make something out of it," I said. "We're good at that. You said Jerry went there to celebrate?"

"Yeah. He wasn't from here, he was Lakota Sioux from Montana. Knew a dance he learned in reservation school. Buffalo dance. Did it pretty good too. Had a tape of the drums and everything. He said he was gonna dance out on the runway, put on a show for the people. Maybe make a few dollars."

"I see," I said. "Jesus. He, ahm, he had a gas can with him."

"Not gas, kerosene," Gesh said. "He needed a fire for the dance. Took my kerosene and wet down some rags so they'd burn in the rain. Musta screwed it up. He was drinkin'. He was always drinkin'. It's all the young people know these days."

"Not so many," I said. "Not anymore. Are you sure it was kerosene he took? Not gasoline?"

"I don't keep no gas here. Got no car or nothin'. Just use kerosene for the lamp, the stove."

"Yeah," I said. "Right. Look, there's going to be a ceremony at the base tomorrow. Would you like to come?"

"No," he spat. "No way. It's a bad place. Haunted. I won't go there."

"Suit yourself. Maybe I could come back here, sometime."

"Why?"

"To talk. I'll tell you how the Cree breed wolves. Maybe I'll even bring a couple beers."

The old man stared at me a long time, reading me. Then he shook his head. "I don't think so," he said quietly.

"No? Why not?"

"Because you ain't comin' back, Delacroix. I ain't stupid, just old. You don't believe me about them ghosts. I read it in your eyes. So you're gonna go see for yourself. Ain't you?"

I didn't want to lie to him. So I didn't answer.

"Thought so," he said, not bothering to conceal the contempt in his tone. "You got some education, I can tell by the way you talk. Jerry didn't know nothin'. Just a sidewalk Indian. But if you go out on that field, you'll be as dead as him. As dead as them dogs."

"I can take care of myself," I said. "I'll be back."

"No," he said. "You won't." And he turned his back on me, shutting me out. As though I were dead already.

"Took you long enough," Jenkins said as I climbed into the Jeep. "You find the shack?"

"I found it. The old man said Buck took a can of kerosene to soak some rags and start a small fire out on the runway. He was going to put on a little show. To celebrate the tribe taking over the base."

"But something went wrong?" Jenkins asked, his tone neutral.

"He'd been drinking. My guess is, he spilled some of the kerosene on himself. And when he lit the fire . . . he burned."

"Yeah." Jenkins nodded warily. "That must've been how it happened. It wasn't suicide, then?"

"No. He didn't go out there to die. He went out there to dance."

"So we can go ahead with the transfer ceremony tomorrow?"

"I don't see why not. Do you?"

"No," Jenkins said, visibly relaxing. "What happened was a damn shame. But we have to move on."

"Yeah, I guess we do. The old man said something odd, though. He said the field's haunted. By the ghosts of flyers who cracked up a plane a long time ago. That the ghosts killed Jerry somehow. That they killed your dogs too."

"I told you he was crazy."

"Is he? If the dogs had been patrolling the perimeter, Buck never could have gotten on the field."

"Yeah, well, they weren't. We had no reason to think anyone would try to penetrate the field, so we shipped the dogs out. Transferred 'em back to Offutt. Wish to hell I'd gone with 'em."

"What about the plane? Was there a crash?"

"Bullock was a Strategic Air Command base," Jenkins said warily. "We flew nuclear missions out of here twenty-four hours a day, seven days a week, for nearly thirty years. There was a cold war on, remember? Even if there were crackups, I couldn't tell you about 'em. It'd still be classified information. You were a soldier once. You know how it is, right?"

"Yes," I said. "I think so."

Jenkins dropped me off at my van and drove off to report to his colonel. I trotted to my Chevy through the rain and scrambled in. And started as a figure sat up in the back seat.

"Hi," Eva Redfern said. "Sorry. I wanted to make sure I didn't miss you. Must've fallen asleep. What did you find out?"

"That Jerry Buck's death was an accident," I said, starting the van. "Sort of."

"I don't understand."

"Neither do I, exactly. Have you got time to take a short ride with me?"

"I suppose so. Where are we going?"

"To the dogs," I said. "Or to where they used to be."

The kennels had been removed, but the chain-link dog runs were still in place, probably more trouble than it was worth to tear down. The concrete runs had been swept clean. But I found what I was looking for in the grass that had grown up beneath the edge of the fence. A chalky white pebble, not much bigger than a marble. I bounced it in my palm a moment, thinking. Then carried it back to the van.

"Well?" Redfern said. "What did you find?"

"A lump of truth," I said, passing her the pebble. "You've got fingernails, see if you can dent that."

"I can . . . scrape it a little," she said, "but I can't dent it. What is it? Chalk?"

"Nope, it's crap. A dog turd, to be specific. Hard as rock. Calcified."

"What?"

"Don't worry, it won't contaminate you. It's old. Probably a dozen years or so. And it was the only one I could find."

"And is this thing—" she tossed the turd into my ashtray and dusted off her hands. "Is this supposed to mean something?"

"Maybe. It might mean that what old Joe Gesh told me about the dogs was true," I said, slipping the van into drive and heading out onto the tarmac. "That they were killed a long time ago. As near as I can tell, no dogs have used those kennels for years."

"But why should that matter?"

"I'm not sure it does, but it makes me wonder if the rest of what he told me is true. About dead flyers. And ghosts that kill in the rain."

"You're not making much sense."

"I'm about to make even less," I said, easing the van to a halt on the runway. "Look, I'm going out there to look around. I'll leave the headlights on, but since I may lose track of them in the rain, I want you to blow the horn in exactly ten minutes. And keep blowing it, once a minute for fifteen minutes or so. If I'm not back by then, go to the air-police barracks, find Sergeant Jenkins and tell him what happened. He'll know what to do. Understand?"

"No! I don't understand any of this."

"Maybe there's nothing to understand," I said. "Maybe the old man really is crazy. It shouldn't take long to find out. One last thing. If I don't come back, whatever you do, *don't* come looking for me. I want your word on it."

"All right, I promise I won't look for you. But why?"

"Because if I'm not back in half an hour, you can offer tobacco to the spirits who haunt this place. I'll be one of them. The stupid one. The one who wouldn't listen to his elders."

I closed the van door on her objections, turned up the collar of Jenkins's raincoat, and trotted off into the rainy dark. I tried to move in a straight line, keeping the headlights directly behind me, but it was impossible. The third time I glanced over my shoulder to get a fix on the van, I couldn't see the lights anymore.

I chose to follow a seam in the concrete instead, hoping it would keep me moving in a more-or-less straight line down the tarmac, away from the van. I didn't meet any ghosts. At least, not at first. There was only the solitary slap of my boots in the puddles, as I trotted along in the sickly glow of the flashlight.

Big airfields have their own special reek, *eau de* exhaust fumes, scorched rubber from rough landings, the acrid stink of wing and windshield de-icer and fuel spills. The stench was strong at first, but seemed to fade as I jogged on. Bullock hadn't been used much for a while, perhaps the rain was rinsing the perfume away. Just as well.

It didn't sound like an airfield either. They're never silent. Always there's the scream of jets, taking off, landing, or just warming up, mingling with the constant rumble of support vehicles. Here there was nothing. Just the whisper of the drizzle. And the occasional whistle of the wind in the wire of the perimeter fencing.

It seemed oddly peaceful, running along in a halo of light, alone, hidden from the world of men by the gunmetal curtain of the rain. No ghosts, no dead dogs, nothing to see. . . . I checked my watch to see how long I'd been running, but the dial was wet and blurry and I couldn't quite make it out.

And then I fell. Hard. I tucked and rolled instinctively, skidding along in the water like an otter on a slide. The flashlight clattered away from me in the dark.

I lay there a few minutes, dazed, trying to catch my breath, gather my wits. God, I was tired, exhausted, heart pounding, head splitting. If I could just rest a bit. . . .

Sweet Jesus. The dogs. They'd died out here. In the rain. Just like this. I forced myself to my hands and knees and crawled toward the faint glow of the flashlight. It was lying beside a puddle, its light diffused, scattered into swirling rainbow bands, by the water, and the nearly invisible turquoise liquid floating on it. I tried to sniff it, but couldn't get a sense of what it was. And realized I couldn't smell anything at all, not the water or the wind. Nothing. And then I recognized the floating slick. Knew it for what it was. It was Death. In the rain. For the guard dogs. And Jerry Buck. And now for me.

I picked up the flashlight, but it was oily, slippery, and I fumbled it away, watched frozen with horror as it tumbled slow-motion down on the tarmac. And winked out.

I turned slowly in a circle, knuckling the rain out of my eyes, trying to get a sense of where I was. It was hopeless. I could only see a few feet. It didn't matter. I had to move, to get away, so I started walking, dazed and aching, stumbling along like a wino, lost in the belly of the beast.

I don't know how long I walked. Years. Then off to the left, I caught a glimpse of a monstrous shape. A ghostly aircraft? It wasn't real. Couldn't be. So I ignored it, and stumbled on. But then I saw a second silhouette, as huge as the first.

I turned and reeled toward them. And found the fence. And the trucks. Toxic-waste tankers, a line of them, a few yards beyond the fence. Waiting their turn at the incinerator. They seemed ugly and misshapen in the rain, foam steaming down their sides like lather, sizzling as the rain reacted to the specks of toxic sludge spatters.

I peered blearily through the fence for a night watchman, anyone. But there was no light, and the exit gate was locked. The tankers might as well have been on the moon. In the shape I was in, there was no way I could climb a fifteen-foot fence and fight through the bayonet wire. And if I got hung up there, I'd die as surely . . .

I heard a groan. A low moan from behind me. I turned, trying to place it . . . And realized what it was. The horn. Redfern had started blowing the horn.

And without thinking, I started running toward it, shambling across the tarmac, a puppet without strings. Veering, stumbling, called on by the horn. And each time it was a little closer. Fifteen. She would blow it once a minute for fifteen minutes. How many had I heard? I couldn't remember. I only knew that to stop running was to die. Like the dogs.

I saw the van. Spotted the faint halo of the headlights ahead, off to the right. I swerved toward them. And fell, tumbling along on the concrete runway, knocking what breath I had out of me. And then Redfern was there, helping me crawl.

I couldn't make it through the van door. I vomited, head down, still on my hands and knees in the rain. I retched and spewed until there was nothing left to give, and then I lost that too.

But it helped. And the drive back toward the gate helped more. I hung my head out the window, drinking the nightwind and the rain, purging my lungs, and my soul.

"Do you have a car here?" I asked. It was the first thing I'd said since she found me.

"We'll leave it. You're going to the hospital in Crater Creek."

"No," I said, coughing. "I can't. If I go there we'll lose everything. And we've already paid too much. Jerry Buck paid for it. We can't back off now. Just stop at your car."

"No. I'm staying with you."

"You can't. There are arrangements you have to make for tomorrow. I want you to talk to Dr. Klein. He'll help us, I think."

"Klein? Why should he help?"

"Because at heart, he's basically a decent man," I said, managing a weak smile. "But more important, he has a . . . warped sense of humor."

"What are you talking about?"

So I told her, and she said I was crazy. And she was right and I knew it. But I was so coldly enraged that I didn't care. I asked for her promise. And she gave it. Probably just to humor me. But she gave it. And that was enough.

"If you won't go to the hospital, at least come home with me," she said. "You can't stay here."

"I'll be all right. I'll rest. But I have one last bit of business to take care of first."

"This time of night? What kind of business?"

"Private," I said. "And personal. Very personal."

In the end she left me alone. She didn't like it, but she did. And I was sorry she did. I was sick and miserable and exhausted, and the only thing that kept me going was the thought that if I stopped for even a moment, I wouldn't get up for a week.

That, and the anger, of course. It was like a fire in my belly, a cold blaze of killing rage. For what had been done to Jerry Buck, and to me. And what they were trying to do to my people.

So I sat in my van, with the windows open, and the radio on, and waited. And thought. And I must have dozed off. Because the next thing I knew there was a wan hint of grey light on the horizon and the deejay was babbling about breakfast. I checked my watch. A little after four A.M. Time enough.

I fired up the van and drove over to the air-police barracks. There was a light in the day room. No others. I unlocked the van's glove compartment and took out my revolver, a smith and Wesson .38. I checked it, and slipped it into my waistband.

I'd hoped they were too shorthanded to post a guard, and there was none. I just walked in. The day room was immaculate, tiled floors gleaming, every magazine aligned. Something clicked in the corner, and I realized the large coffee urn had switched itself on automatically. They'd be up and about soon.

His room was easy to find. It was the largest, and his name was on the door. Chief Master Sergeant Purvis L. Jenkins.

It wasn't locked. I eased the door open, stepped in, and closed it behind me. I waited a moment for my eyes to adjust to the dimness, until I could make out his form on the bed. He was lying on his back, snoring softly, his fingers laced behind his head. I peeled off his sodden raincoat and draped it over him. Then I drew my weapon and switched on the lights.

He blinked instantly awake and alert. I was impressed. He glanced at me, and the gun, and the raincoat. And his eyes widened a fraction. But he didn't flinch.

"Shit," he said softly. "You went out there, didn't you?"

"That's right. I nearly died. Suffocated. Like the dogs."

"What, ahm, what are you going to do?"

"I'm going to ask you some questions. And you're gonna tell me the truth. Because if I even *think* you're lying to me, I'm going to fire this weapon in your general direction. I won't even have to hit you. And your raincoat will explode, and you'll burn. Just like Jerry Buck. Do you understand?"

He nodded, swallowing.

"The plane the old man told me about, the one that crashed. What was it?"

"Look, for God's sake—"

I eased back the hammer of the .38. He read my eyes, and saw his own death there. "It was a tanker," he said, grudgingly, as though each word was an agony. "A KC-135 Stratotanker."

"My God," I said softly. "And it crashed on takeoff?"

"Right. Spilled its whole payload. Nearly twenty thousand gallons of jet fuel. Just dumb luck it didn't explode on impact. But it was raining, and—it didn't."

"Why didn't you recover it?"

"Because by morning, most of it was gone," he said simply. "Drained away, soaked into the gravel bed under the runway. It's low land at that end of the field, next to the marsh. There was no way to recover it short of tearing up the whole damn field, and we couldn't do that. Hell, there was a war on and we had to keep B-52s in the air twenty-four hours a day. Anyway, it was gone. So we went on flying missions, and figured we'd got off lucky. Until it showed up again three years later. And the guard dogs all died."

"In the spring," I said. "In the rain. From the fumes. Gasoline, not kerosene. Buck might have burned himself with kerosene, but it wouldn't have exploded the way it did."

"That's right. Basic physics, jet fuel's almost two pounds a gallon lighter than water, so when the water table rises high enough, we get seepage onto the field. More this year than most. Usually we don't get much, and not for long."

"It was long enough for Jerry Buck," I said. "It was forever."

"Yeah." He nodded. "Look, I'm—"

"Don't!" I snapped, cutting him off. "If you say you're sorry, I swear to God I'll blow you away just for the hell of it. Now, maybe you couldn't clean up the fuel while the base was operational, but it's closing. Why not do it now?"

"Budget," he said bitterly. "With peace breakin' out, they've cut us to the bone. We've barely got money enough to keep a third of our force active. It'd cost millions to tear up the field to clean up the spill. We just don't have it anymore."

"But why us? Why dump it on the Ojibwa?"

"Two reasons. One, because you're broke, and wouldn't have the money to develop the field. We figured you'd open a gift shop or a bingo hall and that'd be it. You'd probably never come across the spill at all. And if you ever did, you likely wouldn't report it and risk losing the land."

"I see. And where does Kanelos fit in?"

"He's a front. If we'd just ceded the base to you, you might've had it inspected. This way it's maybe not the nicest deal in the world, but at least everybody gets something out of it."

"Everybody but Jerry Buck."

"That was an accident. He shouldn't have been out there."

"Maybe he wouldn't have been, if the area was posted as hazardous. And he sure as hell wouldn't have started that fire. Would he?"

"No, I suppose not. What are you going to do?"

"What I have to. Take the deal. Maybe it's a bad deal, but my people have never gotten any other kind. And as you said, at least there's something for everybody. Even for us."

"Good." He nodded. "You're doing the right thing. I'm sorry—"

I pulled the trigger. A reflex. The hammer clicked on an empty cylinder. Jenkins winced, then his eyes narrowed. "You bastard!"

"Easy," I said. "Maybe I just forgot to load one cylinder. Thanks for your—cooperation, Sergeant."

"Look, please try to understand. I was just doing my damn job. Trying to protect my own people."

"Your people?"

"The air force. It's the only family I've ever had. But for what it's worth, I really am sorry. About Buck. And the rest of it."

"I think you know what that's worth," I said.

"Yeah," he said, "I guess I do."

The rain paused briefly at first light, just long enough to reveal a pallid sun, bled white by the storm. But then the sky darkened and the torrent resumed with a vengeance, an icy, wind-driven drizzle, the kind you only see in northern Michigan, or Seattle, or Nome.

Jenkins had told the colonel about my visit. I could tell by the wariness in his eyes as he greeted Eva Redfern and me at the reception center. None of us spoke of it, still the tension was there, like a fuse smoldering just below the surface. An explosion only a word away.

The gathering was almost a repeat of the day before, reporters, a few cameramen, and a gaggle of local politicians. But there were no hors d'oeuvres, no air of gaiety. It was less a celebration than a wake. A vigil for a sidewalk Indian who'd traded the poverty of the reservation for an ugly death, far from his home and his people. A wake for Jerry Buck.

Another difference was the presence of Dr. Klein and a half dozen of his neo-hippie students. I'd thought Colonel Webber might object when they arrived, but I made it clear they were the honored guests of the Ojibwa Nation. Klein and his raggedy clan of peaceniks had protested the presence of nuclear death on this land for years. They'd been ridiculed, harassed, and arrested. Right or wrong, they'd paid their dues, they'd earned admission to this last matinee.

Jenkins surprised me by greeting Klein warmly, and openly. Shaking his hand. Webber's mouth soured in disapproval, but Jenkins's action seemed to defuse some of the tension in the room. If there was going to be trouble, it would have been between these two old adversaries. But there was no animosity left between them. They were like two fighters who go the distance, savaging each other until the final bell, and then embrace. Gladiators, with more spiritual kinship to each other than to those who never bled, no matter what their politics.

The actual transfer was almost an anticlimax. Colonel Webber made a brief speech of welcome, then introduced Mr. Kanelos and his attorneys, Eva Redfern, and me. He then transferred title to the property formerly known as Bullock Air Force Base, Strategic Air Command, to Mr. Frantzis Kanelos, head of Kanelos Waste Disposal. Kanelos in turn transferred the title to the legal representatives of the Ojibwa Nation in exchange for a permanent lease of the waste incinerator and four hundred acres of land adjacent to it. I'd suggested Redfern change the wording of his lease to read: for as long as the sun shall rise, but she said sarcasm had no place in a legal document.

And she was right. The stakes were too high. Native Americans have been swept into the corners of our continent by a tidal wave of history. Our past is over, we can only press on, and struggle to survive in the present. And sometimes that means eating the dirt of injustice and making the best of it.

But not always.

Kanelos signed the final documents with a grin and a flourish, to a smattering of polite applause. And I met Redfern's eyes and they were brimming, with joy or pain, I couldn't tell. Both, perhaps. But there was steel in her glance too. The land was ours again. We had a done deal.

"Ladies and gentlemen," I said, raising my voice, "on behalf of the Ojibwa Nation and its ruling council, I thank you for coming to witness this historic event. But as all of you know, the proceedings were marred by a tragedy, the—accidental death of Geronimo Gall Cobmoosa, known to us as Jerry Buck. To honor Jerry's memory, and to exemplify the brotherhood that now exists between us, we would like to invite Mr. Kanelos to lead a candlelight procession to lay a wreath where Jerry Buck died. Doctor Klein will pass out candles and umbrellas at the door—"

"Wait a minute," Kanelos said, glancing at Webber, "you mean go out there on the runway now? With candles?"

"What's a little rain?" I said. "With a prosperous future—"

"Forget it, Frank," Webber broke in. "Jenkins told me Delacroix was out on the runway last night, damn near got himself killed. This is just his idea of a little joke. He knows it's not safe out there."

"It's not a joke," I said. "It was a fishing expedition. I needed to be sure Mr. Kanelos knew about the fuel spill."

"Even if I did, it won't make any difference to our agreement," Kanelos said uneasily. "My lawyers—"

"Assured you it's rock solid," I finished for him. "I certainly hope so. In any case, since it is a little damp for a candlelight procession, we've arranged alternate entertainment. Ladies and gentlemen, please step to the observation window to view a small display . . ."

Far down the perimeter road, there was a blast of white smoke, and three solitary shafts of light flashed into the gunmetal overcast above the runway. And burst into red flowers of flame, sputtering gamely in the darkness. Candles in the rain.

". . . of fireworks," I finished.

"What?" Webber said, his face going grey. "You can't—"

But it was too late. In slow motion, the flares continued their arc across the sky, and began to fall, raining petals of fire down on the tarmac. There was a deep *chuff*, like a sharp intake of breath, and the runway burst into flame, in scattered spots at first, but quickly dancing across the surface of the water, until the fires united in an inferno a half mile across, howling into the sky as though the gates of hell had opened.

I moved quietly back and stepped out onto the portico, joining Redfern and Dr. Klein at the railing. Reporters and cameramen streamed past us, drawn like moths to the flames. A few minutes later Jenkins sauntered out and stood behind Dr. Klein. Jenkins's face was a carved, ebon mask. I could read nothing in it.

"Quite a bonfire," he said at last.

"Not so bad," Klein said. "Compared to Kuwait, this one's a marshmallow roast. By my calculations, it should burn between five and six hours, depending on how much fuel has evaporated over the years. And that will be the end of it."

"And of the runway, and the incinerator," Jenkins said. "Ain't you worried Kanelos will sue your tails off?"

"I hope he tries," Redfern said grimly. "I'd love to take his deposition under oath, about what he knew and when, about the fire hazard that killed Jerry Buck."

"Good point," Jenkins conceded. "Doubt the government will bother you either. Might try though. The colonel's in there ravin' about sabotage. Ordered me to arrest all three of you, in fact."

"So?" I said. "Are we under arrest?"

"Hell no," Jenkins said wryly. "It just shows how shaky his grip on reality is. We've got no authority to arrest anybody. This isn't a military base anymore. Won't even look much like one in a few hours. Won't be anything left of that runway but gravel and ash. A couple years, you won't even be able to tell it was there."

"There'll always be traces of it," Klein said. "When you cauterize the earth, it leaves scars. I wonder what archaeologists will make of them a thousand years from now?"

"Maybe if we're real lucky, Doc," Jenkins said quietly, "they'll look around and scratch their heads. And won't even be able to guess what it was used for."

Out on the perimeter of the field, the blaze was already burning low, the concrete sizzling and cracking in the drizzle. But on the tarmac near the spot where Jerry Buck died, the inferno still raged on, furiously roiling plumes of oily smoke into the sky. The flames leapt and twisted and writhed, like a ring of ghostly dancers, carrying candles in the rain.

WHEN YOUR BREATH FREEZES

by Kathleen Dougherty

There are seven of us.

I am Sister Ellen: the youngest, the ugliest, the least devout, the most fragile. I need the vast silences of northern Alaska and the imposed silence of this cloister. The souls of these women are quiet, their musings as distant as the Chukchi Sea. The nuns have taken me in for the winter, an act of charity, a charity they might well regret. But they don't know about my special ability, my accursed gift. If they did, they'd shun me as others have. Their unspoken thoughts, though, are safe from me. Nothing could compel me again to peruse the mind of another. What you see there are the ugly shapes of nightmares.

Under my white robes, the color for a novice, are a pair of expedition-weight long johns, the fabric a heat-retaining, sweat-wicking synthetic; then a pair of wind-blocking pile pants. We have no television, no radio, yet we have the latest in underwear.

Off come the sturdy black shoes and on go the insulated knee-high boots. I unpin the white novice's veil from my hair and hang the veil on a wall peg. I slide a black ski mask over my head, position the mouth and eye holes. I like wearing the mask; its blank anonymity hides my facial scars. There is only one mirror here, in the infirmary. I have little use for mirrors.

I wrap my neck with the wool scarf knitted by Sister Gabrielle. I think tenderly of her gnarled hands, twisted by arthritis, the black yarn, and the slow clack of the needles. She had embroidered "Ellen" on a cloth tag. My fingers work a stretch cap on top of the ski mask, then I shrug on the anorak with its thick pile of yellow fleece lining, its rich fringe of fox fur around the hood. The drawstring snugs the hood low on my forehead and up over my mouth. The fur tickles and has that dusty aroma of animal skin.

Last are the glove liners and the padded mittens with Velcro wrist bands. Even before I open the heavy wooden door, I imagine I hear the cows lowing, though that's not possible. The wind's voice whips away sound and, deceptively, mimics the wail of a cat, a distant locomotive, an unhappy ghost.

I flick on the outdoor lights and step beyond the door, pulling it closed behind me. The frigid air steals my breath. Outside all is the white of an unusually bitter February. Though midmorning, there are hours before dawn bleaches the sky. My teeth chatter. It is colder than death out here.

The north wind pauses in its cold rush. I spit. The saliva crackles, freezing in midair, and shatters like glass on the walkway. Cold, very cold, even by the standards of northern Alaska. More than seventy below. Gusts sweep snow pellets, hard as gravel, across the covered walkway to the barn. That wooden structure, like the convent, appears to sprout from the mountainside.

During the Yukon gold rush, miners hewed these caverns, clawing from granite the shelters that shielded them from brutal winters. The south-facing walls are wood; north-facing walls and much of the ceiling are the smoothed underbelly of the mountain. Snaking into the earth from those north walls are tunnels; a few lead to steaming pools of hot springs, potable—though slightly sulfurous—water. After the Second World War, the exhausted claim was purchased by the Immaculata order, and this remote land, once brimming with the harsh voices and greed of prospectors, became the refuge of silent nuns.

The gale blasts against my long skirts and I cover the walkway in a graceless stagger. The barn door sticks, its hinges cranky with cold. I wrench open the door and step inside to rich aromas: cow hide, dung, hay, bird droppings, wood smoke. The miners had used the large room as a barracks. Humid air fogs a tunnel entrance, one which leads to the hot springs, where the nuns take paying guests during the brief summers.

The barn houses two cows, a mangy good-for-nothing goat, and a chicken-wire enclosure with a dozen hens and an irritable cock. The hens set up a comical squawking and fluttering, shocked to their very cores every few hours when I come to tend the wood stove. The cows regard me with their calm brown eyes, aware that it's morning and hoping for fresh fodder. These are, as far as I've seen, the only cows in Alaska, a gift from a rancher in the lower forty-eight. He'd stayed here last summer, Leonidist said, soaking in the convent's hot sulfur springs, and was convinced he'd been miraculously healed of gout.

Pine logs dropped into the wood stove make the coals flare. The stove stands in an isolated hollow scooped from the mountain. The flue disappears into the rocky ceiling.

I milk the cows and the sullen goat, gather eggs from the hens. I slap the cow's haunches, urging them up and down the center aisle. They don't like the enforced exercise, but their shanks tend to develop abscesses. Sister Fiske, a paramedic and our only source of medical expertise during these frozen months, prescribed aerobics. The cows want only to stare into their food bins and meditate golden hay into existence. Their resistance makes the stroll hard work and I wonder about the medical benefits for any of us. After half an hour, I stop, panting. Their bony heads study me quietly, a pitying look which makes me smile.

I muck out the stalls and coop, spread down fresh straw, and rake the soiled material to the far entrance. I switch on the outdoor lights. This part gets tricky. If drifts have built up in the past hours, a path will have to be cleared. That means shoveling for two minutes, dashing into the warmth of the barn and scaring the heck out of the chickens, shoveling another two minutes, and so on.

To my delight, the door swings open easily and the path to the garden appears clear. I rake the straw outside and drag the mound a few yards when a snow-dusted rock catches my eye. A mound of black, a large stone that hadn't been there before . . . and with awful clarity the form resolves into that of a huddled person. My chest tenses with shock. I am kneeling next to the shape without memory of moving closer.

She is curled into the fetal position. The ebony veil, hard and shiny, has frozen into place, covering most of the profile, but there's enough exposed to see the broad jaw, the deep etch of lines from nose to mouth, the dark brown mole with its two stiff hairs stark against ashen flesh. Frost has made a mask of the features, smoothed out the web of wrinkles on her full cheeks, lessened the downward draw of persimmon lips. It is Sister Praxades, our cook, who refuses—refused—to bake white bread. In the kitchen with her black sleeves rolled up over dimpled forearms, she taught me to knead whole-grain dough. She smelled of flour and yeast and discontent.

With my right glove and liner off, I touch her throat where, in life, the carotid artery throbs. Her neck is frozen solid, hard and unyielding.

Her pudgy hands and feet are bare, pale as alabaster. How can this be? No one would willingly tromp barefoot in Alaska's winter.

My thoughts are slow lizards, too long in the cold.

My right hand signs the cross over her body. I mentally begin an Act of Contrition, but retreat to the barn when the air hurts my lungs. Chickens cackle and the goat bleats while I finish the prayer for Sister Praxades, an inadequate charity for a woman who had been more than tolerant of a newcomer.

Tears burn my cheeks. I, who have so little opportunity for love, loved her.

There had been seven of us.

Now there are six.

Reverend Mother thinks in German, a language I don't comprehend. Snatches of words, swirling in her mind-winds, fly out: *schnee, tot, unschuld, verlassen.* She is in her late forties, the youngest except for me, yet authority is a mantle she wears with ease. Her bearing is military, her oval face composed, her gray eyes sharp. Only now her gaze reveals disquiet upon my panicked report of Sister Praxades's death. Reverend Mother's face shutters down; her thoughts whirl. Rosary beads rattle within the folds of her black robes. Her pale lips shape the English words, "Jesus, Mary, Joseph," a favored indulgence of this order. Each nun says this prayer so often that the rhythm becomes one with each inhale and exhale. When the rare words seep from their minds, that is what I sense: JesusMaryJoseph.

Reverend Mother orients on me. Her lapse of control is over. Her fingers sign, *You—lead me—Praxades.* Even now Reverend Mother does not break the quiet meditation.

Her hand halts me as I turn. She shapes sentences fast, too fast, and I shake my head in confusion. She places a long index finger to her lips, then signs, *No tell—others.*

Why not tell the others? They'll know Sister Praxades is missing. I gesture for permission to speak, my sign language inept. Reverend Mother slices her hand in the negative, a command that reminds me of my position here. The shock of finding Sister Praxades has made me exceed my bounds. Flushing, I bow my head in apology, nod compliance, and we exit her office. It is up to Reverend Mother, not the distraught pseudo-novice "Sister" Ellen, to decide when to tell the nuns. If she waits until after the Angelus, before the noon meal when contemplation officially ends, Sister Praxades will not be any less dead for the delay.

In the hall Sister Leonidist, standing on a foot stool, scrapes tallow from a wall sconce. Candle glow highlights the postmenopausal down of her cheeks and chin. Thick red eyebrows shadow her sockets, making her pale blue eyes seem large and black. Leon the Lion, my pet name for her in my head, is the one I'd have gone to first to share the terrible discovery. She performs a modified curtsy from her perch in respect of Reverend Mother as we pass. I look longingly over my shoulder at Leon. She grins and winks, pretends to stick a finger up one wide nostril.

At the side door, before Reverend Mother dons her anorak, she removes her black headdress. Her hair is a flattened, short gray-brown, and its thinness somehow diminishes her authority. I focus on the splintered wood planks, embarrassed. It is disrespectful to see her so. After a moment, she nudges me, not unkindly. It is time to go out into the cold.

One voice: *"Dominus vobiscum."* The Lord be with you.

Five voices: *"Et cum spiritu tuo."* And with your spirit.

It is noon and the hours of silence end. Reverend Mother observes us from the lectern. Her hands clutch the frame on either side of the Bible. Her knuckles whiten. She is, I know, gathering strength to talk about Sister Praxades. The nuns do not speak. Their minds are suspended in a sea of expectation; no gleanings travel from their consciousness to mine, not even the Jesus, Mary, Joseph prayer. Leon catches my attention with a raised bushy eyebrow and looks pointedly at her lap. She signs: *Cook sick?*

The others may think that. We are not allowed in our cells except to sleep or to rest if we're ill. How I wish Sister Praxades were on her pallet, tucked under quilts, resting away a fever instead of curled miserably outside, the door of her mind forever frozen closed. I hope that whatever malady caused her to wander in the snow also prevented the cook from suffering.

My vision blurs and I drop my gaze to the pine table. In front of me and the four seated nuns are blue ceramic bowls of potato soup, our lunch. In the kitchen I simmered the potatoes in chicken stock—no wonder those fowl squawk with such alarm—and added cream, butter, salt, pepper, and a dash of crisp Chardonnay. As Sister Praxades taught, I tasted and added more butter, cream, tasted and added more spices, tasted and added more wine . . . and still the broth seemed bland.

Rich yellow butter dots the soup's surface, my poor attempt to duplicate the dead woman's craft. Only the bread, a thick, sweet rye, can be trusted. The large, round, crusty loaves were baked by the cook yesterday.

Reverend Mother's sharp inhale pulls my attention to the lectern. Her lips press together. "Sister Ellen found Sister Praxades outside this morning. Sister Praxades is dead." The bald statements straighten every spine, including my own.

"No," cries Sister Gabrielle, an old friend of the cook, eldest nun, knitter of woolens for the likes of me. Her misshapen hand fists, hits the table, and spoons jump. Her anguish bolts to my heart. She cries again: "No!"

"Sister Gabrielle," comes the cautioning, authoritative voice of Reverend Mother.

The old nun's mouth gapes, showing too-even dentures. Tears diffuse down cheeks as creased as parchment. She hunches over the table, gasping with hushed sobs, and a thread of saliva descends from her lips. Sister Fiske, the medic, sits next to the stricken woman. Her chin lifts, her eyes narrow behind magnified glasses. A sharp, disapproving line creases between her brows and her mouth thins, a compassionless look from a woman who frets about the abscesses of cows.

At a nod from Reverend Mother, Fiske rises, accompanies the crying Gabrielle into the stone corridor. The old woman's voice muffles in decrescendo. After a moment, the thin creak of the chapel door reveals their location. And in this room . . . silence. Leon stares at her lap. Sister Xavier, our housekeeper, an angular woman with a jaw as square as a box, fingers a soup spoon. She rarely speaks even when conversation is allowed.

Reverend Mother sighs deeply and bows her head. She says, "Why did you doubt?" Stress has made her German accent noticeable. Their shared emotion builds critical mass and penetrates my carefully erected barriers.

Each is deeply, piercingly ashamed.

Reverend Mother restricts me to the kitchen with my bowl of cooling soup while she conducts a private meeting with the others in the dining room. At the pine counter where Praxades taught me to shape loaves of whole wheat, I force myself to finish my lunch. Food is never wasted. Each tight swallow emphasizes my hurt: grief for the cook and, to my chagrin, the wound of being excluded from the nuns' discussion. I don't belong here, I chide myself. Why should Reverend Mother behave as though I'll stay beyond the spring thaw?

After I eat and feed more coal to the stove, the temptation to eavesdrop wins. I press my ear against the swinging door to the dining room. Not even hushed conversation seeps through the wood. Pushing the door open a crack—my toes still on the kitchen floor so there isn't technical disobedience—I see the five blue bowls on the table, still full. The nuns are gone.

Determined to be a help and to demonstrate a charity I'm not exactly feeling, I busy myself in the pantry, planning dinner. Surveying the shelves, my gaze touches opaque brown vials, medicines that Sister Praxades took on a complicated schedule. The names on the labels don't mean anything to me; once she showed me the collection on her chubby palm, pointing out one for blood pressure, another for cholesterol, and so on.

I pop the cap of one bottle and spill out beautiful azure capsules into my hand. Whatever her medications were supposed to do, they hadn't done their job last night. Sighing, I return the pills to their container and scoop the half-dozen prescriptions into my pocket. Fiske will want these returned to the infirmary.

I decide on tuna casserole, a dish I'm unlikely to ruin. I gather the canned fish, mushroom soup, noodles, and a stale bag of potato chips. The planks squeak under my tread and I see Praxades of last night, after dinner, sashaying and spinning her robes in exaggerated mockery of Sister Fiske, floorboards complaining under her weight. Mimicry was her gift and no one, myself included, was exempt, but Fiske was the cook's specialty.

At the sink I twist the crank of the opener around the tuna can and indulge the sweet sorrow of memories. Oddly enough, Praxades was liberal while the much younger Fiske was conservative. Praxades wanted a satellite dish and television so she could learn recipes from Julia Child; she wanted a subscription to *Gourmet* magazine, deliverable by bush pilot when weather allowed. In the common room, the arguments between Praxades and Fiske were high entertainment. Fiske struggled to control her indignation, I'll give her that. However, Praxades was a master of provocation. The cook's suggestions would become more and more extreme: The nuns should forgo habits and wear fleece slacks and shirts, the L. L. Bean catalogue had them in black.

Last night the cook's trump card, so to speak, enraged Fiske to unusual heights. Praxades suggested that evenings be passed by rousing games of stud poker, using holy cards as chips. The silent Sister Xavier grinned. Leon always looked happy, as though her features were incapable of any other expression. Fiske sprang to her feet, hands clenched by her sides, her complexion red; she'd flung her book to the floor. She sputtered, "You . . . you . . . you sacrilegious old fool, you disgusting—"

"Enough," interrupted Reverend Mother, a regal lift to her chin. "Sister Praxades, hold your tongue. Sister Fiske, you allow the cook to bait you every evening. Both of you must learn control and tolerance." However, Reverend Mother's eyes held a glitter of amusement; not, I'm sure, because of Fiske's fury but because of the cook's inane ideas.

Smug satisfaction brightened Praxades's plump face. Fiske retrieved *The Lives of the Saints,* touched the cover to her lips in apology—to the book, which must have been blessed—and returned to her chair, hands trembling. I felt the heat of her hate for the cook, an emotion as searing as any that had touched me in the cities. It is Lent, weeks of sacrifice in preparation for Easter, but she definitely wasn't offering up her aggravation to the Lord. Fiske even lacked the control to school her expression. She darted a withering, mean look at Reverend Mother, then dropped her gaze to her book. Her face was murderous.

The fork in my hand stops scooping out the tuna. An uneasy resonance jingles in my mind. Had Fiske looked surprised at Reverend Mother's dire announcement? I recall only Fiske's disapproving expression over Gabrielle's outburst.

Perhaps Fiske had nothing to be surprised about.

Fiske, while not a physician, plays the part of one by doling out medications. In my habit's pocket, my fingers clutch the containers of pills. No one would know if they had been tampered with. No one, that is, except for Fiske.

No, I think, please. Not here.

Not again.

Reverend Mother imposes an afternoon of silence in memory of the cook. When I enter her office and request permission to speak, she signs, "later." Minutes afterward, swaddled in my anorak, I tromp through the barn, chickens squawking in terror, and exit by the rear door. If Praxades was disoriented by medication, probably Fiske had to lead her outside. Snow squeaks like plastic pellets under my boots. Wind whips up millions of grains as fine as baby powder, shoving me nearly off my feet. My polarized lenses fog. I push the goggles above my eyes with awkward mittens and squint. The body is gone. While I was sequestered in the kitchen, the nuns moved the cook.

The day's dilute glow is muted by dark-bellied clouds, and though

I search, crouching near the ground, crabwalking the path, there's no evidence that anyone has been here: not the dead cook, not the nuns, and—as I look at ground near my boots—not even Sister Ellen. The harsh land of winter has wiped away the traces. A spasm of shivering makes my jaw muscles tremble. I straighten. Abruptly a gale whites out the world and my name floats through the whirl: *"Ellen."*

I pivot, pulse galloping, half-expecting to see Praxades levitating from the ground. That movement is a dangerous mistake. The wind increases, howling and spinning drifts, shoving so hard that I stagger. The mad swirl of snow is blinding. Panic shoots through my very core, more invasive than the cold. Which way is the barn? How long have I been out here? Two minutes? Three? Already my fingers are deadened, ice freezing together my eyelashes, narrowing my view to thin, blurry slits.

I must move. My feet stumble, forcing my body against the wind, and again I hear my name, swallowed by the squall, but definitely from my left. If I'm hallucinating, if hypothermia is creating a false call, then I'm dead. I fight, moving to my left for an eternity of seconds; finally arms grab and pull me into the thick smell and chicken cackles of the barn. Violent shivers drop me to my knees on the straw. The door latch clunks closed. My rescuer drags me to the heat of the wood stove.

My gloves are pulled off, then the liners, and my frozen fingers are clasped in hands so warm they burn my flesh. When the ice melts from my lashes, I'm staring into the kind, silent face of Sister Xavier. I know her the least, yet I know this: She will perform extra penance for the sin of breaking silence when she called my name.

In the infirmary, I proffer Sister Praxades's medicines. Fiske's cold fingers remove the bottles from my palm.

I speak, violating the imposed quiet. "Why would Sister Praxades go outside?"

The woman is still a moment, studying me, and the intensity of her stare and the knowledge of my scars makes my cheeks warm. Then she shrugs, a who-knows gesture. That motion is a lie. I feel her dissembling, controlling body language. She walks across the rough brick floor, twirling her robes in the way that Praxades mocked.

For a moment the mirrored cabinet bounces her image at me, then her double swings away as she opens the cabinet. I follow. "The cook was fine last night. What would make her do such a thing?"

Fiske ignores me, reads the label on one vial, and places it on a shelf cabinet. In my cell, under my pallet, is a list of the prescriptions and one pill from each container. Feeble evidence. The thought strikes me that if Fiske decides to remove any other thorn in her side, by persisting like this, I'm making Sister Ellen the next likely target. Fiske's pinched face last night rises to mind, her seething fury at the cook . . . and, now I recall, toward Reverend Mother.

Anger, however, isn't an omen of murder. "What do you think caused her odd behavior?" I ask, observing her profile as she shelves the remaining vials. "The mix of drugs she'd been taking?"

Her lips curl slightly in contempt. This impugning of her medical care prompts her to talk. "Not at all."

During the next pause, I expect her to announce that Praxades was befuddled by a stroke or low blood sugar. Instead, she closes the wall cabinet. I'm careful not to look into the mirror. Fiske says, "Separation from God."

"What?"

"That's what killed your precious Sister Praxades."

She turns in a flair of robes and for a moment a silly picture forms, a ballet of nuns in long black habits. I catch her by the arm. With slow disdain, she rotates her head to fix a dark gaze on my hand. I don't let go. "She . . . you're saying she died from, what, weak faith? *That's* your clinical diagnosis?"

She raises her eyes to meet mine. Behind thick lenses her irises glint as though forged of hard, shiny metal. "No, Sister Ellen. That's my spiritual diagnosis."

Our gazes lock. I almost do the thing that I vowed never to do again under any circumstances: invade the mind of another.

If I forcibly examine her thoughts, she will know. They always knew. The last time I used this accursed ability, I destroyed everyone around me.

Fiske stares, a smirking, superior look. It strikes me that she knows all about me, but that's impossible. Her hands shape the words *Look, Files, Top, Ellen.* With a nod she indicates the tall file cabinet.

I release Fiske. She strides away, footfalls slapping the brick floor, and exits the infirmary. As I look at the file cabinet, my stomach clenches in sudden, inexplicable fear. I, of all people, understand that some things are better left alone. Yet minutes later I have scanned the thick files bearing my name. Everything is there: the *Journal of the American Medical Association* study about a woman with provable telepathy; the Duke University professor's interview in *People* magazine and a photo of me hooked to an EEG machine; the *Newsweek* and *Time* articles about my assisting with various murder investigations nationwide; the *New York Times* report about how Gardini the Magician, a debunker of so-called psychics, finally paid a quarter of a million dollars to a bona fide mind-reader.

Dozens of newspaper and magazine articles cover the famous psychic's last murder case: Psychic's Husband and Brother Guilty of Business Partner's Murder. Then the same grainy photograph shows up in report after report: my disfigured features after the men my brother hired attacked me with acid. Long before that, though, everyone I came into contact with was leery of me. And weeks before acid ate away my features, I decided never again to snare thoughts from another's mind. After plastic surgeons had done the best they could with flesh that scarred so badly, I sought anonymity, a location where my history and notoriety might be unknown, where I might find, if not peace, at least isolation.

I thought that the nuns hadn't questioned me about my past or my scars due to their otherworldliness. Now I see that they had no need to interview me.

I stand in front of the infirmary mirror, holding the heavy file and gazing at my wretched reflection.

During dinner, while heads bend over a surprisingly tasty tuna casserole, first Leon, then Reverend Mother read passages from the Bible. Dinners are a time to fortify our bodies and our spirits. Reverend Mother, now at the podium, chooses the verses describing Jesus walking on the sea. The expressions of Leon, Xavier, Reverend Mother, and Gabrielle—especially Gabrielle—are serious and downcast. Fiske, to my eye, appears artificially solemn. I swallow a second helping of casserole, eager for the meal to end so that I can interrogate Leon over the dishes. After a minute, the only sound of fork against plate is my own. I look up. Fiske, Xavier, Gabrielle, and Leon are rapt with attention on Reverend Mother. She reads:

> "But when he saw that the wind was boisterous, he was afraid; and beginning to sink he cried out, saying, 'Lord, save me!'
> "And immediately Jesus stretched out His hand and caught him, and said to him, 'O you of little faith, why did you doubt?' "

Reverend Mother closes the Bible, kisses the gold-embossed cover, and returns to her place at the table. Everyone resumes eating, but something has happened which I've missed. The heavy cloud of their mood has lifted. On a psychological level, the dim dining room is bright.

In the cavern, Leon and I wear headlamps to light our way to the spring. The earth-generated heat keeps the temperatures from dropping below fifty, yet the high humidity is chilling. The damp mist blurs her shape and when our buckets accidentally clang together as we walk, my pulse jumps. She appears comfortable with how the cook died. She explains that Sister Praxades was moved to a mining shaft north of the barn. After leaving the corpse, they barricaded the entrance. When the ground thaws and, with the approval of the medical examiner—from two-hundred-mile-away Lygon—and Praxades's relatives, a burial plot will be prepared. Until then, her body will remain frozen and will be safe from the occasional arctic fox.

Her chipper tone nonpluses me. She might be discussing the disposal of the goat. We reach the pool and kneel down to draw water. I ask, "Why can't we have a memorial service now?"

"To mourn her would be to question God's will."

I set my full bucket down impatiently; water sloshes over the lip. "Leon, *talk* to me."

The desperation in my voice must have moved her. She sets her pail next to mine and says, "Of course I miss Sister Praxades. She brought this place alive. She made us laugh." Through the steam I see her grin. "Well, everyone except Sister Fiske," Leon amends.

"Ellen, look at it this way. If you died, would you want those you love to feel grief, to suffer over losing you?"

I wouldn't. Still, I'm troubled by the acceptance of the cook's death. Even the elderly Gabrielle appears adjusted to her friend's absence, though perhaps that's not true. She might be numb with grief.

Leon places her hand on my shoulder. In the steam, her headlamp creates a bright halo. "Perhaps it's easier for us. Our beliefs treat death as a natural part of the soul's journey. It wouldn't make sense for us to behave as though Sister Praxades is gone forever."

I wish I believed in the immortality of the soul. "What if Fiske messed with Praxades's medication?"

Leon is quiet a moment. I know I've surprised her. "I guarantee that Sister Fiske is innocent of everything except anger. She's devoted to safeguarding our health, not endangering it."

Leon could probably find good in Judas. We trudge back through the tunnel toward the living quarters. An aura radiates from her, and in that aura three words ring over and over: JesusMaryJoseph.

I assume the duties of the cook, though joy has evaporated for me. The others appear inexplicably cheered, except for Reverend Mother, who wears a preoccupied expression as though straining to hear a faint voice just beyond the audible range. A snowstorm blankets the grounds with one foot, then two feet of powder. I watch Fiske, who ignores me. The weather rages and we turn inward; the times of silence are natural for them. This spiritual hibernation makes me edgy, though my bread-baking improves. Two days pass.

On the third morning, Gabrielle vanishes.

I sleep. I wake with a start, furious with my failed vigil. Today Leon, Xavier, and I searched outside for Gabrielle, but our efforts were thwarted by the storm's bluster. She disappeared in the night, like Praxades. The spirits of the nuns are visibly leadened, even Fiske's. My mind is groggy; confused speculations stick in my skull. Why is everyone so resigned about Praxades, now Gabrielle? Why does Reverend Mother appear fatigued? She walks hesitantly, as if movement is an effort. Is Fiske poisoning Reverend Mother? Has Fiske killed Gabrielle?

A distant sound travels from the corridor. I sit up. Was that the timbers creaking? I toss off the comforter; chill seeps through my habit, cold slipping like spiders under the thermal underwear. In a few seconds I light the hurricane lamp, pull on my insulated boots, and tiptoe into the dark hall. All but one of the cell doors are closed. I peer into that room and my candlelight glows on an empty pallet. Seeing the tidy vacant room is a blow. I run to the kitchen, the dining room, the infirmary, the sitting room, the chapel, my search as fruitless as I feared. At the entryway door, I yank on anorak, gloves, cap and let myself out into the clear, breezy night, the cold so sharp my lungs inhale reflexively with the shock. It is always like this after a storm, as though fierce weather hones winter to better express its nature. The northerly has swept the entryway clear of all but a half-foot of powder, though drifts smooth the side wall clear up to the eaves. I round the building and find wind and deep snow . . . and heartache.

A figure glows in the frosty moonlight, skin gleaming whitely, a wide sweep of back and jiggling buttocks. "Leon!" I cry. She turns, a statue of salt, merging into the colorless world except for dark thatches of hair at crotch and head. My boots sink deep into the fresh powder as I struggle to her side.

"Please don't worry," Leon said. "I have faith." Syllables slur from frozen lips. "I'm getting warmer. My feet—"

"Leon, for the love of God, *please.*" Unshed tears chill my eyes. "You're not getting warmer. You're freezing."

My own face is ice. My stiff fingers won't grip. I loop my arm under hers and guide her toward the building. She resists; her red-lashed eyes blink sleepily under the narcotic of hypothermia.

"Damn you, Leon, *walk.*"

Her pale mouth opens in a semblance of a smile, the muscles of her jaw stiff with cold. "I'm walking, Ellen," she mumbles. "I'll come back. Reverend Mother did." Her arm slips like mist from mine and she stumbles away, wading through fresh snow, moving with a speed I wouldn't have thought possible. But she is numb. My legs drag through thigh-deep drifts and, trailing her, I fall, flounder deep in powdery whiteness. My freezing arms thrash for purchase in a substance as unstable as flour. Snow blankets my vision. I regain my footing, breathing hard, brushing ice from my face. Every muscle trembles so violently, my body straining to produce heat, that I can barely stand. I am alone in a landscape as pale and barren as the moon, and I suddenly understand who the murderer is.

I race through the corridor to Reverend Mother's room and enter without knocking, throat parched from cold and panic. A single candle flickers from the floor. Reverend Mother lies on her bed in full habit, fingers laced at her waist, thick black socks on her feet. The down comforter and blankets have been kicked to the floor. I lean over her. "I don't know what rot you've been telling these women, but Leon's out there and you're going to help me get her inside. If she hears you calling, she'll come in." Part of me says it's already too late for Leon, but I can't listen to that.

Reverend Mother stares at me, eyes glittering as though a fire blazes inside her skull. "It's Lent. The Lord calls her. She's being tested."

I pull her to a sitting position and her heat radiates like a furnace. Fever has glossed her skin with perspiration. "This is not Christ asking the apostles to walk on water, damn it. This is Alaska and she'll die out there. No one can survive that cold."

Her hands clutch my shoulders with a frenzied strength. "I did."

An odor pierces my hysteria, a fetid smell. It isn't a chamber-pot stink, but a scent of putrefaction and decay. With horror, I look at her feet, which she suddenly tucks under her skirts, a childlike gesture. I pull back the material. She isn't wearing thick, dark socks; frost-bitten toes and heels have swelled, rotted, and blackened. I slide up the polypro of her long underwear. Dark streaks on the calves disappear under the fabric, infection spreading toward her groin. Sickened, I cover her legs. Reverend Mother lies back against her pallet, and whispers a few words in German, the gist of which I understand. "Yes," I nod sadly, "you have faith."

The pilot and I haven't spoken. I'm his only passenger and wear heavy, insulated ear muffs to dull the engine noise; conversation is impossible. I'm also wearing a thin gauze mask that Sister Xavier fashioned at my request before I left the cloister. The pilot didn't ask about it. He probably thinks the mask is a religious garment. Below us is Anchorage, refreshingly green in its springtime mantle.

Xavier and I hunted but never found Leon's body. We speculated that she must have entered an abandoned mine shaft. After the start of the thaw, I found Gabrielle not far from the tunnel where the others had barricaded Praxades, and where we had entombed the corpse of Reverend Mother. I spent the last four months meditating on my own considerable responsibility in these terrible deaths. At first I raged at the twisted beliefs that corralled this small, insular society into suicidal behaviors. After talking awhile with Fiske and Xavier, though, I saw that I could have played a part in bringing a sort of heathen reasoning to their lives. However, my goal was self-protection and isolation, not involvement. Perversely, I managed to neither protect myself nor remain uninvolved. Guilt will always reside within me, a hard, frozen shard of northern Alaska.

After the pilot lands, I step down from the plane, pull the mask below my chin, and walk toward the terminal.

Travelers at the airport stare, but I've taken a gift—and a lesson—from my months in the cloister. In my soul spreads a vast emptiness, images and ideas bright stars with light-years of distance in between.

THE JUDGE'S BOY

by Jean B. Cooper

A thought will jump out at you from behind a door; a memory will rise from the wet napkin under your drink. Everything comes back. Dreams too. This is a good dream, I'll say to myself: naked woman, a curving outstretched form negative against the light coming through a window shade; the room going gold. There is always a woman. Always a woman. Maybe it was the judge who told me that, along with all the other crap he put in my head when I would listen. Then the dream is gone, and it's the face of the judge I see.

When I dream, it's not really about the judge. I see him in my waking hours. I'm driving down 17 and turn off on a Carolina river road that's nothing more than a carriage lane, and there's His Honor the judge leaning against a live oak, rolling a cigaret. I'm tooling through Cottageville to Edisto Beach, going to drink beer, catch a fish, get this low-country fog out of my brain, and standing under the rusted tin roof of an abandoned tobacco house in the middle of a field is the image of the judge, exhausted by his own evil.

The judge is dead. I know he's dead. I was there when they took his body five years ago. It's just the old ways of this sad moist land that keep him before me. It's the religion ringing from the small spare clapboard churches that spring up like ghosts in the marsh as I take the narrow turns at high speeds, trying, maybe, to outrun my guilt, or to find some final pardon.

337

There is always a woman. Now I know when he said it to me (have always known, but the game, see, is to pretend it's dim and slipping away from me, falling off me like old clothes, ancient skin, and me, Ray Ford, emerging new and unscathed).

He said it when we were on the porch of my grandfather's house, a dingy wood-framed cottage that sat at the edge of a pond. A sandy road led to it, and I'd been mildly interested in the cloud of dust I saw coming at me down that road. A visitor. And me just returned to the empty house only the night before. Then I recognized the car, big and black. A 1974 Mercedes. The judge himself. Of course he would know I was . . . back. I almost said "home," but it wasn't home anymore.

The judge had come out of the car like a thundercloud building, one dark billow at a time, his enormous feet in glossy black wing-tipped shoes; next his heavy legs, lifted ponderously; then his dark-suited self, round and rumpled. He wiped his forehead with a handkerchief and gingerly managed the three cement steps to the porch.

"Ray," he said, "I got some business I need you to take care of for me." Like we had been talking to each other at full tilt for hours. Like I had not been gone for ten years away at school, away at work for a law firm I hated. Like the cane-bottomed rocker was warm from him having sat in it all morning. He seemed to remember his manners then. "Well, it's good to see you, son."

We shook hands. Over his wide shoulder I glimpsed his driver, a big solemn black man, Durrell James. "All I have is coffee," I said.

"I don't want no coffee. I got a little business I want you to take care of for me."

"Maybe your man Durrell, there, would like something to drink."

The judge let a slow, yellow, gelid smile part his lips, but the eyes never left mine. "Don't do nothing for Durrell. Let it be."

In our years of growing up, Durrell James and I had never been friends, vying as we had for the attentions of the judge. We had more than once gone at it as boys. There was one fight when Durrell had held a knife at my throat, but the judge had walked in on us. You know there are some frogs that can go underground and live out of sight in the mud. That's what is out there in the swamp. Waiting.

Hate and jealousy can be like that. I looked at Durrell. He was staring straight ahead, intent on marsh grasses.

I decided to be nonchalant in spite of the bile and maybe a wave of fear rising in me. "What in the world could an out-of-work lawyer do for the Honorable Galen D. Pringle, Retired?"

"I don't have time to joust with you, Ray. I will remind you only about who it was taught you everything you know, and I ain't talking about them silly-billies in Virginia, either. What you can do is this: I want you to find somebody for me."

"Find somebody?"

"Yes."

"You want me to find somebody for you?"

He sank into the unpainted rocking chair and sighed to let me know how I wearied him. He decided on a different approach. "Me and your dead granddaddy used to take john boats all over this place. I loved your granddaddy like a brother, but you, Ray, have always been a pain in the ass. Which is why you can't practice in somebody else's law firm. Got to be on your own. Well, that's okay. It's how I did it. But don't give me grief this morning. I'm old, and I'm hot. Do this one thing for me."

He knew before my car turned onto the road that would take me back that I was coming. He knew that I had told one of the top firms in South Carolina they could stuff it, and that I'd walked out. Such were his sources. And because he knew me, he knew I would do what he asked. He was probably discussing it with Durrell as they rumbled down my forlorn road. Not one to waste a motion, the judge had grown fat and slow through excesses of life's pleasures and with economy of activity. He had paid for my education at U-Va. He had fed and clothed me and watched over me, according to his lights, because my mother was dead, my father was long gone, and because he and my granddaddy had roamed these backwaters in john boats in sweet, languid days. Days, the judge said, of his last remembered happiness. So he wanted me to find somebody.

"Whom shall I find for you?" I slung the bitter coffee into the bare, dry yard.

He did not look at me, but handed me a wallet-sized photograph of a black girl of indeterminate age, except to say young. She might have been fifteen or twenty-five. Her hair was pulled back tight and smooth. Her oval, defiant eyes looked at the camera as if she might climb through it. Her full mouth had no trace of a smile. "Who is this?"

"A girl worked for me. Tablue . . ."

"Durrell's little sister?"

"Yes. But not little anymore. A thief and who knows what else."

I held the picture, recalled a skinny little girl, Tablue James, but it was the judge I was watching. He was a wily old cuss, and if he wanted to find this girl, he could have a sheriff on her, the people in these hamlets, farmers, everybody looking for her. Even Durrell.

He shifted his bulk in the chair, flicked nonexistent lint from his trouser leg. "Don't be thinking why can't Durrell or somebody else be finding Tablue for me. This is a sensitive situation. Durrell does not understand sensitive."

I looked again at the man in the car. No, Durrell could not be expected to have sensitivity. What Durrell had was hands like slabs of meat and a neck thick as a tree trunk. "Why is she important to you?" I rested my back against the porch post and prepared for one of the judge's lies.

"She's not important. It's what she took that's important. She took my money."

I tried not to smile.

"I put her in my office, to give her a break, and what does she do but make off with cash from my safe!"

I could see by the pain in his watery eyes that his heart was broken. Parting with cash money for which he received absolutely nothing in return was a mortal wound to him. "I still don't see . . ."

"She took two hundred thousand dollars!" He spat the words at me. They sounded like water on a hot pan. "You think I want people knowing I had that kind of money on me? Durrell don't even know it. And you better not tell him, either."

Things were clearer. The judge had known the right people, done the right things, and had himself put on the family-court bench, which is not a position in and of itself that is a moneymaker, but it has its bennies: You hang in there, don't muck up too much, and you just might get into a juicier position. The word is if you can go along and get along, you'll be around a long time. The judge could do that. He'd made a pile when the South Carolina coastline started developing. Cheap property overnight going through the roof. Somebody here and there dropped a word or two to Judge Pringle, and he knew what to buy and when to buy it. But he had gone to some trouble to let everybody believe he was almost broke all the time. Driving old cars, wearing cheap suits, and eating blue-plate specials at a grill in Walterboro, the county seat. The judge in town for court. The judge in tragic dramatic form. He'd seen *To Kill a Mockingbird* too many times, and probably would have given his left eye to shoot down a dog in the street.

He motioned for me to come closer. I did. He smelled of bourbon and some sweet aftershave. "Ray, I know where she is."

I looked at him. He had broken capillaries around his nose branching out onto his florid cheeks. How old was he now, seventy? "Where is she?"

"She thinks she's so smart." He looked into the middle distance, whether for effect or for real, I do not know. He shook his head sadly. "There is always a woman." Then finally, "She's on Melinda."

The judge owned Melinda Island. His only real-estate deal that did not pan out into big bucks. He'd started to develop it, but the native islanders raised such a stink about it that he dropped it rather than be confronted by the NAACP or whatever investigative news program decided to take him on. The judge did not wish to be investigated by anyone at any time. "How do you know she's there? Why wouldn't she just hightail it out to Canada, the Bahamas, wherever?"

He stood up. Suddenly he did not seem angry or agitated. "I just know, that's all. You go over there and get her for me. She'll remember you. You bring her back to me. It's not even a day trip, Ray. Do this one last thing for me. What with emphysema, gout, and whatall, I won't make it to the end of the year. All debts will be paid between you and me."

The judge had been dying for the last thirty years from some imagined protracted malady or other. In his heart of hearts he really believed he would live forever. "What makes you think she'll come with me?"

He got into the back of the car and was closing the door. "You'll charm her, Ray, just like you've always charmed everyone." Durrell gunned the big car and threw sand back into my face.

A bad deed is best done quickly. That's not quite Shakespeare, but it's close enough. I set out the next morning for Melinda Island. It's isolated. They don't even have mail delivery. Every now and again someone of the few families who live there will boat over to French Island, pick up mail and some sundry things, then go back. You can forget Melinda Islanders even exist. In fact, they wish you would. I took the ferry across to French Island, rented a small outboard, and docked in Melinda about lunchtime. There's only one place to eat there: Loobie's Shack. Loobie is one of three white people who live on Melinda. The other two are his sister and her husband. Loobie's name is Lou B. Dunn. He retired from the navy in Charleston and opened this bait and tackle shop and makes a mean cheeseburger. His beer is cold. I remembered it from my high-school days when the judge would bring me over so he could walk his beautiful but poor island to mourn what might have been. Loobie sneaked me beers then. Loobie told me things he thought I might need to know: how to fish for sheepshead; how to cure a hangover. Loobie said to me things men say to each other as cautionary tales: Ray, watch a man's hands. If a man's gonna hurt you, he'll use his hands.

When I walked into his place, he recognized me, even after ten years.

"Ray!" His grip was firm as ever. He pulled a dripping beer out of his case. "What brings you here?"

We were both ten years older. His military buzz cut was frosty now, but he was still Loobie in a dirty T-shirt, frazzled khakis, and an apron tied at his big belly. I didn't see a health-department rating sign up anywhere, but I breathed in air saturated with crab, beer, hot grease, and salt water. It was good.

"I'm looking for somebody."

"Is that right?" He chewed on his cigar stub. "Who's that?"

I figured he knew. But I played on anyway. I showed him the photo. "Tablue James. The judge wants to talk to her."

"That sonofabitch." Loobie took a hand towel and zapped a fly with it. "Why don't he come hisself?"

We both knew why Judge Pringle would not come to Loobie's. Loobie had told him during the first stages of the judge's real-estate plans that if he set foot in Loobie's establishment, the judge would be gut-shot. "He's getting old." I let Loobie consider that for a beat then I said, "He could have sent Durrell."

"Durrell." Loobie's voice was filled with loathing. Most people steered clear of Durrell James. He was born a menace and lived to prove it. How he avoided jail is a mystery, even with the judge on his side. "You know what they say about him, Ray? I don't know if it's true, but they say he beat up a girl over in Georgetown, and then because she wasn't dead, he set her on fire."

I said, "He's quite a guy, huh?"

"Let the judge send Durrell. I'll cut that sonofabitch from stem to stern. I'll hang him out for the seagulls to pick at. Wouldn't nobody on this island, including his own people, give a rip about it. He's terrorized too many of them for too long."

I turned the beer up. Loobie was mean as death, but he was old and probably slow. Durrell was maybe twenty-nine and didn't know the concept of remorse. Me, I'm the kind that'll either outwit you or sneak up on you. I am, in those things, like the judge, and it hurts me to admit it. "I'm here because the judge wants to talk to Tablue."

Loobie got a beer for himself. "None of my business. You want to see that girl, suit yourself. It's a small island. You won't get no help."

That was true. Most of the people knew my connection with Judge Pringle, and those who did not outright hate him at the least mistrusted him, and would not give up Tablue.

"She ever come by here?"

"Everybody comes by here. Hell, Ray, even you're here." Loobie reached with astonishing speed, caught another worrisome fly with his hand, and shook it silly in his massive fist.

The rain started about half an hour later. It was steady, beating on Loobie's broad glass-front window and his tin roof. He had two booths in the long part of his L-shaped hovel. I slid into the one on the left, sat facing the door, and ate some boiled shrimp. The wind had picked up a little, making the screen door slap. Every time it did I looked up and saw nothing, just more rain on the window. I dozed off a couple of times. Then out of the rain there she was. Tablue James.

She shook the water from her jacket and hung it on a peg by the door. There was only the insistent drumming of the rain, Loobie's hand coming out with a cup which Tablue took, and she headed straight for me. Her dress was black and short, more like a T-shirt, but with the neck cut low. I watched her coming; I couldn't help it. Ten years had grown into long legs and hollows and swells you can't take your eyes off of. She wore no shoes. I stood when she stopped at the booth. She didn't even look at me, but sat in the booth and put her coffee cup on the table.

I said, "Don't the shells hurt your feet?"

She took a sip of the coffee and turned her bronze eyes up at me. "You look the same. Bigger, though."

"You remember me?" I'd been trying since the day before to recall Tablue James, but all I could manage was a skinny little kid standing inside her mama's door when the judge and I would drive out to the ramshackle house to pick up Durrell. And Durrell never said anything about his family.

"You the judge's boy."

There was just the slightest emphasis on the word "boy." I said, "I'm Ray Ford. I worked for the judge when I was a kid."

"My brother, Durrell, he hates your guts."

"Yes, well, Durrell is good at that."

Tablue broke into a wide grin. She had a small space between her top front teeth. It was not unattractive. It was like a little door and you might want to go in there. She said, "He's good at some other things, too." Her grin disappeared. "Why you here?"

I wanted to get it over with. At least that's what I was telling myself. "The judge wants you to come back with me."

"I bet he does." She took a napkin from the dispenser on the table and dabbed at the water on her chest and arms. "And you came to get me. You still work for Judge Pringle? A grown man like you still an old man's errand boy?"

"He says you are a thief. He says he did you a favor and you took advantage of him. Said you stole some money."

Her eyes widened. I thought for an instant she might slap my face like an offended woman in those old black and white movies. Instead she slumped against the back of the booth and shook her head.

I said, "You mean you didn't take the money?"

She was studying the contents of her cup. "Oh, I took the money. I cleaned out his office safe. What gets me is he told you he did me a favor? That's what he said?"

"More or less."

She let out a long sigh. "A favor."

Up at the front, the door continued to bang with the wind, and a fog had gathered, even inside of Loobie's, where it mingled with cooking fumes and steam. The weathered walls were damp. The light was low now. There was a heavy thunderstorm out there. I hoped I had tied up the rented outboard well enough.

She broke into my worry. "The judge does that for people, doesn't he? Did you a favor or two?"

It was not a secret. The Fords had always been backwater people, and who my daddy was never came to light. My mother took that information to her grave. I was eight years old, and they pulled my poor mother out of the creek where the car she had just learned to drive had landed after she took a curve too fast. I was left to Grand-daddy Cleatus Ford, a man aged and failing when I was born, and not able to care for an eight-year-old boy. Judge Galen Pringle, with his powers as a family-court judge, took on my care. It was a favor, but to Cleatus Ford, not to me. I said to Tablue, "I worked for what I got from Judge Pringle. Durrell did, too. There were many times we would have preferred fishing for shad or crappie to shoveling out the judge's horse stalls or washing his car, cutting his grass. We were just kids. I'm not here to talk about me. I'm here to ask you to make everything right with the judge, to come back with me."

Tablue picked up my beer bottles with long slender fingers. "In this weather? No, settle back, Ray. Let's have a talk."

I watched her walk to the front, saw her slender profile as she leaned over Loobie's counter and got two beers. Tablue moved like water coming back to the booth, like an inexorable wave rolling toward shore. From her toes to her sleek head she was liquid and lovely. Yet I felt something wasn't right. I didn't mind she was a thief. I'd lived in big cities, had lunch and kept society with all manner of thieves daily. But still, about Tablue there was something. She sat, and I dismissed that nagging feeling to the effects of, the spell of being back in the South Carolina lowlands again after a long absence. You forget the magic and the mystique of this haunted place. Time is different here, amorphous and intoxicating in its own way. I'm not even sure how long we sat there with the fresh drinks before she said, "I'm not going back."

"He could put the law on you."

"Could. But ask yourself, why hasn't he?"

I had asked myself that on the way to Melinda. I figured:

1. He wants to keep quiet about the money
2. He wants Tablue spared embarrassment
3. He doesn't want the hassle of the law

Maybe. But then I had said to myself: She's got something on him.

"You've got something on him."

Her eyes sparkled and narrowed. She laughed, but without mirth. She was about to say something, but changed her mind. Then: "Your name is Ray. Like in sunshine? Your mama name you that?"

I had not thought about my mother like that for so long that the question caught me off guard. "I don't know. I guess so." I was trying to remember.

"Ray, tell me about your mother."

"She's dead."

"I know. I'm sorry. So is mine. But tell me about your mother anyway."

The rain came, driven sideways at the window in Loobie's, and there was a tight cold howl in the wind. I took a long pull on the beer and a long look at the dripping glass window, vapor condensing because of the heat in the cafe. Down here something is always becoming something else. My mother's face almost came to me, pulled up from those faraway days when her voice was a grace note through Granddaddy's little house. I could remember walking down that road to the house, feeling the warm sand between my toes. My mother was beside me. The sun was hot on my neck. My hand was in hers. She's talking, because I recalled her soft words. . . .

Under the table I grabbed Tablue's ankles and held them, squeezing. "Stand up now."

Tablue's face was blank. Our eyes locked. She stood. It was her feet. I had noticed, but had not seen. She was missing her little toes, from each foot the little toe gone. I looked down at them and felt the tiny hairs on my neck lift. That walk down the sandy road, my feet, my mother's feet. My mother was missing her little toes.

"Ray, the judge likes to own things," Tablue said.

You condition yourself. You force yourself to avoid emotions: fear, sadness, loneliness. The one thing as a man you will allow yourself to have is anger. I was having a feast of it, felt it filling me until I thought my eyes would plop out onto the table and look back at me.

Tablue said, "You don't look so good."

She got up and came back with a soft drink. This time she sat beside me. I felt her press up against me, heard her voice go inside my ear and grab me somewhere low and deep. "Baby, I'm in it up to my nose, and I need your help. These people here on Melinda can help just so much. I got to get away."

I sipped the drink. "Nobody's keeping you, Tablue." I shook my head to loosen the memory of my mother walking.

"The judge is a powerful man. You got to come out of the dark. It's time you saw what's real."

"Tablue, what do you have to say to me?" I did not look at her while she spoke.

Her mother had told her. There'd been talk about it for years. The judge and my mother. I knew Mama'd gotten pregnant at fifteen and whoever the father was had taken off. But Tablue said, shortly after I was born, from the fields her people would see the judge's car snaking through the countryside, my mother in there with him.

Tablue lit a cigaret, picked a piece of tobacco from her tongue. "They say your mama, she was gone leave him. He took her toes. Not too long after that she had the wreck. My mama was there when they pulled her from that water. He was there too, the judge. Mama said he liked to died on the spot, was clawing at the car door for her."

"Yeah? You have a lot of information. You're not trying to tell me that old man is my father." I never would have believed that.

"No. I don't know. Maybe."

"Where do you fit into this, Tablue?"

She got up and sat across from me again. Her mood had changed. We were no longer confidants. There was a childish quality to her voice. "I'm no angel. You been gone a long time. But look around you. What is in this place for me? The judge, he puts me to work in his office, and one thing leads to another."

"So. You and the judge." It was an image I could not manage. Tablue, in her early twenties, and the judge. I'd had enough for one day. "I'm done with this. Get Durrell to help you. He is, after all, your big brother."

This time her laughter was quick, loud, and hoarse. I saw Loobie look back at us. "Who you think held me down when Judge took my toes?"

That I could believe. "You've got two hundred thousand dollars of the judge's money. That'll get you away from him and from your brother. Just leave. It's what I'm going to do."

"You can't go anywhere in this storm. That's three miles of bad water out there now." She leaned across the table to me and said, like she'd just thought of it, "Tell you what. You come home with me. I fix you a nice fish stew, hush puppies, or griddle cakes."

It's a misery to realize that everyone who knows you thinks you're stupid. What had I done or not done to give them that impression? I'd been raised in the inlets, marshes, and swamps by a man whom I always knew was despicable. Children know when things aren't right. Children see what goes on, and eventually they put it all together no matter how it breaks their hearts. Buried deep into my psyche were my mother's missing toes and glimpses of the judge's hand on her shoulder, her hip. I dredged up quick whispers between them. Now the judge had sent me for Tablue. Now Tablue invited me home.

"You want to cook my supper, Tablue?"

"Why not?"

Why not, indeed? "You do look good in that black dress."

She smiled broadly. "I dressed for you."

"I know you did. Does the judge like black?"

She almost lost it a little, but she was good, I'll give her that. "No, honey," she cooed. "He likes white."

* * *

The clouds were bruised and low, but the rain was lighter. The wind was at about sixteen knots. We walked a mile under broad dripping oaks. The worn house where she was staying was dark and silent. Tablue walked ahead of me, stepped lightly onto the porch, and opened the door. She went in. When I did not follow, she came back out. "Ray?"

I went in.

There was no dignity in what we did. It was just something to do, something to kill a rainy night. I lay beside her afterward in the shadowed room. Finally the rain had stopped. The moon broke through the clouds in a tide of truth. Its light shone golden through the window and spilled over Tablue's sleeping body.

There were only a few hours left. The storm had prevented his coming, but now, with the weather right, Durrell would come. It was almost first light when I heard what I'd been listening hard for. Tablue slept on. There it was again. He was so sure of himself, he was coming through the front door. I eased from the bed and pressed my back against the cool wall behind the door. Durrell entered, crouched, ready to spring. I caught him over the back of his head with a brick I'd found by the back porch. He went down. I hit him again.

On the bed Tablue sat frozen, her mouth open. "Is he dead?"

"I don't know." I felt for a pulse. "No, he's alive."

Her words shot at me. "Kill 'im."

"What?"

"Do it! You don't, he's gone come for you sure."

I went outside and came back with Tablue's clothesline. I tied Durrell's hands and his feet. Tablue sat in her bed smoking, furious with me, and not knowing what her next move should be.

I said, "Durrell put you up to taking the money." She was silent except for desperate drags on her cigaret. Her big eyes watched me, tried to fathom how much I knew. "Durrell put you up to it, and you and he were going to, what . . . leave?"

"Durrell is tired of driving the judge's car. What's it matter to an old man like that anyway, sick as he is? Rolling in money he'll never use. Durrell and me, we had some of it coming. That crazy man took my toes off!"

"With Durrell's help."

Her cigarette flared hot as a laser. "I haven't forgot that. Why you think I'm doing what Durrell told me to do?"

"Why do you think he has two cans of kerosene outside the house?" She looked at her cigaret and stubbed it out. "I take it Durrell didn't say anything about that to you, did he? What did he say, 'Just get cozy with Ray Ford, little sister, and let Durrell handle the rest'?" I'd found the cans when I'd gone for the clothesline. They were meant just as much for Tablue as they were for me. She could see that. Durrell was a loner. He had never needed a partner, even if she was his sister.

Tablue got out of bed and walked over to her brother. She kicked him. He did not stir. But soon he would. Maybe I'd cracked his thick skull, but Durrell James was like the rent: He'd just keep going on, just keep getting up. I left them there in that half-light. They could fight it out, do what they would with the money.

Down by Loobie's I untied my boat and started out across the water toward French Island. Halfway across the inlet I heard a muffled noise. Gulls squawked overhead. Looking back at Melinda, I saw a black plume rising to blend with the mother-of-pearl morning clouds. A lick of red flame showed. Tablue had made her move. And she just might get away with it.

The judge lived in an antebellum house badly in need of renovation. I pulled my car into his circular gravel drive and let myself in the front door. It was almost midday, but the interior of the house, with its fourteen-foot ceilings, was cool and dark as a tomb. After a thorough search of the downstairs, I found him upstairs in his bedroom, alone. My heart had raced, wondering whether I'd find some of Durrell's handiwork, but in his big, high bed the judge lay.

When I entered, his eyes opened, and his hand flopped on the counterpane. His bedside table was littered with upset prescription medicine containers. Some pills lay on the floor. When the judge spoke, I could barely hear him. "Ray. That Durrell." I moved to his bedside. His face seemed to have fallen in on itself. He had a bad color to him. It looked to me as if after all his years of complaints, something had finally got to him. But he was still the judge, and he was trying to gather enough of himself into this one place. He pushed up onto his pillows. It was a mighty effort. I watched. "Ray." The old man licked his dry lips. His eyes went to his empty water glass. I stood still. "Ray. Durrell took my money."

"I know."

"I swear I'm dying."

"You just might be."

"Durrell took my medicine and put it over there on the mantel-board." I looked across the room. On the mantelboard sat a prescription bottle. "It's my heart. You hand me them pills. I'll put one in my mouth and maybe pull out of this thing."

I did not move.

He closed his eyes. For a long moment we stayed like that. He then opened his eyes again and said, "Hand me the pills, boy. You know you want to do it. You've always had a sense of the heroic."

I sat over by the window, listened to the doves in the myrtle trees, listened to his breath come out in short rasps. My old granddaddy knew two things: the backwaters and the Bible. It was he who tried to drill into me the Gifts of the Spirit. I'm low in most of them except patience. I can wait. I'm the most patient man there ever was. It took awhile for the judge to die. It was evening, with the sun going down in a flood of orange behind a stand of pines, when I took one last look at the body of Judge Galen Pringle. What had he done to my young ignorant mother? He wasn't my father. We did not look anything alike. I straightened his bedclothes. I set all his medicine bottles, including the longed-for bottle on the mantel, back into position on his nightstand. I called the doctor whose name appeared on the bottles.

I still live here in this low country. I'm Ray Ford, the judge's heir. I own the old house. I own Melinda Island. I practice a little law, and I go fishing with my friend Loobie, who swears that Tablue's house just up and burned that day and the islanders had let it. One of Tablue's cousins had taken her over to French Island. She has not been seen since. Driving these back roads, I do have visions of the judge. Tricks of the mind. They don't bother me. One of these days, if you believe my granddaddy's religion, I'll have to answer for what I did not do for the judge. Meanwhile, the fish are biting, the beer is cold, and the dreams of the absent Tablue are fond and familiar.